Susanna Gregory was a police officer in Leeds before taking up an academic career. She has served as an environmental consultant, worked eighteen field seasons in the polar regions, and has taught comparative anatomy and biological anthropology.

She is the creator of the Matthew Bartholomew series of mysteries set in medieval Cambridge and the Thomas Chaloner adventures in Restoration London. She now lives in Wales with her husband, who is also a writer.

Also by Susanna Gregory

SUSANNA GREGORY

THE CHANCELLOR'S SECRET

THE TWENTY-FIFTH CHRONICLE OF
MATTHEW BARTHOLOMEW

sphere

SPHERE

First published in Great Britain in 2021 by Sphere

1 3 5 7 9 10 8 6 4 2

A CIP catalogue record for this book is available from the British Library.

ISBN 978-0-7515-7948-2

Typeset in ITC New Baskerville by Palimpsest Book Production Ltd,
Falkirk, Stirlingshire

Printed and bound in Great Britain by Clays Ltd, Elcograf S.p.A.

Papers used by Sphere are from well-managed forests
and other responsible sources.

Sphere
An imprint of
Little, Brown Book Group
Carmelite House
50 Victoria Embankment
London
EC4Y 0DZ

An Hachette UK Company
www.hachette.co.uk

www.littlebrown.co.uk

For
Philippa Davies
Heather Evans
Marguerite Jones
and
Laura McKechnie

Wonderful friends

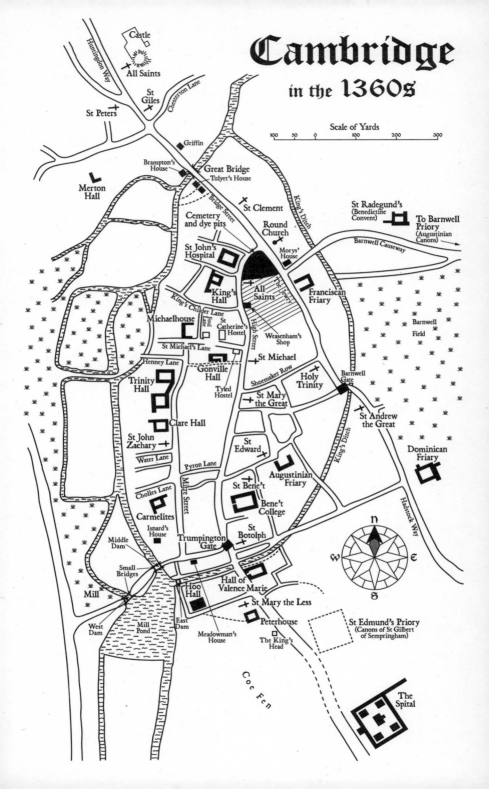

PROLOGUE

Cambridge, early June 1360

John Baldok was pleased with himself. He had been in the castle, delivering a handsome sum of money that had been raised to repair the Great Bridge, when the Sheriff's clerks had been distracted by a commotion in the bailey. It had happened just as they had finished recording receipt of the money in their ledgers, so when they had hurried outside to watch, Baldok had seized his chance. He had grabbed the coins, shoved them up his sleeve, and strolled nonchalantly out through the main gate. No one would ever accuse him of the crime. He was a burgess – one of the men who made important decisions about town affairs – and thus above suspicion.

Yet he did experience a small twinge of conscience. The town had struggled to pay the levy, and its theft meant people would have to dip into their purses a second time. It would cause hardship and suffering. But the ruthless side of him shrugged – it was the clerks' fault for putting temptation his way, so any blame should be laid at their door, not his. Besides, he needed all the cash he could get these days, because his new mistress had very expensive tastes.

He grinned when he thought about Rohese. She was the Mayor's wife, and he loved the thrill of tiptoeing into her bedchamber while Morys pored over his accounts on the floor below. The lovers were discreet, but their affair was an open secret even so. Fortunately, no one was likely to mention it to Morys, because the Mayor was a very unpopular man.

'If you want anything done in Cambridge,' another

1

burgess had informed Baldok at his first guildhall meeting, 'pay Morys. It does not matter what it is – building a new house, diverting water from the river, repairing a road, negotiating trade deals. Nothing will happen until he has had his cut. It is the way things work around here.'

'Why was he elected if he is so brazenly corrupt?' Baldok had asked, bemused.

The burgess shrugged. 'He bought the votes he needed to win, and now nothing – *nothing* – happens until he has been paid. Being Mayor has made him very rich.'

It was an unsatisfactory state of affairs, but Baldok was disinclined to object, as he was not a very honest man himself.

Baldok reached the Great Bridge and hesitated. It had been damaged by spring floods, and should have been closed until it was repaired. Unfortunately, that entailed users taking lengthy detours, and they had objected so vigorously that the council had had no choice but to keep it open. Very heavy carts were banned, and horsemen were advised to dismount, but other than that, people were free to take their chance.

Only one other person was on the bridge that evening, because it was nearly dark and the weather was unseasonably cold. The traders from the surrounding villages had already gone home, and other than one or two priests hurrying towards their churches for compline, the streets were deserted.

Baldok began to cross the bridge, wincing as the handrail swayed alarmingly in time with his footsteps. He did not allow himself to dwell on the uncomfortable fact that repairs might have started that week, if he had not stolen the money.

It was to be one of the last thoughts he would ever have.

*

The next morning, Baldok's body was found on the riverbank beneath the bridge. Sheriff Tulyet came to investigate, and asked the University's Corpse Examiner, Doctor Bartholomew, for a cause of death. Bartholomew deduced that Baldok had died of a broken neck, sustained when he had toppled over the handrail to land on the shore below.

'Are you sure?' asked Tulyet doubtfully; despite its lofty name, the Great Bridge was not very high. 'I could jump off this thing and not suffer so much as a scratch.'

'Not if you went head first,' explained Bartholomew.

'So was it accident, suicide or murder?' asked Tulyet.

'For Baldok to end up in this position suggests a hard push or a vigorous jump, which rules out an accident. Your clerks said he was in good spirits when he left last night . . .'

'Not suicide either then,' said Tulyet. 'So he was murdered?'

'It seems most likely.'

'He had been delivering bridge-tax money to the castle,' said Tulyet. 'It subsequently went missing, although, as it happened when he was left alone with it, I do not need to look very far for the culprit.'

'He *stole* it?' Bartholomew was shocked. 'But he was a burgess!'

'Which is probably why he thought he could get away with it,' said Tulyet wryly. 'Had he lived, he would have learned otherwise.'

'Well, there is no money with him now, so it was either stolen from his body, or someone else took or was given it before he died.'

Tulyet began to investigate, but learned nothing to tell him who had pushed the burgess to his death. Weeks passed, and although he hated the notion of a killer besting him, he was eventually forced to admit that there was no more he could do.

CHAPTER 1

Cambridge, July 1360

Matthew Bartholomew, physician and Fellow of the College of Michaelhouse, was in two minds about getting married in eleven days. On the one hand, he loved Matilde with all his heart, and was looking forward to spending the rest of his life with her. On the other, marriage was forbidden to scholars, which would mean an end to his teaching the mysteries of medicine. He would miss that more than he could say.

He sat in the room he shared with four of his pupils, and stared out of the window into the pre-dawn gloom. Michaelhouse had been his home for the greater part of two decades, and had seen him pass from idealistic youth to pragmatic middle age. Its daily routine was deeply ingrained in his being: rising before dawn for church, breakfast in the hall, teaching and seeing patients until evening, and then preparing the next day's classes.

How would he fare as a 'secular'? Filling his time would be no problem – he was one of few town *medici* willing to tend the poor, either for a nominal fee or free of charge, and they would continue to expect his services regardless of whether or not he was a member of the University. However, when he left Michaelhouse, he would lose his College stipend, so his only income would be what he earned from medicine – which meant he would have to tout for wealthy clients.

He experienced a pang of unease. What if the town's affluent elite declined to hire him? Matilde was independently wealthy, but he could hardly expect to live off her for the rest of his life. Moreover, every spare penny she owned was being funnelled into the school for women she intended to establish, as she considered it an outrage that half the town's population should be denied the delights of education on the basis of their sex.

At that moment, the College bell chimed, telling scholars to assemble in the yard, ready to process to Mass in St Michael's Church. There was a faint glimmer of light in the east, and he could just make out his book-bearer, Cynric, hauling on the bell-rope.

Cynric had been in his service since Bartholomew had been a student in Oxford, but that was something else that would soon change: Cynric had decided to remain at Michaelhouse when the physician left. The book-bearer had made a good life for himself in the College, and did not want to abandon all he had built over the years. Bartholomew knew exactly how he felt.

Slowly, Michaelhouse came to life. Windows were thrown open, bedding set to air, and footsteps clattered. Bartholomew's students were the last to rise, grumbling as usual about the ungodly hour. All four had recently passed their disputations, and would graduate at the end of term, which meant they would be presented to the Chancellor as intelligent men of good character, worthy of receiving the coveted degree of bachelor. Then they would be free to practise medicine on their own, although Bartholomew had reservations about them all: Islaye was too gentle and Mallett was not gentle enough, but the two who gave cause for the greatest concern were Stasy and Hawick. Neither had a genuine vocation, and had chosen to study medicine because they wanted to be rich.

He glanced at them and saw Stasy grin, making him suspect mischief in the offing. Sure enough, there was a furious screech from the kitchens, where Agatha, techni-cally a laundress but in reality ruler supreme of the

5

College's domestic affairs, was preparing the scholars' breakfast.

'What?' Stasy asked, all false innocence when Bartholomew raised his eyebrows questioningly. 'It is not my fault the peafowl ate all her raisins.'

'You had better hope she does not guess you facilitated it,' said Bartholomew tartly, thinking him a fool to risk getting on the wrong side of the fearsome Agatha. 'If she does, your life will not be worth living.'

'Ten days,' sighed Hawick. 'Then we shall leave this boring old College for ever. I cannot wait to be free of all its rules. Have we told you our plans yet?'

Bartholomew shook his head warily. It was Stasy who replied.

'Hawick and I will settle here and earn ourselves a fortune. There are only three physicians and one surgeon for the whole town, so there are plenty of opportunities for two young and talented *medici*.'

This alarming news made Bartholomew think it was just as well he was giving up teaching, as he might need all his time to repair the mistakes the ambitious but inept duo would make. He had been astonished when they had passed their disputations, and only later had it occurred to him that money might have changed hands – he knew for a fact that their examiner had allowed himself to be bought in the past. Unfortunately, by that time, it was too late to do anything about it.

'Isnard, the cripple-bargeman, came here last night,' said Hawick, changing the subject when Bartholomew made no reply. 'He was ill.'

Most people who visited Bartholomew were, but he was more concerned by the news than he would normally have been, because of an outbreak of summer flux. He had tended a dozen new cases the previous day, all from the parish of St Mary the Less, and Isnard lived nearby.

'Not the flux,' said Stasy, reading his mind. 'He has a

head cold, and wants you to cure him. He says he cannot sing with a sore throat.'

Isnard was a member of the Michaelhouse Choir, which had recently changed its name to 'the Marian Singers' in a effort to escape a reputation for tuneless bawling.

'Please do not make him better,' begged Hawick. 'He has a voice like a donkey, yet still wants to perform at our graduation ceremony. It will be much nicer without him – without all of the choir, in fact.'

That was certainly true, and as it would be Bartholomew's last appearance as a University Regent Master, he, too, would be sorry to have it marred by the cacophony that passed as music among the Marian Singers. But Isnard had been his patient for years, and Bartholomew had a soft spot for him, so he would visit him later, and if he could help, he would, despite the unhappy consequences for everyone else's ears.

When Cynric rang the bell a second time, the scholars hurried into the yard, where the Master was waiting to lead them to church for their morning devotions. The current Master was Brother Michael, not only a celebrated theologian and influential Benedictine, but also the University's Senior Proctor. Although proctors were technically answerable to the Chancellor, Michael had been in University politics for so long that the Chancellor answered to him, and it was common knowledge that he made all the important decisions.

As soon as the last student was in line, he led the way through the gate and out onto St Michael's Lane. Even though the sun was not yet up, the streets were already uncomfortably hot, and the scholars' feet kicked up dust as they went. Bartholomew tried to remember when it had last rained, and supposed it was back in May. Trees and crops wilted, several wells had run dry, and he had never seen the river so low.

Bartholomew was fairly sure that the paucity of water was exacerbating the spread of the flux, as the easiest way to use less of it was by cutting down on basic hygiene – most folk now saw water as too precious a commodity to waste on needless hand-washing. Unfortunately, he stood alone in advocating higher standards of cleanliness, because everyone else thought the flux came from a poisonous miasma that seeped from decomposing vegetation or meat, and thus viewed good sanitation as an irrelevance.

The procession wove through the shadowy graveyard and entered St Michael's Church, which was a pretty building on the High Street. It had a low, squat tower and an unusually large chancel to accommodate all the College's students and Fellows; staff and parishioners were relegated to the nave. Inside, Bartholomew inhaled the familiar odour of cool, damp plaster, old wood and cheap incense. When he married, he would have to attend All Saints-in-the-Jewry, which was smaller, shabbier and not nearly so pretty.

It was his turn to assist at the altar, so he took his place and watched Father William riffle through a missal for the readings of the day. The Franciscan had a reputation for being the grubbiest friar in Christendom, and he more than lived up to the description that day. His habit was stiff with ingrained dirt, his hands were filthy, and his hair stood up in oily spikes around an irregularly shaped tonsure.

His other claim to fame was conducting inordinately speedy masses, which the students appreciated, even if the Fellows considered this a dubious skill. He galloped through the Eucharist at an astonishing lick, and had intoned his final prayers while Bartholomew was still fumbling about with the chalice and paten. When the rite was over, Michael led his scholars home again. Bartholomew walked next to William, with the three other Fellows behind, and the students streaming at their heels.

'I am tired of this heat,' the Franciscan grumbled, breaking the rule that scholars were to process to and from church in silence. The students began chattering, too, their spirits high with the looming end of term, and the knowledge that they would soon be leaving for the summer vacation, some never to return now that their studies were complete.

Bartholomew agreed. 'We need rain before the wells run completely dry.'

'The situation would be less dire if Mayor Morys allowed folk to take their drinking water from the Mill Pond,' William went on. 'It is half full, but will he share? No! He forces them to pay for every bucketful. It is brazen robbery.'

'No one should drink from the Mill Pond,' said Bartholomew with a fastidious shudder. 'Although it is better than the river – now Morys keeps the Mill Pond sluices closed, there is almost nothing to wash away all the accumulated sewage and rubbish. It is a filthy grey trickle, yet people still use it for cooking and washing.'

William wrinkled his nose. 'It certainly stinks. I can smell it from here.'

Bartholomew could also smell something, but suspected it was the friar's mucky robe.

'Could this stench be the miasma that causes the summer flux?' William asked uneasily. 'I know you have seen more cases than you can count these last few days.'

Bartholomew did not want to explain his rejection of the miasma theory to a man who was incapable of accepting new ideas, so he kept his answer vague. 'This outbreak is like no other that I have seen. Usually, I can blame a specific well or stream, but this time, the victims appear to be random – small clusters with no or little connection to each other.'

William stole a glance at the students walking behind. 'Stasy and Hawick have vowed to cure the flux when they start their own practice. I hope they fail. They are arrogant now, but if they cure an ailment that confounds you, we shall never hear the end of it.'

'They will not succeed,' said Bartholomew, aware that producing an effective remedy would require a considerable outlay of money and a lot of hard work. His students did not have the first, and were unlikely to bother with the second.

'You should order Morys to open the sluices,' said William. 'Then all the Cam's filth will be washed away and we shall be stench- and miasma-free once more.'

'That will take more than the contents of the Mill Pond,' sighed Bartholomew. 'Too much filth has accumulated in the river, and the only thing that will help us now is rain. *Lots* of rain.'

William was silent for a while, then asked, somewhat out of the blue, 'What do you think of your new brother-in-law? I was astonished when Edith remarried last month, as I assumed she would remain a widow for the rest of her life.'

He could not have been more astonished than Bartholomew. Although his sister's first marriage had been an arranged one, it had been very happy, and she had always maintained that no one could ever take Oswald's place. Philip Chaumbre seemed pleasant enough, but there was nothing remarkable or special about him, and Bartholomew failed to understand why he, of all men, should have caused Edith to change her mind.

'I assume it is a match of convenience,' William went on. 'Oswald left her a cloth business and Chaumbre is a dyer, so the association will benefit them both. Indeed, I would say it has put them among the wealthiest families in the shire.'

'I hope that was not why she accepted him,' said Bartholomew, alarmed by the notion. He loved his sister dearly, and her happiness was important to him.

'Not everyone has the good fortune to wed for love, Matt,' said William, very sagely for a man who would never marry at all. 'Count yourself lucky.'

Since Brother Michael had been elected Master, the College had developed in leaps and bounds. First, he had persuaded wealthy benefactors to pay for repairs and improvements, so the roofs no longer leaked and there was real glass in all the windows. This meant that in inclement weather, scholars were no longer obliged to choose between light and warmth – having the shutters open so they could see what they were doing, or closed so they did not freeze.

Second, he had arranged for the Michaelhouse pier to be upgraded. As it was very conveniently located for the market square, merchants paid handsomely to use it for the goods they transported up and down the river. Thus it now provided the College with a princely and reliable income, most of which was spent on food, so sawdust-filled bread and watery pottage had become distant memories.

And finally, he had elevated Michaelhouse's academic standing by encouraging its Fellows to publish their ideas and send copies to Avignon for papal endorsement. Under his rule, the College's future looked both secure and promising.

He led the way into the hall and took his place on the dais at the far end. He waited until his Fellows and students were standing at their designated places, and had stopped chatting, fussing and fidgeting. Then he intoned a grace in his perfect Latin, before sitting down and indicating that the servants were to serve breakfast.

That day, all the windows were open in the hope of catching a breeze, although with scant success. For some inexplicable reason, breakfast comprised a stodgy pease pudding and roasted meat, which Bartholomew considered unsuitable fare for a sweltering summer morning. Michael disagreed, and set to with gusto.

'How are your wedding preparations coming along, Matt?' the monk asked conversationally, loading his platter with beef.

He was Bartholomew's closest friend, although too busy for his own good as he juggled the duties of Master and Senior Proctor with his teaching obligations. He was a large man, tall as well as plump, and was of the opinion that a princely girth was a sign of healthy living, not because he ate too much.

Bartholomew winced. The wedding was a sore point, as he would have liked a small, private ceremony, as befitted two people well past the first flush of youth, but Matilde had waited a long time to snag the man she loved, and she wanted it done properly. She had asked a friend named Lucy Brampton – a lady of firm opinions and a flair for organisation – to help, and Lucy was determined to provide Matilde with a day to remember. They gaily ignored his pleas for restraint, which meant he had given up being horrified by the growing grandiosity of the occasion, and had settled into a kind of nervous resignation.

'I would rather spend the money on medicine for the poor,' he said, hating the thought of funds squandered on things he deemed unimportant, such as garlands, fine table linen, and the purchase of new-fangled implements from the Italian Peninsula called 'forkes' – although as these were used to spear food, thus obviating the need for filthy fingers plunging in and out of the common bowl, he supposed they had their advantages.

'Do not be such a misery!' chided Michael. 'Your guests deserve to have the time of their lives. And so do you.'

'Have you heard any news about those two missing scholars?' asked Bartholomew, changing the subject because he knew they would never agree; Lucy Brampton was not the only one who liked a party. 'Huntyngdon from King's Hall and his friend Martyn?'

It was Michael's turn to wince. 'None – their where-abouts remain a mystery.'

'They are my patients,' said Bartholomew. 'I do not know them well, but neither strikes me as a man to jaunt off without telling anyone.'

Michael agreed. 'Huntyngdon is the illegitimate but much-loved son of an earl, while Martyn is destined for the Bishop's retinue. Both have promising futures, and their disappearance is out of character. I fear something terrible has happened to them.'

'You think they are dead?'

Michael nodded slowly. 'Although there is no reason to suspect foul play. They are popular with their colleagues, and we have been at peace with the town for weeks now. There have been no brawls since that Spital business back in May.'

'So, what will you do about them?'

'There is no more I *can* do. I have explored every avenue of enquiry imaginable, but learned nothing of use. However, it will not be my concern after today, because I am delegating the matter to my Junior Proctor.'

'Thomas Brampton?' asked Bartholomew, startled. Brampton, the brother of Matilde's friend Lucy, was more politician than investigator, and was unlikely to succeed where Michael had failed. Ergo, by passing the respon-sibility to him, Michael was effectively giving up on Huntyngdon and Martyn. 'Really?'

'I have no choice,' said Michael, so heavily that Bartholomew saw it had not been an easy decision. 'Besides, the case needs fresh eyes.'

'You might fare better getting his sister to do it,' said Bartholomew acidly. 'Lucy is arranging my wedding with terrifying efficiency, so hunting missing scholars will be no kind of challenge at all for her. It is a pity the siblings are not reversed – she should meddle less, and he should do it more.'

'I shall promote him to Senior Proctor tomorrow,' said Michael quietly. 'He is—'

'But *you* are Senior Proctor!' blurted Bartholomew, shocked to learn that Michael was planning to vacate a post that afforded him so much power. He lowered his voice, aware that students were turning to listen. 'Or is this your way of announcing that your ambitions have been realised at last, and you have been awarded an abbacy or a bishopric?'

Michael smiled. 'Not yet, although it is only a matter of time. However, Aynton plans to resign as Chancellor tomorrow, and I have decided to take his place. I cannot be Chancellor and Senior Proctor at the same time, so Brampton must step into my shoes.'

Bartholomew blinked, startled anew. 'Aynton is leaving? But he has only been in post for a few weeks!'

'More than enough time for him to realise that he is unequal to it.'

'How can that matter, when you are Chancellor in all but name?' Bartholomew was unsettled by the news, feeling his entire world was beginning to shift and change, and he did not like it. 'I cannot imagine there is much for him to do.'

'Unfortunately, there is,' sighed Michael. 'We are far larger and more prosperous than we were a decade ago, so there is a lot to handle, even for a figurehead. And Aynton *is* unequal to the task. He is a pleasant fellow, but he is disorganised, feeble and inept, and it has been a struggle for me to manage his duties, as well as my own.'

'So you are glad he is going?'

'I am not,' replied Michael grimly. 'I would rather he acquired a backbone and a modicum of common sense, and worked with me to drive our University into the future. I much prefer directing from the sidelines, as it gives me greater freedom to act. I do not want to be elected Chancellor tomorrow.'

Bartholomew gaped yet again. 'You plan to hold an election *tomorrow*? Is that not rather hasty? You usually claim that these things take months to organise.'

'As they should,' said Michael. 'But we cannot be without a titular head over the summer, as there are several very important matters pending that will require a Chancellor's seal. Aynton has done us a serious disservice by deciding to leave so precipitously.'

'But tomorrow!' breathed Bartholomew, still stunned. 'Why not next week?'

'Because we must be quorate for the vote to be legal, and some of our Regent Masters are already slipping away – they are supposed to wait until the end of term, but we all know this rule is regularly broken. Ergo, I have no choice.'

'So why will you stand? Why not remain Senior Proctor, and find a Chancellor you can manipulate, as you have always done before?'

'If only I could,' sighed Michael. 'Unfortunately, as soon as Aynton announced his retirement, three men raced forward to nominate themselves as his replacement. None are suitable, and would damage the University that I have worked so hard to build.'

'Which three?'

'John Donwich of Clare Hall, who is a diehard traditionalist, resistant to change; Richard Narboro of Peterhouse, who cannot walk past a shiny surface without stopping to admire himself; and Geoffrey Dodenho of King's Hall, whose brain is smaller than a pea.'

'Oh,' said Bartholomew. 'I see what you mean. Donwich and Narboro *would* be a disaster. But surely you can bend Dodenho to your will? He is too dim-witted to know what was happening, and would present all your ideas as his own.'

'I considered it, but I cannot have him involved with the complex negotiations that are scheduled over the summer.

15

He would destroy everything just by opening his mouth.'

'But what happens if you lose tomorrow?' asked Bartholomew worriedly.

Although Michael had done more for the University than any scholar in living memory, there were some who resented his success and would vote against him out of jealousy and spite. It would be none of Bartholomew's business soon, but that did not mean he would stop caring about the *studium generale* and its future.

'I will not lose.' Michael shrugged confidently. 'I am the best candidate. Besides, not only will the others have no time to gather any meaningful support, but it is the Feast of St Benedict on Friday. The founder of my Order will ensure that I am where I need to be on the morning following tomorrow's election.'

'Will he?' asked Bartholomew doubtfully, aware that Michael did not always keep the vows he had made at his ordination, so might not be as favoured as he imagined.

'Of course.' Michael smiled as he wiped his greasy fingers on a piece of linen. 'It will be your last vote as a Regent Master. And perhaps the most important of them all.'

It was always difficult to teach during the last few days of the summer term, when disputations were over, the results were pinned on the door of St Mary the Great, and the students itched to go home to their families. A few slipped away early, ignoring the obligation to 'keep term' – to spend a specific number of nights in Cambridge during the academic year. The rest, however, grew rowdier and more restless with each passing day, especially those who were due to graduate, who felt their studies were now complete.

Most Fellows did not try to give lectures and left their lads free to do what they liked. Bartholomew was the exception, and persisted with a full teaching schedule, as he felt there was still so much more for his students to learn. He drove them hard, ignoring their resentful glares as the College's lawyers, grammarians, philosophers and theologians strolled off to lounge in the orchard or play ball games in the yard.

He kept his pupils at their studies until the bell rang for the noonday meal. While they hurried away to snatch some fresh air before eating, he decided to visit Isnard, to make certain that the bargeman really was suffering from a cold and not the flux. He looked around for a couple of students to take with him, feeling it was a good opportunity to continue their education. His eye lit on Stasy and Hawick, who were by the gate, where the College's assorted poultry had also gathered.

'You want us to go with you now?' asked Hawick in dismay, when Bartholomew told them that they had been chosen for some additional tuition. 'But dinner is nearly ready.'

'And it is too hot for traipsing after customers anyway,' added Stasy, fanning himself with a grimy hand. 'Let Isnard come to us if his complaint is urgent.'

'You will not keep many patients with that attitude,' warned Bartholomew. 'And what are you doing among these birds anyway? Whatever it is, they do not like it.'

'They do not,' agreed a quiet voice, and Bartholomew jumped as John Clippesby, the College's gentle Dominican, emerged from the shadows.

It was generally assumed that Clippesby was either insane or a saint in the making. He talked to animals, and insisted that he understood every grunt, squawk, moo, bleat, bark, mew, cluck or oink directed back at him. What he claimed they told him often made a lot more sense to Bartholomew than the ramblings of his allegedly rational colleagues.

'What are you doing, lurking in the dark?' demanded Stasy, his tone impertinent for a student addressing a Fellow. 'Listening to that gossipy peacock again?'

He exchanged a smirk with Hawick, and Bartholomew

bristled. He was fond of Clippesby, and was not about to stand by while Stasy mocked him, but Clippesby spoke while the physician was still devising a suitable rebuke.

'Peacocks never gossip,' he said, regarding Stasy with wide, innocent eyes. He gestured to the bird in question, a glorious creation with an enormous tail and an ego to match, who belonged to Walter the porter. 'However, Henry did mention that you drove him and his harem into the kitchens last night, with a view to seeing them in trouble with Agatha for scoffing raisins.'

'Then Henry is a liar,' declared Hawick indignantly. 'We did nothing of the kind.'

'Birds do not know how to lie,' said Clippesby, and it occurred to Bartholomew that the same was true of the Dominican himself. 'They see no need for it.'

The peacock strutted towards Clippesby, hoping for a treat. For no reason other than malice, Stasy aimed a kick at him, and as Bartholomew chose that moment to step towards the gate, the flying sandal missed the bird and caught him instead. While Stasy staggered off balance, Henry lunged.

'It bit me!' howled Stasy, holding up a finger to reveal a tiny blob of blood. 'It should not be allowed to roam free. That thing is dangerous!'

'So are you,' retorted Bartholomew, making a great show of hobbling about and rubbing his knee, although the truth was that Stasy's shoe had barely touched him.

'Hey!' came Walter's angry voice. The porter was inordinately fond of his bird, and had recently spent all his life savings on four peahens, because Clippesby said that Henry yearned for female company. 'Come near my flock again and I will kick *you*! Now clear off!'

Stasy shot him a dismissive sneer before loping away towards the orchard, where the medical students tended to congregate at that time of day. Hawick muttered what might have been an apology, and trotted after him.

'Do you want me to fetch them back?' asked Clippesby, leaning down to pick up a chicken that was scratching about nearby; he cocked his head towards her as she clucked. 'Ethel says you wanted to take them to see Isnard.'

'I did,' said Bartholomew shortly. 'But not any more. Were they up to mischief here, John? The birds did not seem very happy when I arrived.'

'Stasy wants to wring Henry's neck,' explained Clippesby. 'So he and Hawick herded all the poultry here, so he could grab him. Ethel heard them planning the attack.'

'What?' cried Walter, shocked and angry. 'He was going to do *what*?'

'Do not worry,' said Clippesby kindly. 'I shall watch over the birds myself from now on. No harm will come to Henry, I promise.'

Bartholomew hoped he was right, for everyone's sake, because if Henry did meet a premature end, murder would quickly follow, and he did not want Walter to hang for it.

The physician felt as if he was in a furnace as he headed towards the river, to take the towpath to Isnard's cottage. The sun burned through his black academic tabard, which was so uncomfortable that he flouted College rules by removing it. Shirt sleeves were cooler, although not by much, and he pitied those who were in the grip of the flux, fevered and lying in houses that were like ovens.

The Mill Pond was a small lake, very deep in the middle, created by the West, Middle and East dams. Each dam had a sluice, which comprised great wooden gates that could be opened and closed as needed. In the past, several mills had operated there, but now there was only one: Mayor Morys's. It stood near the Small Bridges, and the West Dam directed water down a specially constructed spillway that drove its wheel.

Morys's mill ground grain. If the Mill Pond were low or empty, its wheel could not turn and he lost money, hence his determination to hog what little water trickled in from the drought-starved Cam to the south. The river's flow was not cut off entirely, but the dams slowed it significantly, so what water did seep through was so sluggish as to be virtually stagnant. The situation was a little better when the West Dam was opened to drive the mill, but not much, as most of the water was directed along an arm of the Cam that flowed around the west of the town, and only joined the main river once past the Carmelite Priory.

Bartholomew reached Isnard's house, which was near the Middle Dam, and stopped for a moment to look around.

There were not many buildings near the pond, as it had a tendency to flood in wet weather. The exceptions were Isnard's house, which stood on a small rise; a row of cottages occupied by people who had not appreciated the location's shortcomings when they had moved in; and a low, squat ugly building belonging to Peterhouse. This was Hoo Hall, named after an early Master, and currently offered as accommodation for students.

The Mill Pond itself was a hive of activity. Although less than half full, women flocked around its sun-baked shores to do their laundry or to scrub pots and pans; others collected water for cleaning, cooking and drinking. Guards employed by Morys prowled to make sure they paid for what they took. It smelled stagnant and Bartholomew wrinkled his nose in distaste.

'It is no good advising them to use the wells, Doctor,' said Isnard, emerging from his home to greet him; he spoke in a croak and he could not breathe through his nose. 'Most of those have turned muddy, but the Mill Pond is still clean.'

Bartholomew was amazed that anyone should consider

the Mill Pond 'clean', although he knew better than to debate the matter with Isnard, whose opinions were immovable once he had decided upon something. Bartholomew was fond of him, even though events earlier in the year had revealed the bargeman to be an intolerant bigot with a passionate and wholly irrational hatred of strangers.

'Do you drink from the pond?' he asked.

Isnard regarded him askance. 'I do not! And nor will I, unless someone contrives to fill it with ale. But it is too hot to stand out here, so come inside and sit in the shade. Then you can cure me of this vile disease.'

Bartholomew entered to see that Isnard had company – Margery Starre was visiting. Margery was quite open about the fact that she was a witch, which should have been enough to see her hanged. However, she knew how to end unwanted pregnancies, prepare love potions, banish adolescent spots, and ward off evil. Thus she was popular with townsfolk and scholars alike, so the authorities tended to turn a blind eye to her activities.

'I cannot help poor Isnard, Doctor,' she said ruefully. 'I have never been any good at curing common colds.'

Nor was Bartholomew, so the bargeman was horrified when told that he would just have to wait for it to get better on its own.

'What do you mean, you cannot mend me?' he rasped at Bartholomew. 'You must! I can barely breathe, my head aches, my throat is sore, and I feel terrible. I intend to sing a solo at the University's graduation ceremony, and I cannot practise feeling like this.'

'Rest your voice, drink lots of boiled barley water, and let nature take its course,' instructed Bartholomew. 'You should be well in time for your solo.'

'But I need to rehearse or they will give the part to John Godenave!' cried Isnard hoarsely. 'There must be *something* you can do.'

21

'You can try a linctus of blackcurrant, but rest and time are really the only cures.'

'You see, Isnard?' said Margery. 'What did I tell you? We medical professionals are all as helpless as each other when it comes to colds.'

'And the summer flux,' put in Isnard nasally, full of disgust for both of them. 'Neither of you are very good at mending *that* either.'

'He is right, you know,' said Margery, as she and Bartholomew walked along the towpath together a short while later. 'I have had no success with curing this horrible flux.'

Bartholomew did not reply, because he was holding his tabard over his nose and mouth so as not to inhale the stench of the near-stagnant river and its festering cargo of sewage, animal manure and refuse. He used his free hand to flap away the flies that swarmed around his head, determined to prevent them from alighting, as he knew exactly where they had been first. Margery was made of sterner stuff, and neither the insects nor the reek seemed to bother her.

'The flux always comes in summer,' she went on, 'but it is much worse this year. I am rushed off my feet with demands for help.'

Bartholomew glanced up at a brassy sun in a harsh blue sky, and wondered when he had last seen even a wisp of cloud. 'What do you prescribe for it?' he asked, his voice muffled by the cloth.

'Boiled barley water,' came the surprising response. 'It washes out the poisons, see. Of course, mine comes complete with incantations to make it more effective – to God *and* to the older deities, as it is difficult to know who to trust on this matter. I also add a bit of liquorice and mint to make it palatable.'

'That is a good idea,' said Bartholomew approvingly,

then added hastily for clarification, 'Flavouring the water, I mean.'

She smiled smugly. 'Yes, *you* should not try spells; you are not qualified for it. You might want to warn those students of yours against it, too – Stasy and Hawick. They think they will compete with me when they set up business here, but they are sadly mistaken.'

'I imagine they are more interested in competing with me,' said Bartholomew wryly. 'But they know no spells, so do not worry on that score. Magical incantations are not part of the University's medical curriculum.'

'You may not have taught them any, but they certainly think they have learned some on their own account,' countered Margery. 'They are vile boys, and I am surprised you took them on in the first place.'

Bartholomew was not about to confide that they had been foisted on him against his will by a former Master, because the College had been strapped for cash at the time, and they had agreed to pay their tuition fees up front. He turned off the towpath into Water Lane, unable to stand the stink of the river any longer.

'There is Richard Narboro,' said Margery, pointing a gnarled finger at a scholar who strutted along ahead of them. She sniggered. 'Have you heard about him and Lucy Brampton? You know Lucy – she is the one organising your wedding.'

'She certainly is,' muttered Bartholomew, and before he could add that he had heard the story about her several times already, Margery began to regale him with it anyway.

'Ten years ago, Narboro offered to marry her. Her family agreed, so a contract was drawn up. Then he went off to work for the King, but promised to wed her when he got back at the end of the month. The rogue stayed gone for more than a decade. He arrived home a few weeks ago, took one look at her, and called the betrothal off.'

'I wonder when it will rain,' said Bartholomew in an effort to change the subject; he disliked gossip. Unfortunately, Margery declined to be sidetracked.

'He claimed he did not like what the delay had done to her teeth, and announced his intention to remain a scholar instead. And scholars cannot wed, as you know. So poor Lucy spent ten years waiting for him, and now it is too late for her to snag someone else.'

'You cannot know that,' objected Bartholomew, feeling obliged to defend her – she was Matilde's friend after all. 'She looks much younger than her forty summers, and her teeth are not the worst I have ever seen.'

'Her fangs are not the real problem,' averred Margery in conspiratorial tones. 'Her brother is: Junior Proctor Brampton plans to sue Narboro for breach of promise, and no one wants to marry into a litigious family, lest they become victims of a lawsuit, too.'

'I hardly think—'

'Doubtless that is why she is planning your wedding,' Margery forged on. 'Because she was deprived of her own. Of course, I have seen her smiling at other men, so *she* has not given up hope, even if everyone else knows her situation is hopeless. Narboro's rejection of her was cruel, and I am surprised she has not come to me for a spell to punish him.'

'She is not that kind of—'

'I heard this morning that Narboro wants to be Chancellor,' interrupted Margery, and cackled her amusement. 'As if *he* could defeat Brother Michael! However, just to make sure nothing goes awry, I have put hexes on all three of the good brother's opponents.'

'Please do not tell anyone else that,' begged Bartholomew, thinking that Michael's chances of victory might be damaged if it became known that he had acquired the active support of a witch.

'I will not,' she promised. 'I know how scholars fear

matters they do not understand, poor lambs. But just look at that foolish Narboro! He barely has two pennies to rub together, yet he still attires himself like a baron. He will not be able to dress with such extravagance when Lucy's brother has finished with him.'

'I doubt Brampton will persist once he learns Narboro has nothing to give him.'

'You are wrong – the lawsuit is not about money, it is about revenge. Brampton is wealthy, and will use his fortune to crush a man who insulted his family's honour. To him, destroying Narboro is more important than Lucy's future happiness.'

Bartholomew looked at Narboro. As a Fellow of Peterhouse, he was obliged to wear its uniform tabard, but as these garments were rather shapeless, he had altered his to show off his trim figure. He had also dispensed with the hat that went with it, allowing him to flaunt his beautiful golden curls. He held something in his hand, and constantly glanced down at it.

'His mirror,' cackled Margery, watching in amusement. 'He is never without it, because he likes to be able to see himself at all times.'

There was a building with a new window at the corner of the lane, and Bartholomew watched as Narboro admired his reflection as he passed. He was so delighted by what he saw that he failed to watch where he was putting his feet, and he stumbled over a pothole.

'He is so vain!' chuckled Margery. 'His Peterhouse colleagues call him Narcissus Narboro, after a famous Greek person who loved himself so much that he died.'

'Greek mythology,' corrected Bartholomew. 'It did not actually happen.'

'Well, it might happen here,' averred Margery, when Narboro tripped a second time. 'He will break his neck unless he stops admiring himself.'

*

The midday meal was over by the time Bartholomew reached Michaelhouse, so his students had saved him some bread and cheese. He forgot to eat them in the excitement of teaching *De motu thoracis et pulmonis* that afternoon, although his students were less than thrilled about sitting in a stifling hot hall to learn Galen's pontifications on the movements of the chest and lungs. Then it was time for supper, followed by more patients, so it was well past eight o'clock by the time the physician finally repaired to the conclave.

The conclave was a pleasant room off the hall. It was the undisputed domain of the Master and his Fellows, and was where they gathered each evening to read, chat and prepare the next day's classes. Michaelhouse currently had five Fellows – Bartholomew, William and Clippesby, who had been there for years, and Aungel and Zoone, who were more recent appointments.

When Bartholomew arrived, the others were already there, and the atmosphere was one of convivial relaxation. He slumped wearily at the table and opened his copy of Galen's *De ptisana*. It was about the virtues of barley water, which he felt should be revisited now it was his chief weapon against the flux.

'You should relent, Matthew,' admonished William, who was trying to remove a nasty stain on his habit that had been there for weeks. 'It is unfair to drive your lads so hard when the rest of us are winding down.'

It was not sympathy for Bartholomew's classes that prompted the remark, but guilt: William had spent his day dozing in the orchard, and the physician's dedication to his duties made him feel lazy.

Bartholomew shrugged. 'They paid for a year's teaching, so that is what they will get. We do not want them claiming that they have not had their money's worth.'

'Your lads can have no cause for complaint on that score,' said Clippesby, who was in a corner, surrounded by roosting hens. 'You have crammed more inside their heads this term than the last five years combined.' One of the birds clucked, and he smiled. 'Indeed, Ethel has just informed me that no Michaelhouse students have ever worked so hard.'

'There is still so much more that they should know,' sighed Bartholomew. 'Yet in a few days, some will be licensed to ply their skills on real people. Would you want Stasy or Hawick to tend *you* if you were ill?'

'Certainly not,' declared William firmly. 'I shall continue to be looked after by you, even after you are wed.'

'Will you?' asked Aungel stiffly. 'Then what about me?'

John Aungel, until recently a student himself, had been appointed to teach medicine when Bartholomew left. He was young, eager and conscientious, but everyone knew he could never fill his former master's shoes.

'We shall use you both,' said Clippesby, ever the peace-maker. 'For different things.'

'You are better at horoscopes,' said William, and jerked a dirty thumb at Bartholomew. 'Whereas he thinks the stars have no effect on a man's health, and refuses to calculate them.'

Aungel allowed himself to be mollified. 'Then I shall provide them free of charge for anyone from Michaelhouse.'

'I should think so,' said Will Zoone, the last and newest of the Fellows. He was a tall, languid man with black hair, who taught arithmetic. He also designed bridges, castles and siege engines, although there tended not to be much call for these in the University. 'We are colleagues, and I would never think of charging you for *my* services.'

There was a short silence, as the other Fellows tried to think of something Zoone had that Aungel might want. Then Bartholomew went back to his book, aware that the conclave was stiflingly hot. The windows were open, but there was not so much as a whisper of breeze to move

27

the air. In the stillness of the evening, he heard church bells chiming to announce the end of compline. Shortly after, Michael arrived, all important huffing and puffing as he settled in his favourite chair.

'All is set for tomorrow,' he reported. 'The church is ready, and we shall have our election at noon. Donwich, Narboro and Dodenho will doubtless spend tonight preparing their speeches, but I shall just speak from the heart.'

'You will win,' predicted William gleefully, 'and Michaelhouse will be home to yet another Chancellor. Our College continues to go from strength to strength.'

'Although this election has been sprung on us with almost indecent haste,' put in Zoone worriedly. 'It smacks of intrigue.'

'Of course there is intrigue,' said Michael comfortably. 'It is the University.'

They began to discuss the other candidates, so Bartholomew returned to his reading. When he had finished, and was sitting back to rub his tired eyes, the conversation had moved to the two missing scholars.

'I *know* Martyn and Huntyngdon,' Aungel was saying. 'They are steady, reliable men, who take their University duties seriously. They are *not* absconders.'

'But one lodged in the Cardinal's Cap,' said Zoone disapprovingly. 'And the other visited him there. We all know that taverns are forbidden to scholars.'

'The Cap is different,' explained Michael. 'It is where learned men from different foundations gather for intelligent debate. There is never any trouble, so I tell my beadles to turn a blind eye. And yes, the missing men did meet there just before they disappeared – they discussed metaphysics, and left an hour later. Neither has been seen since.'

'Have you questioned the sentries on the town gates and bridges, Brother?' asked Aungel. 'Perhaps Huntyngdon and Martyn did slip away that night, although if so, I am sure they will have a legitimate reason. They are not men for reckless jaunts.'

'I questioned the guards twice,' replied Michael. 'They are certain that no scholars left that evening or the following day. And before you ask, yes, we *can* trust them – they have been vigilant since the fright we had with the threat of a French invasion earlier this year.'

Aungel raised his hands in a shrug. 'Then if they did not leave, they must still be here. But where? There are not many places one can hide for days on end.'

'They are not hiding,' declared Clippesby confidently. 'The College cat would have heard if that were the case, but she assures me that there has been no news on that front.'

At that point, there was a knock on the door and Cynric appeared.

'You are needed, boy,' the book-bearer told Bartholomew. 'By Sheriff Tulyet. There has been an accident on the Great Bridge.'

Bartholomew looped his medical bag over his shoulder. 'What sort of accident?'

'A nasty one,' replied Cynric. 'Perhaps you should come, too, Brother, because the casualty is thought to be Chancellor Aynton.'

CHAPTER 2

The Great Bridge was in the north of the town, and spanned the Cam at a point where it was narrow but deep. The piers and spandrels were stone, but the top part was wood and so in constant need of repair. Despite it being a vital part of the town's infrastructure, no one wanted to pay for its upkeep – Mayor Morys thought the Crown should do it; the Sheriff argued that it was the burgesses' responsibility; and the University thought it should be done by anyone except scholars.

As a result, repairs tended to be only grudgingly made, and it was not uncommon for bits to fall off before any action was taken. The situation was more precarious than ever that summer, as the bridge had been badly damaged by spring floods. Money had been squeezed from the merchants to mend it, and there had been great anger and dismay when Burgess Baldok had made off with some of it in June. Most people considered his subsequent murder to be divine justice, and confidently waited for the money to reappear with God's compliments. It never had, and its whereabouts continued to remain a mystery.

Bartholomew and Michael hurried up the High Street, both grateful for Cynric's reassuring presence at their heels. The town was rarely safe after dark, but it was worse when hot nights drove thieves and robbers out of their beds. Moreover, a large number of beadles were ill with the flux, and without them to keep law and order, trouble was never far away.

'I hope the bridge will be completely rebuilt in stone,' said Michael as they trotted along. 'It will be a lot safer, and will require much less maintenance.'

'Morys promised it would be,' said Bartholomew. 'Of course, that was when he wanted to get elected. Now he is nearing the end of his year in office, he need not bother.'

'Actually, he does,' countered Michael, 'because the King approved the tax that was levied to pay for it, and he keeps writing to Morys, demanding updates on its progress.'

'Someone should tell him that Baldok stole the money.'

'Morys did, but His Majesty just ordered him to collect some more. Then he sent one of his own builders to assess whether the bridge should be rebuilt in stone or patched up with wood. This man will present his findings at the guildhall on Friday, following which the council will make a decision about it.'

Bartholomew was contemptuous. 'The only decisions they make are ones that benefit themselves, so I doubt we shall see a decent bridge any time soon.'

'Do not be so sure, Matt. The King is watching this time, and he even sent a small donation to encourage matters along. Ergo, the council will *have* to do the right thing – and the right thing is a bridge of stone.'

'It is, but I shall only believe it when it happens,' said Bartholomew, who had heard dozens of promises to repair the bridge for good, but none had ever borne fruit.

Their journey took them past Matilde's house, where lamps were lit within. A glance through the open window revealed her sitting with a book in her lap, while Lucy knelt on the floor with a length of cream silk.

'That will be the cloth for Matilde's wedding kirtle,' surmised Michael. 'I wish she was as interested in the minutiae of this marriage ceremony as Lucy, because it might serve to distract her from the school for women she intends to establish.'

'Surely, *you* do not believe that education is only for men?' asked Bartholomew, shocked. 'I thought you were of the opinion that everyone should have a chance to learn.'

'I am – my grandmother would skin me alive if I thought anything else! The thing that concerns me is what happens when these women have completed their studies. What if they demand places at the University?'

Bartholomew shrugged. 'Who is more worthy of one: Matilde and your grandmother, or Father William and Dodenho?'

Michael pursed his lips, aware that there were actually rather a lot of men who had no business claiming to be scholars. 'All I hope is that her venture will not cause me too many headaches at the start of my reign as Chancellor. After a few months, she can do what she likes, because I shall sit so firmly on my throne that nothing will ever dislodge me.'

Bartholomew laughed, although he suspected that Michael had not been joking.

Just past Matilde's house was King's Hall, the University's largest and most prestigious College. One of the missing men was a Fellow there, as was Dodenho, who was no doubt inside at that very moment, labouring over his speech for the next day's election.

Then came the Hospital of St John, which comprised an untidy sprawl of buildings on the left side of the road, and a cemetery with gravelled paths on the right. On the southern edge of the graveyard were four large timber-lined pits, each deeper than a man was tall. They belonged to Philip Chaumbre, Bartholomew's new brother-in-law, who had used them for storing fermenting dye-balls until people complained about the stench. He had moved his festering wares to a site outside the town, but had so far failed to fill in the holes, which represented something of a hazard to anyone walking through the cemetery in the dark.

'He must be short of money, to leave them open for

so long,' said Michael as they passed. 'I can tell you for a fact that your sister bought her own wedding kirtle. As you know, the husband always sees to that, as a token of his devotion.'

Bartholomew regarded him uneasily. 'You mean I should pay for Matilde's?'

Michael gaped at him. 'You have not done it? Lord, Matt! I wonder she has not deserted you a second time. Of course you must! What are you thinking, man?'

'Can I borrow some money? I spent all this term's stipend on barley water.'

'Poor Matilde has no idea what she is letting herself in for,' muttered Michael, and changed the subject as they turned into Bridge Street, where bobbing lights indicated a commotion around the Great Bridge. 'Have you met Mayor Morys's wife Rohese, by the way? She is rather loose with her affections.'

Bartholomew blinked at such a confidence out of the blue. 'Is she?'

'She and Burgess Baldok were lovers, and it is whispered that the affair gave her a taste for dangerous liaisons.'

'Very dangerous,' said Bartholomew. 'Especially for her partners. I would not want to run foul of Morys.'

Michael nodded sombrely. 'He is not a man to overlook being cuckolded, and while he would not sully his own hands with violence, he hails from a clan of Fenland louts who will happily oblige him.'

Bartholomew frowned. 'Is *that* what happened to Baldok? It would not surprise me to learn that Morys ordered his murder, then, finding the stolen bridge money on his body, decided to keep it for himself.'

Michael pulled a wry face. 'If so, it will never be proven. Morys is all-powerful, and the council is steeped in corruption. Of course, Morys is great friends with your new kinsman Chaumbre . . .'

'Chaumbre is great friends with everyone,' said

33

Bartholomew defensively. 'But he left Cambridge years ago to make his fortune in London, and he has not yet been back long enough to forge unsavoury alliances – with Mayor Morys or anyone else.'

'Well, Morys made him a burgess the moment he came home again,' persisted Michael. 'And he does not do that for just anyone. I hate to speak ill of Edith's new husband, Matt, but please be cautious in your dealings with him. I fear he is not all he seems.'

Although mishaps on the Great Bridge were not unusual, they always attracted a lot of attention, so the area thronged with spectators when Bartholomew and Michael arrived. Many had brought lamps, which meant the scene was very brightly lit. The light attracted insects, which swirled around them in a dense cloud. Some onlookers held sleeves over their faces to avoid inhaling them, while others ducked and flapped at the buzzing, fluttering swarms.

A number of students were among the crowd, and a small group of beadles struggled in vain to move them on. In charge was Junior Proctor Brampton, a short, nondescript man who was not very good at imposing his authority on boisterous young men. By contrast, Michael strode forward with a scowl that saw most of them scatter like leaves in the wind. Bartholomew wondered how Brampton would cope when he was Senior Proctor. If he could not break up a peaceful gathering, how would he quell a riot?

'I had it under control, Brother,' he objected stiffly. 'There was no need for you to stamp up, glaring like a great fat gargoyle.'

'You should have yelled at them,' said Michael, manfully ignoring the insult. 'Forced them to listen to you.'

'I *was* yelling,' said Brampton sulkily. 'They just did not hear me.'

'Nor did I,' retorted Michael. 'But never mind this now. Just tell me what happened.'

'I have been too busy keeping the peace to ask questions,' retorted Brampton haughtily. 'Shall we do it now? Together?'

Bartholomew left them to it, and threaded through the onlookers, looking for Sheriff Tulyet. A number of burgesses were there, although not Chaumbre. Then a flash of movement caught his eye, and he saw a boy named Ulf Godenave dart among them. The Godenaves were a family of light-fingered layabouts who lived near the castle – which was convenient, given that at least one of them was usually imprisoned in it at any given time. Although no more than seven or eight years old, Ulf was already a skilled pickpocket, and his coat bulged with what he had stolen that night.

A few bold scholars had not melted away under Michael's basilisk stare, and clustered together near the burgesses. One was Narboro, resplendent in a fine linen robe and extravagantly pointed shoes. Bartholomew watched as Ulf sidled up to him, and dexterously sliced the purse from his belt. As Narboro had not noticed, Bartholomew went to tell him.

'Damn it!' cried Narboro in dismay. 'That contained money I can ill-afford to lose. I would give chase, but running kicks up dust, and there is nothing more unbecoming than a man covered in dirt. Do you not agree?'

He looked Bartholomew up and down, decided the physician could say nothing worth hearing on the subject, and flounced away without waiting for a reply.

Bartholomew walked on, unimpressed to recognise two more scholars who had defied Michael by lingering: Stasy and Hawick. They were with a pair of Fellows from Clare Hall, and he experienced a lurch of alarm. There was no love lost between these two foundations, and he was afraid they might be about to quarrel. If they did, others would join in, and there would be an all-out brawl.

'Go home,' he told his students curtly – he had no

authority over Clare Hall. 'You should not be out at this time of night. You know it is against the rules.'

'We came to see if you needed help,' said Stasy smoothly, although Bartholomew did not believe him, because they had never done it before.

'Go home,' he repeated, and glared until they slouched away. The Clare Hall men started to follow, but Bartholomew contrived to stand in their way, which was enough to make sure they went off in the opposite direction. When they had gone, he resumed his hunt for the Sheriff and found him at the edge of the bridge.

Richard Tulyet was a small man with an elfin face and a wispy beard, although his delicate features disguised a bold warrior and an iron will. He was honest, shrewd and efficient, and was willing to work with the University, which meant there was none of the jurisdictional sparring that afflicted most other shires with powerful academic or religious foundations in their midst. Bartholomew liked him enormously, and considered him a friend.

The same was not true of his son Dickon, a strapping lad who was already bulkier than his sire and would tower over him when fully grown. Dickon's voice had dropped an octave in the last year, and he was growing a moustache that promised to be a lot lusher than his father's. He carried himself like a soldier, despite the fact that his knightly training had been cut short on account of his overly aggressive behaviour. There was a rumour that the Devil had sired him, and most people who knew him were ready to believe it. A collective murmur of approval had echoed all across the town when Tulyet had recently announced that he was sending Dickon to join the King's army in France.

'Your Chancellor has had an accident,' the boy announced before his father could speak. He smirked gleefully. 'One with *lots* of blood. He has fallen on the *ponticulus.*'

The Great Bridge had wooden railings to prevent people from toppling off it, but these were so rotten that they could no longer be trusted. As a temporary solution for pedestrians, a rope bridge had been provided, which hung off the west side of the main one. Everyone called it the *ponticulus* – the 'little bridge'.

Bartholomew hurried forward and saw the Chancellor had evidently been walking over the main bridge when he had crashed through the railings to the *ponticulus* below. He had landed in such a way that one of the posts had speared him through the middle. Unfortunately, it had not yet killed him, and his chest rose and fell as he struggled to breathe. He was alone, although dozens of people peered down at him from the bridge above.

'Where are the other *medici?*' demanded Bartholomew, shocked that nothing had been done to help the wounded man. 'All live closer than me – one should have come at once.'

'Two are away,' explained Tulyet, watching Bartholomew begin to climb down, 'while Rougham and the surgeon are at a feast in Clare Hall. You are the only one left.'

'Donwich invited them there, to celebrate the victory he thinks he will win in tomorrow's election,' put in Dickon, and smirked again. 'They will both be drunk by now.'

'When do you go to France?' asked Bartholomew coolly, feeling that the sooner the lad was out of the country, the better. Even Tulyet was beginning to acknowledge that Dickon was not all that could be desired in a son, while his mother openly admitted that he frightened her.

'Next month,' replied Dickon happily. 'I shall find something interesting to do there, even if tormenting peasants and burning villages is no longer allowed.'

'If you are to win your spurs and become a knight, you must remember the chivalric code,' lectured Tulyet. 'To protect the weak and—'

'Yes, yes,' interrupted Dickon impatiently. 'Although the weak would not be weak if they learned how to fight, so they only have themselves to blame.'

It was not easy for Bartholomew to reach the dying Chancellor, as his fall had caused the *ponticulus* to twist dangerously. He managed eventually, moving with care lest a sudden jolt should pitch them both into the river below. He was not pleased when he felt a thump at his side and saw that Dickon had followed him. He was about to order the boy away when Tulyet called out.

'He is stronger than me and lighter than Michael. He will be of more use to you than either of us, if you need help.'

Bartholomew knelt next to Aynton and told Dickon to hold a lamp so he could see. The post had entered the Chancellor's side and emerged through his back, rupturing vital organs as it went. There was nothing Bartholomew could do to save him, and he was glad that Aynton had lost his senses, so knew nothing of what was happening.

'Shall I haul the rail out?' offered Dickon eagerly. 'I am not afraid of blood.'

'I am sure you are not,' said Bartholomew, regarding him in distaste. 'But neither of us will be doing any hauling. We are going to let him die peacefully and with dignity.'

'You mean you will leave that thing inside him?' asked Dickon, bemused.

Bartholomew nodded, aware that Michael had heard his assessment of the Chancellor's condition, and was already murmuring last rites. Although not a priest, the monk had been given special dispensation to grant absolution during the plague and had continued the practice since. Tulyet began to order the spectators away, to give Aynton privacy in his final moments.

Dickon remained nonplussed. 'So we just kneel here until he stops breathing?'

Bartholomew nodded again. 'So stay back and keep quiet.'

Dickon retreated obediently, although not so far that he could not see what was happening. Then Aynton opened his eyes. Sorry for it, Bartholomew rummaged in his bag for the powerful poppy juice syrup he kept for those *in extremis*, aiming to make him sleep again. The Chancellor guessed what he was going to do and raised a bloodstained hand to stop him.

'I cannot . . . feel anything,' he gasped. 'Am I . . . dying?'

'Yes,' replied Bartholomew, knowing Aynton would not thank him for a lie. 'Michael is giving you absolution. Can you hear him?'

'He is a . . . good man,' whispered Aynton, and shifted, causing a welling of blood. 'He . . . make a fine chancellor . . . The task . . . beyond me . . . I did my best . . . never enough.'

'It does not matter now. Lie still and listen to his prayers.'

But Aynton grabbed Bartholomew's hand to pull him closer. 'Hear . . . confession. You . . . not a priest . . . God will not mind . . . unburden my soul . . . I have . . . grave sins.'

Bartholomew seriously doubted it. 'Michael!' he called urgently. 'Come down.'

'One stains . . . my conscience . . . especially,' Aynton went on, so softly that Bartholomew could barely hear him. 'I must tell—'

There was a loud crack when the monk stepped on the unstable parapet, and Dickon yelped as a lump of wood fell and hit him on the shoulder. Tulyet yanked Michael back before he did any more damage, and Bartholomew saw there would be no confessor coming.

'I . . . brought death . . . on the innocent,' Aynton continued; his grip on Bartholomew's fingers was weak and clammy. 'I sent Huntyngdon . . . to deliver a letter.' He shifted again and more blood gushed. 'To Narboro.'

'He must be babbling,' declared Dickon, who had inched forward to listen. 'Dying men do, apparently, although I have not seen many yet. Look at all that blood! Why is it—'

'Hush!' snapped Bartholomew.

'I was pushed,' Aynton breathed, his eyes full of anguish. 'I . . . was on the bridge . . . a shove . . . and over I . . .'

Bartholomew regarded him in shock. Then he glanced up at the broken railings, and saw it was unlikely that Aynton had fallen through them by chance. The bridge would have been empty at that time of night, with no bad-tempered jostling as there was during the day, so the chances of him stumbling violently enough to snap them by accident were remote. Someone had done to the Chancellor what had been done to Baldok a few weeks before.

'Who pushed you?' Bartholomew demanded urgently.

Aynton's grip tightened, but his voice dropped so low as to be all but inaudible. '. . . *instaribam* . . . *litteratus* . . . do . . . understand?'

Bartholomew frowned. 'It was a learned person? You mean a scholar?'

A spasm of agony gripped the Chancellor, and his voice faded lower still. '. . . *n litteratus* . . . *hoc*. . .'

'What is he saying?' demanded Dickon, craning forward keenly. 'Is it Latin?'

Aynton's eyes closed. He took two more shuddering breaths and the life slipped out of him. For a moment, all that could be heard was Michael on the bridge above as he continued to murmur prayers of absolution. Then Dickon began to clamour questions.

'Is he dead? What was he talking about? Did he tell you that a scholar killed him?'

'I thought so at first, but then it sounded like *non litteratus* – someone without formal learning,' replied Bartholomew, bemused. 'So now I have no idea which he meant.'

It quickly transpired to be impossible to carry Aynton off the twisted *ponticulus*. Bartholomew and Dickon tried, but it tipped at such a precarious angle that they were forced to stop. Then Michael suggested a stretcher with a winch, and hurried away to see what could be organised, leaving the Sheriff to control the ever-expanding crowd of ghouls on the bridge and the nearby riverbanks.

Mayor Morys arrived while Michael was gone, and began dispensing loud, impractical and unwanted advice on how to deal with the situation. He was more concerned with preserving the *ponticulus* than the dignity of the victim, and when he suggested dropping Aynton into the river and retrieving him by boat, Bartholomew's patience snapped.

'He is our Chancellor, not a sack of grain.'

'I stand corrected,' said Morys with an unrepentant smirk. 'Although, in my defence, I should remind you that he resigned, so technically, he is nothing at all.'

Bartholomew did not dignify that remark with a response. He was acutely uncomfortable, kneeling on the swaying *ponticulus* with Dickon. He had placed his tabard over Aynton's upper body, but the jutting rail made it impossible to cover the rest, and the spectators were going nowhere as long as there was an impaled corpse to hold their attention. Time passed slowly, and he wished Michael would hurry up.

'I hope Donwich wins the election tomorrow,' he heard Morys announce to his cronies. 'I could work with him – he is a man who understands the ways of the world.'

In other words, thought Bartholomew sourly, Morys believed Donwich to be more amenable to bribes. He glanced up at the Mayor, noting the sharp eyes, narrow face and expensive clothes. Morys was reputed to have quadrupled his wealth during his year in office, and Bartholomew was glad the man's tenure would expire at the end of the month.

'*I* could work with him, too,' came a woman's voice, and he saw the speaker was Morys's wife Rohese. 'I *like* the men from Clare Hall. They are all very fine specimens.'

She was twenty years her husband's junior and full of sensual vitality. Her lips were painted scarlet, and she had a provocatively undulating gait. He recalled what Michael had said about her, and wondered how much Morys knew about her indiscretions.

'Go home, Rohese,' the Mayor ordered sharply. 'This does not concern you.'

'You said that when John Baldok was killed,' pouted Rohese. 'But he was a friend.'

Morys regarded her coolly. 'This victim is Chancellor Aynton, and I am sure you do not include *him* in your circle of acquaintances.'

'I do not,' she conceded, then smiled. 'Is that young Dickon? What are you doing down there, my lovely?'

'Helping,' replied Dickon proudly, and for the first time ever, Bartholomew saw him blush. 'Because I am stronger than my father.'

'You are a very fine lad,' purred Rohese with a look so sultry that Dickon went redder than ever and, for once, could think of nothing to say.

With a final, smouldering glance that encompassed not only Dickon and Bartholomew, but – somewhat unsettlingly – Aynton, too, she turned and sashayed away.

'She knows my name,' said Dickon in a strangled whisper. 'Did you hear? I did not think she knew me.'

Given his unsavoury reputation, Bartholomew thought it highly unlikely that anyone in Cambridge would be unaware of Dickon's existence. He did not say so, though, because Dickon carried a sword, knives and probably other weapons as well, and might whip one out if he sensed an insult – and the *ponticulus* was far too unstable for a fracas.

When Rohese had gone, another head peered over the bridge. It belonged to a burly, bearded man in a dusty tunic, who carried himself with considerable authority. Bartholomew was about to order him away when he heard Michael's voice.

'You see the problem, Shardelowe? The *ponticulus* has torqued, so carrying Chancellor Aynton off it is impossible and—'

'Ah, the King's builder,' interrupted Morys, nodding approvingly. 'A man used to winching heavy objects hither and thither. It was a good idea to fetch him, Brother. However, whatever is done must not harm the *ponticulus*. It is too valuable.'

'So is our Chancellor,' retorted Michael tartly. 'Now move back so we can retrieve him, if you please.'

Shardelowe assessed the situation with a professional eye, then set about constructing a hoist. While he worked, Dickon whispered in Bartholomew's ear.

'The King sent Shardelowe to look at the bridge. His Majesty plans to come here next year, you see, and he wants to ride across it without being pitched in the river. He even gave us some money to help with the repairs, although my father says he was not very generous.'

Knowing His Majesty's reputation for thrift, Bartholomew suspected he had parted with the barest minimum – enough to ensure the town was forced to do what was necessary, but not enough to make much of a dent in the final bill.

Eventually, the winch was ready, so Bartholomew yielded his place on the *ponticulus* to the builder, who deftly secured Aynton with ropes. Dickon remained where he was, watching with rapt attention. Bartholomew went to join Michael and Tulyet.

'We are lucky this wretched bridge has not claimed more victims,' said Tulyet unhappily. 'Let us hope the council agrees to rebuild it in stone at the meeting on Friday, so that no one else will fall prey to the thing. Wood rots too easily.'

'Aynton told me he was pushed,' said Bartholomew. 'Deliberately.'

'You mean *murdered*?' breathed Michael, horrified and disbelieving in equal measure. 'But who would do such a thing?'

'He did not say. He was insistent, though.'

'*Was* he pushed?' asked Tulyet. 'Can you tell?'

'Not with certainty. However, I doubt he would have stumbled with enough force to have landed where he did. So I believe him – I think he *was* shoved.'

'Did he say anything else?'

'That he gave Huntyngdon a letter for Narboro, but he feared the errand may have caused Huntyngdon's death.'

'What sort of letter?' demanded Michael. 'Personal or University business?'

'There was no time to ask. I heard him say *litteratus*, which made me think he was accusing a scholar, but then I thought he said *non litteratus*, suggesting someone with no claim to education. But which did he mean?'

Michael glared at him. 'Well, you had better decide, Matt, because we *must* catch whoever did this. Not only was he a friend and a colleague, but we cannot have high-ranking University officers murdered with gay abandon.'

Tulyet called his son over. 'Dickon, you have sharp ears. What did you hear the Chancellor say before he died?'

'Not much, because he was muttering,' replied Dickon. 'But I thought he told Doctor Bartholomew that a scholar pushed him. It is probably true – they are a violent horde.'

Coming from Dickon, this was damning indeed.

Bartholomew raised his hands in a helpless shrug. 'I

am sorry, Brother. His voice was just too soft for me to catch.'

They stood in silence for a moment, all thinking of the man they had known for so many years. Then Tulyet became businesslike.

'I used the *ponticulus* just before compline and he was not here then. Ergo, the culprit struck while the office was being recited, because the alarm was raised moments after it had finished. This may help you to establish alibis among your suspects.'

Michael glanced at the Chancellor's body, now suspended in a cocoon of ropes. 'What suspects? A scholar, angry with him for resigning? A townsman, aiming to strike a blow at the University? A common robber, hoping for his purse?'

'Well, if the culprit is a scholar, you have less than ten days to find him,' said Tulyet. 'Most will leave on Saturday week, and some will never return. You must work fast.'

'Brampton will,' said Michael. 'I have an election to win, and then a University to run. But who found the body? Do you know?'

'The vicar of St Clement's,' replied Tulyet, and led the way to where the hapless priest stood wringing his hands in distress, white-faced and trembling.

'I saw no one else in the vicinity,' he blurted as they approached, anticipating their first question. 'And all I heard were awful groans from the victim, which is what made me look over at the *ponticulus*. I shall never forget the horror of what I saw, not even if I live for a thousand years.'

'Nor will we,' said Michael grimly.

It was not long before Aynton was placed gently on the bridge, where Cynric was waiting to cover him with a blanket. Once the Chancellor was safe from prurient eyes, Michael knelt to pray again, while the book-bearer went to recruit bearers to carry him home. Aynton had lived in Clare Hall, where he had accepted a Fellowship after he had been made Chancellor.

Bartholomew stood with Tulyet, waiting for Michael to finish and Cynric to return, and together they watched Shardelowe dismantle the hoist. The builder was not alone for long, because Morys sidled up to him.

'Our *ponticulus* must be mended by dawn, Shardelowe, or it will adversely affect tomorrow's trade,' he began. 'If you do that free of charge tonight, I guarantee that the council will vote for a stone bridge on Friday.'

Shardelowe regarded him coolly. 'I thought we had already agreed that they would.'

Morys shook his head. 'What we agreed was that, rather than putting it out to tender, we will just appoint you to do whatever repairs you recommend. I made no mention of which materials would be used.'

'But it must be stone!' cried Shardelowe angrily. 'Wood would not be worth my time.'

'And I shall ensure it *will* be stone,' said Morys smoothly. 'But only if you repair the *ponticulus* tonight. Well? Shall we shake hands on it?'

Bartholomew would not have trusted Morys as far as he could spit, but Shardelowe grasped the proffered hand and allowed himself to be led away to discuss the particulars.

'Morys did not even have the decency to lower his voice,' he said, watching them go. 'He just offered to fix the outcome of a council meeting, and cared nothing that the Sheriff was within earshot. I shall be glad when he steps down next month, so someone honest can take over.'

Tulyet laughed. 'Morys flourished by being *dis*honest, and his replacement will likely do the same. Indeed, there is no other reason to take the job, unless you enjoy imposing unpopular taxes, dealing with fractious colleagues, and fending off the University.'

'Will you report his antics to the King? Such brazen corruption cannot go unpunished.'

Tulyet grimaced. 'I already have, but Morys greased the palms of a few royal judges, and my complaint was quietly forgotten. However, I have no objection to his machinations this time, because he is right to secure us a stone bridge – even more so, now I have seen what happened to Aynton. But speaking of the University's officers, what is your Junior Proctor doing?'

Brampton was struggling to keep a group of drunken rowdies off the bridge. They were townsmen, so he had no authority over them, which they knew because they were jeering at him. His response was to flap his hands at them, which at first elicited a startled silence, then a chorus of mocking guffaws. Tulyet went to intervene, doing so with such consummate diplomacy that Brampton emerged with his dignity intact, which was nothing short of a miracle. Bartholomew wondered how Brampton would cope with a murder investigation, and hoped Aynton would not be deprived of justice because Michael's deputy was an inept nonentity.

Because the monk had dismissed most of the gawping scholars when he had first arrived, Cynric was having trouble finding anyone suitable to carry Aynton to Clare Hall. Then two students came to offer their services, although Bartholomew was not pleased to see that they were Stasy and Hawick, who had rebelliously ignored his order to return to Michaelhouse.

'I am not letting *them* near a corpse,' hissed Cynric to Bartholomew. 'They may swipe bits of it for dark purposes.'

Cynric was deeply superstitious and spent a lot of time with Margery Starre. He claimed to be a Christian, although the pagan amulets on his hat suggested that he was not a very committed one. He saw the hand of Satan everywhere, even – on occasion – in students.

47

'I do not think—' began Bartholomew, but Cynric cut across him.

'They are not to be trusted. You sent them home, but here they are, clamouring to tote cadavers about. It is not natural. Anyway, I do not like them.'

Nor did Bartholomew, but as the book-bearer had failed to find anyone else to help with Aynton, he had no choice but to accept their help.

'They can take the front, while you and I carry the back,' said Bartholomew, seeing his consternation. 'They will not misbehave while we are right behind them.'

'They might,' countered Cynric. 'But I have a charm that should keep them in line. If they try anything nasty, they will disappear in a puff of smoke.'

Bartholomew knew better than to reason with him, and was about to walk towards the stretcher himself when Dickon arrived with the clear intention of lending a hand, too. The boy was nearly a head shorter than the two students, but considerably bulkier, and Bartholomew had no doubts that he was equal to the task, despite his tender years.

'And he is another who Satan loves,' whispered Cynric, shooting him a venomous glare. 'My charm will work against *him* as well.'

'At this rate, you will be carrying Aynton by yourself,' said Bartholomew.

Cynric regarded him admonishingly. 'It is no laughing matter, boy. Now, keep your distance as we go, because I should not like you to be singed by stray sparks.'

He placed his three helpmeets where he wanted them and they set off. Bartholomew, Michael and Tulyet followed at a respectful distance.

'I still cannot believe that someone killed him,' said Michael, a catch in his voice – he had liked the inept, bumbling, amiable Aynton. 'His tenure was so short that no one can have found fault with it. Virtually no decisions were made, and I took responsibility for the ones that were. Ergo, the culprit must be a townsman – a *non litteratus* – who aims to damage the University.'

'I disagree,' said Tulyet. 'First, we have been at peace for weeks now, and I have not heard so much as a whisper of trouble. And second, it is pitch black and he wore a plain robe, so how could any townsman identify him? Do not lay this murder at our door, when it is obviously a scholar's work. A *litteratus*.'

'But I have just explained why it is not,' argued Michael. 'Aynton was an affable soul, who had no time to accrue enemies among his colleagues.'

'Then his death must be connected to his resignation,' shrugged Tulyet. 'Someone who objects to the fact that his replacement will be appointed tomorrow, and hopes that his murder will slow everything down.'

'I sincerely doubt it! Usually, everyone clamours at me to get a move on, and my colleagues will be delighted by the speed with which I have organised this election.'

'If you ask me, it is *too* fast,' persisted Tulyet. 'Your rivals have had no time to rally support, and they will resent it.'

'In which case, Brampton has his first three suspects,' put in Bartholomew. 'Namely Donwich, Narboro and Dodenho.'

Michael was thoughtful. 'It is possible, I suppose. This election is important, because once I am in post, it may be years before I decide to move on to greater things. My rivals will have a long wait before they can stand again.'

'Would any of them kill to be Chancellor?' Tulyet hid a smile at the monk's hubris.

'We shall have to find out,' replied Michael. 'However, even if one of the three did not strike at Aynton in person, they may have supporters to do it on their behalf. What is wrong, Matt? I can tell something is bothering you, because you are oddly quiet.'

He was right. 'Stasy and Hawick,' said Bartholomew unhappily. 'Why were they out when they should have been home? Why did they linger when I ordered them away? And why do they insist on carrying the stretcher?'

'Does your concern arise from the fact that you think them capable of murder?' asked Tulyet, eyeing him shrewdly.

'I am not sure what to think,' hedged Bartholomew, not about to speak his mind in front of the University's most powerful scholar and the Sheriff, although the truth was that his students were an unpalatable pair who might stoop very low indeed if they thought they would benefit from it.

'So these are the men Brampton must interview tomorrow,' said Michael. 'Donwich, Narboro and Dodenho; any followers they might have; and Stasy and Hawick.'

Clare Hall was the fourth College to be founded in the University, following on the heels of Peterhouse, King's Hall and Michaelhouse. It stood on Milne Street, between Trinity Hall and the church of St John Zachary, and owed its wealth to the generosity of a rich baroness who had taken it under her wing.

Michael tapped on its gate, unwilling to hammer when the hour was late and the residents would be sleeping. He need not have worried, though, because the porter opened the door to reveal a hall that blazed with lights and the sounds of a party in progress.

'For tomorrow,' the man explained. 'Master Donwich anticipates a victory.'

'Does he indeed?' said Michael, startled. 'But never mind that. I am afraid Chancellor Aynton is dead. We have brought him home. Shall we put him in the chapel?'

The porter disappeared towards the hall to ask his Master for instructions, leaving the visitors to set their burden down in the yard while they waited for a response. They were not alone for long: a scholar named John Pulham approached, carrying a lamp.

The Fellows of Clare Hall were all much of an ilk – suave, self-satisfied men whose contribution to academic life tended to be in University politics rather than any intellectual achievements. Bartholomew was not surprised that one of their number intended to run for the chancellorship the following day.

'Aynton?' breathed Pulham, when Michael told him what had happened. 'No! He was a gentle man. Who could have done this terrible thing?'

'Brampton will find out,' promised Michael. 'I would do it myself, but it is the Senior Proctor's responsibility, and I cannot fulfil those duties as well as being Chancellor.'

'Donwich thinks *he* will win,' said Pulham, casting a wry glance towards the hall.

'Where would you like Aynton?' asked Michael, declining to comment. 'The chapel?'

Pulham led the way, asking questions about Aynton's death that the monk was mostly unable to answer. His sadness seemed genuine, and there was a tremble in his voice that would have been difficult to fabricate.

The chapel was small, but boasted beautiful wall paintings, fabulous misericords, and stained glass that was among the best in the town. It smelled of expensive incense and new wood. The bearers set the bier on the floor, then Cynric, Stasy and Hawick went to stand in the yard, while Tulyet and Dickon left to quell a spat in a nearby tavern. Bartholomew waited inside the chapel with Michael, who had knelt to say more prayers. The monk had barely begun when Master Donwich strode in, two more Fellows at his heels.

John Donwich was an impressive figure – tall, elegant and haughty. His two companions were also handsomely attired, but there was a coarseness about them that made them different from the other members of Clare Hall. They were the pair who had been talking to Stasy and Hawick earlier, and Bartholomew wondered again why his students should associate with them when Michaelhouse and Clare Hall had never been friends.

'What is going on?' demanded Donwich. 'Why are strangers in our domain?'

'They brought Aynton to us,' explained Pulham quietly, watching Michael clamber to his feet. 'I am afraid he is dead.'

'*You* gave them permission to enter?' snarled Donwich. 'You overstep your authority, Pulham! I do not want the Senior Proctor and his minions in my College, thank you.'

'Master!' breathed Pulham, shocked by his incivility. 'You cannot—'

'You may leave now,' said Donwich, looking Michael up and down with undisguised distaste. 'Forgive me for not offering you refreshment, but it is late.'

'Not too late for a feast apparently,' retorted Michael, cocking his head at the sounds of continued merriment. 'Will you end your frivolities now that one of your Fellows lies dead?'

'That is none of your business,' snapped Donwich indignantly. 'Gille, Elsham? See him and his lickspittles out.'

'Steady on, Master,' gulped Pulham, acutely embarrassed. 'There is no need to insult the Senior Proctor with such—'

'He will not be a proctor tomorrow,' interrupted Donwich. 'Because I shall dismiss him and appoint Gille and Elsham instead. They have always supported me, unlike *some* people.'

'If you refer to me and the other Fellows,' said Pulham tightly, 'then perhaps you should stop favouring newcomers over old friends.' He glared at Gille and Elsham. 'Moreover, it was wrong to make a bid for the chancellorship without discussing it with us first. The outcome will affect the whole College and—'

'I do not need your permission,' snarled Donwich. 'I am Master, and I can do what I like. Now, if you will excuse me, I have *invited* guests to entertain.'

He stalked out. Pulham glowered at his retreating back, then indicated that Bartholomew and Michael were to walk with him to the gate. Stasy and Hawick hung back, and Bartholomew glanced around to see them talking to Gille and Elsham again. Cynric lurked nearby, and Bartholomew hoped the book-bearer would eavesdrop, because he wanted to know what they were saying to each other.

'I am sorry,' said Pulham, opening the gate. 'As you can see, our Master is rather ungovernable at the moment. Being elected head of house has turned him into something of a despot. Obviously, the rest of us do not condone his behaviour, but as long as Gille and Elsham indulge his every whim, there is little we can do about it.'

'Gille and Elsham are the only two Fellows who support him?' fished Michael, always interested in the internal squabbles of rival foundations.

Pulham nodded. 'The rest of us will not vote for him tomorrow. We want you, Brother.'

Bartholomew was astounded. There was an unspoken law that members of a foundation always stuck together, no matter what, so Donwich must have seriously ruffled his colleagues' feathers to have precipitated such open dissent.

Michael indicated the brightly lit hall. Its occupants were growing rowdier by the moment, suggesting they were already drunk or heading that way.

'Who is celebrating with him, if he has alienated all but two of his Fellows?'

'A lot of hostel men, who he thinks will vote for him,' replied Pulham. 'They will not, of course, and are just enjoying a good night at our expense. And some wealthy burgesses, who he hopes will become benefactors.'

Bartholomew glanced up at the window and was unsettled to recognise the distinctive profile of Philip Chaumbre. What was his brother-in-law doing in such company?

'I pity anyone trying to sleep,' he said, wincing as someone began to bawl a tavern song and others joined in with gusto.

Pulham gave a disgusted snort. 'It will not bother any of our students, because Donwich has let them all go home.'

'Before the end of term?' asked Michael indignantly. 'But only the Senior Proctor has the power to grant that sort of indulgence.'

'I know,' said Pulham tiredly. 'But Donwich thinks that particular statute is perverse, and aims to overturn it when he is Chancellor.'

'He is not Chancellor yet,' said Michael stiffly, 'and I cannot have Masters ignoring the rules to please themselves. There would be anarchy! Clare Hall can expect a substantial fine tomorrow. But tell me, Pulham, would anyone here harm Aynton? It did not escape my notice that Donwich did not ask how he came to die.'

Pulham blinked. 'No, he did not, did he! It was almost as if he already knew what had happened, so did not need an account from you.' Then he shook himself. 'What am I saying? The more likely explanation is that he could not bring himself to beg you for answers.'

'Are you sure?' asked Michael.

Pulham nodded firmly. 'Donwich would never hurt Aynton. On the contrary, he was delighted with him for resigning, as it allowed him a chance to further his own ambitions.'

'Delighted enough to have coerced him into it?' pressed Michael. 'And then killed him lest he changed his mind?'

'Donwich *has* recently revealed a side of himself that none of us knew existed,' acknowledged Pulham. 'But murdering a colleague? No, never.'

'Then what about his henchmen?' asked Michael, lowering his voice so the pair behind them would not hear. 'Are Gille and Elsham the kind of men who would do anything to promote their Master's interests?'

54

Pulham opened his mouth to deny it, then reconsidered. 'I would hope not,' he said eventually. 'They are Aynton's colleagues, too.'

'So, our list of murder suspects has expanded by two,' said Michael, as he and Bartholomew walked home; Stasy and Hawick trailed along behind them, and Cynric brought up the rear. 'Pulham was unable to say with certainty that Gille and Elsham are innocent.'

'Donwich did nothing to eliminate himself either,' said Bartholomew. 'He has always been ambitious, but, as Pulham pointed out, being elected Master of Clare Hall seems to have ignited a lust for even more power.'

Michael counted off the names on chubby fingers. 'Donwich and his henchmen Gille and Elsham; Narboro and any supporters he might have; Dodenho and any supporters *he* might have; and Stasy and Hawick, who are suspiciously friendly with two Fellows from a rival foundation.'

Bartholomew stopped walking and waited until the students caught up. 'What were you discussing with Gille and Elsham?' he demanded bluntly.

'They wanted a remedy against the flux,' replied Hawick, so smoothly that Bartholomew knew he was lying.

'They cannot afford to catch it, because Donwich relies on them so heavily,' put in Stasy with one of his irritatingly sly smirks.

Bartholomew peered at them in the dim light of the lamps lit outside Trinity Hall. 'The only "remedy" anyone can offer is good hygiene, rest, and plenty of fluids.'

Stasy's face was full of smug disdain. 'So you claim, but *we* have invented one, and we shall sell it when we open our practice. However, the recipe is a secret, so do not ask us for it, because we shall refuse to tell you.'

'There *is* no remedy,' insisted Bartholomew firmly. 'And

if you concoct something and sell it, knowing it will not work, you will be guilty of fraud.'

'Which will see you arrested,' put in Michael. 'Not by me, but by the Sheriff, as you will come under his jurisdiction once you leave the University. Moreover, someone will sue you if you promise a cure and it fails. A lawsuit could ruin you before—'

'We learned enough law at Michaelhouse to defend ourselves,' interrupted Stasy dismissively. 'Besides, our remedy *will* work. It will not only mend those who have the flux, but protect those who do not.'

'Impossible!' said Bartholomew. 'It is like the common cold: all we can do is alleviate the symptoms – tinctures to relieve pain, and plenty of boiled barley water.'

Aware that once Bartholomew began talking about medicine, he might wax lyrical for hours, Michael walked on alone. Cynric waited patiently for the lecture to finish.

'You and your boiled barley water,' sneered Stasy. 'You endorse it as the answer to everything. Well, in my opinion, it is worthless, and anyone who swallows it in the quantities you recommend is wasting his time.'

Bartholomew was silent for a moment, and when he spoke, his voice was cold enough to wipe the challenging grin from Stasy's face.

'My advice to patients is based on years of experience and observation, not something cooked up one night in a tavern. Boiled barley water will not cure the flux or a cold – nothing can – but it will help the body to recover lost fluids.'

Having had his say, he turned and strode away. A moment later, he heard Stasy chant in a voice so deep and sinister that all the hair stood up on the back of his neck.

'May Matthew Bartholomew never cure the flux or the common cold,' the student intoned. 'Dark lord, hear the supplication of your faithful servant.'

Bartholomew whipped around, but Stasy was not there.

Nor was Hawick, although Cynric emerged from the shadows.

'They left,' the book-bearer said. 'Do you want me to fetch them back?'

'Did you hear Stasy curse?' demanded Bartholomew, wondering if his ears had deceived him, as the student had sounded very close – within touching distance, in fact.

'I did, but do not worry,' said Cynric. 'Mistress Starre knows how to reverse nasty hexes, and when she has helped you, I shall ask her to turn it on him instead.'

'Please do not,' begged Bartholomew, although he knew he was pleading in vain, as the book-bearer always felt he knew best where witchery was concerned. 'But never mind that – did you hear what he and Hawick said to those Clare Hall men? Gille and Hawick?'

'Every word,' replied Cynric. 'Unfortunately, they chose to converse in French, so I did not understand any of them.'

'Damn!' muttered Bartholomew.

CHAPTER 3

It was difficult to sleep for what remained of the night, as the heat was stifling, even with the window shutters open. Insects seemed to know where the pickings were richest, and legions of them whined and buzzed around Bartholomew's head. He tossed and turned uncomfortably, more sorry than he could say about Aynton, whom he had liked for his gentleness and amiability. He was even more sorry that the man should die on the eve of shedding a role he had found so burdensome.

He glanced across the dark room to where Stasy and Hawick slept. They had arrived home shortly after him, but had vigorously denied chanting curses. They were obviously lying, but it was too hot to argue, so he had let the matter drop. He knew they had lied about the nature of their discussion with Gille and Elsham, too, and wondered why. Because they were embroiled in something illegal or unsavoury that necessitated falsehoods to keep them out of trouble? Or was it just a natural reaction to a teacher prying into their private lives?

He had included them on his list of suspects for Aynton's murder for reasons other than their mysterious association with Gille and Elsham, though. First, there was their refusal to leave the scene of the crime, and second there was their uncharacteristically helpful offer to carry the body. Were these enough to warrant them being turned over to Brampton for questioning? Yet they were unlikely to have had more than a nodding acquaintance with the Chancellor, so why would they kill him?

'Do you need a remedy for restlessness, sir?' came Stasy's voice from the other side of the room.

Bartholomew had assumed the students were asleep, so the question made him jump. It also made him uneasy, wondering if Stasy had somehow read his thoughts. He struggled for insouciance. 'The only remedies I need are a cool breeze and a way to repel insects.'

'Poor Chancellor Aynton,' whispered Stasy, although Bartholomew could not tell if he was sincere. 'He was a spineless fool, but there was no harm in him.'

'Michael will bring his killer to justice,' said Bartholomew, aware even as he spoke that it sounded like a threat.

'Not if Donwich wins tomorrow,' came a rejoinder that sounded full of smug satisfaction. 'He will dismiss Brother Michael and Junior Proctor Brampton, and appoint Gille and Elsham in their places.'

'So *they* will see the killer caught,' said Bartholomew coolly. 'And if they fail, it means they are unequal to their new duties, and Donwich will have to appoint someone better.'

'I am sure they will manage,' said Stasy smoothly. 'Yet I am astonished to hear you claim that Aynton had a killer. I was among the first to arrive after the alarm was raised, and it looked to me as if he had fallen – an accident.'

'He told me he was pushed,' said Bartholomew, and to see how the student would respond, added a brazen lie. 'Indeed, he provided enough information to let us identify the culprit. All we need to do is think it through.'

There was a long pause, during which he could almost hear the lad's mind working. 'Then make sure you pass it all to Gille and Elsham,' he said eventually.

Bartholomew sat up, determined to have some truth from him. 'Why are you really friends with them, Stasy? I know it has nothing to do with remedies for the flux, because they will buy those from an experienced *medicus*, not a pair of untried novices.'

Stasy sighed irritably. 'If you must know, we run a

business together: they collect exemplars from scholars who have finished with them, and we sell them to the students who need them next.'

Exemplars were compilations of essential texts that undergraduates were required to study in depth, and were produced by the University stationer. They were less expensive than purchasing all the original books, but still costly, even so.

'We offer more than Stationer Weasenham gives for second-hand copies,' Stasy went on, 'and we charge our customers less. Thus, our profit margins are smaller, but we do a lot more trade. Scholars know they get a better bargain with us than from him, so they come to us first. We are especially popular with the hostels, which, as you know, tend to be populated with lads who have very little money.'

'Unfortunately, that is illegal,' Bartholomew pointed out. 'Weasenham pays the University handsomely for his monopoly on exemplars.'

'So betray us to him,' challenged Stasy. 'But, if you do, you will hurt the poorest scholars who cannot afford his exorbitant prices. Exemplars should not cost so much that only the wealthy can have them.'

'No,' acknowledged Bartholomew, although he could not see Stasy and Hawick as champions of the penniless, and there was something about the explanation that did not quite ring true. 'So why did you not tell me all this when I asked you earlier? Why respond with a lie about a cure for the flux?'

'It was not a lie – we *have* invented a remedy. However, we could hardly admit that we are undercutting Weasenham while the Senior Proctor was listening, could we?'

Before Bartholomew could ask more, the bell rang, telling the scholars to rise for morning prayers. The other students stood up at once, suggesting that they had been awake and listening since the conversation had started.

It made him suspect that they knew exactly what Stasy and Hawick did in their spare time, and that, as usual, the Fellows were the last to find out.

Bartholomew did not attend church that morning, because he was summoned by Meadowman, Michael's head beadle. Meadowman had the flux, but boiled barley water was not working and he grew worse by the day. The heatwave did not help, and he was uncomfortable in his tiny, badly ventilated cottage. He lived near the Mill Pond, between Isnard and Hoo Hall, so Bartholomew walked there at once. He examined him carefully, then prepared a tonic of poppy syrup, mint and comfrey. As he worked, he nodded to the stinking bucket that the beadle used to catch whatever spilled out of him.

'Where do you empty that?'

'I do not do anything with it,' replied Meadowman miserably. 'I am too ill. If it was not for the kindness of my fellow beadles and the Marian Singers, I would be dead by now. Here is Isnard now, God bless him.'

The bargeman swung inside on his crutches and gave Bartholomew a baleful glare. 'I still have this cold,' he rasped accusingly. 'Your linctus did not work.'

'Nothing will work,' explained Bartholomew patiently, aware that he would have to explain this every time he and Isnard met until the bargeman recovered. 'It will get better in its own time.'

Isnard indicated Meadowman with a jerk of his thumb. 'You said that about him, but *he* will be in his grave unless you do something soon. Do you have nothing to help him?'

Bartholomew was perplexed by Meadowman's case. There was no reason why the beadle should not recover like everyone else, and he was at a loss as to what to do about it. He spent a few moments reassuring him that all would be well – he was far from sure it would, but if

Meadowman lost hope, he would die for certain – and finished by recommending rest and plenty more boiled barley water.

'But I do not like it,' objected Meadowman. 'It is akin to drinking glue. Besides, why would such a mild remedy work on this powerful sickness? I need something stronger.'

'Have you been throwing it away?' demanded Bartholomew, suddenly hopeful that an explanation for the beadle's continued sickness might be to hand.

'I swallow as much as I can bear,' replied Meadowman evasively, then added in plaintive tones, 'Are you *sure* I will not die?'

'Of course,' replied Bartholomew briskly, and remembered what Margery Starre did to make barley water more palatable. 'I will send a different kind when I get home. And you can try some broth. Do you have money for it? I know you have not worked for a week now.'

Meadowman nodded. 'Someone sends me a farthing every other day. I have no idea who. Not Brother Michael – he brings me food, although I cannot face it, so Isnard takes it for the Marian Singers.'

'This anonymous saint gives money to other flux-sufferers, too,' put in Isnard. 'Or rather, he sends it to their parish priests, who distribute it on his behalf. We tried to make them tell us his name, but he swears them to secrecy.'

Bartholomew was surprised to hear it, as most people who provided alms were keen for their largesse to be appreciated. He turned his mind back to the flux.

'Where do you empty the waste bucket, Isnard?' he asked, thinking that if it were the Mill Pond, he would know why the flux continued to claim victims in that area.

'The public latrine by the Trumpington Gate,' replied the bargeman. 'I used to pour it in the river, which was a lot less trouble, but I stopped after you threatened to break my crutches if I did it again.'

Bartholomew blushed guiltily, but then told himself that anything was fair in the war against unhygienic practices. It was true that Isnard was only one man out of hundreds who did the same, but the fight had to start somewhere.

'You caught that cold from the miasma that hangs around the hovels near All Saints next-the-castle,' said Meadowman, as Isnard sneezed violently. 'I told you to stay away from that area. Nasty agues have been breaking out there for weeks – the Godenave family are always sniffing and snorting.'

'I had no choice,' rasped Isnard. 'Ulf Godenave stole my purse, so I went to get it back. That boy will swing before he is much older. He cannot look at anything without filching it.'

'Maybe it was him who burgled Burgess Chaumbre last night,' said Meadowman, more talkative now the poppy syrup had eased his discomfort. 'Did you hear about that? No one knows how much was taken, but the rumour is that it was a lot.'

Bartholomew regarded him in alarm. 'Someone broke into my sister's house?'

'*Chaumbre's* house,' said Meadowman. 'The one in Girton village, where he lived before he moved in with her. As the place was empty, the thief took advantage of it.'

'I wish Chaumbre would fill in those dye-pits on the High Street,' said Isnard, wiping his nose on his sleeve. 'I stopped to relieve myself there last night, and it was only by the grace of God that I avoided toppling into one.'

Isnard liked to drink, which Bartholomew was sure had been a factor in the near-mishap. Still, the dye-pits were a hazard, and he wondered why Chaumbre was taking so long to remedy the matter.

'Beadle Brown told me that Chaumbre had an awful

row with Aynton about it yesterday,' said Meadowman. 'Aynton threatened to take up a spade himself, and Chaumbre told him to mind his own business. The discussion became quite heated, apparently.'

'Did it?' asked Bartholomew, wondering if he should include his brother-in-law on the suspect list, too. Yet people quarrelled all the time without killing each other.

'And before they parted,' Meadowman went on, 'the Chancellor asked Chaumbre if he needed to borrow some money to get it done. Chaumbre was so affronted that he called the Chancellor a meddlesome arse.'

'Well, Chaumbre is not meddlesome enough,' put in Isnard. 'Father William and I asked him to help us persuade Morys to open the Mill Pond sluices, because the river stinks, but he said that challenging the Mayor was not his job.'

'Oh, yes, it is,' averred Meadowman. 'He is a burgess. Who else's is it?'

'People are wary of using the bridge now it has claimed a second life,' said Isnard, jumping to another subject. 'So today, I shall set up a ferry service. It will make me a fortune, so some good has come out of those two deaths.'

Bartholomew was not sure Aynton and Baldok would have agreed.

By the time Bartholomew had finished with Meadowman, it was too late to attend the morning service, but too early for breakfast, so he went to spend a few moments with Matilde. He thought about the flux all the way along the High Street, and only when he reached her house did he turn his mind to happier matters. Or at least, to weddings.

Matilde's home stood in the shadow of All Saints-in-the-Jewry, and was a pretty place with a creamy yellow wash and black timbers. He pushed open the door and stepped into an interior that was cool and smelled of lavender and roses. It was simultaneously practical and elegant, and he knew he would be a lot more comfortable living there than with students who tended to view tidiness and personal hygiene as something for other people.

Matilde stood helplessly in the middle of her parlour, surrounded by shoes, while her friend Lucy Brampton, the Junior Proctor's sister, pondered which ones were suitable for a bride. They did not hear him enter, allowing him a moment to watch the woman who would become his wife in ten days.

To his mind, the passing years had only added to her beauty. There were one or two silver strands in her hair, and the laughter lines around her eyes and mouth had deepened, but she was still the loveliest woman he had ever seen, and his heart always quickened when he saw her. He remained amazed that, of all the men she had ever met, she had chosen to marry an impoverished physician-scholar, somewhat past his prime, with no prospect of wealth or influence. He sincerely hoped she knew what she was doing.

Lucy was older, but still pretty, and knew how to make the best of herself. Her clothes fitted snugly around her trim figure, and judicious use of face-paints hid most evidence of ageing. The only part she could not disguise was her teeth, which were sadly decayed. She had been beside herself with delight when her fiancé had arrived home after his ten-year absence, so Narboro's rejection had been a very cruel blow. Like most of Matilde's friends, she possessed an unusually sharp mind, but Bartholomew would have liked her more if she were less obsessed with his wedding.

'Matt!' cried Matilde. 'What a lovely surprise! Have you—'

'What do you think?' interrupted Lucy, holding aloft two pairs of shoes; behind her back, Matilde rolled her eyes, albeit indulgently, and grinned at him. 'The blue or the red?'

'Blue,' replied Bartholomew, knowing from experience that Lucy expected him to make a choice, regardless of whether or not he had a sensible opinion on the matter.

'Really?' she asked, frowning. 'You do not think they are overly fancy?'

'Red, then,' capitulated Bartholomew.

Matilde laughed. 'He would not notice if I walked up the aisle barefoot – unless it exposed some interesting medical problem with my toes.'

'I was sorry to hear about your Chancellor,' said Lucy, once the red shoes had been put to one side, although Bartholomew suspected the decision would be reviewed at least twice more before it was finally settled. 'He was stuck in his ways, but he was not a bad man.'

'You knew him?' asked Bartholomew curiously. 'How?'

'Through my brother,' replied Lucy. 'Regrettably, Matilde and I quarrelled with him several times, because he wanted to prevent her from opening her school.'

'Did he?' asked Bartholomew, sincerely hoping this did not mean that *they* should be included on the list of murder suspects. 'Did he say why?'

'He thought learning should be the exclusive domain of men, because women's inferior brains are unequal to it,' explained Matilde drily. 'I suggested we organise a public debate on philosophy between Lucy and Father William. Oddly enough, he declined to allow it.'

'He also claimed that if women learned their letters, it would signal the end of the world as God intended it,' added Lucy, and humour flashed in her eyes. 'When I asked how he could be so sure, he said he had read it in a book, but refused to tell me which one. It was obvious that he was making it up.'

'Perhaps he could not remember it on the spur of the moment,' said Bartholomew, more charitably.

Lucy shot him a disbelieving look, but declined to argue further. 'There was no malice in him, though. It is men

66

like Father William who represent the real danger to our venture. Did you know that he has written to the Pope, asking for us to be suppressed? We have not even opened our doors yet!'

'William writes to the Pope most weeks,' said Bartholomew, 'but I doubt the Holy Father reads his rants, so do not worry too much about papal condemnation.'

Lucy smiled, and reached for her hat – a green affair with yellow feathers. 'That is good to hear. And now I shall leave you two to discuss lace, while I visit the glover. My brother wanted me to break my fast with him, but I am disinclined to give him the pleasure of my company as long as he insists on suing my former suitors. I shall eat with the glover instead.'

'Lace?' asked Bartholomew warily, when she had gone.

'For my kirtle,' explained Matilde. 'There are many different kinds, and she is determined to have the one that will best match the cloth she has chosen. I have no particular feelings on the matter, but she does – very strong ones.'

Bartholomew grimaced, feeling that while he was happy to snatch a few precious minutes with his fiancée, he was disinclined to do it if it meant debating lace. Then he recalled what Michael had told him about paying for the kirtle.

'How much will it cost?' he asked uneasily.

Matilde knew exactly why he wanted to know. 'More than Brother Michael can lend you, so keep your money for your patients and I will buy the kirtle myself. But what did you think of Lucy today? Did she look pale to you?'

'Not especially,' replied Bartholomew. 'Why?'

'Because being rejected by Narboro was bad enough, but her brother has made things far worse with his lawsuit. Without it, she might have found another man, but no one will wed the sister of a man who sues. And pity is hard to bear, too – people feeling sorry for her and saying so.'

'I think she had a narrow escape,' said Bartholomew. 'Narboro is an empty-headed fool and she deserves better.'

'That is what I tell her, but folk nudge each other and point whenever she goes out anyway. It is why she spends so much time with me – my house is a refuge from well-meaning but unwanted sympathy.'

As he walked home, Bartholomew glanced up to see the sky was a flat, pale blue, with not so much as a wisp of cloud to break the monotony. It was going to be another sweltering day, and although he liked summer, he found himself longing for the cool grey clouds of autumn.

He waved to his sister and her new husband as he went, although they were laughing at something together, so caught up in the joke that neither noticed him. He remembered Chaumbre's friendship with the corrupt Morys, and Michael's warning about him. All he hoped was that Edith would not be hurt by the man she had married with such curious haste.

He stepped through Michaelhouse's gate just in time to witness a commotion involving Stasy and Hawick. They had been walking towards the kitchen, but the peacock released such a cacophony of screams that they were forced to beat a hasty retreat. Then the chickens united in what sounded uncannily like a taunting cackle. Clippesby was watching.

'It is because Stasy tried to kick Henry yesterday,' the Dominican told Bartholomew. 'Peafowl have long memories, so it is just as well that Stasy will leave at the end of term, because he will never know a moment's peace here now.'

Bartholomew watched the two students flee to the orchard, after which the rumpus died down. Then he glanced at Clippesby, who had the College cat under one arm and a stray dog in the other, although neither looked particularly pleased with the arrangement, and there were hisses and warning growls aplenty.

'I do not suppose you were near the Great Bridge last night, were you?' he asked hopefully. 'When Chancellor Aynton was killed?'

The Dominican liked to slip out at night to commune with his animal friends, so he often saw and heard things as he stood quiet and unnoticed in the shadows. Unfortunately, his way of reporting them invariably took some decoding, although Bartholomew had learned that the effort was often worthwhile.

'No,' came the disappointing reply. 'I was here, working on my next treatise.'

Earlier that year, Clippesby had stunned everyone by producing a dissertation on the complex issue of nominalism and realism, which was so insightful that it had won instant papal approval. It had been presented as a discussion between two hens, and was commonly known as the Chicken Debate. A second discourse had followed, and he was now working on the third, which was eagerly awaited by the academic world.

Clippesby gave one of his vacant smiles. 'But I can tell you two things about your new brother-in-law. First, his Girton home was burgled last night.'

Bartholomew nodded. 'Beadle Meadowman mentioned it, but I saw Chaumbre laughing just now, so it cannot have been too serious.'

'On the contrary,' said Clippesby, his eyes wide. 'The newt who lives in his garden says an enormous sum was stolen. Chaumbre rarely goes to that house now he lives with Edith, and has left it in the care of two elderly servants. It is no secret that it is vulnerable, so the newt was not surprised when a burglar chanced his hand.'

'According to Edith, most of his money is still in London,' said Bartholomew. 'I can only assume he will not miss what was taken from Girton.'

'Perhaps, but the second thing I have to tell you comes from the High Street rats, who saw Chaumbre quarrel with Aynton about those dye-pits yesterday morning. Harsh words were exchanged, and Aynton accused Chaumbre of not being as rich as he lets everyone believe. They parted on sour terms.'

Meadowman had mentioned that, too, and Bartholomew's heart sank again. He did not want his brother-in-law to be a murder suspect – Edith would never forgive him. 'Please tell me no threats were issued.'

'None that the rats heard. But ask the Junior Proctor, because he was there, too. They saw him lurking behind a grave while it was happening.'

'Lurking?' echoed Bartholomew warily.

'Hiding, so he could eavesdrop without being seen,' elaborated Clippesby. 'I do not know why, and nor do the rats.'

'What do you think of Brampton?' asked Bartholomew, who had a lot of respect for the gentle Dominican's opinions, bizarrely presented though they were.

Clippesby was thoughtful. 'I would like him more if he was not so close to Donwich. The Clare Hall robin tells me that Donwich will be livid when he loses the election today, which will put Brampton in an awkward position: will he stay loyal to his friend Donwich, or to Michael, the man who will promote him to Senior Proctor?'

'Is that all you know about Brampton?'

'Well, he inherited a fortune from his father. He refuses to share it with Lucy, though, because he thinks a husband should provide for her. Unfortunately, she will never get one now he is going after Narboro in the law courts. She has begged him to drop the suit, but his affection for her is less than his indignation at Narboro, so he refused.'

Bartholomew went to pass Clippesby's report to Michael. The monk was unsurprised by the news that Brampton had spied on the Chancellor, leading Bartholomew to draw an obvious conclusion.

'So *you* sent him to do it,' he said heavily.

'He had no orders along those lines from me this week, although perhaps he should have done – then I might have been able to stop Aynton from resigning. Do not look so disgusted, Matt! Watching the Chancellor comes under the remit of all Junior Proctors. One will be minding me after today. It is all part of our system of checks and balances.'

'But Brampton acted of his own volition on the day that Aynton was murdered?'

'Yes,' conceded Michael. 'However, there is nothing suspicious about that, although I will ask him about it later anyway. Leave him to me.'

'I think he should be on our list of suspects for Aynton's murder.'

Michael blinked his surprise. 'Do you? Why?'

'First, Clippesby says he is friends with Donwich, whom he may prefer to you. Second, he spied on the victim hours before the murder, but not on your directions. And third, he seems meek and inept, but there is something about him that I cannot like.'

Michael puffed out his cheeks in a sigh. 'Well, if you do not like him, he *must* be a killer. I shall order his arrest immediately.'

'I am serious, Brother!'

'So I see, and between you and me, I am not overly enamoured of him either. But he is not a murderer. Besides, he knows he will do well with me as Chancellor. He will do nothing to jeopardise that.'

Bartholomew was unconvinced, but knew there was no point arguing. 'Matilde and Lucy quarrelled with Aynton, too, but obviously they are not the culprits.'

'No,' agreed Michael. 'Not least because they took pity on four hot, tired and thirsty beadles last night, and invited them into Matilde's house for a cool drink. Their compassion has given them reliable alibis for the murder.'

'For an amicable man, Aynton seems to have argued

with a lot of people,' mused Bartholomew. 'However, the one that concerns me most is Chaumbre. The notion that my sister might be sharing her home with a man who shoved a scholar over a bridge . . .'

'Edith would not have married a killer, Matt. Yet I do question Chaumbre's choice of friends – not just Morys, but Donwich, too. He was at the Clare Hall feast last night – I saw him through a window when we delivered Aynton's body. Morys was also there, although that is no surprise – he wants Donwich to be Chancellor because he thinks he will take bribes.'

'How can Morys have been at Clare Hall? We both saw him on the Great Bridge last night, making sly agreements with Shardelowe the builder.'

'According to my beadles, he was there earlier in the evening, but left "on business" some time before Aynton died. Shall we include him on our list? I cannot abide the man, and if you can put Brampton on it for simple dislike, then I am having Morys.'

Shortly afterwards, Cynric rang the bell for breakfast, and there was the usual mad scramble towards the hall. Bartholomew had never understood why there had to be a stampede, as no one could start eating before every man was standing in his place and grace had been said anyway. Michael eyed Bartholomew balefully as he sauntered up the stairs last, making everyone else wait.

When he had finished his prayers, Michael sat, so at ease in the Master's chair that anyone watching might have been forgiven for thinking that he had occupied it for years, not just a few weeks. He rubbed his hands in gluttonous anticipation as the servants brought fresh bread, pats of yellow butter and platters of cold meat. Bartholomew asked Agatha to fetch him some fruit, disinclined to eat heavy fare in the heat.

'Fruit!' spat Michael, helping himself to an enormous

portion of beef, then topping it with an even larger portion of lamb. 'It is a proven medical truth that brains work better when fuelled by meat and bread.'

'Is it indeed?' said Bartholomew, who had been regaled with this particular 'fact' many times before, although the monk always declined to cite a written reference for it.

'What you see is a perfectly balanced diet,' Michael went on authoritatively. 'Anything else is a waste of stomach space. I have ordered Agatha not to bother with fruit and vegetables any more.'

Bartholomew was aghast. 'But that will cause—'

'No one knows more about food than me,' interrupted Michael. 'And who would not rather eat a chop than a carrot? However, I shall allow the occasional vegetable to sully the table next term, if you help me today.'

'That is blackmail, Brother! Besides, how will I know whether you have honoured the agreement? I shall have left Michaelhouse by then.'

'You will just have to trust me,' said Michael blithely. 'Besides, there is no need for you to teach today: the disputations are over and everyone else is having fun. You are the only one who persists with a rigid timetable of classes.'

'Because there is still so much for my lads to learn and—'

'Please, Matt,' said Michael quietly. 'We must solve Aynton's murder as quickly as possible, but Brampton and I will be busy with the election today. Hopefully, I shall be free to help you tomorrow.'

Bartholomew was alarmed. 'You expect me to look into it on my own?'

'Why not? You have plenty of experience. More than Brampton, actually.'

'But I have no authority to—'

'Here is a writ to say you do,' interrupted Michael, producing a handsome document that smacked of sly pre-planning. 'And while you are out and about, ask after those missing men – Huntyngdon and Martyn – as well.'

'You expect me to solve a mystery that has defeated you? That is not going to happen!'

'Fresh eyes, Matt. You may see something that I have missed.'

'And my classes? What happens to them while I am doing all your work?'

'Aungel will take them,' said Michael. 'It will be good practice for him, ready for next term. And if you will not help me out of loyalty to your dearest friend, then I shall pay you for your time – enough for a donation towards Matilde's new school, which I am sure she would much rather have than a marriage kirtle.'

Bartholomew was silent, trying to balance his desire to do something good for the woman he loved with the fact that every day of teaching was precious now that he had so few of them left.

'Very well,' he said eventually, hoping the case would not be as complex as some he had undertaken with Michael, and answers would be easy to find.

'Thank you. Just do not forget to vote for me at noon.'

As soon as breakfast was over, Michael went to St Mary the Great to oversee preparations for the election. There was already a buzz of excited anticipation in the air, although the number of scholars who nodded, winked and smiled at Michael as he hurried past suggested the other three candidates were likely to be disappointed.

Meanwhile, Bartholomew decided to start his enquiries with Geoffrey Dodenho. He had known him for years, and was sure he was no killer, but questioning him first would allow him to practise on a man who would not bite his head off or threaten eternal war between King's Hall and Michaelhouse for the insult.

The University's biggest and grandest College had an

enormous Fellowship, which included not only Dodenho and the missing Huntyngdon, but Junior Proctor Brampton, too. Ergo, Bartholomew had three tasks to complete at King's Hall that day: questioning Dodenho and any supporters he had about Aynton's death; seeing what Brampton had to say about spying on Aynton – Michael might accept his deputy's innocence, but Bartholomew would make up his own mind; and asking if there was any news about Huntyngdon.

King's Hall was more fortress than College. Its walls and gatehouse were battlemented, there were arrow slits for archers, and a portcullis hung over the door. Such precautions were wise, as its brazen wealth and privilege made it vulnerable to attack by resentful townsfolk. A liveried porter opened the door, and Bartholomew was asked to wait in the courtyard while Dodenho was informed that he had a visitor. The physician was not left alone for long.

'Good morning, Bartholomew,' said a quiet, razor-witted scholar named Ufford. He was a son of the powerful Earl of Suffolk, so was destined for a glittering career at Court, where his intellectual talents would be wasted. 'Is someone ill?'

'I suppose it is this flux,' said the man who was with him. William Rawby did not have influential kin to support him, but he was a gifted lawyer, and the connections he made at King's Hall would help him to rise rapidly through the ranks of the judiciary. 'I heard half the beadles are down with it.'

'No one is ill,' said Bartholomew. 'I have come to see Dodenho.'

Rawby raised his eyebrows. 'Not to offer him your support in today's election, I hope? We love him dearly, but our votes will go to Michael.'

Bartholomew felt his jaw drop. College loyalties ran especially deep in King's Hall, and he was amazed that

Rawby should openly express a preference for an outsider. Seeing his shock, Ufford began to explain.

'The University is not what it was ten years ago. It is now larger, stronger and becoming a rival to the other place in Oxford. We need a charismatic leader, who will continue to drive us forward, and that man is not Dodenho, much as it pains me to say it.'

'King's Hall needs Michael,' elaborated Rawby. 'It is no good being Fellows at the most prestigious College in a second-rate university. We want to belong to the most prestigious College in the *best* university. Michael can make that happen, the others cannot.'

'Does anyone else in King's Hall feel the same?' asked Bartholomew, astonished.

Rawby winced. 'All of us. Poor Dodenho is entirely oblivious, and will have a nasty surprise at noon. But we will make it up to him. We like the man – we just do not want him as our Chancellor.'

Bartholomew was glad when the conversation was cut short by the return of the porter, as it was disconcerting to see scholars abandon their old ways and adopt new ones. Perhaps it was just as well this was his last term, he thought as he nodded a farewell to Ufford and Rawby and followed the porter across the yard, because he was finding it all very unsettling.

Dodenho was in his quarters, a pleasant suite of rooms overlooking the gardens. He was practising the speech he aimed to give that day, but although he loved to hear himself speak, he was not nearly as good an orator as he believed himself to be.

'Ufford and Rawby suggested that I canvass support among the other Colleges last night,' he told Bartholomew. 'But I think I will win more votes with an erudite speech. It was good of them to encourage me to stand, but I know best.'

Bartholomew frowned his bemusement. '*They* encouraged you?'

'Yes, after Donwich put his name forward. Some scholars are uneasy with the University's recent rapid expansion, you see, and will vote for Donwich, because he has promised to put an end to it. But not everyone likes Donwich, so Ufford and Rawby said I should offer an alternative, as I would like to prevent unseemly progress, too.'

All became clear: Dodenho's candidacy would ensure the anti-Michael faction was divided. Dodenho might be a fool, but he was a congenial one, and there would be many traditionalists who would baulk at voting for the unlikeable Donwich. Bartholomew changed the subject, unwilling for Dodenho to learn from him that he was being used.

'Where was I during compline last night?' said Dodenho, repeating the question to make sure he had understood it correctly. 'In our refectory, working on my election speech.'

'Can anyone confirm it?'

Dodenho wagged an admonitory finger. 'I know what you are doing, Matthew – you aim to gauge its quality and report back to Michael. Well, for your information, it is perfect. Ask anyone. The Fellows were with me from dusk until midnight, and the students from midnight until we went to church this morning.'

'So you had company from sunset onwards?' pressed Bartholomew.

Dodenho preened. 'Yes, because they all love my orations. They did ask me to keep my voice down a few times, but that was because they wanted me to save something new for them to enjoy today. But I must get back to it, if you will excuse me.'

Bartholomew bowed and left, and the students and Fellows he met on his way back to the porter's lodge confirmed that Dodenho had indeed spent the entire night in the refectory. And, as none of them wanted him to be Chancellor, he had no supporters to shove Aynton off the bridge on his behalf. With a sense of satisfaction – albeit a modest one, as Dodenho was never a serious contender – Bartholomew crossed him off the list.

He asked the porter if Brampton was there – a perk of being a proctor was Brampton being allowed to live where he pleased, and he elected to sleep in his handsome Bridge Street house, although he still took most of his meals in King's Hall.

The porter nodded. 'He arrived an hour ago, but before you see him, Warden Shropham begs a word.'

'Why?' asked Bartholomew. 'Is he ill?'

'No,' replied the porter. 'I think he wants to talk about Huntyngdon.'

'Good,' muttered Bartholomew. 'So do I.'

Shropham's quarters were large but modestly furnished, as befitted an ex-soldier who disliked ostentation. He was entertaining guests. One was Brampton, which pleased Bartholomew, as it meant he would not have to waste time searching the College for him afterwards. The other was a man whose clothes and bearing suggested high birth. Sure enough, Shropham introduced him as Guichard d'Angle, the Earl of Huntyngdon, father of the missing scholar.

'Do you have news of him?' the Earl asked eagerly, when Shropham introduced Bartholomew, rather misleadingly, as Michael's deputy.

When the physician shook his head, d'Angle demanded to know what was being done to find his son, and as Bartholomew had no answers, he gestured to Brampton.

'Perhaps the Junior Proctor can tell you, My Lord. It is his enquiry now.'

'*Senior* Proctor,' corrected Brampton smugly, and

indicated the document that lay on the table in front of him. 'That arrived a few moments ago. Michael has resigned, and his last act in office was to appoint me as his successor.'

'This monk must be very confident of victory,' mused the Earl.

'Oh, he is,' Shropham assured him. 'And with good cause. He has our support, and all the hostels like him. He will make a fine Chancellor.'

'Then let us hope my son is here to see it,' said the Earl sombrely.

There was a short, respectful silence, then Bartholomew began to ask his questions.

'Chancellor Aynton told me that he gave Huntyngdon a letter to deliver the evening he disappeared. Do you know anything about it?'

'Huntyngdon did mention a mission of some delicacy,' nodded Shropham. 'Indeed, it is why he went to the Cardinal's Cap that night. He would say no more about it, but delivering a missive for the Chancellor would certainly fit the bill. What did this letter entail?'

'We do not know,' admitted Bartholomew. 'But it was intended for Narboro.'

'For *Narboro*?' echoed Shropham in astonishment. 'I cannot see *him* being the recipient of anything vital. The man is an ass – a very *vain* ass.'

'Even so, Aynton wrote to him, and Huntyngdon was charged to deliver it. Aynton thought it was important, because he spoke of it with his dying breath.'

Bartholomew decided not to mention Aynton's fear that the business had killed Huntyngdon until he knew more about it, out of consideration for the young man's father.

The Earl gave a faint smile. 'I am not surprised Aynton chose my son to oblige him. William is discreet, reliable and conscientious.'

'He is,' agreed Shropham, 'which is why I am so concerned about him vanishing without a word. It is out of character.'

'What about Martyn?' asked Bartholomew. 'Would you say the same about him?'

Shropham nodded. 'He is another respectable, steady young man. He has no College or hostel affiliation yet, so he lodges in the Cap. I shall offer him a Fellowship here next term.'

'Would you like to see my son's room?' asked the Earl, standing abruptly. 'As Michael's deputy, you will be well qualified to read a man's true nature from his quarters.'

Ignoring the derisive snort from 'Senior Proctor' Brampton, Bartholomew followed him to a building that overlooked the river. Huntyngdon's room was small, but clean and neat. The book-loaded shelves suggested a man who was serious about his studies, and a glance at the table told Bartholomew that its occupant was writing a treatise on civil law.

'There was no letter from the Chancellor here,' said Shropham helpfully. 'We would have found it when we scoured the place for clues as to where he might have gone. That means he either delivered it as charged, or it is still on his person – wherever that may be. Did you ask Narboro if it arrived?'

'I will do it this morning,' promised Bartholomew.

'Thank you,' said the Earl, and his face crumpled. 'William is very dear to me, so please do all you can to find out what has happened to him. I am not a fool – I realise there may be an unhappy ending to the matter – but the uncertainty is unbearable.'

Moved to compassion, Bartholomew found himself promising to do all he could, but once away, he wished he had held his tongue. He could not afford to take on work that would keep him from teaching, and Brampton was clearly irked with him for agreeing to meddle in matters that came under the Senior Proctor's jurisdiction.

'You will inform *me* if you uncover anything pertinent,' he said coldly, as he escorted Bartholomew to the gate. 'No reporting to the Earl or Shropham first.'

The curtness of the order made Bartholomew determined to ignore it. 'Congratulations on your appointment,' he said, to change the subject. 'You must be pleased.'

'It is no more than I deserve,' shrugged Brampton. 'And I shall be Chancellor when Michael goes on to become an abbot or a bishop.'

'Will you indeed?' murmured Bartholomew, amazed that Brampton thought he could step into Michael's enormous shoes. In an effort to avoid saying so, he turned the conversation to Aynton, asking if Brampton had considered the Chancellor a friend.

'I did not,' replied Brampton shortly. 'I had no respect for the man, and he should never have accepted the post, because he was entirely unequal to it. I will be much better.'

'So will Michael,' said Bartholomew, to remind him that the position was not his quite yet. 'Better than your friend Donwich.'

Brampton gave an unfathomable smile. 'Donwich does have much to learn before he can run a university. Rather like Aynton did, in fact.'

'Is that why you spied on Aynton?' asked Bartholomew baldly. 'I know you eavesdropped on a quarrel between him and Chaumbre.'

Brampton's expression became even more difficult to read. 'I did witness a spat, although I cannot see how it is relevant to Aynton's death. They were arguing about the dye-pits – specifically the fact that Chaumbre cannot be bothered to fill them in. Have you seen my sister today, by the way? We were meant to meet for breakfast.'

Bartholomew was taken aback by the abrupt change of

subject, but had the presence of mind not to blurt that she had opted for a glover's company instead. 'Not recently,' he hedged.

'I imagine she is engrossed in some aspect of your wedding,' sniffed Brampton, 'which is much more important to her than a mere brother.'

'Only because she is unlikely to have one of her own,' said Bartholomew pointedly.

'Thanks to Narboro,' spat Brampton, his small face turning hard and cold. 'I will destroy him for what he did to her, or rather, to me, as it was *my* honour he impugned.'

'Are you sure it might not be wiser to overlook—'

'I would sooner die than ignore what he did,' snarled Brampton. 'His rejection of her was a public slap in the face for my family's honour, and I shall never forgive it.'

Bartholomew was disconcerted by his vehemence, which he thought was disproportionate to the offence. He changed the subject before the new Senior Proctor could begin a rant. 'Will you visit Peterhouse to ask if Huntyngdon delivered the letter to Narboro? Or would you rather we did it together?'

'I would rather you went alone,' replied Brampton shortly. 'I am needed at St Mary the Great to help with the election. Report back to me as soon as you have finished.'

Bartholomew inclined his head, but he was not at Brampton's beck and call, and decided that if the new Senior Proctor wanted information, he could go to Peterhouse and find it himself.

CHAPTER 4

Peterhouse was an ancient foundation located outside the Trumpington Gate. It harboured no ambitions to rival other Colleges in terms of size and wealth, and its Fellowship was small, although it still produced lawyers and theologians of outstanding quality. Bartholomew was conducted into its hall, which, as at Michaelhouse, doubled as lecture room and refectory. All the Fellows were seated at their high table, except the one he wanted to see.

'Narboro never dines with us,' said a quiet, intelligent priest named John Gayton. 'So I assume he is in his quarters.'

Bartholomew was surprised to hear it, as attendance at meals tended to be obligatory in Colleges – communal dining was seen as a good way to forge bonds of scholarship and lasting loyalty. Gayton read his mind and gave a thin smile.

'Eating together *is* compulsory, but we do not enforce the rule with him. To be frank, we prefer it when he is not here.'

'You do not like him?' fished Bartholomew.

'Not particularly,' replied Gayton. 'Especially after his scandalous treatment of Lucy Brampton. Her brother would never have sued him if he had broken the marriage contract quietly and discreetly. Instead, he bellowed offensive remarks about his betrothed's teeth. Of course Brampton leapt to defend her.'

'She is better off without Narboro,' declared a very old Fellow named Stantone. 'He has nothing to commend him, other than perhaps a perfect coiffure. However, a contract is a contract, and I dislike men who break their word. They can never be trusted.'

'No,' agreed Gayton. 'Which is why I shall vote for Michael today. Narboro may be a member of Peterhouse, but he will not make a very good Chancellor.'

So yet another College aimed to reject its own candidate, thought Bartholomew in astonishment, as a murmur of agreement rippled around the other Fellows.

'Chancellor Aynton wrote Narboro a letter,' he said, moving to another matter, 'and he asked Huntyngdon to deliver it. I need to know if it arrived.'

The Fellows exchanged glances of mystification. 'Why would Aynton write to Narboro?' asked Gayton. 'I cannot imagine they had much to say to each other.'

'Unless Aynton wanted advice on hair care,' put in Stantone acidly. 'Narboro is good for nothing else.'

'He must have some desirable qualities,' said Bartholomew, feeling their dislike was painting a picture that was almost certainly unfair. 'He was a royal clerk for ten years, and such posts are competitive. He would have been dismissed if he was inept or stupid.'

'Perhaps he taught the Court popinjays how to nurture their tresses,' sniffed Stantone. 'Because I cannot believe what he told us: that he was the King's favourite clerk.'

There was a rumble of agreement from the others.

'What will he do now he has decided not to marry?' asked Bartholomew. 'Stay here?'

'He will not,' declared Gayton fervently. 'His Fellowship expires at the end of term and will not be renewed. We cannot recall what he was like ten years ago, but we deplore what he has become today.'

'But to answer your original question,' said Stantone, 'we know nothing of any letter from Aynton, and Huntyngdon was never here, delivering messages or anything else.'

'Has there been any news of him or Martyn?' asked

Gayton, and grimaced when Bartholomew shook his head. 'Pity. I like Martyn in particular. He lectures here on occasion, and is very good.'

'He is,' agreed Stantone. 'I had business in Bottisham this week, so I took the liberty of visiting his family on my way home. They have had no word of him either, and are at a loss as to where he might be. There is a rumour that he and Huntyngdon were killed by a drunken townsman, but I do not believe it. Neither were men for a brawl.'

'I imagine you want to ask Narboro about this letter in person,' said Gayton, heaving himself to his feet. 'I shall take you to Hoo Hall, where he lives.'

Hoo Hall was located on the edge of a marshy area called Coe Fen, and could be reached in one of two ways: along a tiny causeway across the bog, which was only practical in very dry weather, or via a lane leading off the Trumpington road. Bartholomew would have chosen the lane, but Gayton elected to use the more direct route over the swamp. It was an unpleasant journey, as every step they took disturbed hordes of biting insects. There was not so much as a breath of wind, and the air was full of the reek of rotting vegetation.

'Our students hate Hoo Hall,' confided Gayton flapping furiously at the flies that swarmed around his head. 'They spent one year there, and threatened to defect to another College unless we offered them alternative lodgings.'

'What is wrong with it?' asked Bartholomew.

'It is wet and cold in winter, you can only reach it by boat when there is heavy rain, and you cannot sleep for the insects that invade during summer,' explained Gayton. 'Moreover, Morys's mill is noisy and sometimes operates at night.'

'But Narboro does not mind these problems?'

A sly expression crossed Gayton's face. 'It was the only

place available when he returned here, demanding his rights and privileges as a Peterhouse Fellow. But it has one advantage – he has the place all to himself.'

'It is a handsome building,' said Bartholomew, admiring the tile roof and stone walls, and thinking that most scholars would give their eye-teeth to live in such a place, regardless of its defects.

'Hoo was our very first Master,' said Gayton. 'Although I cannot see him being pleased to have a house in a bog named after him. It was originally a warehouse for goods arriving by river, but it became redundant when the dams were built to make the Mill Pond. We should have let it fall down, because it was a mistake to convert it into student housing.'

The notion of Narboro's company was evidently too distasteful for Gayton, because he escorted Bartholomew to the door and left without another word. Bartholomew knocked, and when there was no reply, he walked in, thinking to search Narboro's quarters on the quiet if the Fellow was out.

The house was simple, with a hall on the ground floor and a dormitory above. Because it had originally been used to store perishable goods, the hall was lower than the ground outside, like a cellar, and had no windows. As a result, it was dark, cool and musty.

It was nicely furnished, though, with long tables, polished benches, and shelves for books. As Narboro was not there, Bartholomew aimed for the upper floor, which was reached via a flight of stone steps built up the opposite wall. At the top of the stairs was a door. It was open, so he walked through it into a long room with large windows. It was beautifully light, but stiflingly hot, and he appreciated why the students had not liked it.

Narboro stood at one of the windows. He held a mirror in his hand, and turned his head this way and that as he checked his hair.

'I am busy,' he said curtly, his eyes not moving from his reflection.

'So I see,' said Bartholomew. 'But I want to ask you about—'

'Can it not wait?' snapped Narboro. 'I shall be elected Chancellor in an hour, and I am not happy with the lie of my fringe.'

'It looks all right to me,' said Bartholomew.

Narboro tore his gaze away from himself and studied the physician, whose black mop was damp with sweat and had not seen a comb in days.

'You are not qualified to judge,' he determined, returning to his primping. 'And appearance is important, given that a Chancellor will mingle with kings, princes and bishops.'

Bartholomew turned to his questions, keen to leave the dormitory before he melted. 'Chancellor Aynton sent you a letter, which was delivered by Huntyngdon. May I see it?'

Narboro frowned. 'I received no letter from Aynton. Of course, it does not surprise me that he wrote. I am a favourite of the King, and many men clamour for my acquaintance.'

'How well did you know Aynton?'

'I met him once, when I informed him of the high standing that I enjoy with powerful members of Court. I could tell he was impressed. Then he asked for the name of my barber.'

Aynton had been a polite, friendly man, and Bartholomew suspected he had posed a question that he knew Narboro would enjoy answering – it had not sprung from a genuine desire for information. However, it did not sound as if the conversation had been one to warrant further correspondence in writing.

'Did you know Huntyngdon?'

'I exchanged words with him twice,' replied Narboro crisply. 'Both times to admire what he was wearing. He responded politely enough, but made it clear that he was more interested in philosophy than clothes.'

'Then did you ever meet his friend Martyn?'

'I saw him at the Cardinal's Cap on occasion, but all he wanted to do was debate metaphysics, so we had nothing in common.' Narboro lowered his voice. 'He is like my Peterhouse colleagues, who prefer scholarship to sourcing a decent haircut. And forgive my impertinence, but you could do with paying some attention to your personal appearance yourself. Look in this – you will see what I mean.'

He handed Bartholomew his mirror. It was of surprising weight and quality, and when the physician examined it more closely, he saw a painting of a woman on the back, resplendent in a green hat with yellow feathers. The image was almost worn away – rubbed off, because its user preferred the reflection on the other side.

'Lucy Brampton owns a hat like that,' he mused, then wished he had held his tongue when he recalled how they were acquainted.

'She gave me this when we first became betrothed,' said Narboro, taking it back. 'It was a thoughtful gift, and has been very useful.'

'A "lovers' mirror",' mused Bartholomew. 'I saw those in Venice. They represent unity – one face reflected and the other painted, but both on the same object. However, I think men usually give them to women, not the other way around.'

Narboro smiled. 'Lucy knew how to please me. Unlike her brother. Have you heard that he aims to sue me?'

Bartholomew nodded, and tried to bring the conversation back to the letter. 'Did you—'

'Hopefully, he will drop his case when I am elected Chancellor. I pray he does, because I cannot pay the kind of money he wants for "causing offence to his family".' Narboro's face turned ugly with contempt. 'But the insult was to *me*. How dare he expect me to marry a woman I *do not love – with rotten teeth into the bargain!'*

'The letter,' said Bartholomew forcefully. 'Are you sure you never received it?'

'Quite sure,' replied Narboro. 'Now, do you want any-
ng else from me? If not, I must set out for St Mary the
. or I will be late.'

on was murdered during compline last night,' said
mew, opting for bluntness when he saw the inter-
w was about to be terminated. 'Where were you then?'
rboro regarded him in astonishment. 'I hope you
me of killing him. I barely knew the
y would I do such a thing?'

e someone did, and those aiming to fill his
our prime suspects.'

ro eyed him coolly. 'The news of his resignation
over the University hours before compline, so you
t say I killed him in order to take his place. But
king of taking his place, are Dodenho, Michael and
nwich on your list, or do you confine your nasty insin-
tions to me alone?'

'Michael was with a dozen monks, reciting his daily offices, while Dodenho has alibis in a large number of colleagues. How about you?'

'I was here,' replied Narboro, gesturing around the empty room. 'Applying curling devices to my fringe in readiness for my victory at St Mary the Great today.'

'Can anyone else verify this?'

Narboro smiled thinly. 'No – you must take my word for it, as a man of honour.'

A man of honour who broke promises, thought Bartholomew, watching Narboro stalk towards the door, and wondering whatever had possessed the intelligent Lucy to accept him as a suitor in the first place. Or had he changed radically during his ten years away?

*

As he still had a little time before the election at noon, Bartholomew went to the Cardinal's Cap, where Martyn had lodged and where the missing men had last been seen. It was a quiet, respectable inn, where senior scholars often went for intelligent conversation. It was popular among those with friends in rival foundations, who wanted to meet them in a place where they would not be glowered at by less liberal-minded colleagues.

Unfortunately, most of its regulars had already gone to St Mary the Great, and all the landlord could remember about the night in question was that Huntyngdon had tied a red sash around his waist before he left, which was odd enough to have stuck in his mind.

'I have reviewed that evening again and again,' he said unhappily, 'but nothing unusual happened, other than the sash. I can only repeat what I told Brother Michael – that Martyn is the perfect lodger. He is clean, quiet and always pays on time.'

He showed Bartholomew the scholar's room, a pleasant chamber at the back of the building. Bartholomew went through it carefully, but there was nothing to tell him what had happened to its occupant.

'Was Aynton here that night?' he asked, following the landlord back down the stairs.

'The Chancellor? Yes, he spent a few moments talking to Huntyngdon and Martyn, and then he left. They went out a short time later – not so quickly as to suggest they were following him, but as soon as they had finished their drinks.'

'Did you see him give them anything?'

'No, but it was busy that night, and all my attention was on keeping my patrons supplied with ale. He might have done, but if he did, I did not notice.'

Bartholomew hurried home, and washed in water that was warm, faintly malodorous, and did nothing to refresh him. He donned a clean shirt, then struggled into the thick woollen robes that were obligatory attire for formal occasions like elections. Feeling he might expire in them, he trotted out into the yard, where he found Michael waiting for him. The monk set off at once, moving at a leisurely pace so as not to arrive looking like a beetroot.

'Well, Matt?' he asked. 'Is Aynton's killer safely behind bars?'

Bartholomew shot him an irritable glance. 'I can report that Dodenho has alibis galore, so we can cross him off our list. He does not have any passionate supporters, so we can eliminate that avenue of enquiry, too.'

'Fair enough. What else?'

'Narboro was alone in Hoo Hall. I could not gain his measure at all, Brother. He cannot really be as vain as he makes out. If he were, Peterhouse would never have accepted him as a Fellow ten years ago.'

'People change, Matt. I vaguely recall him back then, proposing to Lucy. However, I have no recollection of him being obsessed with his appearance.'

'Are you ready for today?' asked Bartholomew, as they turned into the High Street, and a group of scholars from Gonville Hall cheered when they saw him.

Michael smiled. 'Of course. And now the hour has come, I am looking forward to being Chancellor in name, as well as doing all the work.'

St Mary the Great was Cambridge's most prestigious church, and the only building in the town large enough to hold every Regent Master – scholars eligible to vote – at the same time. This was necessary whenever they met to make important decisions, or for ceremonies like the one at the end of the academic year, when successful students were formally awarded their degrees. No townsman had been surprised, a century before, when scholars at the fledgling University had informed them that they were taking it for themselves. Of course, that did not mean they were happy about it, and resentment had festered ever since.

Elections for Chancellor were significant events, and no Regent Master wanted to miss one, so the church was packed. Many surged forward to shake Michael's hand or express their good wishes as he sailed through the door, making it abundantly clear who would win that day. Even so, there was an order of ceremony to follow: an opening prayer; a summary of the rules by the Senior Proctor, who then introduced each candidate; speeches by each hopeful; the vote; the formal announcement of the result; and the winner's victory bray.

Michael had always run elections with such smooth efficiency that no one could remember them being any other way. Brampton's performance that day made everyone realise that they had taken the monk for granted. First, he was so nervous that he forgot the prayer, which had to be slotted in after his stammering explanation of electoral procedure. Then he had a moment of panic when he could not remember Narboro's name. And finally, he fled the podium before announcing which candidate was to speak first.

'It is a pity he is not as good at proctoring as he is at suing his sister's suitor,' muttered Doctor Rougham of Gonville Hall disparagingly. 'No man will ever look at Lucy again, and she will end her days as a spinster in his house.'

'Perhaps he wants a companion for when he is in his dotage,' shrugged Father Aidan of Maud's Hostel. 'She is clever and amusing, so I can see why he wants to hang on to her.'

As Brampton had no idea how to decide the order in which the four candidates would address the gathering, he suggested they drew lots. It was hardly dignified, and resulted in disapproving mutters from those who were close enough to see what was happening. Dodenho's straw was the shortest, so he went first.

His splendid voice filled the church, but he said nothing original or interesting, and as the church was stifling and the Regents were uncomfortable in their ceremonial robes, they grew increasingly restless as he boomed on. Eventually, they began to lob scrunched-up balls of parchment in the hope of making him stop. When someone exchanged parchment for a shoe, Warden Shropham hastened to drag him off the podium before he was hurt.

Narboro went next, and made much of the noble and royal connections he had forged during his time at Court. He directed most of his remarks to a spot near the altar, and when Bartholomew eased around a pillar to see if he had singled out a friend, he saw a shiny brass plaque: Narboro preferred to address his own reflection than any of his learned colleagues.

When Narboro finished, Donwich strutted forward, and did not endear himself to his audience by starting with a snide remark about the stench of sweat and cheap wool. It was intended for his small but avid cluster of supporters, but the podium was in a part of the church that amplified sounds, so his words carried to others as well. A murmur of offended indignation rippled down the nave.

Eventually, it was Michael's turn. He won instant approval by announcing that he saw no need to make everyone stand in a hot church on his account, because there was not a man among them who did not know him, and he would not insult them by listing his skills.

Once the speeches were over, every scholar was instructed to approach one of three tellers, and whisper the name of his preferred candidate. The tellers then recorded his choice in writing. Within moments, Michael had so many votes that the tellers ran out of space on their parchment, and more had to be fetched. It did not take long to assess the result: three-quarters of the ballot went to Michael, while the rest was divided more or less equally between Donwich and Dodenho. The only vote won by Narboro was his own.

'Will you make a victory speech, Brother?' asked Brampton. 'It is your right.'

'No, it is too hot,' said Michael, much to everyone's relief. 'And everyone here knows that I will do my best.'

'Congratulations, Brother,' said Dodenho pleasantly, coming to grasp the monk's hand. 'Although I shall give you a run for your money next time. I *shall* try again, you know.'

'Dodenho has a hide like old leather,' whispered Gayton to his Peterhouse colleagues. 'Anyone else would have been mortified – slunk home in shame. But not him!'

'Look at Narboro,' spat Stantone in disgust. 'He is stunned by his defeat, because he cannot believe that everyone prefers a competent leader over one with a few friends at Court. What a fool he is!'

Brampton declared the ceremony closed, and everyone turned to leave, keen to be out in fresher air, but an imperious voice rang through the church, stopping them all in their tracks. It was Donwich, standing on the podium with one hand raised for attention. His henchmen, Gille and Elsham, stood on either side of him.

'This election was illegal,' he declared. 'And I shall write to Canterbury today, ordering the Archbishop to launch an enquiry. Until we hear from him, Michael must stand down.'

There was a startled silence, which lasted until Michael chuckled good-naturedly. 'Nice try, Donwich, but I am afraid there is nothing to contest. Everything was done according to the statutes. Ask any lawyer here.'

'Clare Hall disagrees,' shouted Gille, the shorter and more pugilistic of Donwich's two minions. 'So you must step aside until the Archbishop gives his official ruling. Until then, I declare Donwich to be Chancellor, as he had the next-largest number of votes.'

'You will embarrass yourselves if you persist with this,' warned Michael. 'I know the statutes, and none were broken today.'

'I challenge the result on two points of order,' stated Donwich haughtily. 'First, the election was arranged with unseemly haste, so your rivals had insufficient time to prepare. And second, it was rigged and *that* proves it.'

He pointed to two casks of wine, which were waiting to be carried outside and served to any Regent who wanted some. As Bartholomew looked at them, he spotted Stasy and Hawick nearby – students were not allowed to attend elections, so they had no right to be there. They scuttled out of sight when everyone began to turn in their direction.

'What are you talking about, Donwich?' demanded Stantone impatiently. 'How can barrels of wine invalidate an election?'

'Because *he* brought them in expectation of victory,' snarled Donwich, jabbing an accusing finger at Michael. 'It means the outcome was known *before* the vote was taken.'

'Nonsense!' cried Michael, affronted, while Bartholomew recalled Clare Hall's victory feast the night before, and wondered how Donwich thought that was different. 'The wine is provided because it is hot and we are all wearing heavy robes. It is to be shared by us all, regardless of who won.'

'It will not be shared today,' declared Donwich, 'because there has not been an official election – not if I contest it. If you refuse to step down, Brother, the University will have *two* Chancellors, because I am going nowhere.'

'Michael is Chancellor as far as most of us are concerned,' shouted Ufford of King's Hall. 'So if you refuse to withdraw, you will be known as the *Anti*-Chancellor. It is not a title any sane man would accept – it sounds sinister.'

'It does,' agreed his friend Rawby. 'And if you persist with this nonsense, Ufford and I will ride to Ely, and tell the Bishop what you have done. He will not approve of you making trouble in the University.'

Donwich smirked triumphantly. 'Bishop de Lisle is not in Ely – he is with the Pope in Avignon, trying to evade charges of murder, kidnapping, assault and theft. Our prelate is nothing but a common felon.'

'And he is Michael's close friend,' put in Gille slyly. 'It is common knowledge that the monk is his spy, and sends him reports on all our doings.'

'Of course I send him reports,' said Michael irritably. 'He is our Bishop, regardless of what crimes he may or may not have committed. Ergo, there is a legal requirement for me to keep him informed. Read the statutes – they set it out quite clearly.'

'Well, I care nothing for de Lisle's opinion,' said Donwich loftily. 'I shall only accept one – that of the Archbishop of Canterbury.'

Michael's smile was rather wolfish. 'Then you are in luck, because his vicars-general are in Ely as we speak. They will hear your claim on his behalf.'

'Rawby and I will ride there at once,' declared Ufford. 'We shall fetch these vicars, and they will be here tomorrow.'

Donwich's face fell. 'Tomorrow? But I was expecting a delay of several weeks to prepare my case and gather support. Besides, I want the Archbishop himself, not his lackeys.'

'Vicars-general are not lackeys,' said Michael impatiently. 'They are men appointed by him to make rulings in his name. And even if they had not been nearby, he would have sent them to deal with your quibble anyway. It is the way these matters work.'

'You would be wise to reconsider, Donwich,' advised Gayton quietly. 'You will make an ass of yourself if you persist. We do not want you – we want Michael.'

'Besides, your challenge looks like sour grapes,' put in Father Aidan. 'And no one likes a bad loser.'

Donwich glared at them. 'I will *not* give up my claim. There *are* grounds for appeal. Call me Anti-Chancellor if you will, but if you do, I shall remember it when the vicars-general find in my favour. Be warned, all of you.'

But before anyone could respond, there was an outraged screech from Prior Pechem of the Franciscans, a dour, unsmiling man with no sense of humour.

'Witchery! Heresy! Those boys are chanting curses. I heard them.'

With horror, Bartholomew saw Pechem was pointing at Stasy and Hawick.

Pandemonium ensued. Naturally, a church full of scholars, many of whom were friars, monks and priests, reacted with horror at the notion that someone might be committing diabolical acts under their noses. Instinctively, Michael surged forward to lay hold of the culprits, but then recalled that he was no longer Senior Proctor. Brampton only watched with detached interest, and it took a sharp word from Warden Shropham to remind him of his duty.

Stasy and Hawick were in the north aisle, crouching between a pillar and the two barrels of wine, hidden from all but the most observant of eyes. Bartholomew hurried forward, ready to explain that his students might be fools for invading a Regents-only gathering, but they were certainly not heretics, when he saw a pentangle sketched in charcoal on the floor. He faltered uncertainly.

'They were about to a lay curse on our wine,' shouted Prior Pechem, beside himself with righteous rage. 'I heard them summon a dark power.'

'No!' cried Hawick, frightened. 'We never did – we were just guarding it from the men of Corner Hostel, who aimed to steal some before the ceremony was over.'

The accused men clamoured vigorous denials, although one quickly hid a mallet behind his back – the kind used to remove bungs from casks – which was an unusual object to have brought to an election.

'Then explain *that*,' screeched Pechem, pointing at the five-fingered star. 'It is not a symbol that has any place in church, and *you* put it there.'

'We never did,' countered Stasy, far less flustered than his crony. 'It was there when we arrived. Someone else drew it.'

'Liar!' spat Pechem. 'But if you refuse to acknowledge the symbol, then what about the words I heard you chant – your petition to the Devil?'

'You misheard,' shrugged Stasy, although Hawick continued to look terrified.

'There is nothing wrong with my ears,' snarled Pechem, 'and you will be damned for all eternity for lying in a church – a sacred place, where God and His angels are watching.'

Stasy did not look as concerned by this threat as he should have done, and Bartholomew began to worry that his two students had indeed been up to no good, especially in light of the curse he himself had heard Stasy recite just the previous evening. He had a sudden awful feeling that Pechem was right to accuse them of witchery.

'I am not lying,' retorted Stasy insolently. '*You* are.'

There was a collective intake of breath, as Regents were unused to students answering back. Bartholomew looked for Brampton, whose duty it was to end the confrontation before it escalated any further, but the new Senior Proctor just stood with his arms folded and made no attempt to take control. Bartholomew experienced a surge of anger towards him. It was *his* fault that Stasy and Hawick were in the church at all – the proctors were supposed to prevent unwanted invasions, and he should have put beadles on the doors to act as guards.

'These boys are from your College, *Chancellor*,' said Donwich, so gloatingly that Bartholomew wondered if he had put them up to it. 'So what will you do? Fine them? Refuse them their degrees? Burn them in the Market Square?'

Michael was in an impossible position. He could not downplay an accusation of heresy when proof of it was on the floor for all to see. Nor could he defer the matter to another day, as that would smack of indecision and weakness. There was really only one option open to him. He drew himself up to his full height.

'Stasy and Hawick,' he boomed, 'you are hereby expelled from the University.'

Stasy gaped at him. 'But you cannot! We are due to graduate Saturday week.'

'You will not be permitted to do so,' declared Michael. 'And if you had already won degrees, I would have revoked them. By your disgraceful antics today, you have forfeited all you have worked for these last few years.'

'No,' gulped Hawick unsteadily. 'Please, Brother! We were not really chanting spells – it was just a jape. We see now that it was in poor taste. We are sorry!'

'I am sure you are, but the damage is done,' said Michael. 'Brampton? Escort them home, where they will pack their belongings and be gone from Michaelhouse by nightfall.'

Stasy opened his mouth to argue, but Hawick knew better than to prolong the situation. He scuttled after Brampton with his head bowed and tears flowing down his cheeks. By contrast, Stasy's face flared red with rage as he stalked down the nave, roughly shouldering stunned Regents out of his way.

'Lock your doors tonight, Brother,' murmured Bartholomew. 'Stasy means to have his revenge. I can see it in his eyes.'

'Let him try,' said Michael between gritted teeth. 'However, I am more concerned with this challenge of Donwich's. He cannot really think the Archbishop's representatives will find in his favour, can he?'

'I believe he does,' said Bartholomew. 'Being voted Master of Clare Hall has opened the floodgates of his ambition.'

'What an idiot!' muttered Michael. 'It will not end well for him, but we must go through the motions of his appeal, I suppose. Listen to him now – bawling that I am unfit to lead the University because I am unduly harsh. If I had opted for a lesser punishment he would have accused me of laxity.'

'You had better talk to him, Brother. He is so puffed up with his own rectitude that he will explode unless you find a way to release some of the hot air.'

Oblivious to or uncaring of his colleagues' hostility, Donwich began to give an impassioned speech about Michael's shortcomings. It was a serious misjudgement on his part – the Regents objected to being informed that the candidate they had chosen was unsuitable. They reacted with catcalls and jeers, and before the situation grew any more unedifying, Michael ordered everyone home. No wine was offered, lest it encouraged them to linger.

'*You* cannot dismiss anyone,' snarled Donwich furiously. 'I still have a lot to say, and you have no authority over me – over any of us. I do not acknowledge you as Chancellor.'

'Then I suggest we continue this discussion in my office,' said Michael with quiet dignity. 'Such screeching is hardly commensurate with our status.'

And with that, he turned and sailed away, leaving Donwich shaking with impotent rage. The monk led the way to the handsome room in the nave, which had been the Chancellor's until he had decided to take it for himself, relegating the University's titular head to a small chamber near the back door.

Unfortunately, a whole host of scholars wanted to see

more of the confrontation between the man they had elected and his challenger, and once they had all crammed themselves inside, the office was even hotter and more crowded than the nave had been. Present were Donwich and his two henchmen; Ufford, Rawby and Shropham from King's Hall; all the Fellows from Michaelhouse and the Hall of Valence Marie; and the heads of roughly fifteen hostels. Then Brampton arrived with two clerks.

'An official record must be made of this gathering,' he announced importantly, as the secretaries fought for sitting space at the table. 'For the vicars-general to see.'

'Yes,' acknowledged Michael. 'But *you* are meant to be minding Stasy and Hawick.'

'Cynric is doing it,' explained Brampton. 'He said he would be better at it than me.'

That was certainly true, thought Bartholomew, relieved that the pair would be under a more reliable eye than the inept new Senior Proctor's.

'I am sorry about Stasy and Hawick, Matt,' whispered Michael, as Donwich began another rant. 'It probably *was* just some asinine prank, but what else could I do? I cannot believe they were so stupid!'

'It is not your fault, Brother,' Bartholomew whispered back. 'It is Brampton's, for letting them sneak inside in the first place.'

'Better blame the flux then,' said Michael. 'Half the beadles are laid low with it, so none were available to stand watch at the doors. The fit ones are needed to keep order among a lot of students who think that the looming end of term gives them licence to run riot.'

At that point, their attention was snagged by a growing spat between Donwich and the men from King's Hall.

'. . . your mistress,' Ufford was saying accusingly. 'Oh, yes, we know all about your nocturnal visits to Bridge Street, Donwich. No wonder you are such good friends with our new Senior Proctor! His house provides the venue for your trysts with his sister.'

Bartholomew blinked his astonishment. 'Are they saying that Donwich has taken *Lucy* as a lover?' he breathed. 'I do not believe it! For a start, Matilde would have told me.'

'I imagine she considers it none of your business,' replied Michael, an answer which told Bartholomew that the revelation was not news to him. 'But why the shock? Why should Lucy not form an attachment to someone else, now she is free of Narboro?'

'Lucy is *not* my mistress,' yelled Donwich, so full of red-faced rage that he could barely speak. 'She is a friend. There is nothing in the statutes that forbids me from visiting respectable townswomen.'

'Read them again,' drawled Rawby. 'You will find there is.'

'Does Brampton know about this relationship, Brother?' asked Bartholomew in a low voice, then answered the question himself. 'I suppose he must, if they meet in his house. And he condones it?'

'Perhaps he feels she deserves a chance to snag herself a spouse,' shrugged Michael.

'But if Brampton and Donwich collude to facilitate that sort of thing, it means they are closer than we thought,' said Bartholomew in alarm. 'You may not be able to trust your Senior Proctor when you are Chancellor.'

'Brampton knows where his loyalties lie.'

For his sake, Bartholomew hoped he was right. At that moment, he happened to glance at Gille, who had been pushed up against the table by the press of scholars who crowded in behind him. It allowed the Clare Hall Fellow to palm one of Michael's pretty jewelled ink-pots, a gift from a grateful Bishop of Ely. It happened so fast that Bartholomew wondered if his eyes had deceived him.

'Why do you support the monk over me?' Donwich

demanded of the trio from King's Hall. 'You have never sided with Michaelhouse before, and our two Colleges have always been allies. Reconsider your position, and I shall reward you well.'

'That is a good point,' whispered Father William to the other Michaelhouse Fellows. 'Why *are* Ufford and Rawby so keen to help Michael? It is suspicious if you ask me.'

'They simply support the better candidate,' replied Zoone. 'And this challenge of Donwich's is ridiculous. There is nothing in the statutes to say that Michael must acknowledge the pitiful claims of a defeated rival, so why does he?'

'It is odd,' agreed Clippesby, cuddling a hedgehog. 'But perhaps he has been listening to the badgers, who are democratic to a fault. Their elections are always—'

'Hush!' hissed William, looking around in alarm. 'No peculiar animal-inspired opinions here, if you please. It will reinforce the rumours that you are barking mad.'

'We should go, if we are to reach Ely by nightfall,' said Ufford to Rawby, and turned to Michael. 'Do we have your permission to leave, Chancellor?'

Michael inclined his head. 'Bring the vicars-general as soon as possible.'

'You can rely on us,' said Rawby, and then he and Ufford were gone, shouldering their way through the throng and treading on not a few enemy toes on the way.

'Yes, bring them quickly,' called Donwich to their retreating backs. 'Because Michael's reign will soon degenerate into chaos. Nearly all his beadles have the flux, so he no longer has a personal army to support him.'

Michael stepped forward and addressed the gathering in a voice that was eminently calm and reasonable, which made Donwich look petty and ill-mannered by comparison.

'Master Donwich has lodged his complaint and we have all heard it. All that remains now is to put it in writing.

He and I will nominate two men to witness the deed, after which we will sign it and affix our seals. The rest of you may as well go home.'

Donwich opened his mouth to argue, but most scholars had had enough of being squashed and sweaty, so there was a murmur of agreement and a concerted move towards the door. Bartholomew was about to follow when Michael grabbed his arm.

'Donwich will be tied up here for a while, so go to Clare Hall and find out where he, Gille and Elsham were when Aynton died. At the moment, they head my list of suspects. I would do it myself, but you will appreciate why that would not be a good idea.'

Bartholomew did indeed.

CHAPTER 5

Bartholomew was relieved to leave St Mary the Great, even if it was to embroil himself in the distasteful business of murder. He stepped through the door and felt himself wilt in the sun. He pulled off his heavy woollen robes, bundled them under his arm, and set off along the High Street, much more comfortably clad in loose shirt and knee-length breeches.

He was just turning into Gonville Lane when a small figure barrelled into him. Instinctively, his hand went to the purse on his belt, where it met some hot little fingers trying to unfasten it. It was Ulf Godenave, who abandoned his prize when he realised he was about to be caught, and darted away, pausing only to make an obscene gesture. The incident was witnessed by Shardelowe, the builder who had helped to retrieve Aynton's body.

'Little brat,' he growled. 'He will be hanged before he can grow a beard unless he mends his ways.'

'I do not suppose you were on the bridge when Aynton was killed, were you?' asked Bartholomew with more hope than expectation.

The builder shook his head. 'I only came when I heard that a man with my expertise was needed to retrieve the body. It was a good thing I was available, because your Chancellor would have been pitched into the water – and you with him – if an amateur had tried to do it.'

Bartholomew recalled the conversation he had overheard the previous night between Shardelowe and the Mayor.

'The King sent you to assess the bridge, but now it seems you will win the profitable task of carrying out the repairs, too.'

Shardelowe looked decidedly shifty. 'Only if the town council votes for the Mayor's recommendations. Of course, they would be fools not to – they need an experienced builder to solve the problem, or Aynton will not be the only man to fall foul of the thing.'

'It has claimed another life this year already – a burgess named Baldok.'

'I know nothing about him, but Aynton died because the rotten railings snapped under his weight when he was pushed against them. Had they been stone, they would have held.'

Bartholomew regarded him curiously. 'How do you know he was pushed?'

Shardelowe shrugged. 'I must have been told. I cannot recall by whom.'

He hurried away, and Bartholomew watched him go. Should the builder be included on the list of suspects, because he had decided that the best way to ensure himself a lucrative contract was to make sure the bridge suffered another fatality? He shook himself impatiently. He was seeing plots where there were none. Or was he?

Before he had taken many more steps along the lane, Bartholomew saw Edith walking towards him. His sister had raised him after the early death of their parents, and they had always been close. He had witnessed with painful helplessness her grief after losing her beloved husband, and sincerely hoped that her sudden, inexplicable decision to marry Philip Chaumbre would not end in tears, too.

Oswald's death had aged her, so her once raven-black hair was now streaked with grey, although little of it could be seen under the matronly wimple she had favoured since she had become a widow. She wore a dress of pale blue, and looked cool, fresh and relaxed, which made Bartholomew even more aware of his own uncomfortable sweatiness.

She greeted him with a smile. 'Matilde and Lucy are currently agonising over wedding flowers. Well, Lucy is agonising – Matilde would rather think about her school for girls, but humours Lucy because she knows it will help her deal with the shame of what that scoundrel Narboro did to her. You have caught yourself a good woman, Matt.'

'Yes,' he agreed. 'Although I have just learned that Donwich is courting Lucy, so perhaps she will follow us up the aisle yet.'

'I hope not,' said Edith with distaste, 'for her sake. Philip is friends with Donwich, but I do not approve. Donwich is not very nice.'

'No,' agreed Bartholomew, and tried to make his next remark sound casual, although his heart was in his mouth as he spoke. 'Beadle Meadowman, Clippesby and Brampton mentioned a recent quarrel between Philip and Aynton – about the dye-pits.'

Edith raised her eyebrows. 'Philip did not mention it to me, although I know Chancellor Aynton disapproved of him leaving them open. Aynton disapproved of the possibility of a stone bridge, too, and I overheard an angry spat between him and Mayor Morys about it yesterday afternoon. Matilde was with me – she will tell you that tempers ran high.'

'I suppose I had better speak to Morys then,' said Bartholomew without enthusiasm, and hastened to explain. 'Michael wants me to help him find Aynton's killer, so we are talking to everyone who knew him.'

Edith shot him a cool glare. 'Well, you can leave Philip out of it. *He* is no killer. You cannot speak to Morys either – at least, not today. He is visiting kin in the Fens – the ones he uses to bully political opponents. He will be back for tomorrow, though, obviously.'

'Why "obviously"?'

'Because it is when the council will decide about the bridge – whether to fund a new one in stone, or patch up the old wooden one. Morys will want to make sure they vote for stone. Of course, he is right – stone is the only sensible option. However, I hope it will not entail closing the whole thing while the work is carried out – that would be very inconvenient.'

Edith's cloth business relied on trade from the north, so shutting the bridge would have a direct impact on her. It would affect Bartholomew as well, as he used it to reach some of his patients.

'The King sent some money,' she went on, 'and the University has offered to contribute a little, but the bulk of the outlay will come from merchants like me. Thank God for Philip! I would be in dire financial straits without him.'

Bartholomew was bemused. 'I thought you were doing well.'

Edith winced. 'I did not want to worry you, Matt, but Richard got himself very badly into debt again recently. Once all his creditors were paid, everything was gone – the business, my home, our warehouses . . .'

Richard was her son, a debauched young man who was considerably less charming as an adult than he had been as a boy.

'*You* paid his debts?' demanded Bartholomew, stunned and angry. 'But why would—'

'He found a loophole in Oswald's will that left me no choice,' explained Edith. 'I was in despair, but then Philip came along. He has been in London these past thirty years, making his fortune in dye. He is an old friend, and when I confided my plight, he suggested an arrangement.'

'What arrangement?' Bartholomew grew more horrified with every word that fell from her lips. Why had she not told him? Because he never had two pennies to rub together, and so was useless to her? Or because she was afraid he would storm to London and make sure Richard would never hurt her again?

'He bought my house and the business. My workers' jobs are safe, and he lets me run things as I like, while he concentrates on his dyeing. The only difference is that Richard no longer has a claim on any of it.'

'In return for what?' asked Bartholomew, feeling sick.

'Companionship,' replied Edith. 'I was apprehensive at first, but now I *like* him in my parlour of an evening, to tell him about my day and listen to him talk about his own. We play board games, he reads to me, and we laugh. He makes no other demands.'

Well, that was something, thought Bartholomew, as he struggled to come to terms with the enormity of what she had done. No wonder she had told him of her decision one day and married Chaumbre the next – he would have tried to talk her out of it if he had known the whole story, but she had been thinking about the two dozen people who relied on her for their livelihoods.

'What would Oswald have thought?' he breathed, then wished he could bite out his tongue. It was a question that should have remained unspoken.

'He would have approved,' replied Edith quietly. 'He liked Philip when we were all youngsters together, and he would not have wanted his home and warehouses in the hands of men to whom Richard owed money.'

'No,' acknowledged Bartholomew. 'But even so . . .'

'Philip has not only been generous, but accommodating, too,' Edith went on. 'He could have insisted that we move to his house in Girton, but he offered to live in Milne Street instead. His own home lies empty, and we shall rent it out as a hostel next term.'

'Meadowman said it was burgled last night, and that a lot of money was taken.'

Edith was dismissive. 'Philip says it was nothing. But here he comes now. Watch how his face lights up when he sees me.'

She was right: Chaumbre gave a grin of such unbridled

delight when he spotted his wife that it was clear she meant a great deal to him. He was not an attractive man: his nose was too big, his chin was too small, and he had more hair sprouting from his ears than from his head. Bartholomew regarded him unhappily, sincerely hoping for Edith's sake that the dyer's quarrel with Aynton had not resulted in murder.

'Matthew!' Chaumbre cried merrily. 'Is it not a beautiful day? I have been for a lovely walk along the river.'

'Have you?' asked Bartholomew warily, unable to see that a stroll along a festering sewer would be pleasant at any time, but especially in the heat.

'I took the scenic route home after examining my dye-pits. People clamour at me to fill them in, but why should I? They are doing no harm.'

'Isnard nearly fell down one,' Bartholomew pointed out.

'Then he should not stagger around dark cemeteries after spending all evening in a tavern,' chuckled Chaumbre.

'I am sorry to hear you were burgled. Your Girton home—'

'My *home* is with your sister,' interrupted Chaumbre, casting Edith such an adoring look that Bartholomew cringed. 'And what is losing money when you have found love?'

Bartholomew changed the subject hastily, embarrassed by the saccharine display of affection, although Edith did not seem to mind it. 'I understand you argued about the dye-pits with Aynton,' he began.

Chaumbre sighed. 'He ordered me to fill them in at once. I pointed out that he had no authority to boss me around, and, to my eternal shame, I called him a meddlesome arse. We argued about the bridge as well, because he wanted wood rather than stone. I regret it all now, of course, and wish our last exchange had been more congenial.'

110

'Do not take it to heart,' said Edith kindly. 'He *was* meddlesome, and you are not the only one to have told him so over the years. He had opinions about everything – although that is true of most scholars, to be frank.'

'It is,' agreed Chaumbre ruefully. 'I was invited to a feast in Clare Hall last night, where I learned that Donwich has some very opinionated friends. I was glad to leave.'

'You were there all night?' fished Bartholomew.

'I slipped out just before compline, to check on a batch of fermenting dye.'

'Did anyone see you?'

Chaumbre laughed. 'Of course not! I do not keep my people working that late – it would be most unreasonable. I wanted to go home to Edith afterwards, but felt duty-bound to return to the feast, where I stayed until Donwich announced the news about Aynton. I told Edith about it the moment I arrived back.'

'He did,' said Edith, and because she knew her brother well enough to understand why the questions had been put, added pointedly, 'which he would not have done if he had been the one to push Aynton to his death.'

Chaumbre blinked, then gave a great guffaw of laughter. 'You think *I* killed Aynton over our spat? What foolery! I am a happy man, Matthew, and happy men do not kill.'

Bartholomew sincerely hoped he was right.

Clare Hall was oddly quiet when Bartholomew arrived, and he recalled that Donwich had sent all the students home early, confident that he would win the election and change the statute that forbade anyone to leave before the end of term. A porter led him to the conclave, where all the Fellows – other than Donwich and his two henchmen – had gathered.

'We are mortified by Donwich's challenge,' said Pulham the moment he saw Bartholomew, while his colleagues nodded vigorous agreement. 'It reflects badly on the

whole College. Will Michael believe that we had nothing
to do with it?'

'I imagine so,' replied Bartholomew. 'He is not stupid.'

'Unlike Donwich,' said Pulham bitterly. 'I barely recognise him these days. Did you know that he has threatened
to expel any Clare Hall man who contributes funds for
mending or rebuilding the Great Bridge? That sort of
stance will cause all manner of strife with the townsfolk.'

'It will,' acknowledged Bartholomew. 'So perhaps you
should elect a different Master.'

'If only it were that easy,' sighed Pulham.

'Michael sent me to ask more questions about him.
Shall we start with Donwich's premature victory feast?'

'None of us were invited,' said a canon lawyer named
Peter March, another smugly confident man who was
better at politics than scholarship. 'Only Gille and Elsham.
However, no Fellow likes his College invaded by a lot of
outsiders, so we monitored the event very closely. What
does Michael want to know?'

'Was Aynton also excluded?'

'No, Donwich wanted *him* there,' replied March. 'His
presence would have implied that he considered Donwich
the best man to take his place.'

'But Aynton would not have resigned if he thought
anyone other than Michael would succeed him,' put in
Pulham. 'He told us that the University is about to enter
a new and important stage in its development, and he
wanted Michael to oversee it.'

'Michael would have preferred Aynton to remain
Chancellor, while he himself worked quietly behind the
scenes,' said Bartholomew. 'As he has always done.'

Pulham nodded. 'We know, but Aynton was aware of his
own limitations, and he was terrified of making mistakes
that might cause damage. He was a good man.'

'Was Donwich angry when Aynton refused to endorse
him?'

112

The Fellows exchanged the kind of glances that suggested Donwich had been livid.

'Not enough to push him over a bridge though,' put in March. 'He is not a killer.'

Bartholomew would make up his own mind about that. 'If you monitored the feast, can you confirm that Donwich was there all night, so has an alibi for the murder?'

This time, the looks that flashed between the Fellows were more uncomfortable.

'He slipped out for an hour,' admitted March reluctantly. 'And before you ask, it *was* during compline, when we understand Aynton died. However, Donwich did not kill him.'

'Do you know where he went?'

'Bridge Street.' March grimaced. 'He has taken a liking to Lucy Brampton, and often visits her there. I thought he would stay here that night, to fawn over his guests, but . . .'

'His hypocrisy is embarrassing,' said Pulham harshly. 'He tells scholars not to pay for the bridge, but where would *he* be without it? Lucy lives on the other side!'

'What about Gille and Elsham? Did they leave the feast, too?'

'Yes, about an hour before compline,' replied March. 'They reappeared shortly before you arrived with Aynton's body, and we have since learned that they watched him being hoisted off the *ponticulus*. When it was done, they hurried back here to report to Donwich.'

'But they did not bother to share the news with us as well,' sniffed Pulham. 'We only learned what had happened when you arrived with the bier.'

'Do you know what they did when they were out?' asked Bartholomew. 'Other than watching Aynton being retrieved?'

'Not escort Donwich to his mistress, certainly,' replied March. 'He went there alone.'

113

'How do you know?'

'Because Donwich was sweaty and agitated when they went over to him,' replied Pulham, 'and I heard Gille ask him what was wrong. He would not have had to do that if they had been together, would he? But we have no idea what Gille and Elsham did while they were out. You will have to ask them.'

'So what *did* make Donwich "sweaty and agitated"?' asked Bartholomew.

Pulham shrugged. 'He spun some tale about seeing robbers and running for his life. It may be true – the town is dangerous for a lone scholar at night.'

Bartholomew was gratified to learn that his prime suspect for Aynton's murder not only had no alibi, but had returned from his nocturnal foray all of a fluster – as anyone might be after pushing a colleague to his death.

'None of the rest of us left the College,' said Pulham, anticipating Bartholomew's next question. 'We were too busy monitoring Donwich's guests.'

'Except me,' put in March. 'I was in the chapel with our two chaplains, praying for Donwich to revert to the man he was before we elected him Master.'

'So everyone has an alibi,' finished Pulham. 'Other than Donwich, Gille and Elsham.'

'But Donwich is no killer,' said March firmly. 'I can assure you of that.'

Bartholomew ignored him. 'What was Aynton doing while you defended Clare Hall from the Master's guests?' he asked.

'He was with us for the first part of the evening, but he slipped out shortly after Donwich did,' replied March, and glanced uneasily at his colleagues. 'He . . .'

'We think he followed Donwich,' said Pulham, willing to voice his suspicions, even if March could not bring himself to do it. 'To prove once and for all that Donwich's friendship with Lucy is not as innocent as Donwich maintains. Aynton deplored their liaison, you see, because it set a bad example to our students.'

'Which is why Donwich sent them home early, of course,' said March bitterly. 'Damn the man! He does Clare Hall great harm with his lust and his greed for power.'

'Do you have proof that Aynton was spying on Donwich?'

'No, but it stands to reason,' replied Pulham unhappily. 'Why else would he have been on Bridge Street at such an hour?'

'Did Aynton and Donwich like each other?'

'Not really,' replied March. 'Donwich considered Aynton weak and foolish, while Aynton found Donwich arrogant, selfish and rash.'

Bartholomew regarded each Fellow in turn. 'So, to summarise: Donwich despised Aynton's timidity, went out alone just before the murder, and returned home hot and agitated after it. Moreover, Aynton had offended him by refusing to support his bid for the chancellorship and condemning his relationship with Lucy.'

'You twist what we have told you,' objected March, alarmed. 'Donwich would never resort to violence. I repeat yet again: Donwich is no killer.'

'What about Gille and Elsham?' asked Bartholomew. 'Are they?'

'No,' replied Pulham, but his voice lacked conviction, and none of the others would look him in the eye. It told Bartholomew all he needed to know about the unsavoury pair.

The physician barely noticed the wall of heat that hit him as he left Clare Hall, and he walked slowly, head bowed in thought. Had Donwich spotted Aynton shadowing him and killed him for it? After all, no College Master would take kindly to a colleague trying to expose him as a philanderer. All Bartholomew hoped was that Michael

115

would find time to interrogate Donwich, because *he* did not fancy doing it again.

His reverie was broken by Ulf Godenave, who scampered up, begging him to visit the hovels near All Saints next-the-castle, where his grandmother was ill with the flux.

'The sickness is up there now?' groaned Bartholomew, one hand on his purse lest the boy should try to steal it again, although he would win scant pickings if he did. 'All the other cases have been in the south of the town.'

'Deadly miasmas drift where they please,' said Ulf sagely. 'Now, the Carmelites gave me a nice pair of shoes today, and you can have them if you make my granddam better.'

'That will not be necessary,' said Bartholomew, sure they would be stolen.

'Money, then,' said Ulf, flashing a halfpenny. 'A rich saint told the priest to give it to us for food. I was going to buy bread, but she needs your services more . . .'

'Buy the bread,' ordered Bartholomew. 'She will want it when the flux leaves her.'

He followed Ulf over the Great Bridge, noting that the railings and the *ponticulus* had been so skilfully mended that there was nothing to show they had been the scene of a painful death. He stopped and looked over the parapet to see Shardelowe on the riverbank below. The builder was dictating notes to a clerk, ready for his report to the council at the guildhall the next day. He also saw Isnard, who had indeed established a ferry service, and was doing a roaring trade from those who did not want to take their chances on the bridge.

It was early evening when he finished tending Ulf's grandmother, by which time Aynton's death had slipped to the back of his mind. His tentative theory that the Mill Pond was responsible for the flux had been well and truly quashed, because the Godenaves never went anywhere near it.

The flux was distressingly familiar in summer, but that year's outbreak was unusual for three reasons. First, it was concentrated in specific areas, although no one source seemed to be to blame. Second, there were more cases than normal. And third, the symptoms were different – generally milder, but taking longer to shake off. He feared that it might be some new form of the disease, one that was more resistant to the few remedies in his arsenal.

He began to walk home, and was halfway along Bridge Street when he heard his name called. He turned to see Tulyet and Dickon. The Sheriff was eager for news about Aynton's murder, lest it affected the town. Bartholomew summarised the little he had learned.

'So Donwich is the most likely suspect,' he concluded. 'Although I should speak to Morys before drawing premature conclusions. Apparently, his quarrel with Aynton was quite heated.'

'Be careful, 'warned Tulyet. 'He will not appreciate being interrogated by a scholar.'

'And he has rough kin to set on you, if you offend him,' put in Dickon with inappropriate relish. 'Most are useless louts, but his cousin John is nice. He is showing me how to kill people with my bare hands.'

'How to wrestle,' corrected Tulyet, and hastened to elaborate. 'Hand-to-hand combat is a necessary skill for any warrior, one I have often had occasion to use myself. John Morys is a knight at the castle, so I hired him to train Dickon.'

'I see,' said Bartholomew, thinking that the boy was dangerous enough as it was, without teaching him more ways to menace the general populace. 'How do you feel about helping me with Morys tomorrow, Dick? He may cooperate with you there.'

'I will come,' offered Dickon eagerly, fingering the

sword that he liked to carry at his side; Bartholomew noted with alarm that it was larger than his father's. 'I will threaten to spill his innards if he refuses to talk.'

'It is a kind offer, but no,' said Bartholomew firmly.

Dickon looked crestfallen. 'That is a pity. He deserves it, because he is corrupt. His wife Rohese is lovely, though.' He smiled rather dreamily. 'I met her today. She called me a fine, strapping lad, so I told *her* she is a fine, strapping woman.'

'That must have swept her off her feet,' drawled Bartholomew, unsettled that Dickon was now old enough to show an interest in the opposite sex. It did not seem that long ago that he was a babe in arms. Where had the time gone?

It was nearing dusk when Bartholomew parted from Tulyet and Dickon. He felt hot, tired and soiled, not just from visiting the hovels near the castle, but also from the sordid business of murder. He wanted to wash in cool, clean water, don fresh clothes, eat a light meal – not one of Michael's meat-loaded repasts – and go to sleep. Thoughts of the monk seemed to conjure him up, because, at that very moment, he emerged from the Hospital of St John. Bartholomew told him about the visit to Clare Hall.

'So things are not looking good for Donwich,' mused Michael. 'However, he is a lawyer, so we shall need solid evidence before challenging him.'

'What have you been doing since we parted company?' asked Bartholomew, hoping the 'we' meant Michael would do it himself.

'Arranging accommodation for the vicars-general and their retinue. King's Hall has offered to house the most important ones, while the rest will lodge here in St John's. I would have delegated the matter to Brampton, but I could not find him.'

'Perhaps he went to destroy any evidence that points

to him as the killer,' said Bartholomew sourly. 'He is on the suspects list, after all.'

'On yours,' countered Michael. 'Not on mine.'

'I still do not understand why you chose him to replace you. He does not have an ounce of authority, and will . . . what is *he* doing?'

He peered through the gathering gloom towards the hospital cemetery. Lamps had been lit near the dye-pits, where Narboro was holding forth to a group of influential burgesses, although Chaumbre was notable by his absence.

Michael chuckled. 'He fell down one of the holes earlier, and had to pay for a donkey to pull him out. He is of the opinion that Chaumbre has left them open deliberately, so that anyone injured will need a physician – namely his brother-in-law.'

Bartholomew was horrified. 'Does anyone believe him?'

'I doubt it, but the burgesses are obliged to hear his complaint anyway. They all like Chaumbre, but Narboro is a scholar – and an unpopular one at that – so nothing will come of his grumbles. Come away, before he sees you. You do not want to be dragged into something that will waste your time.'

As they turned into the High Street, they met Matilde and Lucy, who had been visiting Weasenham the University stationer regarding some exemplars that Matilde had ordered for her school. Judging by the women's dark expressions, the texts were still not ready.

'Do not worry,' Lucy was saying. 'I shall put it about that his scribes make critical errors, so his texts are not to be trusted. After a week of falling sales, Weasenham will be only too glad to complete our order.'

'He cannot bear the thought that women are as clever as men,' said Matilde angrily. 'So he aims to thwart our plans by refusing us supplies. But now you are Chancellor, Brother, you can *command* him to cooperate with us.'

'And I shall,' promised Michael. 'As soon as the vicars-general have been and gone.' He turned to Lucy. 'I was proud to appoint your brother as my Senior Proctor today. I am sure he will serve me well, and make a name for himself in University politics at the same time.'

Lucy smiled wryly. 'He certainly thinks so. However, I fear his suit against Narboro will overshadow all else. Perhaps *you* can persuade him to drop it.'

'I have already tried,' sighed Michael. 'But the insult rankles and he refuses to listen. Of course, Narboro does not help by flaunting himself about the town. He makes it hard for Brampton to forget about him.'

'Narboro is his own worst enemy,' agreed Matilde. 'But speaking of legal challenges, I hope you have a plan to defeat Donwich. It will be a disaster if he is Chancellor: he will anger townsfolk by refusing to help fund the new bridge, *and* he opposes my school.' She glanced at Lucy. 'I do not know what you see in him.'

'He is always very charming to me,' replied Lucy defensively. 'A different man altogether from the one who offends his colleagues and aggravates the town.'

'Did you see him last night?' fished Bartholomew. 'Around compline?'

'Yes, he visited me briefly, but I told him to return to his guests at once. I felt it was rude to abandon them in order to spend time with me. As far as I know, he did as I suggested.'

Bartholomew frowned. March had said that Donwich had been gone for an hour. Was this evidence that he had taken the opportunity to kill the man who refused to endorse his candidacy, and who dared to spy on his romantic liaisons into the bargain?

'Your friendship with him has become common knowledge,' he warned. 'It may harm your reputation if it continues.'

Lucy grimaced. 'I would rather be seen as a fallen

woman than as an object of pity. Besides, Donwich will keep me amused until someone better comes along – assuming another man is brave enough to risk my brother's litigious nature, of course.'

'I forgot to mention it earlier,' said Matilde to Bartholomew, 'but Edith and I overheard Aynton quarrel with Morys yesterday afternoon, and it occurs to me that it might be relevant to finding his killer.'

'Edith told me they argued about the bridge,' said Bartholomew.

Matilde nodded. 'Our Mayor wants an expensive stone affair, but your Chancellor said that the University will pay only one tenth of the cost of a wooden one, and not a farthing more. At one point, Morys told Aynton that he would regret his decision.'

Bartholomew stared at her. 'And within hours Aynton was dead?'

'I think Morys meant that wood is only a temporary solution,' explained Matilde, 'and that Aynton would be sorry if he failed to look further into the future.'

Bartholomew was not so sure, but at that moment the town's bells began to chime for evening prayers, and Matilde said it was time for her to go home. Bartholomew offered to accompany her there.

'Then allow me, madam,' said Michael, offering Lucy a plump arm. 'Escorting you to your house will be no trouble, as I can use the opportunity to discuss University business with my Senior Proctor.'

Bartholomew was pleased to have Matilde to himself, especially when she listened patiently and with interest to his ideas about the flux.

'So the culprit seems to be ale one day, and water butts the next,' he finished. 'With wells and the Mill Pond thrown in totally at random. It is all very perplexing.'

'Have you considered the possibility that water has nothing to do with it?' she asked. 'All the other *medici* say it is a miasma, which is certainly the accepted wisdom on the subject. Or perhaps it is bad food or this terrible heat.'

'The heat exacerbates the problem but does not cause it, while food cannot be to blame because there is no common supply. I understand why people think that miasmata – tiny airborne particles of rotting matter – cause diseases, but this does not explain why some folk fall ill while others are spared. I am missing something.'

'Well, I am sure you will work it out,' said Matilde comfortingly. Then her eyes narrowed and her voice turned angry. 'Look at him, slinking along like some common felon. I shall never forgive him for what he did to Lucy. He is a rat!'

Bartholomew followed her pointing finger, and saw Narboro, who had finished regaling the burgesses and was returning to Hoo Hall. He was clearly uneasy to be out alone after dark, so was trying to keep to the shadows in the hope of remaining invisible.

'Did you hear how he came to fall down Chaumbre's dye-pit?' she went on scathingly. 'He was admiring himself in that hand-mirror of his, and did not look where he was going.'

Bartholomew laughed. 'Was it the one Lucy gave him to remember her by, with the painting of her on the reverse?'

Matilde nodded. 'Yes, but her image is all but rubbed off, because he prefers what he sees on the other side. Did he show it to you? The man has no shame! Perhaps Brampton is right to destroy him with the law.'

'Would Lucy take him, if he offered himself again?'

'Not if I have anything to do with it – she deserves better. A *lot* better. But here we are at home. Will you come in?'

It was late by the time Bartholomew arrived back at Michaelhouse. He had been so busy since the election that he had forgotten about Stasy and Hawick, and was startled when he opened his door to find them stuffing the last of their belongings into a sack. Cynric stood over them impatiently.

'I keep telling them to hurry,' he growled. 'But they are slower than snails.'

'They cannot leave the town now,' said Bartholomew, alarmed for them. 'The King's highways are dangerous after dark, especially for travellers with baggage. They will stay here tonight, and go in the morning.'

'We have no intention of leaving Cambridge, not tonight or any other time,' declared Stasy indignantly. 'We are going to appeal Michael's decision in front of the Archbishop's emissaries, and they will reverse it.'

'And thank you for the offer, but we refuse to spend one more night in this nasty old place,' said Hawick, looking around with studied distaste. 'We shall go to the shop we have rented in Shoemaker Row – the one we shall open to patients tomorrow.'

'And there is nothing you or your fat friend can do to stop us,' put in Stasy fiercely. 'We do not need degrees to heal the sick and make lots of money.'

'No,' acknowledged Bartholomew. 'But—'

'You should have stood up for us, sir,' blurted Hawick, defiance crumbling as he remembered again all he had lost. 'To be expelled for a harmless jape after all our hard work! It is not fair.'

'Prior Pechem heard you chanting spells, and there was a Satanic symbol on the floor,' Bartholomew pointed out tartly. 'What did you expect? A monk can hardly turn a blind eye to that sort of thing in the University church, especially in front of all the Regent Masters.'

'We are sorry,' said Hawick tearfully. '*Please* talk to him and plead our case.'

Bartholomew did not want to, but reminded himself that they *had* been his students for years, so he should at least try to help them.

'Very well,' he said tiredly. 'But I doubt Michael will change his mind.'

'Do not bother,' spat Stasy. 'We want nothing from you or anyone else at this stupid College. And Michaelhouse will be sorry – I can promise you that.'

'You threaten us?' asked Cynric dangerously, fingering the dagger in his belt.

'Not in the way you think,' gulped Hawick with an unconvincing smile. 'You know we are in the used-exemplar business? Well, we shall no longer sell our wares to Michaelhouse students. That means they will have to pay the stationer's exorbitant prices, so the College will be very sorry indeed that its Master has crossed us.'

'Come on, Hawick,' said Stasy, picking up his bag and slinging it over his shoulder. 'It is time to go. Wait for me by the gate – I need to use the latrine before we leave.'

Bartholomew was glad when they had gone, although he was not alone for long, as Islaye and Mallett sidled in, confessing sheepishly that they had not liked to be there while the other two were packing. However, they soon wished they had steeled themselves to the poisonous atmosphere, because their erstwhile roommates had not confined themselves to their own belongings when loading up their bags. The cries of outrage were cut short by a screech from Agatha, followed by a tremendous racket from the peafowl. Bartholomew and Islaye ran outside to see Stasy streaking across the yard with several birds in hot pursuit.

'He must have tried to steal food from the kitchen,' surmised Islaye. 'But Agatha hates him, so when her howl woke the birds . . . well, they do not like him either.'

'My prayer book has gone!' shouted Mallett, rushing out to join them. 'The one my mother gave me. Come on, Islaye – help me get it back.'

They tore after Stasy, but the ex-student had too great a start, and was gone before they could reach him. Cynric also gave chase, but not for long, because he knew a lost cause when he saw one. He came back to talk to Bartholomew.

'I do not believe Hawick's claim that they will only avenge themselves by withholding cheap exemplars,' Bartholomew told him. 'Will you warn everyone to be on their guard?'

'I already have,' said Cynric. 'But they will not get in here again, especially now the birds have taken against them. They were fools to make enemies of peafowl – Master Clippesby says they are the most vindictive of all God's creatures. Well, other than people.'

They had certainly seen Stasy on his way, thought Bartholomew, watching the Dominican help Walter round them up and chivvy them back to their roost.

'We are protected by spells and charms, too,' Cynric went on. 'Ones I asked Margery Starre to prepare. She will not let us down, so you can sleep safe in your bed tonight, boy.'

Bartholomew nodded a terse goodnight and trudged to the conclave, hoping to spend an hour relaxing with his colleagues before bed. He was tired, but he was too tense to sleep after the confrontation with Stasy and Hawick.

The conclave was stuffy, even though only one lamp was lit. Moths circled it in a fluttering cloud, and their shadows danced on the walls. He arrived at the same time as Clippesby, who reported that all the birds had settled back down for the night, sure the physician would want to know. Then he went to sit in a corner, where he produced two mice from his sleeve, and proceeded to hold a conversation with them.

Michael had returned not long before, and was sitting in his chair by the hearth, while William and Zoone regaled him with their opinions about the election.

'*You* said that today was an auspicious date for it, because St Benedict would ensure that you woke up as

Chancellor on his feast day, tomorrow,' said William, rather accusingly. 'But you will not. Perhaps you should have petitioned my founder – St Francis – instead.'

'Of course I shall wake up as Chancellor,' said Michael impatiently. 'Everyone knows that Donwich's ambitions will never be realised.'

Zoone regarded him narrowly. 'You seem remarkably composed about all this, Brother, almost as if you do not care that he called you a cheat. I would be incandescent with rage, but you only smile, and radiate wisdom and tolerance.'

Michael shrugged. 'Which is how a Chancellor *should* behave. No one would thank me for aping Donwich's manners.'

'You will need help to overthrow him,' declared William. 'So I suggest you make me Junior Proctor. I did it once before, and I was very good at it.'

'Thank you, William,' said Michael, tactfully not pointing out that William's narrow-mindedness and bigotry had been a real liability. 'But I shall not appoint anyone until the situation is resolved. To do otherwise would be like prodding an angry hornet.'

'True,' acknowledged Zoone. 'Hopefully, Ufford and Rawby will be in Ely by now, and they will bring the vicars-general tomorrow. This business *must* be resolved before term ends, or our scholars will carry news of the situation to all corners of the civilised world. What is Donwich thinking? It is almost as if he *wants* to harm the University.'

'He does not care about reputations,' averred William. 'How can he, when he is enjoying a lustful liaison with the Senior Proctor's sister?'

'Not lustful,' said Michael mildly. 'They are friends.'

William laughed coarsely. 'Is that what you call it? But perhaps you should persuade him to marry her, Brother – he cannot be Chancellor then, and Lucy is in need of a husband. Of course, she could do a lot better than that arrogant ape . . .'

Zoone was thoughtful. 'Perhaps the rule about women is another statute Donwich aims to change if his challenge is successful. He told me himself that he will abolish the keeping of term, allowing students to come and go as they please.'

'The Clare Hall blackbird says he wants to let scholars visit taverns and carry weapons, too,' put in Clippesby from his corner. 'And as such a policy will lead to violent and drunken brawls with townsfolk, she hopes he is never in a position to do it.'

'He must be stopped,' agreed Zoone. 'So, what can I do to help, Brother? I am an engineer, so shall I arrange an accident? I can make it a non-fatal one, if you prefer.'

Michael laughed, although Bartholomew suspected that Zoone had not been joking. 'I think we can trust the vicars-general to make the right decision without resorting to that sort of tactic, Zoone. But it is late and it has been a long day. I bid you all good night.'

CHAPTER 6

During the night, Bartholomew received two summonses from patients. The first was Zoone, who had failed to drink enough during the day and had given himself a bad headache – the pain eased after two jugs of the ubiquitous boiled barley water. The second was Walter the surly porter, and Bartholomew's heart sank when he recognised the first symptoms of the flux. Thus far, Michaelhouse had escaped it.

'What have you eaten or drunk outside the College?' he asked, hoping there would be a tavern involved, so he would be able to isolate one source of infection.

'Nothing,' groaned Walter, both hands to his stomach. 'It is too hot for wandering about, and I have not left the porters' lodge in days.'

'You must have gone out to check the gates or to admit visitors. Or to feed the poultry.'

A weak smile lit Walter's surly features: his birds were the only creatures that had ever truly touched his heart, and he loved them far more than any human.

'I might have slipped to the kitchens to fetch them treats,' he admitted. 'But I do not leave my lodge to meddle with gates or escort visitors about. That is what students are for.'

As security was clearly a low priority for Walter, Bartholomew went to see if Cynric would guard the College until Stasy and Hawick no longer posed a threat. The spiteful pair would certainly know about Walter's relaxed attitude to his duties, and he did not want to make it easy for them, should they attempt to exact revenge for their expulsion.

Cynric was in the kitchen with Agatha. Bartholomew was not surprised to be informed that the laundress had not left it since the heatwave had begun – being stone-built and low, it was the coolest part of the College, and thus a very comfortable place to be.

'Do not worry, boy,' said Cynric, pleased his skills were needed. 'They will not get in, I promise. And we *should* be on our guard, given all the curses they mutter. Margery is going to be very busy on our behalf as long as they are at large.'

'They had better not have cursed me,' declared Agatha belligerently. 'If they have, I shall trounce them with a ladle. Where are they now, Cynric?'

'In the shop they rented in Shoemaker Row,' replied the book-bearer. 'They worked on it all night, and opened this morning as *medici*. I reminded them that they never got their degrees, but they said they do not need one to practise medicine.'

'They do not,' sighed Bartholomew, aware that anyone could declare himself a healer, regardless of education, knowledge or skill. He had asked for the profession to be regulated, but neither the University nor the town thought it necessary. 'As long as they do no obvious harm, and do not annoy the apothecaries and barber-surgeons, they can do what they like.'

'They will not do it for long,' predicted Cynric darkly. 'The Devil will want to gather two such dedicated servants to his bosom before they have second thoughts and become Christians again.'

'My nephew Robin came late last night,' said Agatha, who was related to half the town; Robin was a sergeant at the castle. 'He told me that Stasy has invented a remedy for the flux and will start selling it today.' She glared accusingly at Bartholomew. 'But *you* said nothing will cure it, other than time and boiled barley water.'

'If every remedy was required to work, no *medicus* or

apothecary would ever be able to prescribe one again,' said Bartholomew wryly. 'Ergo, Stasy and Hawick will claim what they like, and blame any lack of success on the patient's stars or abnormal humours, just like all the other charlatans. All I hope is that whatever they have concocted is harmless.'

'We shall find out soon enough,' said Agatha. 'Because Robin told me that they sent a pot to Beadle Meadowman. They feel sorry for him, because he has been ill for so long, and you have failed to mend him.'

Bartholomew decided to visit the beadle immediately, lest the remedy contained something to make him worse.

'Here,' said Cynric, tossing Bartholomew a tiny packet. 'If Stasy and Hawick come for you with evil intent, throw this in their faces. Margery says it will stop them dead.'

Bartholomew tried to hand it back. 'I cannot be seen deploying magic powders. I do not want to follow Stasy and Hawick in being expelled from the University.'

'You will not be part of it for much longer anyway,' said Cynric carelessly. 'But it is not a magic powder – she knows you are frightened of those – it is fine-ground pepper. She says it will sting their eyes and stop them from bothering you.'

Bartholomew poured some into his hand, and saw the book-bearer was right; it *was* just pepper. 'I still cannot accept it. It is far too expensive for—'

'She likes you,' interrupted Cynric. 'And she does *not* like them. Take it, boy. It may save your life, should they launch an attack and I am not there to protect you.'

'He is right,' said Agatha. 'Take it and be grateful that such an important lady thinks so highly of you. The poor Chancellor was thrown off the bridge to his death, and we do not want the same thing happening to you.'

'You think Stasy and Hawick killed Aynton?' asked Bartholomew uneasily.

'I would not put it past them,' replied Agatha. 'They are malicious, greedy and callous.'

'There are rumours that another scholar killed Aynton,' put in Cynric. 'Master Donwich or Narcissus Narboro, for example, who want to be Chancellor themselves.'

'Narboro!' spat Agatha. 'I felt sorry for Lucy when he spurned her, but now I think she is the luckiest woman alive. Can you imagine what it would be like married to him? She would never get the chance to check herself in the mirror, because he would hog it all day.'

'Perhaps you should throw pepper in *his* eyes,' suggested Cynric. 'Being blind for a while would give him the opportunity to think about something other than his hair.'

'He made a terrible fuss about falling down a dye-pit yesterday,' chuckled Agatha. 'So much that Robin says Chaumbre was forced to fill it in at once – the man he hired worked all night. Of course, now Chaumbre has done one, he will forget about the others. Personally, I think he hopes to store his dye-balls there again one day.'

'I do not like those holes,' said Cynric, and shuddered. 'They look like something Satan might have dug with his claws.'

Bartholomew left when book-bearer and laundress began a sharp disagreement about whether the Devil would use his nice sharp talons for such menial work, or ask familiars like Stasy and Hawick to get a spade out.

It was still dark when Bartholomew arrived at Meadowman's house. The beadle was no better, and as it had been more than a week since the illness had started, he was beginning to look thin and haggard, with lines of pain around his mouth. Bartholomew inspected the boiled barley water – from a batch flavoured with honey and camomile – that he had sent the previous day, and saw that very little, if any, had been drunk.

'Your students came at dawn,' Meadowman whispered.

131

'They told me you were cursed and could never make me well. They left me that.'

He nodded to an expensive-looking phial on the windowsill. Bartholomew picked it up and smelt it warily. All he could identify was mint, although he knew there were very dangerous substances that would take more than a sniff to detect.

'Have you taken any of it?' he asked uneasily.

'A tiny sip,' admitted Meadowman. 'I know I should have resisted, given that they are sorcerers, but I have been ill for so long that I yielded to temptation.'

At that moment, Isnard arrived, full of mucus and unpleasant snorting noises. His eyes were bloodshot and when he spoke, his voice was an octave lower than normal.

'I met your students – the warlocks – on my way home from the Griffin last night,' he growled. 'It was hot, so they recommended a cooling dip in the Mill Pond. It sounded like a good idea, and I only remembered once I was in that I cannot swim.'

'Ale will kill you one day, Isnard,' said Meadowman. 'You might have drowned.'

'I nearly did,' said Isnard. 'Luckily, Master Gayton from Peterhouse fished me out. I swallowed half the Mill Pond before he arrived, so if you notice it is emptier this morning . . .'

'Other than your cold, how do you feel?' asked Bartholomew, thinking of the myriad diseases which lurked in that foul body of water. 'Any nausea or sickness?'

'No, but this ague is killing me. I do not even have the energy to pull my ferry, and had to hire some of the Marian Singers to do it for me. Are you sure you do not have a remedy hidden away somewhere, Doctor? I will pay whatever you ask.'

'I wish I did,' sighed Bartholomew. 'But no one does, including Stasy and Hawick, so if they offer to sell you one, do not buy it.'

Isnard sniffed revoltingly. 'I will not – not after they tried to kill me last night. Once I was in the Mill Pond, screaming for help, they raced away sniggering. If Master Gayton had not happened past, I would have died.'

'They left you?' asked Bartholomew, shocked, although he supposed he should not be surprised that the malevolent pair should strike at him by targeting his patients.

'The moment they were sure I was in trouble,' replied Isnard. 'But they will not hurt me a second time. If they come anywhere near me again, I shall punch them.'

'Senior Proctor Brampton came last night,' Meadowman told Bartholomew, 'to assess if I was malingering. More beadles have the flux, you see, so he is desperately short of men. He said the University cannot pay us while we are laid up, so thank God for that saint – the man who gives money to the priests to help us.'

Bartholomew poured him a beaker of barley water. The beadle took it, and very cautiously used it to wet his lips.

'You need more than that,' said Bartholomew. 'Lots more.'

'But I do not like it,' objected Meadowman, trying to hand it back. 'And I only sick it back up again, so what is the point? Besides, such insipid medicine cannot possibly cure this terrible sickness. How could it?'

Bartholomew had explained several times about the importance of replacing lost fluids, and knew that repeating it again would be futile. Instead, he rummaged in his medical bag for the pepper from Margery Starre. He did not usually deceive patients, but Meadowman's plight had grown desperate, and the beadle could just as easily die from refusing to drink as from the flux.

'This is a very potent powder,' he said, and put a pinch on the back of Meadowman's hand, hoping the beadle would be unfamiliar with expensive condiments, and so would not recognise the taste. 'Touch your tongue to it and see.'

'Goodness!' gasped Meadowman. 'That *is* strong. Is it dangerous?'

'Very, in the wrong hands,' replied Bartholomew gravely. 'I will add a dose to the barley water, but you *must* drink the whole jug this morning, or the flux will . . .' – he flailed around for a pretext that the beadle would take seriously – '. . . will burst out of your nose and kill you. I will send a student with more this afternoon.'

Wide-eyed, Meadowman took the beaker, and Bartholomew watched him drain it. If the ploy worked, he could conclude that the beadle's reluctance to follow medical advice was responsible for his abnormally slow recovery.

When Bartholomew returned to Michaelhouse, he found his colleagues assembling in the yard. He was bemused, because dawn had broken while he had been with Meadowman, and they were usually in church by now. Then Michael appeared in his best habit, and the physician recalled that it was the Feast of St Benedict. Michael always marked the occasion with later morning prayers, to which he invited fellow Benedictines. There were not many Black Monks in Cambridge, as the University tended to be more popular with the mendicant Orders than the monastic ones, but there were enough to make the ceremony noisy and joyful even so.

At one point, Bartholomew spotted Stasy and Hawick at the back of the nave, although they had gone by the time the rite had finished. He and Cynric inspected the spot where they had been, and found a lot of grease on the floor.

'They want one of us to slip and break his neck,' surmised the Welshman. 'I had better follow them today, to make sure they try nothing else to hurt us.'

'Be careful,' warned Bartholomew. 'I do not want them targeting you in the hope of avenging themselves.'

Cynric sniffed his disdain. 'They are no threat to me, boy. But I hope I do catch them doing something illicit: as they are no longer scholars, they cannot claim protection from the University, which means I can hand them to the Sheriff. Or better yet, to Dickon.'

On that note, he padded off to begin. Bartholomew returned to Michaelhouse, where an especially fine breakfast had been provided in honour of the Master's favourite saint. When it was over, and Bartholomew was in his room preparing for the day ahead, Michael came in.

'Summarise where we are with Aynton's murder,' he ordered. 'Who is still on our list?'

'Donwich is at the top,' replied Bartholomew. 'He has no alibi, he was at loggerheads with Aynton over his affair with Lucy, and he was furious that Aynton refused to endorse his candidacy for Chancellor. Moreover, when Donwich returned from visiting Lucy on the night of the murder, he was "sweaty and agitated".'

'As anyone would be after dispatching a fellow scholar,' mused Michael thoughtfully. 'Who is second on the list?'

'Narboro,' replied Bartholomew. 'Who also has no alibi, and may have killed Aynton to make sure the election went ahead. He makes me uneasy, although I cannot say why. Perhaps it is his narcissism, which is so extreme that I find myself wondering if it is real.'

'Third?'

'Donwich's henchmen, Gille and Elsham, who are eager for him to be Chancellor, because he will make them his proctors. They were absent from the feast during compline, when Aynton was killed . . .'

'Have you asked them where they were? No? Then that must be done today. Fourth?'

'Stasy and Hawick – they were among the onlookers when we found Aynton and refused to go home. Further, they harboured malicious intentions towards the University even before you expelled them – why else would they have cast spells in St Mary the Great? They were never my favourite pupils, but they revealed a new side to themselves yesterday.'

'To me, too, and it makes me wish I had expelled them sooner. When you next speak to them, find out where they were when Aynton was killed. Fifth?'

'Mayor Morys, who wants Donwich to be Chancellor, because he is bribable. He may not have pushed Aynton himself, but he has kinsmen who will do it for him. Dick has offered to interview him with me today.'

'Good. Sixth?'

'Brampton. You see nothing amiss with the fact that he spied on Aynton, is full of venom, did not tell you about the quarrel he witnessed between Aynton and Chaumbre, and is good friends with Donwich, but I do.'

'Include him if you must,' said Michael, rolling his eyes. 'But if you do, I want Chaumbre, who also argued with Aynton and who left Clare Hall's feast to look at dye, which no one can corroborate. He may be lying. Next?'

'Those are all so far. I suppose you want me to question them on my own today, because you will be too busy fighting off Donwich's challenge.'

'Actually, I want you to teach. Your students are disturbed by the expulsion of two of their number, so it is important to make sure they follow their usual routines today. Thus you will lecture, and I shall investigate murder.'

Bartholomew blinked his surprise. 'Truly? You do not need my help?'

'I will take Brampton instead. It will be good for him. Besides, I cannot do anything about Donwich's claim until the vicars-general arrive, but Aynton clamours at me for justice. Perhaps I shall have his killer by tonight. If not, though, I will need you tomorrow.'

Bartholomew did not hear the last part – he had hurried away before Michael could change his mind.

*

To make up for lost time, Bartholomew drove his students hard that morning, and was astonished when the bell rang for the midday meal, feeling as though he had barely started. As he ate, he noticed that some of the food was on the verge of spoiling, despite being bought fresh that day. Again, he wondered when the weather would break.

Before he could resume his gruelling schedule, a message came from the Spital, where several residents had the flux. He left Aungel to lead the discussion he had planned on Galen's *De ptisana* and hurried out, feeling the sun burn through his hat as he walked. It was the hottest part of the day, and the air was thick with the scent of scorched earth. Trees wilted, their leaves curled, brown and crisp from the lack of rain.

He tended his patients, and was just passing the Gilbertine Priory on his way back when he met Michael. The monk reported that he had spent his morning racing after Morys, but had missed him at every turn. As he looked cool and fresh, Bartholomew suspected that he had not so much raced as strolled, with plenty of stops for refreshment along the way.

'While I was tearing about like a March hare,' the monk went on, 'I met Donwich and his henchmen in St Mary the Great, Brampton and Chaumbre in the Market Square, and Stasy and Hawick in Shoemaker Row. I questioned them all but learned nothing useful.'

'Did you press them on their alibis?'

'Of course. Brampton said he was on University business, although he has no one to confirm it; Chaumbre was looking at dye, which we know; and Stasy and Hawick claim they were with each other, which is no answer at all.'

'Is Dick helping you hunt for Morys?'

'He is busy – something about a new clue for the murder of Baldok, which he still hopes to solve – so he sent Dickon in his stead. I endured the brat's company for an hour, but sent him home when he suggested prising information from our suspects with a sword.' Michael grimaced. 'Although I wish I had accepted his offer with Stasy and Hawick.'

'They were uncooperative?'

'Naturally enough. I expelled them, after all.'

'Hawick wants you to reconsider. Is there any way to let them have their degrees?'

'They can appeal to the vicars-general, but my decision is unlikely to be overturned – the Archbishop's men cannot be seen condoning witchery either. Hah! There is Narboro. Shall we question him together, as he is here?'

They walked towards where Narboro was adjusting the buckles on his elegant shoes. He straightened as they approached. Michael opened his mouth to speak, but the Peterhouse man cut across him.

'You should know that I have lodged proceedings against Philip Chaumbre for leaving those great holes in St John's cemetery,' he declared haughtily. 'I fell down one and suffered a grievous injury yesterday, so it is only right that he compensates me with money.'

'Let me see it,' ordered Bartholomew. 'I may be able to help.'

'That would be unethical,' blustered Narboro, backing away. 'You are related to the defendant.'

'Anyone can see there is nothing wrong with you,' said Michael sternly, 'and that your sole aim is to win some easy money. If you have any sense, you will drop the suit before it lands you in trouble.'

Narboro's expression turned sulky. 'Well, how else can I raise the vast sum that your Senior Proctor demands of me for not marrying his sister?'

'I do not understand why you agreed to wed her in the first place,' said Michael. 'You must have known ten years ago that she was not the right lady for you, or that you might prefer to remain unattached.'

'I was young and reckless back then,' sniffed Narboro. 'And she had all her teeth.'

As Bartholomew and Michael walked towards the Trumpington Gate, they saw Morys, who was engaged in a furious altercation with the sentries.

Cambridge lay on a major highway, so all traffic paid a toll to pass through the town – money that was then used to keep the road in good working order. As there was always a shortfall between what was collected and what was needed for repairs, individual householders along the street were obliged to pay the difference. Naturally, they resented it, so to keep costs to a minimum, the guards were assiduous about what they allowed in. Any cart deemed too heavy was ordered to divide its load or divert to another route.

That day, an enormous wagon had arrived, piled high with huge blocks of stone, and drawn by eight oxen. It would mangle the road if permitted to trundle on, and the guards were right to stop it. Unfortunately, Morys had decided that he had the authority to grant an exemption.

'But look at the thing!' one soldier shouted. 'It will destroy the High Street!'

'Nonsense,' stated Morys in a voice that brooked no argument. 'Now step aside before I dock your wages for insolence. Carter? Proceed.'

The sentries watched in dismay as the great vehicle began to lumber forward. It knocked a chunk off the gate when the driver misjudged its width, and its wheels left deep furrows in their wake. As he passed, the carter winked conspiratorially at Morys and tossed him a purse. Michael was outraged and stormed over to say so.

'The guards are right – that thing should never have been allowed through,' he declared angrily. 'Look at the ruts it has made! Who will pay to mend them? You?'

'Those were already there,' lied Morys. 'Besides, it is none of your business.'

That was true, but rather than admit it, Michael began to interrogate him about the Chancellor's murder instead. 'You and Aynton quarrelled on the day he was killed. Why?'

'It was not a quarrel, it was a difference of opinion,' retorted Morys. 'And it did *not* result in me shoving him off the bridge, if that is the direction your thoughts have taken.'

'So where were you when he died?'

'At Clare Hall, with a whole roomful of witnesses.'

'Not during compline, which is when Aynton was killed,' countered Michael. 'We have reliable witnesses who say you left long before then.'

'Oh, so I did,' said Morys smoothly. 'I remember now. However, I am not at liberty to divulge more, because my errand concerned confidential guildhall business.'

'Then tell us who you met,' ordered Michael. 'Because I am sure you want to help us by eliminating yourself from our list of suspects.'

'I am not in the habit of breaking council secrets,' retorted Morys loftily. 'So you will have to take my word that I was nowhere near your Chancellor when he died.'

'Do I indeed?' muttered Michael. 'Then tell me about your argument with Aynton instead. What was the "difference of opinion" about?'

'The bridge,' replied Morys, and his expression turned sly. 'He agreed to pay half the cost of a stone one, so I expect you to honour his promise.'

Michael shook his head in disbelief. 'Aynton thought wood would suffice, and was vehemently opposed to building in stone. Do not lie to me, Morys.'

Morys smirked, unrepentant. 'It was worth a try, and if you had believed me, I would have won something good for the town. The truth is that he offered to pay a tenth of a wooden one, but that is miserly, and I am sure the new Chancellor will want to reconsider in the interests of good town–University relations. Yes?'

Michael raised his eyebrows. 'Legally, we are not obliged to pay anything at all, so be grateful for what you have. However, I want to know *precisely* why you argued with Aynton. Did you demand more money of him, as you have just done with me?'

'Our discussion was private,' said Morys archly. 'But I cannot stand around gossiping with you all day – I should be at the guildhall. You do know that the burgesses will vote to build a stone bridge today, do you not?'

'How do you know what they will decide?' asked Bartholomew, although even as he spoke, he recalled the discussion on the bridge after Aynton's murder, where Morys had promised Shardelowe that very outcome in exchange for free repairs on the *ponticulus*.

'I have a nose for such things,' replied Morys blithely. 'Besides, it is the right thing to do. It will be expensive though, so I shall expect *everyone* to reach into his purse to pay for it – the University *and* the town.'

'The town will refuse,' predicted Michael. 'They have already given a fortune for the bridge – a fortune that you recklessly entrusted to the thieving Baldok. Why should they hand you more?'

'Baldok did not steal that much,' argued Morys. 'Just one instalment. We still have the bulk of it.'

Michael ignored him and forged on. 'Some were almost beggared by the first levy, and even wealthy merchants like the Mortimers, FitzAbsolon, Chaumbre—'

Morys interrupted with a laugh. 'I shall not be troubling Chaumbre, because he is not as rich as he would have everyone believe. But the University *will* pay its share. I can promise you that.'

'I think we had better attend this meeting, Matt,' said Michael, watching the Mayor strut away. 'He is up to something, and I want to know what.'

CHAPTER 7

The guildhall was a large black and white edifice with elegant plasterwork, located near the Market Square. Inside was a porch leading to the massive central chamber where the burgesses did their business. A good deal of money had been spent on it in the past, although funds had been tight in recent years, so its grandeur was fading into shabbiness.

It was unusually full that day, because the meeting was open to any interested parties – and there were lots of those, as the Great Bridge affected everyone who lived in Cambridge. All twenty burgesses had shown up, and sat with Morys at a table on the dais. Those who wanted to listen to their deliberations perched on benches in the body of the hall or stood at the back, and included not only merchants, but knights from the castle, an assortment of priests, and a number of scholars, ranging from the principals of impoverished hostels to the heads of wealthy Colleges. Donwich was among the latter.

The chamber was swelteringly hot, despite all the windows being open, and there were complaints aplenty about the airlessness. Bartholomew was called to help Mistress FitzAbsolon, wife of the town's cutler, who was on the verge of passing out.

'Watch Morys today, Matthew,' she warned, as he took her outside. 'He is a sly rogue, and your University should not trust him.'

Inside again a few moments later, the roar of conversation had grown deafening. He saw Edith talking to Gayton of Peterhouse and Warden Shropham from King's Hall, so he eased through the throng to join them, arriving at the same time as Michael, Tulyet and Dickon. Even as they exchanged greetings, Morys called the meeting to order.

'We all know why we are here,' he began. 'The Great Bridge *must* be repaired – the King himself insists on it. The decision we shall make today is whether to mend it with wood that will rot again in a year or two, or with stone that will last for ever.'

'Nothing lasts for ever, Morys,' called Prior Pechem piously. 'Except God.'

'The Great Bridge has claimed two lives this year alone,' Morys went on. 'Namely Baldok and Aynton. I feel it is time to end such needless suffering, and build in stone, for safety and permanence. So first, I invite Doctor Rougham, the University's most eminent medical man, to give his professional views about the situation.'

Rougham looked startled to hear himself so described, and cast an anxious glance at Bartholomew before taking the floor, evidently afraid of being challenged. He was currently building his College a chapel, and was always looking for new ways to pay for it – Bartholomew could only suppose his testimony had been bought.

'The Mayor is right,' Rougham began. 'The Great Bridge is a serious hazard to public safety. Not only is it unstable, which has led to distressing mishaps, but the river below festers with vile diseases. No one who falls in it will survive.'

This was patently untrue, as children swam in it every day, but Bartholomew did not object to the exclamations of alarm that rippled through the hall, feeling it was not a bad thing for people to be reminded that the filthy Cam represented a significant danger to health.

After Rougham came more witnesses, all of whom were in the pro-stone camp, until it was time for the last and most important opinion of all: Shardelowe, sent by the King to provide an official verdict on the matter. The builder presented such a bleak picture of the bridge's current condition that there was not one person present who did not wonder how it could still be standing.

'So my advice to you,' he said in conclusion, 'is to keep the granite piers and spandrels, but to strengthen them with a limestone balustrade and a durable cobbled pavement. And I am the man to do it for you.'

'Why is that, Shardelowe?' prompted Morys, nodding encouragingly.

'Because I am cheaper than anyone else,' replied Shardelowe, 'and because the King admires my work so much that he sent me to assess the situation here. After all, what is good enough for His Majesty should be good enough for anyone else.'

Aware that Morys had already promised Shardelowe the work, and that the council's decision would thus be a foregone conclusion, Bartholomew's attention wandered. His gaze fell on Chaumbre, who had left the dais to stand with Edith instead. The dyer took her hand and gave her the sweetest smile imaginable. She returned it and Bartholomew saw there was genuine affection between them. It made him feel treacherous for having Chaumbre on his list of suspects, and he hoped the man could be eliminated before she found out, or she would be furious with him.

Next to him, Dickon sighed and fidgeted with boredom. Then the boy remembered that he had a catapult in his scrip. He pulled it out and began flicking an assortment of missiles at people he did not like. When these included Father William, Bartholomew took it away from him, earning himself a malevolent glower in the process.

'But who will pay for this extravagant stone creation, Morys?' called Burgess FitzAbsolon worriedly.

'All of us,' replied Morys smoothly. 'Shardelowe and I have negotiated an excellent price, and the money sent by the King, plus what we have already collected in taxes, will cover three-fifths of it. Show them, John.'

The order was directed at his cousin, the battle-honed knight who was training Dickon in hand-to-hand combat. John flung open the lid of a chest that stood nearby to show it was full of coins. There was an appreciative sigh from those close enough to see them.

'What says the University?' asked Morys. 'You promised a tenth of the cost of a wood bridge, but that is unfair, given that you use it just as much as we do. What about dividing the outstanding amount between us – one fifth from you and one fifth from the town?'

'So *that* is why he called an open meeting,' breathed Bartholomew in understanding. 'Not to persuade the council to his point of view, because he has probably already bought most of them, but because it is more difficult for us to refuse with half the town looking on.'

'No,' called Donwich, before Michael could respond. 'We are not obliged to contribute anything. The cost must be borne by the town alone, as is right and proper.'

'You cannot speak for the University,' said FitzAbsolon crossly. 'You are not its Chancellor. I want to hear what Brother Michael—'

'I am the *Anti*-Chancellor,' interrupted Donwich grandly, 'which means I have just as much authority as he does. Besides, it is only a matter of time before the Archbishop's agents find in my favour, so you would be wise to watch your tongue.'

'Brother?' asked Morys, while most townsmen regarded each other in bafflement that such a peculiar situation could exist. 'Will *you* show your contempt for the good people of Cambridge by refusing to part with a little of your University's fabled wealth?'

He and Donwich exchanged a quick glance of triumph, and Bartholomew wondered how much Donwich had been paid to back Michael into an impossible corner. To refuse to contribute to the scheme would antagonise the town, but to agree would allow Donwich to bray to their

145

colleagues that *he* would not allow himself to be bullied by the Mayor.

'The University will provide one tenth of the total,' said Michael tightly. 'Which is a considerable increase on the amount we originally agreed for repairs in wood. It is a fair offer, especially as we are under no obligation to pay anything at all.'

'Done!' said Morys before anyone could argue. 'When can we have it?'

Michael blinked. 'It will take some time to—'

'You have until next Wednesday,' determined Morys. 'Shardelowe will begin work at once, and I suggest we all walk to the bridge now, so he can outline his plans in more detail.'

The Mayor's declaration signalled the end of the meeting, and Bartholomew noted that the motion to rebuild in stone had been bulled through without the council's vote. The burgesses looked relieved, presumably so they could deny culpability later, should things go wrong.

As people began to file out of the guildhall, Donwich came to inform Michael that he had no right to squander the University's money, and that *he* would not allow himself to be manipulated by the Mayor when he was confirmed as Chancellor.

'You will refuse to give what I promised, if the vicars-general find in your favour?' asked Michael, his voice loud enough to carry. 'You will leave the town to pay it all?'

Donwich's smirk slipped at the immediate growl of anger from the people who heard. 'We shall see,' he hedged. 'However, I shall ensure that our scholars know it was your idea.'

'What a loathsome worm!' exclaimed Gayton, watching him strut away. 'It is obvious that he had all this worked out with Morys in advance. I hope the vicars-general reject his claim soon, Brother, because he could do a lot of damage in the interim.'

Once outside, most folk disappeared to their homes or places of business. Bartholomew and Michael were among the few who followed Shardelowe to the bridge, along with Zoone, who, as an engineer, had valid opinions about the builder's plans. Donwich decided he should be there, too, and was flanked by a tight knot of supporters that included Gille and Elsham. Morys and half a dozen burgesses came next, with Tulyet and Dickon bringing up the rear.

When they reached the bridge, Shardelowe made the point that it would have to close while work was under way.

'But we cannot manage without it for months on end!' cried FitzAbsolon. 'It will cost us a fortune in lost revenue and tolls, not to mention the harm it will do to trade. I *knew* we should have opted for a wooden one. Morys was wrong to persuade us otherwise.'

'If you buy the supplies as they arrive, and agree to pay me and my men the moment the work is completed,' said Shardelowe, 'you will have a new stone bridge in eight days.'

'Eight days?' echoed Tulyet, while gasps of disbelief came from everyone else. 'That is impossible! Besides, rushed men make mistakes, and we do not want a shoddy result.'

'Or deaths and injuries among your workforce,' put in Bartholomew.

'We are professionals,' stated Shardelowe loftily. 'We do not have accidents, and our work is exemplary. If you leave us alone to get on with it, I promise to finish by Saturday week – in time for the University's graduation ceremony.'

'It cannot be done,' argued Tulyet impatiently. 'Tell him, Zoone.'

Zoone rubbed his chin. 'Actually, it is theoretically possible, if they work night and day, and there are no unforeseen difficulties. Of course, that assumes all the materials arrive promptly – the deadline will be missed if even one delivery goes astray.'

'Leave all that to me,' said Shardelowe briskly. 'I shall offer my men a bonus if we finish on time, and there is nothing like a fat purse to motivate a fellow. Of course, it will cost a little extra, but nothing that cannot be recouped tenfold by an early resumption of tolls. What do you say?'

'Yes,' said Morys, so quickly that Bartholomew was not alone in surmising that he and the builder had already discussed the bonus and agreed on it. 'Shall we put it in writing?'

Gille offered his services as a scribe, and when he produced the materials he needed to prepare the contract, Bartholomew recognised the jewelled inkpot as the one he had filched from Michael's office in St Mary the Great the previous day.

'I know,' said Michael, when Bartholomew pointed it out to him. 'But now is not the time to accuse him of theft. It will make me look petty – which is exactly why he is flaunting the thing, of course.'

'Lord!' muttered Bartholomew, astounded by the depths to which Donwich's cronies were prepared to sink to score points.

For the rest of the afternoon and early evening, Bartholomew listened to Zoone and Shardelowe discuss the minutiae of the project. He was fascinated by the complex calculations involved, although they left everyone else with glazed eyes. Then he felt a tug on his sleeve, and turned to see Cynric. The book-bearer nodded to where Stasy and Hawick stood nearby, waylaying anyone who would stop to listen to them.

'They are touting for business,' the book-bearer explained. 'They started at dawn and have not stopped since – I have watched them the whole time. There will be trouble soon, because they bought a load of Margery Starre's remedies and are passing them off as their own. She will not be pleased.'

Bartholomew imagined she would not, and thought they were reckless to antagonise a self-confessed witch, whose hexes were generally believed to be effective.

'What will she do about it?' he asked uneasily.

'Oh, just something to ensure they never do it again,' replied Cynric airily. 'But they have been maligning you, boy. They tell folk that you cannot cure the flux or a common cold, but they can, which makes *them* better physicians.'

Bartholomew was unconcerned. 'When their "remedies" fail, they will discover that they have done themselves great harm by making reckless claims.'

When Cynric had gone, Bartholomew went to the side of the bridge and looked down. In the narrow gap between it and the *ponticulus*, he could see the river. Its stench made his eyes water, and he wondered how Isnard could bear to operate a ferry on it – the bargeman had a steady stream of customers, who would rather use his boat than risk the bridge.

His gaze wandered to the nearby houses. To his left was Tulyet's, a handsome mansion that provided him and his family with a comfortable alternative to the spartan accommodations at the castle. To his right was Brampton's, smaller than the Sheriff's, but newer and more ornate, with glass in every window and a fine tile roof, all of which showed the Senior Proctor to be a man of considerable wealth. Bartholomew wondered if that was why Donwich was courting Lucy – with no children, the Senior Proctor was likely to leave all his worldly goods to his sister, and Donwich had always been interested in money.

At that moment, a loud shout caught his attention, and he looked up to see two carts attempting to pass each other. Unwilling to be mashed into the parapet while they manoeuvred, he left the bridge and walked down to the riverbank. A ragged band of children, led by Ulf Godenave, scampered along its shores, playing chase. Some took refuge behind the wreck of a small boat, which jutted into the river, impeding its flow and snagging anything that floated too close. It was then that Bartholomew saw the hand.

'You are mistaken,' called Morys, when Bartholomew shouted the news to the people on the bridge. 'It is a dead fish or a bit or rubbish.'

But Bartholomew knew a human hand when he saw one. He began to slither across the mud towards it. Ulf and his friends stopped playing to watch him, while towns-folk and scholars clustered at the edge of the bridge. Some squashed Donwich into the rickety balustrade, and there was an ominous creak.

'Back, back!' he cried in alarm. 'It is not strong enough to withstand you shoving at me, and I do not want to end up like poor Aynton.'

'No,' agreed Tulyet drily. 'So perhaps you should recon-sider your objections to helping us pay for repairs. Careful there, Matt. That mud is very slippery.'

'I know,' snapped Bartholomew, aware that it was ruining his only good shoes – the ones he would wear to his wedding, given that he had no money to buy more. 'So will someone come down here and help?'

'Not me,' averred Donwich in distaste. 'Grubbing about in the filth comes under the Senior Proctor's remit. Where is Brampton?'

'In St Mary the Great,' replied Michael, evidently deciding that the task was below the dignity of the Chancellor, too, as he made no effort to join Bartholomew in the slime. He shot Donwich a cool glance. 'He is *calculating* how much each College and hostel will have to pay towards Shardelowe's improvements.'

Donwich retorted that *he* was not the one who had agreed to throw away the University's money, and a spat immediately blossomed between his coterie and those who felt Michael had done the right thing. With an irritable sigh, Bartholomew resigned himself to ploughing through the muck alone. Then someone joined him.

'It is me,' announced Dickon grandly. 'My father says not to let you fall over in front of everyone, because they will laugh at you. Take my hand for balance.'

Reluctantly, Bartholomew did. He was surprised by the strength of the boy's grip, and was reminded yet again that Dickon was going to be a veritable titan when he was fully grown. Together they picked their way across the slick surface, each holding the other up when he slipped or skidded. It felt like an age before they reached the boat.

'It *is* a body!' cried Dickon with unseemly glee, and before Bartholomew could stop him, he poked it with his sword. 'And it is *very* dead!'

The corpse was not fresh, and maggots abounded, although Dickon was unfazed, and watched with unflinching interest as Bartholomew examined the victim.

'It is Huntyngdon,' the physician announced. 'There is still a purse on his belt . . .'

'Does it contain Aynton's letter?' called Michael urgently.

It was Dickon who whipped out a dagger and sliced through the cords to retrieve it. He opened the filthy, muck-impregnated object carefully.

'No documents,' he announced, relishing the fact that all eyes were on him. 'No money either. Wait there, Brother. I shall bring it to you, so you can see for yourself.'

He slithered up the bank and vanished around the end of the bridge, before padding up to present the filthy

151

item to Michael with a courtly flourish. The monk peered at it, but fastidiously refused to touch it himself.

'Is Martyn down there, too?' called Tulyet.

'No, but you should send Dickon upriver to look for him,' replied Bartholomew, 'given that he is the only one willing to do anything useful.'

The remark was intended as a rebuke to the Sheriff and Michael, both of whom he felt should be helping him, so he was disconcerted when Tulyet began issuing his son with instructions. Dickon stood a little taller, thrilled to be entrusted with such a task – and one that suited his sense of the grisly into the bargain. He strutted away importantly.

Meanwhile, Bartholomew accepted Isnard's offer to lift the body into his boat and take it to the pier at the foot of the bridge, then went to report to Michael. Tulyet came to join them, glaring at would-be eavesdroppers until they moved out of earshot.

'Huntyngdon was stabbed,' began Bartholomew, struggling to wipe the filth from his shoes on a patch of grass. 'A single wound to the back.'

'How long has he been dead?' asked Michael.

'It is impossible to say, but the landlord of the Cardinal's Cap told me that he tied a red sash around his waist on the night he disappeared, and there is a sash on the body. I suspect he died not long after he left there, which accounts for the level of decomposition. And we know why he went out that night: to give Aynton's letter to Narboro.'

Michael stared at him. 'You think he was murdered to prevent him from delivering it?'

'Well, we know he went to the Cap to undertake a "mission of some delicacy", and that Aynton spoke to him and Martyn, after which they took their leave. We also know that Narboro never received the letter, but nor is it in Huntyngdon's purse.'

Michael scrubbed at his face. 'All this does not bode well for Martyn being alive. Are you sure it is murder?'

'Yes, although it did not happen here. He was killed elsewhere and the river carried him downstream, probably last night, which explains why no one saw him sooner.'

'How can you tell he was not killed here?' asked Tulyet curiously.

'Because of the leaves caught in his hair. No plants are growing around the bridge, so they must have come from upstream – between here and the Mill Pond.'

'Morys's mill was operating yesterday evening,' mused Tulyet, 'which means water was released through the West Dam sluice to drive it. It must have been enough to dislodge him. Dickon will find the place. Perhaps he will find Martyn's corpse there, too.'

'I hope not,' said Bartholomew unhappily.

It was a short but sad journey from the bridge to King's Hall, carrying Huntyngdon on a bier borrowed from St Clement's Church. When they arrived, Bartholomew quickly searched the dead man's clothes, to make sure the letter had not been secreted elsewhere, but there was no sign of it. He had just finished when Huntyngdon's father burst in, his face white with grief.

'Stabbed, you say?' the Earl whispered hoarsely, after Michael had told him what they knew. 'By whom?'

'We will find out,' promised Michael. 'Senior Proctor Brampton, Matt and I will do our utmost to see your son has justice.'

'You see this sash?' the Earl asked in a strangled voice. 'He wore it whenever he did something important. I brought it from Avignon, where it was blessed by the Pope himself.'

'So Huntyngdon believed that giving Aynton's message to Narboro was important,' whispered Michael to Bartholomew, once they had stepped back to give the Earl

153

some privacy. 'Or do you think he was charged with another mission that fateful night? It makes more sense, as I cannot imagine anything involving Narboro as being of great significance.'

'If so, there is nothing on his body to suggest what it might have been.'

'His purse is empty. Perhaps this is just a simple case of robbery – he was obviously wealthy, and that sash is ostentatious.'

'Where is the purse?' asked Bartholomew. 'Do you have it?'

Michael grimaced when he realised it was nowhere to be seen. 'That wretched Dickon must have kept it as a memento. What a vile little ghoul he is!'

'We will get it back when he has finished scouring the riverbanks for bodies,' promised Bartholomew. 'Which he is not qualified to do, by the way, no matter how highly Dick rates his talents. Will you ask a beadle to do it as well? It would be terrible to miss Martyn, and leave him rotting until he washes down the river in pieces.'

'Unless Martyn killed Huntyngdon, then fled the town,' said Michael soberly. 'But we should not speculate without all the facts. We shall wait and see what the searches turn up.'

At the Earl's request, Bartholomew examined Huntyngdon's body again, doing so with all the respect he could muster. But there was nothing to tell them who had killed the young man or why, and all he could say when he had finished was that Huntyngdon had probably had no idea he was in danger until it was too late.

'He would have felt a brief, piercing pain, then nothing,' he told the ashen-faced Earl. 'It would have been over very quickly.'

He left the Earl to grieve in peace, and went to wash his hands in a bucket of clean water. Then he and Michael walked outside, where dusk had fallen. Insects swarmed around the amber light shed by a lantern on a post, and bats flitted among them, feasting. The air was hot, dusty and still, but the town was far from silent. There was a rumpus emanating from the High Street taverns as towns-folk slaked their thirst with ale, while All Saints opposite was holding a service that entailed a lot of tuneless hollering.

'Is that your choir, Brother?' asked Bartholomew, aware that no other body of 'musicians' was equal to creating such an unholy racket.

Michael shook his head. 'It *is* practice night, but I cancelled it when Donwich challenged my election. I do not want him accusing me of assembling an army of townsmen to back my bid.'

It was a good point, as the Marian Singers were devoted to the monk, and certainly would object to anyone they thought meant him harm.

'So who is singing?' Bartholomew asked, wincing as a particularly strident *Gloria* began. The tune was Michael's, although the Latin words were all but unrecognisable.

Before Michael could reply, the gate opened and a cavalcade clattered in. The riders dismounted, beating dust from their clothes and stretching stiff limbs. It was Ufford and Rawby, bringing the vicars-general and their retinue from Ely.

'Good – all three of them came,' said Michael approvingly. 'I was afraid one might stay behind, which would have been problematic if the opinions of the other two were divided. Now we can be sure of getting a decision.'

'I am amazed they did not just send one,' countered Bartholomew. 'Donwich's claim is a nonsense, and anyone with sense can see it. Moreover, having three vicars-general come running lends his challenge more importance than it deserves.'

Michael went to greet them, and Bartholomew followed, raising his eyebrows as yet more horses trotted through the gate. The vicars had brought an impressive train of clerks, chaplains and men of law. Donwich would doubtless be pleased by the fuss he had generated, but Bartholomew thought it was a waste of a lot of people's time.

The vicars-general were named William Teofle, Thomas Ely and John Tinmouth. Teofle was a tall, patrician Dominican; the other two were short, plump Franciscans.

'We are glad to be here, Brother,' Teofle informed Michael warmly. 'Although I was deeply saddened to hear of Aynton's death. I have known him for years, and considered him a friend. I hope you have the culprit behind bars.'

'Not yet,' replied Michael. 'But he will not elude us for long, I promise.'

'Good,' said Ely briskly. 'Now, I suggest we begin work straight after our devotions tomorrow morning. Is that acceptable to you?'

'Of course,' said Michael. 'I shall inform Donwich that you have arrived.'

'Ah, your "Anti-Chancellor",' said Teofle, running the words around in his mouth as though tasting them. 'I am not sure an English university has ever had one of those before.'

'No,' agreed Michael. 'And I am glad it is his title, not mine.'

Ely slapped more dust from his habit. 'We were astonished when we heard that Aynton had resigned, leaving you holding the reins. Do you know why he did it?'

'He said he felt unequal to leading the University into the future,' explained Michael quietly. 'We should respect, not condemn, him for recognising his limitations and acting on them.'

'Ineptitude has never bothered chancellors before,' said Ely. 'And he had you to guide him, so I fail to understand why he chose to duck his responsibilities. Shame on him!'

'I do not envy you spending time with him,' muttered Bartholomew, watching the Franciscan stalk towards his lodgings, his two companions at his heels. 'He seems rather sanctimonious.'

'He does,' acknowledged Michael. 'So let us hope that Teofle and Tinmouth are more amenable.'

CHAPTER 8

The next day was Saturday, and Bartholomew was horrified to emerge into the yard to discover the weather was hotter than ever, even though it was still dark. He wondered if it would kill all the crops, so there would be food shortages and starvation that winter.

On a brighter note, Walter was recovering, which Bartholomew attributed to Agatha, who had forced the porter to drink all the boiled barley water he had been prescribed. Walter was still in some discomfort, but no longer needed to dash to the latrines with distressing haste. He sat in his lodge, his loyal peacock at his side, and when he began to grumble about the students, Bartholomew knew he was feeling better.

Unfortunately, there was an outbreak of flux around the Gilbertine Priory, and Bartholomew arrived to discover that Stasy and Hawick had been there before him, offering a remedy that they claimed would cure it. Desperate and miserable, the sufferers had paid up, although Bartholomew saw a mark on one pot that identified its contents as having been made by Margery Starre. She would be livid when she found out, especially as they had sold it at twice the price she usually charged.

On his way home, Bartholomew stopped to see Meadowman, and was pleased to see colour in the beadle's face for the first time in days. He was sitting up, listening to Isnard describe the fun had by the Marian Singers in All Saints the previous evening, where they had arrived en masse to help with the St Benedict's Day celebrations.

'The congregation was not expecting us,' Isnard

chuckled, and although he was still hoarse, his cold seemed to be retreating. 'So they had quite a shock.'

'I can imagine,' said Bartholomew drily. 'Did they mind?'

'Why would they mind?' asked Isnard indignantly. 'Everyone loves the joy and enthusiasm we bring to public events.'

'Like Doctor Bartholomew's wedding,' said Meadowman with a sweet smile, 'where the choir also plans to make a surprise appearance.'

This was news to Bartholomew, who was sure Matilde would not appreciate such a rabble performing on her special day – and Lucy certainly would not. Isnard scowled at Meadowman, who gaped his dismay when he realised what he had let slip.

'It is this wretched flux,' said the beadle defensively. 'It has robbed me of my wits.'

'It is not the flux, it is that medicine from Stasy and Hawick,' said Isnard crossly. 'You should not have sipped it, especially as they are now going around braying that one gulp cured you instantly. You should shout the truth – that it was the special powder Doctor Bartholomew put in your barley water.'

'I am not the only one who has given them cause to brag,' countered Meadowman. 'Your cold is getting better, and they are taking the credit.'

'Then they are liars!' spat Isnard. 'They did present me with a phial, but I threw it away. I will never trust them again after they almost saw me drowned in the Mill Pond.'

Satisfied that both patients were on the mend, Bartholomew left. He saw Stasy and Hawick on Milne Street, emerging from the house of a wealthy saddler – a man who was friends with Edith, and who Bartholomew had assumed would never annoy her by defecting to another *medicus*. But he could tell from his old students' gloating expressions that the saddler had done just that.

'People have heard about our success with the flux,' crowed Stasy with the kind of smirk that would make anyone want to slap it off him. 'Poor Meadowman would be dead by now, were it not for us.'

Bartholomew was not about to demean himself by arguing. 'Where were you around compline time on Wednesday?' he asked, supposing he might as well quiz them about Aynton, since they were there.

'Out,' replied Hawick defiantly. 'With each other, as we have already told Michael. And do not accuse us of killing Aynton, because we never did.'

'Besides, you said that Aynton had provided enough clues to let you identify the culprit,' flashed Stasy challengingly. 'Which means that either you lied or he did. Either way, you have no right to interrogate us.'

Their replies did nothing to persuade Bartholomew to delete them from his list of suspects. Unfortunately, he knew that badgering them would not convince them to cooperate, so he opted for affability instead. After all, he had taught them for years, and while they had never much liked each other, most of that time had passed without antagonism or hostility.

'I hear you have set up in Shoemaker Row,' he began pleasantly, although it was not easy to disguise his irritation. 'I wish you success of it.'

Stasy regarded him suspiciously, although Hawick took him at his word and grinned happily. 'We shall make a fortune there. People already flock to buy our services – not just our remedies, but horoscopes and urine readings, too. You taught us well.'

'Donwich has promised to give us our degrees when he is Chancellor,' put in Stasy gloatingly. 'He thinks our expulsion was unfair, and wants to make things right.'

'We shall continue our used-exemplar trade as well,' Hawick went on. 'That is very lucrative. The profits allowed us to rent the shop *and* buy remedies to sell.'

160

'Margery Starre's remedies,' warned Bartholomew. 'She will not appreciate you passing her wares off as your own, so you might want to be careful.'

'Come, Hawick,' said Stasy haughtily. 'We do not need business advice from a man who barely makes ends meet, and who will be deep in debt when he leaves his College.'

Bartholomew sincerely hoped he was wrong. They strode away, and he jumped when he heard a soft voice in his ear – he had forgotten Cynric was shadowing them.

'Do not worry about the remedies. Margery knows about them, and she has a plan.'

'What plan?' asked Bartholomew, alarmed.

Cynric grinned. 'One that will discredit them so badly that they will leave the town and never be heard of again. And good riddance!'

And with that, he hurried after his quarry.

Bartholomew arrived in the hall just as Michael was saying grace. It was already stifling and the students had been given permission to wear whatever they found most comfortable after two of them had fainted. The result was a sea of colour, as everyone had leapt at the chance to don something other than the prescribed black.

Agatha, flushed and flustered, came to report that the butter had turned rancid and the meat had spoiled overnight. The meal therefore comprised dry bread and an eclectic selection of boiled vegetables.

'The heat is dismal enough,' said Michael, regarding his platter in dismay. 'But when it affects my victuals . . .'

'It will rain on Tuesday, after which we shall have forty cool, wet days,' declared Zoone with such confidence that the other Fellows regarded him in surprise. He began to elaborate. 'A change in wind direction tells me that a wet spell is on the way, while Tuesday is the Feast of St Swithun. And, as everyone knows, rain on St Swithun's Day means forty soggy days always follow.'

161

'Rank superstition!' exclaimed Michael. 'I am surprised at you, Zoone.'

'I have seen many a dry summer ended by that venerable saint,' countered Zoone, 'and this time will be no different. I am an engineer, do not forget – my structures will not stand firm unless I take weather patterns into account. Ergo, I know a lot about them.'

'The swallows anticipate a change soon, too,' put in Clippesby, who had carried two peahens into the hall, and was feeding them grain picked from his bread. 'They are also tired of the drought, as there is no wet soil for repairing their nests.'

Father William's eyes narrowed. 'Someone has been leaving bowls of mud all around the College, and I should have guessed it was you. I tripped over one last night, and look at the state of my best habit.'

Everyone did, although the new stains were barely visible among ones that were fouler and had been there for a lot longer. Seeing he was going to get no sympathy, William changed the subject to Narboro.

'I dislike him for being a peacock,' he declared, then glanced at Clippesby's avian guests. 'No offence, ladies. He is an empty-headed fool, and I do not believe that the King considered him an indispensable part of his retinue.'

'It is difficult to imagine,' agreed Zoone. 'However, I was in London once, and I saw Narboro with the royal party. I cannot say if he was indispensable, but he was certainly there.'

'Probably sharpening the pens,' sneered William. 'Or polishing His Majesty's mirrors, thus allowing him to admire himself at the same time.'

While the friar held forth, Bartholomew turned to Michael. The monk was immaculate – freshly shaved, his tonsure a perfect circle, and his habit spotless. He exuded authority and confidence, although Bartholomew knew him well enough to detect unease behind the elegant demeanour.

'You are worried about the vicars-general,' he surmised, keeping his voice low so that no one else would hear. 'But I doubt you have cause for concern. Donwich's challenge is absurd, and they will see it in moments.'

Michael gave a brief smile. 'I am not worried about Donwich, Matt. I just want the vicars to see me at my best.'

'Because they will report to the Archbishop, and he is someone with the power to award you an abbacy or a bishopric?'

'Oh, no – he cannot be more dazzled by me than he is already,' replied Michael, never a man to waste time with false modesty. 'I need to impress them because I now embody the University. This chancellorship carries a heavy burden of responsibility.'

'One you have carried for years,' said Bartholomew, wondering if there was more to his friend's disquiet than he was telling.

'True,' acknowledged Michael, and sighed. 'But the constraints of the post – especially now the vicars are here – make it impossible for me to investigate these murders, and it is hard for me to watch you struggle alone. I itch to join you.'

Bartholomew regarded him balefully. 'It is hard for me, too. Every teaching day I have left is precious, but I am forced to sacrifice them in order to do the Senior Proctor's work. Brampton should—'

'While I am closeted with the vicars, Brampton *must* begin collecting the bridge money,' interrupted Michael. 'If he does not, Morys will bray that the University reneges on its promises and there will be trouble. And you are the only person I trust to win justice for Aynton and Huntyngdon. You liked them – you will not deny them what they deserve.'

'Appoint a Junior Proctor,' suggested Bartholomew, disliking the way Michael was backing him into a corner. 'Narboro has already offered, and William would do it in a heartbeat.'

Michael grimaced. 'They could not solve a murder if they saw one committed right in front of them. It *must* be you who investigates these crimes, Matt. Obviously, I would rather do it myself, but that is impossible now the vicars-general are here. However, if you do this for me now, I swear that I will never make another demand of you again.'

Bartholomew started to laugh at a promise he knew would never be kept, but then he saw the agonised expression on Michael's face. The monk *did* hate not being able to pursue the killer himself, and agreeing to become Chancellor had cost him more than anyone realised. Bartholomew was suddenly ashamed of his selfishness. He nodded agreement, and turned his mind to what they knew so far.

'The deaths of Huntyngdon and Aynton are connected, linked by the letter that one gave the other to deliver. However, it would make a lot more sense if Aynton had written to someone other than Narboro. I do not see anyone involving *him* in something serious enough to warrant murder.'

'No, but Aynton wrote to him nonetheless. Perhaps his vanity is an act, a ruse to conceal the real man. Speak to him again today, and see what you can find out. But first, go to the castle and retrieve Huntyngdon's pouch from that thieving Dickon.'

'Why? I cannot imagine the Earl will want it.'

'Actually, he does. Besides, I want to be sure it really is empty – that Dickon did not dismiss a mere letter as unimportant, because only weapons and money matter in his eyes. If the little ghoul refuses to part with it, take it by force.'

'"Take it by force"?' echoed Bartholomew in disbelief. 'Would you have him run me through?'

Michael snorted his disdain. 'He is all swagger, but a coward at heart. He would never dare attack you lest you hit him back. But if you are averse to violence, threaten to give him spots. That will bring him to heel, as no youth likes looking like a leopard.'

'True.'

'When you have the purse, deliver it to King's Hall, and while you are there, ask again about Huntyngdon's business with Aynton. Why was *he* chosen to deliver the letter, rather than someone from Aynton's own College? And try to learn more about Huntyngdon's relationship with the conveniently absent Martyn.'

'Did you charge a beadle to scour the riverbank?' asked Bartholomew. 'I assume Dickon found nothing, or we would have heard.'

'He unearthed a wealth of dead animals, all of which he presented to his horrified sire. And yes, I sent a beadle to investigate, too, but he found nothing useful either.' Michael chuckled. 'Dickon was offended that we wanted to look for ourselves, and shadowed him every step of the way, barking orders and advice. The poor man was quite unnerved.'

Bartholomew was not surprised – he would not have been happy with Dickon dogging his footsteps as he hunted for corpses either.

'What if Narboro and King's Hall have no answers?' he asked.

Michael raised his hands rather helplessly. 'Speak to our main suspects again: Gille, Elsham, Stasy, Hawick, Chaumbre, Morys and anyone else you think merits attention. Not Donwich, though – leave him until we have solid evidence to confront him with.'

'Brampton is on the list, too,' said Bartholomew pointedly.

'I know,' said Michael drily. 'But I need him to collect bridge money for the next few days, so leave him alone, too.'

In his room a short while later, Bartholomew issued Aungel with a long list of texts he wanted his students to study that day, although he could tell by the incredulous expression on the young Fellow's face that his demands were unlikely to be met.

'I will try,' said Aungel. 'But no one else is teaching, and all our lads can think about is going home. It is difficult to make them sit still, let alone get them to listen.'

'Well, do your best,' said Bartholomew, wondering if he was the only scholar in the entire University who thought students were there to learn.

'Of course, it will be far easier without Stasy and Hawick,' said Aungel, perching on the windowsill to chat. 'They were a bad influence on the rest – disruptive.'

'They were no worse than some of the others,' said Bartholomew, tempted to point out that Aungel had not always been an ideal pupil either.

'You would not say that if you knew them as well as I do,' sniffed Aungel. 'Michael was right to expel them. Graduates of the University are supposed to be men of upright and moral character, which they are not.'

'No?' asked Bartholomew absently, most of his mind still on the list of texts.

'They think spells can take the place of proper medicine. I wish they would leave town, because they will be a nuisance here. People are superstitious, and will always opt for charms over the real weapons against disease – urine reading, phlebotomy and horoscopes.'

As far as Bartholomew was concerned, there was not much to choose between them, but he held his tongue, aware that Aungel was something of a traditionalist, despite all he had done to convince him to open his mind.

'You speak as if casting spells is something they did a lot,' he said, picking up his medicines bag and looping it over his shoulder.

Aungel shrugged. 'It is – they have been at it for years now.'

Bartholomew raised his eyebrows. 'And you never thought to mention it to me?'

'Too right I never! They would have cursed me, as they have cursed you. But do not worry, sir. I am sure Cynric and Margery Starre will find a way to reverse the hex.'

The town baked under the relentless sun, and even though it was still early morning, Bartholomew could feel the heat of the road burning through his shoes. He tried to keep to the shade, but everyone else had the same idea, so there was lots of irritable jostling. It also meant zigzagging from one side of the street to the other, depending on the height and position of buildings, and at one point, he was sure someone was replicating his every move. He stopped to look behind him, but saw nothing amiss.

Yolande de Blaston, part-time prostitute and wife to one of the town's carpenters, had left a bowl of water outside her house for thirsty animals. It thronged with small birds until Ulf Godenave darted forward and kicked it over. The birds scattered in alarm, and the water trailed into a nearby pothole. Ulf's spiteful laughter turned to a startled yelp when someone shot from the house and cuffed him around the ear.

'Got the little sod!' crowed Yolande, as the boy raced away before she could do it again. 'It is the fifth time he has kicked that bowl over, and I am tired of lugging water from the well. And he bit our dog.'

'Did he?' asked Bartholomew, startled. 'Why?'

'Because she barked at him. He did it to shut her up, lest I came out to see what he was doing – which was stealing the laundry I set out to dry in the sun.'

Bartholomew hoped Ulf would have the sense to keep his distance for a while, as Yolande was not a person to aggravate. He asked after her enormous brood of children – fifteen at the last count – but before she could reply, their attention was taken by a screech and some pithy swearing. Narboro, flouncing along elegantly, had not watched where he was putting his feet, and had stumbled into the water-filled pothole.

'Look at my robe!' he cried angrily. 'Wet and filthy! It is your legal duty to look after the street outside your home, madam, but you have allowed this great pit to develop.'

Householders were responsible for their bit of the road, but the de Blastons could barely afford rent and food, so repairing potholes was well beyond their means.

'No harm has been done,' said Bartholomew, pulling Narboro away before Yolande smacked him over the head, too; he could tell from her scowl that she was considering it.

'No harm?' snarled Narboro, although a glance at Yolande's furious face warned him against marching back to have it out with her. 'I am drenched!'

Bartholomew studied him out of the corner of his eye, trying to determine if he really was an empty-headed fool, or something else entirely. He could not do it, so he began to talk, hoping a conversation might reveal the truth about the man.

'I assume you know that Huntyngdon is dead,' he began. 'The scholar who was last seen setting off to deliver a letter to you.'

'I did hear, but all I can tell you is what I said last time: that Aynton may well have written to me, given my important Court connections, but no letter from him ever arrived, delivered by Huntyngdon or anyone else.'

'It is probably connected to his murder,' Bartholomew

went on. 'So if you know anything about it – anything at all – now is the time to tell me.'

Narboro regarded him in alarm. 'Are you saying that I might be in danger, too?'

'You might,' said Bartholomew, although the truth was that he had no idea. 'So it is in your interests to help me catch the killer before he strikes again.'

'But I cannot think of anything,' wailed Narboro, unsettled. 'Other than that Aynton must have wanted me to secure him a position at Court once he left the University.'

'That cannot be it,' said Bartholomew, exasperated. 'Aynton had no intention of abandoning Cambridge – just shedding the onerous responsibility of being Chancellor. Besides, Huntyngdon seemed to think the letter contained something important.'

'Begging favours of *me* is important,' countered Narboro huffily. 'And I honestly cannot think of any other reason for him to write.'

'Could it have been about your refusal to marry Lucy?'

Narboro blinked. 'If so, it was none of his business!'

'Perhaps he thought it reflected badly on the rest of us. A scholar's word should be his bond, and you broke yours.'

Narboro glared at him. 'It is all very well for you to take the moral high ground – *your* fiancée is pretty. Worse yet, I returned home to discover that Lucy had spent the last ten years educating herself. No man wants a wife who thinks she is cleverer than him.'

'Especially if it is true,' muttered Bartholomew.

'Now, if there is nothing else, I am busy.' Narboro stalked away, leaving the physician less sure than ever what to make of him.

Bartholomew began to traipse towards the castle, which stood on a hill to the north of the town, aiming to retrieve Huntyngdon's purse from Dickon. His feet kicked dust from the hard-baked mud of the streets, staining his clean white shirt brown. He turned into Bridge Street and found it thronged with people. At first, he did not understand why it was so busy, but then he remembered that the bridge was closed so that Shardelowe could rebuild it.

He eased through the commotion, and saw that the only way to cross the Cam – short of swimming – was on Isnard's ferry, as the *ponticulus* had also been shut. A long line of people waited to use it, and Bartholomew sagged, aware that queuing would be uncomfortable in the full glare of the sun.

Then it occurred to him that Dickon might be in the Tulyets' Bridge Street house, rather than at the castle. He did a right-angled turn to cross the road, and for the second time that day, was assailed by the feeling that someone had just changed course to follow. But when he stopped to look behind him, there was nothing to see.

He knocked on Tulyet's door and was admitted to the solar, a lovely room with views down the river. The window shutters were closed that day, though, partly to exclude the stink of the water, but mostly to mute the racket made by the builders and those waiting with ever-increasing fractiousness to use the ferry.

Neither Dickon nor his father was in, but Mistress Tulyet was there, entertaining a large group of women that included Edith, Matilde and Lucy. Rohese Morys was there, too, wearing a bodice that was cut precariously low, while her lips and cheeks were painted so scarlet that there was a moment when Bartholomew wondered if she was suffering from a hectic fever. Everyone's attention was on a piece of embroidered cloth.

'I am not sure,' Lucy was saying. 'It is rather coarse, and we want the best.'

'I agree,' said Rohese. 'You should send these back,

Matilde. After all, it is a day you will remember for the rest of your life, and it should be perfect.'

Bartholomew realised they were talking about his wedding, and was appalled that Lucy had chosen to discuss it with so many other people. He glanced behind him, wondering if he could escape before he was trapped into answering questions on matters he knew nothing about. He caught Matilde's eye, and saw she was amused – not just by Lucy's obsession with the event, but by his obvious fear that his own opinion might be solicited.

'I doubt most of our guests will notice the table linen,' she said, smiling indulgently at her friend. 'Just the food and wine placed on it.'

'I agree,' said Edith. 'These are perfectly adequate, Lucy.'

'Oh, they are *adequate*,' sniffed Lucy. 'But who wants adequate when she can have exceptional? No, these will not do. We shall hold out for something better – something *superior*.'

'What do you think, Matthew?' asked Rohese, eyeing him as if he was something to eat, and making him more uncomfortable than ever.

'Well,' hedged Bartholomew, and glanced at Matilde, pleading silently for her help. She struggled not to laugh, but took pity on him.

'Enough, Lucy. We should move on to the *real* business of the day: our school. We have raised sufficient funds to rent a house, pay teachers, and establish a small library. Now we must decide where to put it.'

'On the High Street,' replied Lucy promptly. 'Where it will be seen.'

'I think we should start somewhere more discreet,' countered Edith. 'We can always flaunt it later, once the University's bigots have stopped trying to shut it down.'

'Our current finances allow us to offer lessons not only in reading, writing and grammar,' said Matilde, her eyes alight with enthusiasm, 'but in arithmetic, music, philosophy, theology, Latin, Greek and medicine.'

'Matt will teach the medicine, of course,' put in Edith.

'I will?' gulped Bartholomew, not liking to imagine what his colleagues would say about it. Then it occurred to him that it would not matter, because he would no longer be a member of their University. He could do what he liked, no matter how controversial. He smiled suddenly at the prospect of new challenges, already compiling mental lists of the texts he would want his classes to study.

'Stasy and Hawick offered their services,' said Lucy with a moue of distaste. 'But I declined. Our school will be a respectable place, and they are warlocks.'

'But *they* can cure the flux and the common cold,' countered Rohese.

'So can Satan,' said Lucy tartly. 'But I would not advise soliciting *his* help, either. Stay away from them, Rohese. They are poison.'

At that point, Mistress Tulyet stood and indicated that Bartholomew was to follow her into the hallway, where they could speak without an audience. Unlike her husband, she accepted that Dickon was not very nice – she had seen him bully servants, terrorise other children, and make visitors think twice about calling. She might love her son, but she did not like or understand him, and was less inclined than Tulyet to excuse his disagreeable personality as a 'passing phase'.

'What has he done now?' she asked, anxious and resigned in equal measure.

'He borrowed something belonging to Huntyngdon and I need it back,' replied Bartholomew, deciding that she had enough to contend with regarding her son, so did not need to hear that he was a corpse-robber as well. 'Is he here?'

She winced. 'He should be – we hired a tutor to teach him his letters.'

'But?' prompted Bartholomew.

'But he escaped through a window, and is probably at the castle. Dick . . . well, he lays down the law, but he is secretly delighted to see such spirit in the boy. He thinks he will make a fine warrior one day.'

'I know he does,' said Bartholomew ambiguously.

Hoping to be spared a journey to the castle, Bartholomew asked to search Dickon's room. His mother made no objection, although the missing purse was not there. There was, however, an alarmingly large collection of knives, and some crudely drawn sketches of naked women. Mistress Tulyet gaped her horror.

'My students have some of those,' Bartholomew informed her reassuringly. 'It is quite normal for adolescent boys to—'

'I do not care about the pictures,' she interrupted. 'I am more concerned about the weapons. Does he aim to declare war on the town single-handed?'

Bartholomew would not put it past him. 'He is just preparing for France,' he said soothingly. 'Do not worry.'

He took his leave and turned towards the Great Bridge. As he went, he caught a flicker of movement out of the corner of his eye. Someone *was* following him! Quick as a flash, he ducked down one of the alleys that ran to the river, then slipped into a doorway to wait. Moments later, Gille and Elsham hurried past. They reached the end of the lane, and looked around irritably when they saw he had vanished.

'Looking for me?' he called, watching with satisfaction as they jumped in alarm.

'Of course not,' snapped Gille, rather too quickly. 'We saw that young pickpocket – Ulf – scamper down here. He stole Elsham's purse the other day, and we want it back.'

No one had entered the lane other than the three of them, so Bartholomew knew they were lying.

'I am going to the castle,' he said coolly. 'Then King's Hall. Will that make dogging my footsteps any easier for you?'

Gille looked set to continue blustering, but Elsham knew the game was up. 'You are Brother Michael's closest friend. Of course we must monitor you, lest you launch a scheme that will benefit him at Donwich's expense.'

'Actually, I am trying to find out who pushed Aynton to his death.'

'He intends to accuse Donwich of it,' said Gille to Elsham. 'Michael cannot weave a web of lies himself, not with the Archbishop's men demanding his presence in St Mary the Great, so he has ordered his henchman to do it instead.'

'Donwich will not be accused unless there is evidence to warrant it,' said Bartholomew shortly. 'But perhaps you can exonerate him. Was he with you two during compline on Wednesday?'

'No,' replied Elsham. 'He was—'

'We do not need to tell you anything, Bartholomew,' interrupted Gille angrily, glaring at his friend for being ready to cooperate with the enemy. 'And do not think of accusing *us* of harming Aynton. We went nowhere near him.'

'Can you prove it?' asked Bartholomew and raised his hands when both looked indignant. 'All I want is to eliminate you from the enquiry. Surely you cannot object to that? He was a member of your College, after all.'

'Not a very loyal one,' muttered Gille. 'He should have supported Donwich, but instead he told everyone to vote for Michael. It was an outrage, and we would have ousted him from Clare Hall had he lived.'

'So you had a good reason to want him dead,' pounced Bartholomew. 'Revenge.'

'There are other ways to destroy a man besides murder,'

said Gille in a voice that was full of menace. 'As you will learn, if you try to meddle in our affairs.'

'Enough, Gille,' said Elsham tiredly. 'You are making him think we are guilty.'

'Let him,' snarled Gille. 'It will waste his time and serve him right.'

'But mud sticks,' Elsham pointed out crossly. 'And if he asks impertinent questions about us all over town, people will assume we *do* have something to hide. That will harm us, Donwich *and* Clare Hall.'

'It will,' agreed Bartholomew. 'So I repeat: where were you when Aynton was killed?'

'About an hour before compline, we decided to go out,' began Elsham, ignoring his friend's angry sigh. 'As we left the College, we saw Aynton hiding near the main gate. He was waiting to see if Donwich would visit Lucy, aiming to follow him, and then accuse him of breaking one of the University's rules.'

'The most ridiculous one,' growled Gille. 'Namely, forbidding red-blooded men access to women. It runs contrary to nature!'

'We assumed Donwich would remain in the hall with his guests that night,' said Elsham. 'So we surmised that Aynton was wasting his time.'

Gille laughed coarsely. 'But the lure of his lady love proved too much. Donwich left not long after we did, although we never saw him.'

'We went to the Swan Inn,' Elsham went on. 'John Godenave drinks there on a Wednesday, and he owes us money – we wanted to collect it. We had a few ales with him, but left when we heard the commotion as Aynton's body was found.'

'Ask anyone in the Swan,' said Gille with a gloating smirk. 'They will tell you that we have plenty of alibis for when Aynton was killed.'

As the Swan was just across the road, Bartholomew

decided to do what they suggested. Godenave was there, and confirmed that two surly brutes from Clare Hall did indeed come to demand money from him on the night of the murder. There had been a spat when he had tried to short-change them, which every patron remembered. Without a shadow of a doubt, Gille and Elsham had not killed the Chancellor.

However, they had said nothing to make Bartholomew think Donwich was innocent, so their Master remained firmly at the top of his list.

CHAPTER 9

Bartholomew arrived at the Great Bridge to find it frantic with activity, with workmen swarming all over it. Many were skilled strangers, who had been waiting to offer their services the moment the call went out for specific types of craftsman, and the rest were casual labourers from the town. The wooden balustrade had already been dismantled, and the rest of the structure was swathed in scaffolding and rope.

Several boats were moored at the pier below. This was a ramshackle affair that was rarely used, as most bargemen preferred the sturdy structure owned by Michaelhouse, with its easy access to the market. All were laden with ready-hewn lumps of limestone. The cumbersome wagon that Morys had allowed to pass through the Trumpington Gate the previous day was there, too, and masons had already started to carve decorative corbels from the fine stone it had carried.

The first person Bartholomew saw as he joined the back of the ferry queue was Chaumbre, who looked uncomfortably hot in his fine clothes. He was smiling, though, and hummed happily under his breath.

'Shardelowe has made impressive progress,' remarked Bartholomew, watching the whirlwind of organised chaos with the builder at its centre. 'Moreover, it usually takes weeks for supplies to arrive, but his are here already.'

Chaumbre pulled a wry face. 'Morys is Mayor and Shardelowe can afford bribes, so the council's decision was never in doubt. But building in stone is the right thing to do. Aynton disagreed, of course – he liked to say "wood is good" and was passionate about it.'

177

'You mentioned discussing it the day he died,' said Bartholomew, also recalling that Chaumbre had called Aynton a 'meddlesome arse', which he now professed to regret.

'I did,' said Chaumbre. 'You referred to it as a quarrel, and wondered if it had given me cause to kill him.'

Bartholomew was alarmed – not that Chaumbre knew he was a suspect, but that he might tell Edith. 'You mistook me,' he blustered. 'Of course I do not think you are a killer.'

Chaumbre laughed at his discomfiture. 'Do not worry, Matt. I understand why you had to ask those questions, and I am not offended in the slightest. But I gave you my answers and you were satisfied with them, so let that be the end of the matter. Agreed?'

Bartholomew nodded, although Chaumbre's answers had *not* satisfied him, given that his 'alibi' was inspecting a batch of dye on his own. He began to quiz him anew, hoping to learn something that really would knock him off the list – or allow him to be arrested and thus safely removed from Edith.

'What else did you discuss with Aynton, besides dye-pits and the bridge?'

Chaumbre continued to chortle, and Bartholomew wondered if he was in his right wits, as this was hardly a subject for humour. 'Nothing on that particular occasion. He just stalked up and ordered me to fill my pits, then called me a fool for wanting a stone bridge.'

'How did he know what you thought?'

'Well, I made no secret of it. But he was determined to have wood, because he had promised that the University would pay one tenth of the cost – a negligible amount with wood, but a considerable outlay for stone.'

Bartholomew considered the information. Morys would not have wanted Aynton making a case for wood, so perhaps *he* had decided to silence him. Moreover, the timely arrival of craftsmen and materials was indicative that Shardelowe had invested a lot of his own money in advance of the council's decision. It was a strong motive for murder, so the builder became a suspect, too.

He looked to where Shardelowe stood, busily barking orders at his workforce. He had two lieutenants to see his instructions carried out, and Chaumbre told him they were named Gilbert Bernarde and John de Lyonnes. Bernarde was short, fat and English, while Lyonnes was tall, thin and French. The three of them looked tense and serious, their eyes everywhere, and their voices urgent, revealing that they were under considerable pressure to achieve what Shardelowe had promised.

'Bernarde is a pleasant fellow,' Chaumbre went on. 'Always laughing. Lyonnes is more sombre, but both are good men. If anyone can see this finished in a week, it is them.'

'It is too fast,' said Bartholomew worriedly. 'Safety will be compromised, and someone will be hurt or killed. Shardelowe is overly ambitious.'

Even as he spoke, one man slipped and almost fell. His workmates jeered at his clumsiness, although a sharp word from Lyonnes saw them turn their attention back to their duties. Bartholomew cringed when Bernarde ordered several huge pieces of stone set on the edge of one section of scaffolding, ready to be used for strengthening the existing spandrels below.

'Someone only needs to stumble against one of those things and it will fall,' he objected disapprovingly. 'It is bad practice – a needless risk.'

'I am sure they know what they are doing,' said Chaumbre, and as the queue shuffled forward a few feet, he changed the subject. 'I am glad Isnard had the foresight to hire some friends to help him with his ferrying. He could not have managed all this on his own.'

'Especially as he has a cold.'

'He woke up this morning feeling much better. Your old students claim they cured him, but he is adamant that he never swallowed their remedy. Unfortunately, people believe Stasy and Hawick, as everyone knows that Isnard will drink anything that comes in a bottle.'

'They are right,' said Bartholomew with a sigh. 'He will.'

It was tiresome having to wait to cross the river, and Bartholomew was not the only one who realised he had taken the bridge and the *ponticulus* for granted. The line inched forward slowly, until he was able to see the ferry operation below.

Responding to the greater demand, Isnard had expanded his operation from one ferry to two, the second being big enough to take a horse, if required. He had strung a pair of ropes across the river, which were then used to haul the boats from bank to bank. As it was exhausting labour, his crews worked in relays. Given that the only alternatives involved a lengthy detour or a swim, he and his men were making money hand over fist.

The waiting passengers were hot and irritable from being forced to stand in the sun. Moreover, some had animals with them, so agitated lows, bleats, clucks and barks mingled with the cacophony of irascible human voices.

Bartholomew turned his attention back to the workmen, sure his services would be needed before the day was out. Bernarde encouraged his team with merry winks and good humour, whereas Lyonnes preferred to snarl and belittle. Needless to say, Bernarde's people were making better progress. Lyonnes happened to glance up and spot Chaumbre.

'Have you filled your dye-pits yet?' he called in a thick Auvergne accent. 'Because if not, we have plenty of rotten wood you can use. It will save us dumping it all in the river.'

'You craftsmen!' laughed Chaumbre. 'Always jesting.'

'It was not a jest,' retorted Lyonnes, who looked as though he had never cracked a joke in his life. 'I am serious. You can have it for free.'

'It is a generous offer,' said Chaumbre, struggling for a straight face. 'But one cannot fill large pits with rotting wood. We shall use hard-core rubble, which will be carefully laid down and compacted.'

'Why?' demanded Lyonnes crossly. 'They are just holes, for God's sake. It does not matter what goes in them, just as long as they are filled.'

'Someone will build over them one day,' explained Chaumbre patiently. 'And if we use wood, there will be subsidence. Ergo, no rubbish will go in them.'

Lyonnes spat his disbelief and returned to work. His interjection caused the pits to become a topic of conversation among the waiting passengers, with most folk of the opinion that Chaumbre was taking far too long over what was a very simple task.

'I have filled two,' the dyer whispered to Bartholomew, stung by the censure. 'And I shall deal with the others in my own time. I will *not* be rushed. But all is in hand. Indeed, I am going to my house now, to collect more money to pay for it.'

It was a moment before Bartholomew remembered that Chaumbre owned a place in Girton, although he lived with Edith on Milne Street. 'Oh, yes – the one that was burgled.'

Chaumbre's smile slipped a little. 'Fortunately, the culprit did not get very much, and I have another cache buried in the garden. Do not worry – I still have plenty to keep your sister in the style to which she is accustomed.'

'I hope you have more than that,' said Bartholomew. 'She intends to help fund Matilde's school for women, which will be a very costly venture.'

The smile faded a bit more. 'I am sure Matilde has

181

plenty of others to call upon. You, for example. I imagine her new husband will be eager to make the biggest donation of all.'

Bartholomew might be eager, but he would never be able. He would have his paupers' medicine to provide, not to mention his share of household bills that had hitherto been paid by Michaelhouse – rent, food, clothes, fuel, candles and all the rest. He made no reply, and instead listened to two women behind them, who were discussing the mysterious benefactor who gave money to the parish priests for the poor, sick and needy.

'He is a saint,' declared one warmly. 'But only the vicars know his name, and they refuse to tell anyone.'

Well, the saint was not Chaumbre, thought Bartholomew, glancing at his brother-in-law out of the corner of his eye, not if he dragged his heels over filling in holes and was looking for ways to duck his wife's contribution to Matilde's school. Then Chaumbre began to hum again, a sound so irritating that Bartholomew told him he was going to the castle to speak to Dickon, just to make it stop.

'I hope Tulyet lives a very long life,' Chaumbre said fervently. 'Because I shall not remain in Cambridge if Dickon becomes Sheriff.'

'Nor will I,' agreed Bartholomew. 'But fortunately, he is too young.'

'He will not stay young forever. The post is not hereditary, but he will certainly apply for it if his father dies or retires, and the King will be too frightened to refuse.'

Bartholomew laughed. 'The King will not let Dickon intimidate him.'

'The redoubtable Lady Joan de Hereford thought she could control the little hellion,' said Chaumbre, 'and the whole town heaved a sigh of relief when she took him away. But he was too much, even for her. Sometimes, I believe the tales that the Devil sired him, because he is not a normal child.'

'Mistress Tulyet would not have countenanced Satan in her bed,' said Bartholomew stoutly, although there had been times when he had wondered the same.

'The Devil is cunning,' averred Chaumbre. 'She would not have noticed.'

Bartholomew changed the subject to something less controversial. 'I am sure it is hotter today than it was yesterday.'

'It is,' agreed Chaumbre. 'And as soon as I have retrieved my hoard, I shall go to the Cardinal's Cap for a jug of cool ale.'

'Aynton liked the Cardinal's Cap.'

'He did,' agreed Chaumbre. 'Especially when Huntyngdon and Martyn were there.'

'They visited the place together?' asked Bartholomew, although it was galling to hear this from a non-scholar. Why had no one else mentioned it? Or was it untrue, and Chaumbre aimed to mislead the investigation for reasons of his own?

'Not always, but often. He once told me that he hoped they would follow him into University politics. If they had, they would have been better at it than Donwich, who lacks the necessary tact.'

Bartholomew regarded him through narrowed eyes. 'I thought Donwich was your friend. He likes you well enough to invite you to his College for celebratory feasts.'

Chaumbre chuckled. 'He does, and I am very fond of him, too. However, that does not mean I am blind to his flaws, and he was more likeable when he spent less time with Gille and Elsham.'

As far as Bartholomew was concerned, Donwich had never been likeable.

It was not a pleasant journey across the Cam, as the ferry – the larger of the two – was overloaded and very low in

183

the water. Bartholomew was crammed between two tanners and a goat, the latter of which breathed hot, moist air down the back of his neck for the duration of the journey. Fortunately, it was not a very long one, and they were soon clambering out the other side.

'Thank you, Isnard,' said Chaumbre graciously, pressing an extra coin into the bargeman's eager palm. 'Buy yourself an ale when you finish work.'

'But no more than one,' warned Bartholomew. 'Boiled barley water is much better after a day of labouring in the sun.'

'So you say,' muttered Isnard, telling Bartholomew that the advice would go unheeded.

Although Chaumbre offered to keep company with Bartholomew as far as the castle, he kept stopping to exchange cheery greetings with friends and acquaintances, and Bartholomew did not want his mission to take all day. He excused himself and hurried on alone.

The castle had started life as a simple motte and bailey, some three hundred years before, but was now a formidable fortress. It rarely saw military activity, and was mostly administrative. It comprised a circular keep on a mound, and curtain walls studded with towers. Inside the walls was a bailey that boasted barracks, stables, storerooms, a chapel and a large open space for the men to practise their fighting skills.

Tulyet's office was in the keep, and Bartholomew was conducted to it by Sergeant Robin, one of Agatha's many relations. The Sheriff grimaced in annoyance when he learned that Dickon had given his tutor the slip.

'He will be exercising with the men,' predicted Robin. 'It is sword-work today, and you know how much he loves that.'

Sure enough, Dickon was with the soldiers. Although younger than all of them, and smaller than most, he was putting up an impressive show of sparring, his thick features a mask of concentration as he went through his paces with a bulky bald-headed knight.

'That is John Morys, the Mayor's cousin,' said Tulyet, although Bartholomew remembered him from the guild-hall. 'He is the only man Dickon has ever admired.'

'No surprise there,' muttered Bartholomew, thinking if the brat was going to hero-worship anyone, it would be a rough, battle-honed bruiser with scars. 'Are you sure you should encourage their association? John seems rather . . . pugilistic.'

Tulyet shrugged. 'He has already taught Dickon far more about combat than he learned from Lady Hereford's people. It is a pity he is illiterate, or I would ask him to teach Dickon how to read as well. Dickon would listen to him.'

'Will it be John who takes him to France?' asked Bartholomew, hoping it would be soon, because Dickon, fully trained as a warrior, loitering idly around Cambridge, was not an attractive proposition.

'I wish he would – Dickon would be safe with him – but John says he has had enough of war, and would rather stay home.'

Dickon was furious to be dragged away from something he was enjoying, and his face was as black as thunder. Only John's cautionary hand on his shoulder prevented him from snarling something that would see him in trouble.

'I want the pouch you took from Huntyngdon's body,' said Bartholomew, not bothering to mince his words.

'Why?' demanded Dickon, although he moderated his tone when Tulyet eyed him warningly. He forced a smile. 'I mean, why is it important? There was nothing in it. Some thief must have found the body first, and stripped it of valuables.'

'Almost certainly,' agreed Tulyet. 'Indeed, I am surprised it was not relieved of its fine clothes as well.'

'The maggots,' explained Dickon ghoulishly. 'It probably put the thief off. It did not bother me, though. *I* did not mind reclaiming the purse for Brother Michael.'

'And now Huntyngdon's father wants it,' said Bartholomew. 'So where is it?'

With obvious reluctance, Dickon rummaged inside his own scrip and handed the thing over. Some effort had been made to clean it, although it was still not something Bartholomew would have chosen to keep on his person.

'I tried to give it to Brother Michael yesterday,' said Dickon defensively, 'but he refused to take it. As it was going begging, I decided to sell it to Margery Starre. She always buys things belonging to corpses, because they have special powers.'

'You had no right,' scolded Tulyet. 'You should have replaced it on the body.'

'But the body was dead,' objected Dickon, bemused. 'And thus past caring.'

'His kin will care,' explained Tulyet, although Bartholomew felt the boy was old enough to have worked this out for himself. 'And you cannot do business with Mistress Starre anyway. She is a witch. You must distance yourself from such people.'

'Your father is right, lad,' murmured John. 'Listen to him.'

While they talked, Bartholomew examined the purse, daring to hope that Aynton's letter would be in it – that Dickon had overlooked it because he was uninterested in documents himself. But the purse was empty, and he could only assume that the boy was right: an opportunistic thief – or the killer – had taken whatever had been inside.

'It was like this when you found it, Dickon?' he asked, to be sure. 'There was nothing you threw away because it was wet or dirty?'

Dickon shook his head. 'I was very careful, and if anything had been in it, I would have passed it to Brother

186

Michael at once. Why? Are you looking into Huntyngdon's death as well as the Chancellor's? Can I help? Awkward witnesses always cooperate when I draw my sword.'

Bartholomew was sure they did. 'It is a kind offer, but I can manage, thank you.'

The discussion over, Dickon scampered away before he could be ordered back to his books. Grinning indulgently, John followed.

'So how are your enquiries?' asked Tulyet, walking Bartholomew back to the gate.

'I eliminated Gille and Elsham this morning, but the list is still quite lengthy. It is a pity I could not make out what Aynton said as he lay dying – *litteratus* or *non litteratus*. If I had, I could narrow it down to either scholars or seculars.'

'So who is still on it?'

'Donwich, Narboro, Stasy, Hawick, Morys, Brampton, Shardelowe and Martyn,' recited Bartholomew. 'My brother-in-law, too, but he assures me that he is innocent.'

'I imagine he is, Matt. Chaumbre is a nice man, and Edith is lucky to have found him. Have you tackled Morys yet or do you still want my help? If so, I cannot do it today, because I have reopened my investigation into Baldok's murder – he also died on the bridge, if you recall, and Aynton's fate has prompted me to look into it again.'

Bartholomew frowned. 'You think the two are connected? I do not see how, other than both happening on the Great Bridge.'

'You are probably right, but there is no harm in being sure.'

Bartholomew returned to the ferry, and found another long line of people waiting, this time to cross into the town. Tempers flared as the sun beat down, and there was a lot of irritable pushing and shoving. He decided to sit in St Giles' Church for a while, in the hope that the queue would be shorter when he emerged, but had second thoughts when he saw Ulf Godenave and his ragged friends there, trying to fry eggs on the hot stones in the porch.

He glanced along the Chesterton road, where tall elms offered shade and a place to lie, but the river stank so badly that it would not be a pleasant thing to do. Then he looked at the Griffin tavern, the thick stone walls of which would offer a cool refuge. But others had had the same idea, and the place was packed and noisy.

He was still debating what to do when something landed at his feet. It was a half-cooked egg, and he knew Ulf had lobbed it when the brat raced away sniggering. His play-mates scampered after him, unwilling to linger and take the blame for something he had done. The incident made Bartholomew remember the boy's ailing grandmother, so he walked to the nearby hovels to see how she was.

The Godenave family regarded him suspiciously when he arrived, and only when he assured them that he was not there to collect a fee was he allowed inside. The old woman was recovering well, thanks to the parish priest, who had brought her food and extra barley water, all paid for by the anonymous 'saint'.

As Bartholomew left, he saw Gille and Elsham lurking, evidently not trusting him to tell the truth about his movements that day. They made no attempt to conceal themselves, and only regarded him with unfriendly eyes – until Ulf lobbed eggs at them, too, after which they kept their distance.

'He should be wary of antagonising that pair,' Bartholomew warned the boy's granddam. 'They are not gentle, and one thinks Ulf stole his purse.'

'Our Ulf would never have done that,' objected the crone indignantly. 'Besides, that pair are thieves themselves. I saw Gille stick his hand in the poor box with my own eyes, while his friend Elsham stole the Mayor's wife.'

Bartholomew raised his eyebrows. 'You mean Rohese?'

'She has been looking for a new lover ever since John Baldok died, and she found one in Elsham. But he should watch himself – Morys will not appreciate being made a cuckold again, and he has violent kin in the fens . . .'

Although Bartholomew had been told before that Rohese liked male company, he was sure she would never stoop to Elsham. The Clare Hall Fellow was reasonably good-looking and his stipend was generous, but he was sullen, brutish and unlikely to be much fun. Bartholomew dismissed the claim as groundless gossip.

When the paupers in the little community around All Saints next-the-castle heard that a physician had given a free consultation, they flocked to him in droves. There were several cases of flux, but also some interesting diseases of the lungs and skin. Bartholomew lost himself in his work, so it was late afternoon before he finished. Then he realised with a guilty start that he had done virtually nothing to find Aynton's killer that day.

He hurried to the river, where the queue was now much shorter – on his side, at least. There was a long line on the other bank, as folk who had completed their business in town were making for their homes in the outlying villages. Isnard and his men were tired and hot, but very cheerful, suggesting their labours had bagged them a fortune. Bartholomew joined the back of the line, and was surprised to see Chaumbre there.

'My business in Girton took much longer than I anticipated,' sighed the dyer. 'Poor Edith will wonder what has happened to me, as I promised to be back by noon, to run a few errands for her friend Lucy.'

Bartholomew listened in mounting horror as Chaumbre

explained that his tasks for Lucy included visiting milli-
ners, glovers, cobblers and grocers, all to collect items
ordered for the wedding. Why were so many things
needed for a ceremony that would be over in the blink
of an eye? Seeing his dismay, Chaumbre changed the
subject, and began to talk about the difficulties he had
experienced while mending the window that had been
broken by burglars two days before.

'I could not saw the wood to the correct size, and it
took four attempts before I got it right. I should have
hired a carpenter to do it, rather than struggling myself.'

'What stopped you?' asked Bartholomew absently, most
of his thoughts still on Lucy's wild extravagance.

'The expense,' replied Chaumbre, then smiled. 'I know
I am wealthy, but why waste good money? However, I shall
know next time to leave it to the professionals.'

He burbled on, and Bartholomew tuned him out as
he looked at the bridge. Astonishing progress had been
made in just a few hours – most of the wooden super-
structure had been dismantled and replaced by scaffolding,
so that the workmen could identify any crumbling or
broken stone on the piers and spandrels, and replace it
with new. Work was as frantic as ever, and Shardelowe
was there to make sure no one slacked.

Unfortunately, the labourers were hampered by Ulf
and his friends, who had slipped under the barriers
erected to keep people out, and were larking about on
the *ponticulus*. Ulf had 'acquired' a new hat since
Bartholomew had last seen him, and he wore it at a jaunty
angle. He and his playmates were too quick for the
workmen to catch, and Bartholomew could see Shardelowe
growing exasperated by their antics.

'There will be an accident in a moment,' the physician
remarked, as Ulf leapt from the *ponticulus* to the scaffolding, where he bumped into one of the stones that
Bernarde had balanced there earlier.

'That boy is a nuisance,' agreed Chaumbre. 'And I am sure I have seen that hat somewhere before . . .'

It felt like an age before Bartholomew reached the front of the queue. After an earlier mishap, during which an overloaded boat had capsized and wet passengers had demanded a refund, Isnard set limits on the number of people in each craft. Bartholomew, Chaumbre and three others were allowed on the smaller of the two ferries, after which Isnard and his assistants prepared to push off. As always, Bartholomew was impressed by the barge-man's agility on boats, aware that he was more sure-footed than many folk with two good legs.

'Wait!' came an urgent voice. It was Gille, forcing his way to the front of the throng and brandishing a groat – a princely sum, far in excess of the set charge. 'Two more.'

Isnard eyed the coin greedily, which was enough to see the Clare Hall men hop aboard, much to the outrage of those who had been patiently waiting their turn. Gille elected to stand in the prow, while Elsham sat on the gunwale.

'They have a family emergency,' Isnard informed those who immediately began to bellow their objections.

'Liar!' cried Burgess FitzAbsolon furiously. 'I shall raise the issue of bribery and corruption at the next guildhall meeting.'

Elsham gave a sharp bark of amusement. 'You think Mayor Morys will uphold an objection to something he has refined to such an exquisite art?'

There was no answer to this, and FitzAbsolon was wise enough not to attempt one. He watched with sullen resentment as the ferry pushed off, Isnard and his crew grunting with the effort of the additional weight.

The boat was halfway across when trouble erupted. Some of Ulf's friends began to pelt the builders with bits of broken wood, while a couple of their cronies were back on the *ponticulus*, where they raced to and fro with whoops of glee, causing it to sway violently. Ulf himself was on the riverbank, snatching up handfuls of mud, which he lobbed at the ferry, eliciting yells of anger from those he hit.

Bartholomew saw something fast-moving out of the corner of his eye, but before he could shout a warning, there was a tremendous crash followed by a fountain of water and flying splinters. A huge piece of stone had toppled off the scaffolding and crashed through the *ponticulus* to land on the ferry below. Chaumbre and Elsham went cartwheeling into the water, while everyone else struggled to cling on as the crippled craft tipped precariously. Chaumbre surfaced a few feet away, and began to screech that he could not swim.

Bartholomew considered jumping in to rescue him, but drowning was not the worst thing that could happen to someone who immersed himself in the Cam. Instead, he grabbed one of Isnard's crutches, and stretched it towards the flailing dyer. When Chaumbre seized it, Bartholomew was able to pull him aboard.

When they reached the opposite bank moments later, willing hands were waiting to assist the sodden passengers ashore. Chaumbre was soon sitting on an upturned crate, being fussed over by well-wishers. There were a lot of them, all genuinely concerned, and Bartholomew saw that his brother-in-law was a popular man. There was only one dissenting voice.

'Perhaps God gave you a soaking for failing to fill in your dye-pits,' called Narboro nastily. 'Now *you* know what it is like to fall into a place where you do not want to be.'

He stalked away, head in the air, although he was obliged to break into a run when Chaumbre's friends took exception to the remark and one or two started after him.

While he waited for Chaumbre to recover, Bartholomew looked at the crowd that had gathered to watch the aftermath of the incident. Shardelowe and his crew stared down from the scaffolding that swathed the bridge, while several dozen people were ranged along the top of both riverbanks. Among them were Mayor Morys, Brampton, Donwich, Stasy and Hawick. Cynric was nowhere to be seen, and he wondered if his erstwhile students had given the book-bearer the slip.

Isnard glared up at the workmen. 'One of you pushed that stone on purpose! You have been moaning about us all day, claiming that we are in the way of your delivery barges.'

'We did no such thing,' objected Shardelowe. 'What happened was an accident.'

'Then one of those brats was responsible,' put in Stasy. 'I notice they are now nowhere to be seen.'

'They are not strong enough,' countered Bernarde. 'Blame the sun instead. It must have heated the stone, causing it to tip.'

That sounded unlikely to Bartholomew. 'Where is Elsham?' he asked, recalling that Chaumbre was not the only one who had been knocked off the ferry.

'There, on the bank,' replied Isnard, hobbling towards a prostrate figure. 'He must have swum to safety. Come on, lad, up you get. You are not . . . *help*!'

Bartholomew could see at once that something was badly wrong. An examination revealed that the stone had landed square on Elsham's back, crushing his spine. His limbs were floppy, and he shook his head when Bartholomew asked if he could feel his hands or feet. His face was white, and Bartholomew knew he was dying. So did Elsham.

'I need absolution,' he whispered. 'I have done things . . .'

'Brampton! Fetch a priest,' shouted Bartholomew urgently. 'And where is Gille?'

193

'He was here a moment ago,' replied Isnard, scanning the silently watching faces. 'Perhaps he went home for dry clothes. Do you want me to fetch him back?'

'Yes,' said Bartholomew tersely, sure Elsham would want his friend with him in his final moments. 'Hurry.'

'The priest,' gasped Elsham. 'Please! I must unburden my soul.'

'He is coming,' said Bartholomew gently. 'It will not be—'

But Elsham could not wait. 'I killed Huntyngdon,' he rasped, his eyes huge in his frightened face. 'I stabbed him as he walked along the towpath. He was going to deliver a letter from the Chancellor, but I got to him first. I hid the body, but it must have rolled into the river and floated downstream . . .'

Bartholomew stared at him. 'Why would you do such a thing?'

Elsham would not meet his eyes. 'As a favour for . . . a friend.'

'Who?' asked Bartholomew, wondering what manner of friend would demand that sort of boon. 'Donwich?'

'I cannot say, lest he disturbs my afterlife,' breathed Elsham, each word now an agony of effort. 'Besides, I can only confess my sins, not someone else's.'

'And Martyn? Did you kill him, too?'

'I know nothing about him.'

'I do not understand,' said Bartholomew helplessly. 'Why did your "friend" want Huntyngdon dead? What was in Aynton's letter that was so important?'

'He never told me. I just did what he asked.'

'Did you take the letter after you . . . after Huntyngdon died?'

'I was meant to, but I . . . forgot. I suppose some beggar stole it when his body was washed down here, along with the money in his purse. Not that there was much of that – just a few farthings.'

Bartholomew had so many questions that he did not know which ones to ask first. 'Was Gille with you when you killed Huntyngdon?'

'No, he was in the Brazen George.'

'Then is he the friend who compelled you to kill on his behalf?'

'Of course not!' breathed Elsham. 'He is more brother than friend. You must absolve me, now. Please! I will . . .'

His eyes slid closed, and he did not open them again. A priest arrived, and by the time he had finished murmuring prayers of absolution, Elsham was dead.

CHAPTER 10

'So, you have solved a murder,' said Michael the following day. It was Sunday, with breakfast later than usual because of the extended service in the church. 'All on your own and within hours of me asking for your help. Perhaps I should make you a proctor.'

'I solved nothing,' said Bartholomew unhappily, looking at his food and thinking he would be inundated with demands for laxatives if Michael continued to provide his colleagues with nothing but bread and meat. 'Elsham confessed. And if you did make me a proctor, it would be a very short appointment. I leave the University in six days.'

'Next Saturday,' sighed Michael. 'By which time I hope to have some good news to announce to our scholars, after which I shall declare the University in summer recess.'

'Good news about you being recognised as Chancellor?'

Michael nodded, but Bartholomew was seized with the sudden conviction that it was not what the monk had meant at all. He started to quiz him about it, but Michael raised a hand to stop him.

'I cannot say more, Matt – I am sworn to secrecy. Suffice to say that I shall be busy for the next few days, so you will have to continue the investigation on your own.'

'But—'

'We now have another murder to solve,' the monk went on. 'Because I cannot believe that Elsham's death was an accident – that Huntyngdon's killer just happened to be beneath a lump of rock that plummeted down and crushed him.'

'I spoke to Shardelowe afterwards,' said Bartholomew.

'He showed me how the stones were set. They *were* close to the edge, but none would have fallen without being pushed fairly vigorously.'

'But no one saw who did it?'

'Ulf and his friends were making a nuisance of themselves at the time, and everyone was either watching them or ducking their missiles. No one was looking at the stones.'

'Could Ulf have done it? I would not put it past him.'

'He was on the riverbank. And it was not his friends either, before you ask – they were on the *ponticulus*, and it was lucky the stone did not hit one of them on its way down. Besides, Shardelowe says it would have been too heavy for any of them to budge.'

'So who are your suspects? I assume you have some?'

Bartholomew nodded. 'Most are already on the list for dispatching Aynton, and all were near the bridge when the stone was pushed. They are Donwich, Brampton, Narboro, Stasy, Hawick, Morys and Shardelowe.'

Michael nodded. 'But Chaumbre and Gille are eliminated, because they were on the ferry when Elsham died, and if the killer of Elsham and Aynton are one and the same . . .'

'I had already discounted Gille as a suspect, because he has an alibi for Aynton's murder. He and Elsham were in the Griffin, with witnesses to prove it.'

Michael considered. 'Obviously, the culprit is Elsham's mysterious friend. This person ordered Huntyngdon dispatched, but when Elsham failed to hide the body in a place where it would never be found, he exacted a terrible revenge.'

'I would say the friend is Donwich, but he will need all the help he can get if he is to make himself Chancellor, and I do not see him dispatching a loyal ally just yet. Moreover, he was distressed when he learned that Elsham was dead – genuinely so, I believe.'

Michael was not so sure. 'He has changed since

becoming Master of Clare Hall, and has grown harder and colder. It would not surprise me if he killed a crony to suit himself, then feigned grief.'

Bartholomew supposed it was possible. 'Then there are Stasy and Hawick. I have seen Elsham conferring slyly with them on three separate occasions. They claim it was about selling second-hand exemplars, but why should we believe them?'

'You think either of that lowly, disreputable pair could force a brute like Elsham to kill on their behalf?' asked Michael doubtfully.

'Well, Elsham refused to give me the name of this friend, lest he disturbed his afterlife, and you expelled Stasy and Hawick for witchery . . .'

'That is an interesting point. However, I do not believe that a lump of stone can be shoved off a bridge with no one seeing. There *will* be witnesses – we just need to find them.'

'I tried, Brother,' said Bartholomew tiredly. 'I questioned everyone who was there, but no one saw anything. And they would have told me if they had, not to win justice for Elsham, but because Chaumbre was also a victim, and people like him.'

'I will set a couple of beadles to ask around the taverns,' said Michael. 'There are a few townsfolk who will never share information with a scholar, not even to benefit one of their own, but they talk to the beadles. Did you believe Elsham when he claimed he did not know what was in Aynton's letter?'

Bartholomew nodded. 'I had the impression he did not *want* to know – that he "forgot" to take it lest he inadvertently found out. He says Huntyngdon's purse held a few farthings when he left, but it was empty by the time Dickon cut it free. I suspect the thief emptied it out and threw the letter away, not realising its importance.'

'Pity,' said Michael.

'What about Huntyngdon's father?' asked Bartholomew. 'Could *he* have killed Elsham? Perhaps he is a better investigator than me, and did not need a dying man's confession to learn the truth about what happened to his son.'

'Elsham died when the Earl – and everyone else at King's Hall – was burying Huntyngdon. Well, everyone other than Brampton, who was out collecting the University's share of the money for the bridge.'

'I see,' said Bartholomew, filing the last piece of information away in his mind.

Michael rubbed his chin. 'I accept your reasoning for why Gille cannot be this sinister friend, but I do not like the fact that he disappeared the moment the ferry touched land.'

'Especially as Elsham said he was more brother than friend – yet he abandoned him without a backward glance.'

'Well, find him, and force him to reveal the name of the mysterious person who bent the loutish Elsham to his will.'

'Find Gille?' echoed Bartholomew warily. 'On my own?'

'I have ordered the beadles to be on the alert for him, while Dick has done the same with his soldiers. You are not on your own.'

Bartholomew sighed. 'I suppose I could see if he went home to Clare Hall . . .'

'As soon as I heard what happened, I sent beadles to apprehend him there, but he had already packed a bag and left. Innocent men do not vanish with such suspicious haste, so he definitely has something to hide. Speak to his colleagues and see what you can learn.'

'I doubt they know anything – they do not like each other. Donwich might, though.'

'If he does, he will not tell you, so do not waste your time on him. When you have finished in Clare Hall, visit the Brazen George to see if Gille really was there when

199

Huntyngdon was murdered. Then speak to our other suspects – Morys, Narboro, Stasy, Hawick and Shardelowe.'

'Brampton was also near the bridge when Elsham died. He was chatting to Donwich.'

Michael made a moue of irritation. 'I imagine he was trying to convince him to pay Clare Hall's share of the bridge money. I hope he succeeds, because if not, other foundations might follow suit, and we will be unable to meet our obligations.'

'Are you sure Brampton is the right man for the task?' asked Bartholomew doubtfully. 'It will take a forceful character to sway the likes of Donwich, and Brampton is hardly what you would call assertive.'

'He scaled the greasy pole of University politics without too much trouble, so I imagine he will find a way. Leave him be until Wednesday, by which time he will have collected everything we must pay the town. You may question him then, assuming we are still looking for a culprit. Agreed?'

'You really think he can do it?' asked Bartholomew, sure he would fail, as scholars were notoriously good at finding ways to avoid parting with money.

'I do,' replied Michael. 'Do not underestimate him – he has many hidden skills.'

Bartholomew was interested to hear it, and wondered if sly murder was among them.

As work on the Sabbath was forbidden, there were never classes or lectures on Sundays. Some Colleges allowed their students to roam free, but Michaelhouse had learned that letting dozens of bored – and sex-starved – young men loose in the town was unwise, so the Fellows always made sure there was plenty for them to do at home. Activities usually revolved around amusing talks, games or light-hearted debates.

That day, it was Zoone's turn to provide the necessary

distractions. In deference to the heat, he eschewed anything energetic, and set up a bridge-designing tournament instead. As he offered a monetary prize for the winner, and most students were short of cash so late in the term, everyone was keen to chance his hand. Before that, however, there was to be a mock disputation on the subject of gluttony.

All eyes turned immediately to Michael, who looked up from his post-breakfast cake in astonishment, startled to find himself the centre of attention.

'Why are you staring at me?' he demanded. 'I know nothing about gluttony.'

'Then allow me to enlighten you,' offered Zoone, oblivious to the students' smirks. 'According to Aquinas, there are five different kinds: eating too soon, too expensively, too much, too eagerly, and too daintily. To these may be added eating too wildly.'

'What nonsense!' cried Michael. 'There is no such thing as eating "too soon" or "too much", while eating "too eagerly" is just a man's way of complimenting his cook.'

'Quite right,' put in William, who was something of a glutton himself.

'Moreover, the "expense" of food is outside our control, given that we must eat what we are given,' Michael went on, blithely ignoring the fact that he monitored every aspect of College victuals with an eagle eye. 'And I have no idea what eating "too wildly" means. However, I concede that eating "too daintily" is a nasty habit.'

'So there,' said William, this particular response being his idea of incisive disputation.

'Animals and birds only eat when they are hungry,' put in Aungel tentatively. 'So I suppose you could never accuse them of gorging.'

Clippesby laughed as he stroked the iridescent feathers of the College's lead hen, who perched on his lap. 'You would not say that if you knew them, Aungel. Ethel and her flock always have room for raisins, even when they are full of grain. So do the peafowl.'

'You give our precious raisins to birds?' demanded William, aghast. 'Do you know how much those cost, man?'

'No, and neither do they,' replied Clippesby serenely. 'It does not matter to a chicken if a raisin costs a farthing or a hundred marks – she will enjoy it equally. Aquinas could never accuse a hen of eating "too expensively", because money means nothing to her.'

'That is untrue,' countered William. 'When I bought a cheaper feed for them last term, they refused to touch it, and Ethel sent me a message – which *you* delivered – quoting Aristotle, who condemned those who put the accumulation of wealth above good living.'

'Enough!' said Michael, laughing. 'You can save these fascinating insights for the debate. I only wish I could be there to hear it. Unfortunately, the vicars-general demand my presence in St Mary the Great today. There is much work to be done and—'

'On a Sunday?' interrupted William, immediately puffing up with righteous indignation. 'When all labour is forbidden by God's holy commandments?'

'Blame Thomas Ely,' Michael flashed back. 'It was his idea. But he is a Franciscan, so what can they know about pious living?'

'More than Benedictines,' retorted William, predictably leaping to defend his Order. 'And if Ely suggested it, then I withdraw my objection. We Grey Friars know what we are doing when it comes to theology.'

The students trooped out of the hall, and Bartholomew was about to follow when the peafowl set up a tremendous cacophony near the porter's lodge. He looked through the window and spotted someone lurking in the shadows, but whoever was there beat a hasty retreat when Walter emerged from his lair to see what was going on.

'Birds are better than any guard dog,' said Clippesby,

coming to stand at Bartholomew's side. 'I am sure that was Stasy, trying to sneak in while we were all at breakfast. But Henry remembers being kicked, and will not allow him past.'

Cynric appeared from nowhere. 'Stasy is up and about?' he demanded. 'I assumed he was still in bed – as he was yesterday and Friday, when there was no College bell to summon him to church. I had better go and—'

'I assume you watched them at the Great Bridge yesterday,' interrupted Bartholomew. 'Does that mean I can discount them as suspects for shoving the stone on Elsham?'

Cynric winced. 'They are clever. They know I am keeping an eye on them, so they separate, forcing me to choose which one to follow. But as it happens, I was not with either when Elsham died. Stasy knocked Margery over, see – he says by accident – and I was helping her up.'

'So they distracted you at the salient time?' pounced Bartholomew.

Cynric nodded. 'I imagine they *are* your killers, boy. They are warlocks, and the sooner they are hanged, the happier I shall be.'

And this coming from a man who revered a witch, thought Bartholomew.

Cambridge boasted more than a dozen parish churches, not to mention chapels in convents and Colleges, and nearly all had bells of some description. As it was Sunday, every one of them was in clanging action, calling the faithful to their devotions. They created a tremendous cacophony, the deep bass of St Mary the Great booming over the tinny clanks of St Botolph and Trinity Hall.

Although Bartholomew was ready to begin his enquiries immediately, his patients had other ideas, and his morning was taken up with them. There were several new cases of flux, in places as far apart as the Dominican Friary and the cottages along the Chesterton lane. He was hungry when he had finished, so he returned to Michaelhouse to beg bread and cheese from Agatha – the noonday meal was already under way and he did not want to stroll into the hall late. He ate in the yard, thinking it was a good time to catch the scholars of Clare Hall, who would also be gathered in their refectory.

'You seem better,' he remarked to Walter, whom he passed on his way out.

The porter nodded, although his face retained its habitual scowl. 'But *not* because of Stasy and Hawick, no matter what they claim. I refused to swallow the tonic they sent me, lest it was poisoned. I poured it away. Incidentally, a priest came earlier. He left you this, to help with the flux. It comes from the same person who has been helping the sick beadles.'

It was a heavy purse, containing enough to buy medicine for his poorer patients for a month. It was not unusual for people to leave Bartholomew charitable donations – Edith was generous in that respect, and so were several scholars, burgesses and town guilds. However, none had given him such a large sum before.

'Who is this person?' he asked, touched and grateful. 'I should thank him.'

'The priest would not tell me,' replied Walter crossly. 'And believe me, I tried to prise a name out of him. All he would say is that it comes from someone who appreciates what you are doing, and wants to help.'

'Do *you* have any idea who it might be?'

'The Earl of Huntyngdon,' replied Walter promptly. 'The King's Hall porters told me that he is indebted to you for finding his son's killer.'

'I did not find him – he confessed. Besides, why would the Earl care about sick beadles and paupers? Or make his donation anonymous?'

'True,' acknowledged Walter. 'Someone else then . . .'

'Have you heard any rumours about who killed Elsham?'

204

'None,' replied Walter. 'Although no one mourns him, least of all Clare Hall. Well, other than its Master. Oh, before I forget, Mayor Morys wants you to call, because his wife has the flux. When you visit, overcharge him. He cheats everyone else, so it will serve him right to be on the other end for a change.'

Bartholomew glanced at the dye-pits on his way to Morys's house, and saw that while two had been carefully filled in, nothing had been done to the others. Naturally, the ones that remained were the largest and deepest. He heard people talking about Chaumbre as he passed them, and it seemed the dyer's near-drowning had granted him a reprieve – he was popular, and folk were so glad that he had survived his dip in the Cam that they were willing to forgive him almost anything.

By contrast, Morys was not popular at all, and his mansion near the Round Church showed signs of having been bombarded with muck at various points during his residency. It was a pity, as it was a lovely house – its plasterwork was picked out with gilt and every window had real glass. Bartholomew was conducted to a room that was full of natural light, and after Morys had welcomed him, a maid brought them rose-water sherbets.

'Is this *ice*?' asked Bartholomew, regarding his goblet in astonishment.

'I have it imported,' replied Morys smugly. 'It is costly, of course, but I deserve it.'

The fragment had melted by the time Bartholomew looked back at his cup again, but the drink was still beautifully cold. He swallowed it quickly, before it took on the ambient temperature of the room, thinking that if Morys could afford such a wild luxury, then he was richer than anyone knew, because not even kings and princes spent money on something that had invariably turned to water by the time it arrived.

'My condolences for Elsham,' said Morys, while they waited for the maid to come back and tell them that Rohese was ready to receive the physician. 'His death is very sad.'

He did not look sad, and Bartholomew remembered what Ulf's grandmother had said: that Rohese had taken Elsham as a lover. He had been sceptical at the time, but perhaps it *was* true. If so, it was a strong motive for murder, and Bartholomew had seen Morys near the bridge shortly after the stone had been pushed.

'Did you know Elsham?' he fished.

'Not really, although Donwich said that Elsham and Gille are the only Clare Hall Fellows to remain loyal to him – the others are all treacherous dogs.' Morys smiled. 'He will make a fine Chancellor, much better than Michael, who is overly honest and friends with the Sheriff into the bargain. I cannot do business with a person like that.'

'An incorruptible one, you mean,' said Bartholomew. 'Although it will not matter by the end of the month, because you will no longer be Mayor.'

Morys smiled enigmatically. 'No, I suppose not.'

'Did you see what happened on the bridge yesterday when Elsham died?'

'I am afraid all my attention was on the brats who were throwing mud and bits of wood. Little ruffians! The Sheriff should hang the lot of them. They are no good to man nor beast.'

'Can you think of anyone who might want to kill Elsham?'

'Oh, dozens!' replied Morys, eyes glittering slyly. 'Most of the University thinks Michael should be Chancellor, and Elsham supported his rival. All of them should be on your list of suspects. As should the monk himself.'

Bartholomew saw he had been overly optimistic to think he could learn anything useful from Morys, who was far too clever to be trapped into saying something he would rather keep to himself.

At that point, the maid appeared to say Rohese was ready, so Morys led the way to the back of the house, where the lady in question lay on a bed that was loaded with silken covers. She was pale, and even as they entered the room, she lurched towards a bucket. Repelled, Morys beat a hasty retreat, leaving Bartholomew to tend to her on his own.

'It is not the flux,' said Bartholomew, when he had finished examining her. 'But I imagine you already know that. You are with child.'

Rohese wiped her mouth with the back of her hand. 'Yes, but you cannot tell my husband, because we have not . . . well, he will know he is not the father.'

Bartholomew could not bring himself to ask if that honour belonged to Elsham, when she lay so helpless and miserable. 'The sickness will pass soon,' was all he said. 'Until then, the best remedy is rest, and perhaps a mild infusion of peppermint or raspberry leaf.'

Rohese shot him a rueful glance. 'My predicament will do *you* no favours. If I keep vomiting like this, my husband will tell everyone that you have failed to cure me of the flux.'

'He will guess the truth sooner or later, so you should consider how to deal with the situation before it arises. He is not a gentle man.'

She winced. 'Unfortunately, I am not sure who is responsible for my . . . predicament. Perhaps I should say it is Dickon, as even my husband will be wary of challenging *him*.'

Bartholomew eyed her askance. 'Is Dickon really a possibility?'

She sniffed. 'I do not couple with children, not even strong and handsome ones like him. The two most likely candidates are Baldok and Elsham. Unfortunately, both are dead.'

'Does your husband know about Elsham?'

'I thought not.' Rohese looked away. 'But perhaps I was wrong.'

'Is he the kind of man to kill your lovers?'

'Whose husband is not?' shrugged Rohese. 'He would not do the deed himself, of course, but he has family in the Fens who are willing to exchange violence for money. You will never prove it, though, so do not waste your time trying.'

'Do you feel safe here? If not, Matilde will find you somewhere to hide.'

Rohese gave him a lopsided smile. 'I am safe for now, although I shall have to run eventually. However, it will be at a time of *my* choosing, and I refuse to be rushed.'

Bartholomew took his leave, feeling soiled by the encounter – and burdened, too, with a secret he wished he did not have. He hurried down the stairs and was just walking along the corridor when Morys emerged from a door to one side. The Mayor pulled it shut behind him, but it swung open again to reveal a flight of steps leading down to a cellar. At the bottom was his cousin John, the knight, who knelt by a chest of coins. It was the box containing the money raised for the bridge, which Morys had displayed at the guildhall meeting.

'Well?' demanded Morys, closing the door again to prevent the physician from seeing more. 'Have you cured her?'

'She needs to rest,' replied Bartholomew ambiguously.

'Will you prescribe some of your magical barley water?' asked Morys. 'Because I do not like the thought of her being sick on the coverlets. Vomit stains, you know.'

Outside, the heat hit Bartholomew like a furnace, and he wondered how much longer the sun would bake the town. Then he remembered Zoone's prediction for two days hence, and hoped he was right about rain in the offing. Of course, then the superstitious would say it 'proved' their claims that a downpour on the Feast of St Swithun's Day would presage forty more wet days. The likes of Cynric, Margery and Zoone would milk it for all it was worth.

He had not taken many steps along the High Street when he was hailed by a familiar voice. It was Meadowman. The beadle was pale and walked with a stick, but it was a huge improvement on their last meeting, when Bartholomew had been desperate enough to add pepper to his barley water and lie about it. He was delighted that the ruse had worked.

'I shall be able to return to work soon,' the beadle said happily. 'I wish you had given me that powerful powder sooner.'

As he seemed unsteady on his feet, Bartholomew helped him home. He emerged from the beadle's cottage only to be intercepted by a Peterhouse student, who said that Narboro needed to see him in Hoo Hall at once.

Bartholomew walked there quickly, noting that the Mill Pond was emptier than ever as the drought continued. Morys had doubled the guards around it, to make sure people paid for the water they took. It reeked horribly, which was not surprising, with virtually no through-flow to prevent it from turning stagnant.

Hoo Hall was dark after the glare of the sun, so Bartholomew waited for his eyes to grow accustomed to it, then descended the steps to the cellar-like hall. Since his last visit, it had come into service as a store for perishable food, which was sensible, as it was deliciously cool. He walked across the hall, and climbed the stairs on the opposite wall to the dormitory, where Narboro lay on his bed.

'What happened?' blurted Bartholomew, when the man turned his head towards him and he saw his face. 'Did someone hit you?'

'That bad?' whispered Narboro miserably. 'Lord! What shall I do? I cannot go out looking like this. People will think I have been brawling.'

Bartholomew sat next to him. 'Who punched you?'

'No one – I fell down one of Chaumbre's pits. It is *his* fault that I am bruised and bloody, and I am going to sue him for every penny he owns. You can tell him that.'

'Best not,' advised Bartholomew. 'His lawyers will request the opinion of a *medicus,* and any physician will testify that you cannot have suffered this injury from a fall. You will be dismissed as a liar.'

Narboro deflated. 'Damn! Getting free money from Chaumbre seemed like the answer to all my problems, because unless I can pay off Brampton, he will destroy me. Very well. The truth is that I butted a tomb with my face.'

Bartholomew blinked. 'What for?'

Narboro shot him a nasty glance. 'It was not deliberate, I assure you. If you must know, it was after Elsham died yesterday. I saw his body carried past and I thought I might be sick, so I ran to the nearest open space – St Clement's cemetery. As my head went down to vomit, my nose smacked into a grave.'

Bartholomew's first inclination was to laugh, and his second was to treat the tale with a healthy dose of scepticism. Elsham had not been an especially terrible sight, and it occurred to Bartholomew that the only person it might disturb was a guilt-stricken culprit. He struggled to keep his expression professionally noncommittal. 'Do you usually have such extreme responses to the dead?'

'Always,' declared Narboro. 'I am sensitive, not like the ghouls who surged forward for a better look. I do not know how you could bear to touch the thing. I hope you washed your hands afterwards.'

'Many times,' Bartholomew assured him. 'The University is determined to catch Elsham's killer. What do you know about what happened to him?'

Narboro appeared to consider the question carefully. 'Well, I saw Donwich watching events unfold with unseemly interest, but he cannot be the culprit, because he liked Elsham. Indeed, there were tears in his eyes when he learned the identity of the victim.'

'Why mention him in particular?'

'Because he was whispering with Mayor Morys shortly before the incident, and as I was sure they were up to no good, I tried to eavesdrop.'

'Why on Earth would you want to do that?'

'I hoped they might say something that would allow me to blackmail them,' replied Narboro bluntly. 'I am so desperate for funds to give to Brampton that I will stoop to any depths to get some. But Morys's cousin John feinted at me with a knife, so I beat a hasty retreat.'

'So you do not know what they discussed?'

Narboro smirked. 'I do, actually, because John did not notice me immediately. In essence, Morys was paying Donwich for speaking at the guildhall. Apparently, his remarks forced Michael to contribute a lot more towards the bridge, and the whole "disagreement" was part of a plan devised by Morys to make our University do what he wanted.'

'We suspected as much,' said Bartholomew. 'Although your testimony is proof of it.'

'And that is not all. Donwich will use the incident to show the vicars-general that it makes Michael unfit to be Chancellor. When they appoint him instead, he will force Michaelhouse to pay the University's entire contribution on its own.'

Bartholomew made a mental note to warn Michael. 'So *will* you use all this to extort money from Morys? Or Donwich?'

'I tried, but they both threatened me with violence, so I decided to leave it. Perhaps I should invent a yarn about them dispatching Elsham instead, and you can buy my testimony. They cannot hurt me if they are hanged for murder, can they.'

'We would rather have the truth,' said Bartholomew coolly. 'So, speak honestly now: did you hear anything to implicate them in Elsham's death?'

Narboro grimaced. 'No, not a thing, unfortunately.'

Bartholomew was growing exasperated. 'Look, Narboro, this is important: we know Huntyngdon was murdered – by Elsham – after Aynton gave him a letter for you. You *must* have some idea what it was about.'

Narboro sighed irritably. 'But I do not! How many more times must I say it? All I can think is that he wanted me to get him a Court post for when he retired. It is normally the sort of favour one begs in person, but I was away when you say he gave Huntyngdon this letter, so he must have decided to write instead.'

Bartholomew frowned. 'You have not mentioned this before. Where were you?'

'On a personal errand,' replied Narboro haughtily. 'Which is none of your business.'

'Then you can sit in the proctors' gaol until you tell me,' blustered Bartholomew. 'This is a murder enquiry. It is no time for secrets.'

'You cannot throw me in a cell,' cried Narboro, alarmed. 'I have done nothing wrong!'

'Then tell me where you were.'

Narboro scowled. 'If you must know, I went to Linton to order a new mirror. You see, Lucy spotted me using the one she gifted me ten years ago, and it made me feel like a scoundrel. So I decided to replace it.'

Bartholomew had no idea if he was telling the truth. 'Is that all? I thought it was something important.'

'It *is* important,' declared Narboro indignantly. 'The situation with Lucy is delicate, and not just because her brother aims to ruin me. I cannot have her thinking that I might change my mind about marrying her, just because

I am attached to a present she once gave me. I ordered another mirror – without her painting on the back – and was home four days later.'

'Four days?' echoed Bartholomew in disbelief. 'For a journey to Linton? You could have been there and back in a quarter of that time.'

'There were decisions to be made,' said Narboro stiffly. 'I had to choose the wood, the design *and* the size. Besides, I was glad to get away from Cambridge, to be frank. I am tired of Brampton glaring at me every time our paths cross. I would have stayed away longer but the glazier needed his spare room back.'

'Can you prove you were away all that time?'

Narboro pondered. 'Well, Aynton saw me leave, although he is not in a position to say so, regrettably. I ran into him by the Barnwell Gate, and he asked why I was leaving during term. To avoid him reporting me – I cannot afford a fine – I confided my tale.'

Bartholomew narrowed his eyes. 'You told the Chancellor that you were breaking University rules to buy yourself a new mirror, and he just let you go?'

Narboro looked sheepish. 'Actually, I told him it was for the King, who wanted it urgently. He believed me, thankfully.' He brightened. 'It will be ready soon, and I shall go to Linton to collect it.'

'But, as you pointed out, Aynton is dead, so cannot confirm or deny your tale.'

'No,' sighed Narboro, 'which is why I did not bother telling you in the first place.'

'What about the glazier?' asked Bartholomew. 'Will he verify your claims?'

'Bartholomew, you are a genius!' cried Narboro. 'Why did I not think of that? Of course he will! I stayed with him for three nights, so he will remember me well.'

He provided the glazier's name so readily that Bartholomew was sure he was telling the truth. And if he had been away when Huntyngdon had been dispatched, the chances were that he was innocent of murdering Aynton, too. Bartholomew had eliminated another suspect, but the mystery of the letter remained, and he was not sure how to resolve it.

CHAPTER 11

Bartholomew did not want to visit Clare Hall and ask questions about where Gille might have gone, lest he ran into Donwich who was sure to be hostile, so he dragged his feet all along Milne Street. As he passed Edith's house, she hurried out to take his hand and kiss it.

'Thank you for saving Philip yesterday,' she said, tears in her eyes. 'He says he would have drowned if you had not raced to the rescue.'

Bartholomew had hardly raced, and was uncomfortable with her gratitude. He tried to resist when she drew him inside her house, but she was insistent. Once through the door, he breathed in deeply, savouring the comfortingly familiar scents of baking cakes, herbs and the cloth in the warehouses behind the house. It reminded him of his happy childhood, when Edith had been more mother than sister, and he had not been obliged to dabble in the murky business of murder.

She led him to the solar, where he was pleased to see Matilde, although he was less delighted to note that Lucy and Chaumbre were there, too. The women were sitting at the table, and Lucy explained that they were discussing a new dress for Edith. Chaumbre looked on indulgently, while Matilde's eyes twinkled with humour at the seriousness with which her friend was taking the subject.

'But Edith has several dresses already,' said Bartholomew, bemused. 'Why would she need another?'

'To wear to our wedding, of course,' explained Matilde gravely, although he could see she itched to laugh. 'Obviously, none of us want to clash.'

'No,' agreed Lucy fervently. 'So this is important.'

Bartholomew glanced at Chaumbre, who lounged in a cushion-loaded chair, being fussed over by servants. He saw the retainers were genuinely fond of him, perhaps because they knew who had stepped in to save them when Edith's son had sold the roof from over their heads.

'I shall never forget what you did for me yesterday, Matt,' the dyer said, coming to clasp Bartholomew's hand, although the physician managed to snatch it back before he could follow Edith's example and kiss it. 'Thank God Shardelowe is rebuilding the bridge, because I shall never set foot in a boat again.'

'Good,' said Edith, squeezing his arm affectionately. 'I could not bear to lose you.'

At that moment, there was a tap on the back door, and a maid came to say it was a carter wanting payment for bringing a load of alum.

'Where is my purse?' asked Chaumbre, patting around his belt before giving a grimace of annoyance. 'Damn, I keep forgetting! It is at the bottom of the river, along with everything else I collected from my Girton hoard. Do you have a few shillings I can borrow, Matt?'

Bartholomew had the money from the anonymous benefactor, but he could hardly part with that, as it was not his to lend. Fortunately, Matilde was able to oblige.

'I will give it back on Friday,' promised Chaumbre, beaming at her. 'The monks at Ely have promised to pay me for thirty ells of cloth then. I shall be rolling in money.'

Uneasily, Bartholomew wondered if Morys was right to claim that Chaumbre was not as rich as everyone thought, and hoped Edith had not married a man who would exacerbate, rather than alleviate, the financial difficulties arising from Richard's profligacy.

'How are your murder enquiries proceeding, Matt?' asked Edith conversationally.

'Slowly,' he replied, and glanced hopefully at Chaumbre. 'I do not suppose you saw what happened at the bridge, did you? You are the only one I did not ask yesterday. You seemed too shocked to talk.'

'I *was* too shocked,' averred Chaumbre. 'However, before I nearly died, I noticed a lot of children racing around.'

'The builders are sure they did not push the stone. None are strong enough apparently.'

'Yes,' acknowledged Chaumbre. 'But I did not say I saw a child push the stone – I said they were *racing around.* Some were on the *ponticulus*, while others lobbed mud and bits of wood. It was very distracting. And it all happened at once.'

He gave Bartholomew a meaningful look, all pursed lips and waving eyebrows.

Bartholomew frowned. 'Are you claiming that their antics were a diversion – one to let the culprit kill Elsham?'

'Yes,' replied Chaumbre. 'It did not occur to me at the time, but with hindsight, I see that was *precisely* the plan. But what makes you think Elsham was the target? I cannot imagine it is easy to direct a large lump of rock with any degree of accuracy.'

'Well, who else could warrant that sort of attention?' asked Bartholomew. 'The other passengers on the ferry comprised two nuns and the town's surgeon, so I doubt it was them. Or are you suggesting that you were the target?'

'Of course not,' said Chaumbre indignantly. '*I* am not the one investigating murder.'

'You think Matt was the intended victim?' cried Matilde, and turned to him in alarm. 'You must promise to keep Cynric with you until the villain is caught, because I do not want to be a widow ere I am wed.'

'Like me,' muttered Lucy gloomily, before Bartholomew could tell her that Cynric was too busy protecting the College from a pair of warlocks. 'I am a widow in all but name.'

217

'You seem to have found solace in Donwich's arms,' said Chaumbre baldly, although his smile was amiable enough.

'Not his arms,' corrected Lucy stiffly. 'His company. We are just friends.'

'It is more than that for him,' said Chaumbre. 'He is besotted with you.'

'And Chancellor Aynton was so concerned about the liaison that he followed Donwich the night he was killed,' said Bartholomew. 'It is why he was out alone.'

Lucy sniffed. 'Well, he need not have bothered. My relationship with Master Donwich is entirely innocent, much as he might wish it was otherwise.'

'What will you say if he offers to marry you?' asked Edith curiously. 'He may, because Philip is right to say he is in your thrall. I suppose you could do worse. He is wealthy, reasonably attractive, and would at least try to make you happy.'

'And I doubt any other suitor will be brave enough to take you,' put in Chaumbre bluntly. 'Not after seeing your litigious brother destroy Narboro.'

Lucy's smile was pained. 'Your observations are irrelevant, because Donwich does not want a wife. He loves University life too much to give it up for marriage.'

'He would rather have a mistress, would he?' asked Matilde. 'I suppose he thinks that once he is Chancellor, he will abolish the statute that keeps scholars away from women.'

'He will never be Chancellor,' said Lucy, surprised she should think so. 'The vicars-general will confirm Michael's election, and poor Donwich will retreat to Clare Hall to lick his wounds. He is not like you, Matthew – prepared to sacrifice an academic career for love.'

She turned away to hide the tears in her eyes. Matilde went to comfort her, and for a while there was a tense silence. Eventually, Chaumbre broke it.

'Narboro had two black eyes when I saw him earlier,'

he said conversationally. 'I thought someone had punched him, but he claimed he had fallen down my dye-pits again.'

'He is a liar,' declared Edith. 'Ignore him, dearest. Now, tell us about these murders, Matt. Who are your suspects?'

Bartholomew listed them, although he omitted Brampton out of courtesy to Lucy.

'Donwich is not a killer,' objected Chaumbre, startled to hear his friend on the list. 'He is rude and conceited, but I do not see him resorting to violence. Of course, he did associate with Gille and Elsham, who are not very honourable. Thieves, in fact.'

'Gille certainly is,' agreed Edith. 'He stole from my warehouse. He pretended to be looking at cloth, but when he left, a spool of ribbon had disappeared. I was tempted to challenge him about it, but decided it was not worth the aggravation.'

'Stationer Weasenham thinks he filches exemplars,' put in Lucy. 'He loses several every week, nearly always after Gille has been in the shop, browsing.'

Bartholomew raised his eyebrows. 'Stasy and Hawick sell exemplars passed to them by Gille and Elsham. I wonder if they know they are handling stolen goods.'

'I imagine they do,' said Edith wryly. 'They are not very honourable either. But next time you visit Clare Hall, ask to search Gille's room. If you find Weasenham's texts, it will prove that Gille is a felon. And while you are there, look for my ribbon, too.'

'No,' said Matilde at once. 'Supposing the falling stone *was* intended for you, Matt? The killer might be anyone, and going to Clare Hall could be dangerous.'

'I was not the target,' said Bartholomew firmly. 'First, it would be a lot easier to strike when I am out alone at night, visiting patients, and second, I am sure Elsham's death is connected to his murder of Huntyngdon. There is no need to worry.'

But he could see from her anxious face that he had failed to convince her.

Clare Hall was not a happy College. Bartholomew sensed it the moment the porter opened the gate and conducted him to the conclave. It was not surprising. Aynton and Elsham were dead in suspicious circumstances, Elsham had confessed to a murder, Gille had absconded, and their Master was engaged in an unedifying dispute that entailed him being awarded the dubious title of Anti-Chancellor.

The Fellows were in the conclave, their faces lined with worry. They were sitting around the table, and it was clear that Bartholomew had interrupted an impromptu meeting. Before he could speak, there were footsteps in the corridor outside, and Donwich swept in.

'What are you all doing, gathered here so furtively?' he demanded. 'Plotting against me?' Then he saw Bartholomew and grew angrier still. 'And *you* can get out!'

'The Chancellor sent him,' said Pulham coolly. 'And if you oust him, everyone will think we have something to hide.'

Donwich regarded him haughtily. 'By "Chancellor", do you refer to that impostor Michael? I do not recognise his authority, and neither should you.'

Pulham returned his glare levelly. 'Aynton and Elsham died horribly, and Bartholomew has been appointed to investigate. If we want answers, I suggest we cooperate.'

'Let us talk to him, Master,' urged March pleadingly. 'You can go and prepare for your interview with the vicars-general instead.'

'I have no need to prepare,' retorted Donwich arrogantly. 'Michael called the election with indecent haste and then he cheated. That is all they need to know.'

The vicars-general would dismiss his claim out of hand if he took that attitude, thought Bartholomew. Then

Pulham asked what had transpired on the riverbank the previous day. Donwich had been about to stalk out, but he stayed to listen to what Bartholomew had to say.

'So Elsham confessed to stabbing Huntyngdon,' the physician finished, 'but he claimed it was a favour for a friend. Not Gille, but someone else.'

'In other words, Elsham was innocent,' said Donwich. 'A helpless victim, who was bullied into committing a crime against his will. And Gille fled in terror of his life.'

'Elsham had just four friends,' said Pulham, ignoring his Master's self-serving interpretation of events. 'Gille, Donwich, Stasy and Hawick. No one else liked him.'

'Now just a moment,' began Donwich angrily, 'I am not—'

'Gille has absconded, Master,' interrupted March sternly. 'He raced here shortly after Elsham died, packed a bag and bolted. I told him that running away smacks of a guilty conscience, but he refused to listen. Assuming he had taken refuge with Stasy and Hawick, I went to Shoemaker Row, aiming to reason with him again. He was not there.'

'We have been racking our brains for other places he might be,' Pulham told Bartholomew. 'But with no success.'

'I have it on good authority that he is a thief,' said Bartholomew. 'Perhaps *that* is why he ran – he cannot risk being questioned too closely, lest it leads to his exposure as a felon.'

'How dare you!' cried Donwich, incensed anew. 'That is slander.'

'If he is innocent, prove it by letting me search his room,' said Bartholomew, feeling he had cornered the Master rather nicely. He certainly expected to find stolen goods there, but more importantly, there might be something that would tell him where Gille had gone.

The Fellows agreed at once, although Donwich spluttered

his outrage. They ignored him and conducted Bartholomew up the stairs, their Master stamping along behind them, muttering venomously under his breath.

Gille and Elsham had occupied a pleasant room overlooking the river and the water meadows beyond. Bartholomew began to search it.

'Where is Elsham's Book of Hours?' demanded Pulham, who loved beautiful texts, and always noticed the ones other people owned. 'He kept it on this shelf, but it has gone.'

'I imagine Elsham bequeathed it to Gille,' shrugged Donwich. 'So Gille took it with him when he left. They were friends, after all.'

'No, he left it to Clare Hall,' countered Pulham. 'I drew up the deed myself. He also wanted us to have all his jewellery, but that is missing, too.'

Incensed that their College might be the victim of a crime, everyone – including Donwich – began to hunt for the items listed in Elsham's will. They were not in the room, although they did discover a spool of ribbon and a pile of exemplars under a loose floorboard.

'Just a moment!' cried Pulham, examining the find. 'Two of these exemplars are mine! I assumed a student had borrowed them to study over the summer, but now it becomes apparent that Gille took them.'

'So Gille is a thief and Elsham was a murderer,' said March heavily, and gave Donwich an unpleasant look. 'Charming men you appointed as Fellows, Master. We were right to voice our reservations, and you should have listened.'

'There must be some mistake,' blustered Donwich, struggling to conceal his dismay. 'Or more likely, a conspiracy, designed to discredit me in front of the vicars-general. Next, you will be claiming that *I* am the "friend" who ordered Elsham to kill Huntyngdon.'

'We know you would never do such a thing, Master,'

said Pulham, although Bartholomew thought his voice lacked conviction.

Then the porter appeared to announce the arrival of another visitor – Senior Proctor Brampton, resplendent in his new robes of office. Brampton listened to March's account of what had been found, then turned imperiously to Bartholomew.

'Clearly, Gille and Elsham deceived poor Donwich most grievously. However, as one is dead and the other has vanished, we shall say no more about it. The matter is closed.'

'It is *not* closed!' objected Bartholomew, astonished that Brampton should think so. 'We need to find Gille so he can be questioned. How else will we establish the identity of Elsham's so-called friend?'

'I doubt he exists,' said Brampton dismissively. 'And if he does, it will likely be Stasy or Hawick. They sell charms and spells openly now, so we know they are not respectable men. The rot is in Michaelhouse, as well as Clare Hall, so I advise you to keep your mouth shut about what you think you have discovered here.'

Bartholomew gaped at him. 'Is this how you will keep order in the University? By looking the other way when crimes are committed?'

Brampton opened his mouth to respond, but Donwich spoke first.

'You are a good friend, Brampton. I shall make you my deputy when I am Chancellor.'

Donwich took Brampton to his quarters for refreshment, taking care to let Bartholomew know that he was not invited. The snub mattered not at all to the physician, who would not have accepted anyway, but the Fellows were mortified by Donwich's shabby manners, and sought to make up for it with offers of pies, cake and ale. As he had not eaten much all day, Bartholomew accepted, and listened while they talked about the growing rift between them and their Master.

'Perhaps things will be easier now his henchmen have gone,' said March hopefully. 'He cannot intimidate us so easily without them. However, I hope Brampton does not intend to step into their shoes. I do not understand him at all. Michael promoted him, so why does he fawn over his patron's rival?'

'Hedging his bets,' said Pulham darkly, and turned to Bartholomew. 'We will write to Gille's students, asking if they know where he has gone. If we hear anything, we will inform you at once. Meanwhile, please tell Michael that we are cooperating with your investigation, and have nothing to do with whatever Gille and Elsham were embroiled in.'

'Donwich toadies to Brampton because he is Lucy's brother,' said March, refusing to let the subject drop. 'He aims to make the man his friend, so he can inveigle himself into her company more often. I hope to God this infatuation burns out soon. It is embarrassing.'

'Have you ever heard Brampton giving Donwich orders?' fished Bartholomew. 'Or making suggestions that Donwich then followed?'

'You think Brampton might be the "friend" who is the author of all this trouble,' surmised Pulham shrewdly. 'That he told *Donwich* to kill Huntyngdon, but Donwich could not do it, so he issued the order to Elsham instead.'

'Donwich has many faults, but ordering the murder of colleagues is not among them,' said March firmly. 'He is not a man for violence, as I have told you several times already.'

'Not even to please the brother of the woman he loves?' pressed Bartholomew. 'Perhaps in exchange for a promise of freer access to her?'

'Not even then. He is not a killer – just a silly man who has lost his way.'

224

Bartholomew left Clare Hall, his mind buzzing with thoughts and suspicions. It was early evening, and the intense heat was fading, leaving in its wake a sultry, reeking, sweaty stillness. He was waylaid twice when people begged him to visit victims of the flux, at which point he forgot murder and turned his mind to the spread of the disease that defied all logic. It was late when he had finished, and his route home took him along Shoemaker Row. As he was passing, he decided to visit Stasy and Hawick.

The ex-students' shop was large, freshly painted, and they had commissioned a sign to hang above the door, on which was painted the serpent-entwined staff of Asclepius, the Greek god of medicine. Bartholomew arrived at the same time as Tulyet and Dickon, who had come to investigate a complaint made against the new *medici* by Margery Starre.

'For buying her wares and passing them off as their own?' asked Bartholomew. 'Or for competing in an area where she considers herself to rule supreme?'

'For knocking her over on Bridge Street yesterday,' replied Tulyet. 'Cynric saw it happen, and agrees that it was deliberate.'

Bartholomew told him what he had learned about the murders since they had last met, while Tulyet confessed that he had made no progress at all on the death of Burgess Baldok. As they spoke, Dickon amused himself by lobbing pebbles at the sign, and succeeded in giving it several nasty dents. Neither Bartholomew nor Tulyet told him to stop.

Inside, the shop was pleasantly light and spacious. There was a large dispensary at the front, with a smaller chamber at the back, presumably for private consultations. Both smelled of the fresh rushes on the floor, while the shelves were loaded with the tools of their trade – urine flasks, astrological tables and jars containing remedies. All the pots were labelled in Latin, although a closer inspection told Bartholomew that the names were humorously fictitious and most were empty, there for show rather than actual use. The owners came to greet them.

'People will come here because they like the professional ambience,' bragged Stasy, looking around his new domain with undisguised pleasure. 'The other physicians cannot compete, so will be driven out of business.'

Tulyet laughed. 'You will steal Matt's paupers and treat them for free, will you? And most of his paying customers have been with him for years, so are unlikely to defect.'

'They will,' countered Stasy, bristling. 'I visited Master Chaumbre today, and offered him a very favourable rate. He promised to think about it.'

But Edith would never permit her husband to use another practitioner, while Chaumbre was still grateful for being fished out of the river. Bartholomew knew Stasy was lying.

'Did you rent these premises with money earned from selling stolen exemplars?' he asked, gratified when the pair blanched.

'Stolen exemplars?' pounced Tulyet. 'Now you are no longer members of the University, that sounds like a crime *I* should explore.'

'We never stole anything,' gulped Hawick. 'Gille and Elsham provided the goods – we merely sold them on to needy students.'

'Then you will not mind me looking around upstairs,' said Tulyet smoothly. 'Just to be sure that Gille has not imposed himself on you without your knowledge.'

He disappeared before they could object, taking Dickon with him. Bartholomew was left with a nervous Hawick and an angrily blustering Stasy.

'If the texts were stolen, we knew nothing about it,' Stasy declared. 'Gille assured us that everything was legally obtained. We had no reason to doubt him.'

'Other than the fact that he is an unsavoury lout,'

muttered Bartholomew. 'However, I am more interested in the fact that Elsham claimed a "friend" ordered him to murder Huntyngdon. He had four confidants, and you two comprise half of them.'

'We know nothing of murder,' cried Hawick in alarm.

'And we liked Huntyngdon,' shrugged Stasy, less easily rattled. 'We would never have done anything to harm him. Indeed, we had hoped to acquire him as a client, given that he was rich.'

'Perhaps you tried and he refused,' suggested Bartholomew. 'So you arranged his death before he could tell everyone else in King's Hall to do likewise.'

Stasy scowled. 'Now you are clutching at straws! You cannot prove such an accusation, and it is nothing but malicious conjecture.'

'Then who else had enough power over Elsham to force him to kill?' pressed Bartholomew. 'Someone who knew that he and Gille stole exemplars for you, thus threatening a lucrative source of income?'

'No one else knew – we kept it to ourselves.' Hawick winced when he realised he had just admitted that they had not been ignorant of Gille's felonious activities after all.

'Talk to Rohese Morys,' said Stasy quickly, in the hope that Bartholomew had not noticed the slip. 'Elsham's secret lover. He would have done anything for her, even though she was not very faithful in return.'

'True,' agreed Hawick, nodding vigorously. 'She was seeing Baldok at the same time – that burgess who died in the spring. There were others, too: Hugh FitzAbsolon, Doctor Rougham, Thomas Mortimer the baker . . .'

'Who else had influence over Elsham?' asked Bartholomew, more interested in the murder victim than a list of Rohese's conquests.

'Donwich,' replied Hawick spitefully. 'The Master of his College.'

'And Brother Michael,' added Stasy, a sly cant in his eyes. 'There must be some reason why he is not investigating this business himself – we all know how he loves a good murder to solve. Moreover, Donwich's challenge should not take that long to resolve, so what is he really doing in St Mary the Great with these vicars-general?'

'Gille is not here,' reported Tulyet, clattering down the stairs before Bartholomew could reply. He held a book aloft. 'But this has Elsham's name written in the front, so why was it under your bed?'

'It is Elsham's Book of Hours,' said Bartholomew, taking it from him, 'which Gille stole before he fled Clare Hall. That means he *was* here.'

'He must have sneaked in while we were out,' shrugged Stasy. 'Perhaps to apologise for involving us in his dishonest schemes. When he found we were not here, he left.'

'A likely tale,' said Tulyet contemptuously. 'You two are playing with fire, and I strongly advise you to cooperate before it is too late.'

'We *are* cooperating,' snapped Stasy. 'We are standing here with you, answering all your inane questions, are we not?'

'What is that?' asked Bartholomew suddenly, pointing to a dried toad on a shelf.

'It is used for medicine,' replied Stasy with calculated insolence.

'Not any medicine I taught you,' retorted Bartholomew. 'Or do you use it for the kind of spells that have made Margery Starre famous?'

'Witchery?' asked Tulyet coldly. 'I hope you are wrong, Matt, because I will not tolerate that sort of thing in my town. If you two are really warlocks, I shall hang you.'

'You will hang us, but turn a blind eye to Margery Starre?' demanded Stasy incredulously, a question that Bartholomew thought was actually not unreasonable.

'*She* was not expelled from the University for chanting spells in St Mary the Great,' Tulyet pointed out. 'But speaking of her, she has made a complaint against you for assault.'

'She was drunk,' Hawick declared angrily. 'She was reeling all over the place, and we were nowhere near her when she toppled over. Cynric will doubtless concoct a web of lies about it, but we speak the truth.'

'And if you are wondering why Cynric is not here,' said Stasy, with one of his aggravating smirks, 'it is because he thinks we are tending flux victims in the Griffin. We gave him the slip because we do not like him dogging our every step. He has no right to do it, so call him off before he has an accident.'

'Is that a threat?' asked Bartholomew, sure the pair would be no match for Cynric, so not unduly concerned.

'It is friendly advice,' replied Stasy smoothly. 'Tell him to desist.'

'Or we will turn *him* into a dried toad,' muttered Hawick.

'I saw you at the Great Bridge when Elsham was killed,' said Bartholomew, ignoring the bluster, although he suspected Cynric would take it seriously if he ever found out about the toad. 'Did you see who pushed the stone onto him?'

'No, because we were looking at Margery,' said Hawick. 'She was howling drunken curses at us, so we never saw what happened to Elsham.'

'You should put these questions to Donwich,' said Stasy slyly. 'Elsham and Gille talked a lot about him when they were in their cups. He is in love with Brampton's sister, and will do anything for her. Look to him for your answers, and leave us alone.'

CHAPTER 12

'You did not do as well yesterday as you did the day before, Matt,' said Michael as he led his scholars home from church the following day. 'You spent too much time with patients, and too little time chasing the killer.'

'The flux is important, too,' objected Bartholomew. 'Look at Meadowman – there was a point when I thought he might die.'

'But he did not, and now he assures me that he will soon be fit enough to return to work, for which I am inordinately grateful, as we are seriously short of beadles. But we should discuss your investigation, as neither of us has time to waste today.'

'There are rumours about why the vicars-general are taking so much time with you,' warned Bartholomew, who had been regaled with them when he had visited the sick. 'As opposed to Donwich, whose audience with them was over in a few moments.'

Michael's smile was strained. 'There is nothing I can do about that. I wish I could tell you more, but as I have said before, I am sworn to secrecy. Now, the murders. I assume we have a single culprit, who dispatched Aynton and Elsham, and convinced Elsham to stab Huntyngdon. So, who remains on our list?'

'Well, not Chaumbre and Gille,' said Bartholomew, 'given that they were on the ferry with Elsham at the time. Although Gille disappeared with suspicious haste and there is something about Chaumbre that continues to bother me . . .'

'But those concerns may have nothing to do with our investigation: Gille likely fled because he is a thief, and

Chaumbre might well be hiding something, but if he is, it will probably relate to some dubious business dealings.'

Bartholomew raised his eyebrows. 'Is that supposed to make me feel better?'

'Yes, it is. All merchants dabble on the wrong side of the law – they cannot help themselves – but dishonesty is not murder, so put Chaumbre from your mind for now. So who else can we cross off the list? Narboro?'

Bartholomew nodded. 'He was not in Cambridge when Huntyngdon was stabbed. Ergo, the remaining suspects are Donwich, Stasy, Hawick, Brampton, Shardelowe, Morys and Martyn, if he is alive. Five who can lay claim to being a *litteratus*, and two who cannot.'

Michael sighed. 'If only Aynton had spoken a little more clearly with his dying breath. We might have solved this by now.'

'Of course, there may be others we have not yet considered,' Bartholomew went on. 'You said you would ask the beadles to look for witnesses to Elsham's death. Did you?'

'Yes, but it transpires that everyone was watching the children run amok.'

'Chaumbre thinks that was a diversion,' recalled Bartholomew. 'Ulf is their leader, and he will do anything for money, so it is possible. I will speak to him today.'

'Will he cooperate? The Godenaves have a bad reputation, and Ulf is the worst of them all. He knifed a beadle last year. It was a glancing wound, but the intention to kill was there.'

'Then why is he still free?' asked Bartholomew, shocked. Ulf could not be more than eight, which was young for so serious a crime.

'Because Morys paid a clever lawyer to defend him – claimed he was protecting an innocent child against the unequal might of the University. However, I suspect they share some felonious past, which the Godenaves threatened to reveal unless he intervened.'

231

'Morys and a family of felons,' mused Bartholomew. 'Interesting.'

'Very, so bear it in mind when you corner Ulf. Now, you did not visit the Brazen George yesterday to confirm Gille's alibi for Huntyngdon's murder, so do that first, then speak to Ulf. After that, interview Morys again – he claims he was on town business when Aynton died, but they quarrelled that afternoon so we should press him for more details.'

'Very well.'

'And bear in mind that Elsham was making a cuckold of him.'

'Stasy and Hawick suggested questioning Donwich more forcefully,' Bartholomew told him. 'He has never been likeable, but he has grown greedier, nastier and more ambitious since he was elected Master of Clare Hall. He is still at the top of my list. Him and Brampton, who transpire to be better friends than we realised.'

'Brampton is wooing him because he hopes Clare Hall will relent and pay its share of the bridge money,' said Michael. 'But, I accept your reservations, and I will speak to him this morning. I shall see if I can escape the vicars-general for an hour to tackle Donwich, too.'

'Then let us hope that one of us solves the mystery today, Brother, because there are only five days left before term ends. I would rather spend them teaching.'

You and me both,' muttered Michael.

It was another swelteringly hot day, and Henry the peacock coped by remaining inside the porter's lodge, where there was a cool stone floor to sit on. The bird stirred himself when a delivery arrived for Cynric, though, and the yard rang with his shrill cries.

'It is a spell from Margery Starre,' Cynric told Zoone and Bartholomew, both of whom had come running to see if Michaelhouse was about to be invaded by Stasy and Hawick. 'To change the weather.'

232

'You should have saved your money, Cynric,' said Zoone. 'Because it will rain tomorrow anyway. And as it is St Swithun's Day, the downpour will continue for forty days.'

'Exactly!' said Cynric. 'We do not want floods on the heels of a drought, so this spell will make sure we get a nice gentle drizzle, not a ferocious deluge.'

'Regardless, rain of any description will hinder progress on the bridge,' said Zoone. 'Such work is always more difficult in inclement weather. When I was building a drain in Linton . . . well, you do not want to hear about slippery planks and watery cement.'

'Linton?' pounced Bartholomew. 'Did you meet a glazier there, who makes mirrors?'

'I did,' said Zoone. 'He is reputed to be the best in the country. Why? Do you want one for Matilde as a wedding gift? If so, you have left it too late – they take a while to craft.'

Bartholomew told him about Narboro's alibi for Huntyngdon's murder, and was pleased when Zoone offered to write to the glazier for confirmation of the tale. Then Michael bustled up, all angry indignation.

'I shall have to accompany you to the Brazen George, Matt,' he said crossly. 'Agatha has just confessed to polluting my morning pottage with vegetables.' He shuddered. 'I cannot manipulate the vicars-general with that rubbish inside me. I need meat.'

'What is wrong with vegetables?' asked Zoone, bemused.

'They are dangerous,' stated Michael in a tone that brooked no argument. 'They fester in the heat and have a tendency to explode.'

Bartholomew laughed. 'Where do you *get* these "facts", Brother?'

Michael elected not to reply, and shouted for William instead. The friar was informing the undergraduates that he could have won the debate on gluttony the previous

233

day, if he had not been tricked into admitting that he committed each different kind on a regular basis.

'What?' barked William, irked to be summoned while correcting the misunderstanding that caused students to smirk and pat their stomachs whenever they saw him.

'Something urgent has come up,' lied Michael. 'So you must preside at breakfast.'

'Good,' said William grimly. 'Then we shall see who is a glutton.'

The Brazen George was a cut above most Cambridge taverns, because its food and ale were of high quality, and Landlord Lister only served patrons he deemed to be respectable. It was Michael's favourite establishment, and because he was such a regular customer, a chamber was set aside for his exclusive use. It was a convenient perk, as it was difficult for the monk to fine other scholars for frequenting taverns if he was seen doing it himself.

Grumbling that the ground was so hot that it was burning through his sandals, Michael hurried to the High Street, Bartholomew at his side. He glanced around to make sure no one was looking, then slipped down the lane that led to the tavern's back door. Once inside, he opened the door to his private room – and stopped dead in his tracks.

'I thought you would be unable to resist the lure of this place for long,' drawled Donwich, who had made himself comfortable in Michael's favourite chair.

Lister stood behind him, wringing his hands in distress. 'I am sorry, Brother. I tried to stop him, but he shoved past me.'

Donwich smirked nastily. 'I wanted to see your nasty little den for myself, so I can report every detail to the vicars-general. Teofle, Ely and Tinmouth will have plenty to say about your hypocrisy, I am sure.'

Michael smiled sweetly. 'Perhaps, although you should

be aware that it was Teofle's idea. He has an identical arrangement in Canterbury – a tavern that is always available for confidential meetings or solitary contemplation. He recommended years ago that I should do the same here, and maintains it is the only way busy men can keep their sanity.'

Donwich's face underwent a gamut of emotions within a very short space of time: astonishment, shock, anger and disbelief. 'You lie,' he said eventually.

'Then ask him,' shrugged Michael. 'But be careful how you do it, because he will not take kindly to sanctimonious criticism. Well? What are you waiting for? If you leave now, you will catch him breaking his fast in King's Hall.'

Donwich stood reluctantly. 'I . . .'

'Is there anything else or may Matt and I discuss how to proceed with these nasty murders? Aynton and Elsham were members of your College, so you must want answers.'

'You will not talk about that,' sneered Donwich, struggling to regain his composure. 'You are just here to gorge. And while we are on the subject of Elsham, let me tell you now that he had nothing to do with Huntyngdon's unfortunate demise. Bartholomew fabricated this so-called confession to embarrass Clare Hall.'

Manfully, Bartholomew fought down his indignation at the insult. 'He knew details about the crime that only the killer could have had.'

'Now we must identify the "friend" who urged him to do it,' said Michael, and eyed Donwich meaningfully.

'Well, it was not me,' said Donwich firmly. 'I barely knew Huntyngdon.'

'Then tell us about the night that Aynton died. You cannot prove your whereabouts, although we understand that you returned to your College in a state of high agitation.'

'I did *not* kill Aynton,' declared Donwich, growing angry. 'I liked him.'

Michael raised his eyebrows. 'But he offended you by refusing to support your candidacy for the chancellorship, and he went out the night he died to catch you in a compromising position with Lucy.'

'My relationship with her is chaste,' snapped Donwich, although he blushed like a schoolboy at the mention of her name. 'And my personal life is none of your business, so keep your vile insinuations to yourself. Brampton will be livid when I tell him you besmirch his sister's good name.'

'I do nothing of the kind,' said Michael irritably. 'I merely remind you that Aynton knew about your friendship with her, and he was killed when he went out to expose it.'

'Have you had any thoughts about where Gille might have gone, now you have had time to reflect?' asked Bartholomew, when Donwich had no reply.

Donwich regarded him with dislike. 'If I had, I would not tell you. You will concoct lies to see *him* accused of crimes he did not commit, too.'

'We have no need to concoct lies,' said Michael sharply. 'Not with the evidence he left behind in his room. And do not accuse Matt of planting it there – most of it was found by your own Fellows. Or are you saying that they are dishonest, too?'

Donwich scowled. 'I shall dismiss the lot of them when I am Chancellor. And the vicars-general *will* uphold my challenge – I have never been more sure of anything in my life. If you have any sense, Brother, you will resign before they oust you in disgrace.'

Amusement sparked briefly in Michael's eyes. 'We shall see.'

Donwich regarded him suspiciously. 'Yet you do not respond by suggesting that *I* withdraw instead. Why not? What are you plotting in that sly mind of yours?'

'Just go, Donwich,' said Michael, suddenly tired of sparring with him. 'I have neither the time nor the inclination to bandy words with you. Lister? See him to the front door.'

As being ejected directly on to the High Street would attract unwanted attention, Donwich turned abruptly and scuttled through the back entrance before Lister could oblige.

'Perhaps you *should* have told him to withdraw,' said Bartholomew when Donwich had gone. 'Then the vicars-general can go home, leaving you to investigate the murders yourself.'

'He has a right for his claim to be heard,' shrugged Michael, and turned his attention to ordering one of his gargantuan feasts.

'Are you satisfied with the answers Donwich gave?' asked Bartholomew, once they were alone. 'Because I am not. A flat denial is hardly evidence of innocence.'

'No,' agreed Michael, 'and I shall tackle him again later. But he disconcerted me by invading my sanctuary, and I was not really ready for him. I will be next time.'

Lister was used to Michael being in a hurry, and the table was soon loaded with bread and meat, which the monk began to devour more quickly than was healthy. When the landlord lingered, gabbling more apologies for allowing such an unpalatable guest to bully his way inside, Bartholomew took the opportunity to question him about Gille's alibi.

'He most certainly was not here the night that Huntyngdon went missing,' declared Lister indignantly. 'I do not want his sort as a customer, thank you very much! He and Elsham are thieves.'

'How do you know?' asked Bartholomew, taken aback by his vehemence.

'Because I saw them steal exemplars from Stationer Weasenham with my own eyes.'

Michael looked up from his repast. 'Then why did you not report them to me?'

'They threatened to burn down my tavern if I did. But now one is dead and the other has vanished, I am free to speak the truth.'

'So why did Elsham say Gille was here?' wondered Bartholomew, bemused.

'I was busy that night, so I imagine he did not expect me to recall whom I served,' replied Lister. 'But he underestimated me, because I *always* remember when undesirables invade my domain. I repeat: neither Gille nor Elsham was here.'

'Your busy night explains why Elsham chose the Brazen George for his lie,' said Bartholomew. 'But not why he gave Gille a false alibi in the first place.'

'As a last act of friendship,' surmised Michael. 'He knew his confession meant we would question Gille – the man who was "more brother than friend" to him. However, now we know he lied, it is even more important that we find Gille and discover what role *he* played in Huntyngdon's demise.'

While he finished eating, Michael was distracted and uncommunicative, his mind on the looming encounter with the vicars-general. The moment the last platter was empty, he hurried away to St Mary the Great, while Bartholomew went in search of Ulf.

As he was passing, he stopped to spend a moment with Matilde. He opened her door, and his stomach gave a little flip when he saw her brushing her hair in front of a mirror. She really was beautiful, he thought, and wondered again why she had agreed to marry him when she could have had so many others.

'You look hot and out of sorts,' she said, turning to smile at him. 'Is something wrong?'

'Just the murders,' he sighed. 'And the pressure of solving them while Michael is busy with the vicars-general.'

'I have every confidence in you,' said Matilde, taking

his hands in hers. They were cool and soft. 'No sly killer will best you, so do not worry. And everything will be better tomorrow, when this wretched heatwave will end.'

'How do you know that?' he asked, startled. 'Did Margery Starre tell you? Or Zoone?'

Matilde laughed, and the sheer bubbling joy of it made Bartholomew's stomach lurch again. 'They have many talents, but predicting the weather is not among them. No, I know because I saw clouds in the south-west this morning. That always heralds a change, and—'

She was interrupted by a sudden clamour in the street outside, and opened the door to see Morys involved in a fierce altercation with Shardelowe. Unsurprisingly, it concerned money. The quarrel had already attracted onlookers, including some of Bartholomew's suspects, so he supposed it was as good a time as any to observe them unseen.

First, there was Donwich, oddly solitary without his henchmen. His eyes were fixed on Lucy who stood with her brother, his expression one of almost frantic passion. He was arrogant, ambitious and ruthless, and Bartholomew suspected that he *had* known about his Fellows' felonious antics, but had chosen to overlook them, despite his denials to the contrary. Did that mean he had ordered Elsham to kill, too? But why would he do such a thing? Because Aynton had written something unflattering about him in the letter Huntyngdon was to deliver to Narboro?

Next to Lucy, Brampton was trying to order scholars home, lest the spat degenerated into a brawl. None took any notice, and Bartholomew wondered again why Michael had promoted him to Senior Proctor. He might be a talented administrator and good at collecting money, but it needed more than that to keep order in the University.

Not far away, Stasy and Hawick were using the opportunity to tout for business. They had written a résumé of their skills on small squares of parchment, which they handed to anyone who they thought might be literate. Although Bartholomew had taught them for years, the last few days proved that he had not known them at all. A week ago, he would have said they could not be killers. Now he was far from sure.

'Look at Narcissus Narboro,' whispered Matilde. 'He has disguised his bruises so well with face-paints that they are barely visible. I must ask him how he did it. If he can hide injuries so consummately, imagine what he could do for wrinkles and sagging skin.'

But Bartholomew's attention was taken by the burgeoning spat.

'You promised to pay for materials as they arrive,' yelled Shardelowe, waving the document that proved it – the one that Gille had drawn up using ink stolen from Michael's office. 'Now you renege. We have four barges of cobbles waiting, but none will be unloaded until you give us the money.'

'The delay will hurt you more than me,' shrugged Morys. 'You will lose your bonus if you fail to complete the work by the time agreed. And I *cannot* pay the bargemen today, because the money is still being counted. Is that not so, John?'

He turned to his cousin, who was fingering a sword. Shardelowe started forward angrily, but his assistants Bernarde and Lyonnes grabbed his arms to stop him, aware that attacking an armed knight was rash, even if the builder was too blinded by rage to see it.

'Then give us what *has* been counted,' said Lyonnes, struggling to hold the furious Shardelowe. 'Because you cannot break a legally binding contract.'

'I will do what is best for the town,' declared Morys loftily. 'Now get back to work, or I shall shave ten per cent off what we pay you when you finish.'

'No!' spluttered Shardelowe, outraged anew. 'This is not how business is done.'

'He is right, Morys,' said Bernarde, his voice quiet and eminently reasonable. 'You cannot change an agreement once it is in writing.'

'And if you do, we will walk away and leave you without a bridge at all,' blustered Shardelowe. 'It will not be long before you *beg* us to come back.'

'Cambridge men do not beg,' averred Morys loftily. 'Besides, you will not leave. Not only have you invested a lot of your own money in this scheme, but abandoning a job halfway through will ensure that you are never hired again.'

'You are not the only one who can destroy reputations,' yelled Shardelowe, beside himself with rage. 'No builder will ever finish your bridge, because *I* shall put it about that you are all cheats and liars, not to be trusted.'

'Gentlemen, please,' said Bernarde, raising one hand in a gesture of peace. 'There is no need for harsh words. We can resolve—'

'I will cut out your tongue for slandering my town, Shardelowe,' hissed Morys viciously, and turned to his cousin. 'Well? Go on, John. Do it!'

No one found out whether John would have obliged, because there was a flurry of movement, and Tulyet and Dickon arrived to separate the two factions. Dickon held a dagger, but Tulyet did not need steel to impose his will on anyone. John backed off at once, and so did Bernarde, pulling Shardelowe with him. Unfortunately, Morys's last threat had been one too many for Lyonnes. He released Shardelowe's arm and drew a knife.

'Out of my way, boy,' he snarled at Dickon. 'I am going to teach this bastard a lesson.'

'You?' sneered Morys, although he ducked smartly behind John for safety. 'You are a worm, beneath my contempt.'

'Worm, am I?' screeched Lyonnes furiously, and waved

the knife in a way that made it obvious he did not know what to do with it now it was out.

'Slice out *his* tongue, Lyonnes,' yelled Shardelowe, fighting to free himself from Bernarde. 'He is a liar. Hearing his voice is an affront to honest ears.'

Morys addressed the watching crowd. 'Everything I do is for you, to ensure your taxes are used wisely. Or should I let these rogues fleece us?'

Lyonnes was red with rage. He darted forward, but to reach Morys, he had to get past first Dickon and then John. The boy blanched in fright at the sight of an armed man bearing down on him. He dropped his dagger and struggled to draw his sword. It hissed from its scabbard, and more by luck than skill, managed to knock the blade from Lyonnes' hand. Seeing him defenceless, Dickon went after him with more confidence, driving him back with a series of increasingly fancy swipes.

'Enough, Dickon,' said Tulyet hastily, before there was a mishap. 'Sheathe your weapon. You have made your point.'

'Yes, sheathe your weapon, Devil's spawn,' snarled Lyonnes, determined to have the last word. 'And if you come near me again, I will plant a blade in your nasty little gizzard.'

'If you try, I shall chop off your stupid head,' countered Dickon, his face dark with indignation. 'My sword is sharp enough. I hone it for hours every night.'

Lyonnes' response was to spit on the ground at Dickon's feet, and stalk away. Livid, Dickon made as if to follow, but Tulyet forbade it with a few sharp words. Dickon wavered, and for one horrifying moment, Bartholomew thought the time had finally come when the boy defied his father and did what he pleased. But Tulyet fixed him with a steely glare, and Dickon slid his sword back in its sheath, albeit with very ill grace.

'Show me the contract, Shardelowe,' ordered Tulyet,

242

turning to the builder. 'If Morys did agree to pay for supplies as they arrive, then that is what will happen.'

'Now just a moment,' objected Morys. 'It has nothing to do with you, Sheriff. You cannot come here and start dictating—'

'Some of the bridge money came from the King,' interrupted Tulyet sharply. 'And I am his representative. So, unless you want to challenge *his* authority, I suggest you shut up.'

Ignoring Morys's furious glower, he took the document and held it so that Dickon could read it, too. The boy's lips moved as he struggled to decipher the first few words, but he soon gave up and went to brag to John about his 'defeat of the murderous Frenchman'. Everyone else watched Tulyet, and Bartholomew was not the only one holding his breath for the verdict. Eventually, the Sheriff handed the contract back.

'Shardelowe is right,' he said. 'So Morys will provide payment for these cobbles by the end of the day. Any money-counting should be finished by then, so there can be no reason to defer it any longer. Agreed?'

Shardelowe opened his mouth to say he wanted it there and then, but Bernarde pulled him away before he could prolong the confrontation. Morys scowled at Tulyet, then stalked off in the opposite direction.

'Dickon really is horrible,' murmured Matilde to Bartholomew, watching the boy draw his sword again and strut about importantly in the hope of being noticed by Rohese Morys. 'Obviously, I do not believe he is the Devil's son, but, even so, I shall be glad when he goes a-killing in France.'

'So will he,' said Bartholomew.

The physician lingered outside Matilde's house for some time after the spat was over, because it had happened on her doorstep, and he wanted to make sure it did not reignite. Tulyet and Dickon also stayed, and so did Brampton. The Senior Proctor should have ordered the remaining scholars home, but he chose instead to corner Father Aiden and demand Maud's Hostel's share of the University's contribution to the bridge.

'Michael's replacement is useless,' declared Dickon, watching in disdain. 'I bet you anything that he will not have the bridge money by Wednesday. Some scholars will refuse to pay it, and he does not know how to make them. Perhaps *I* should show him.'

He drew his sword yet again, and began to practise more of the moves he had learned from John. Tulyet did not order him to desist, because the sight of Dickon with a naked blade was driving the last of the spectators away rather nicely.

'I cannot imagine what Morys thought he was doing,' Tulyet said to Bartholomew. 'He was in the wrong and he knew it. All I hope is that his needless aggravation of the builders does not leave us with a sub-standard bridge.'

'I think we might get one of those anyway,' said Bartholomew. 'How can it be otherwise when the work proceeds at such a breakneck speed?'

'Perhaps that is why Lyonnes is so bad tempered,' put in Dickon, still waving his sword around. 'He is tired and needs to rest.'

'I wonder what they are talking about,' said Tulyet, nodding to where Chaumbre and Shardelowe were deep in conversation.

He started to stride towards them, but the builder saw him coming and hurried away.

'We were discussing my dye-pits,' said Chaumbre with a pleasant smile when the Sheriff put the question. 'He thinks it is a pity such handsome structures must be filled in.'

'Is that why you procrastinate?' asked Tulyet, startled. 'You like the workmanship in the things? Well, I am afraid you will have to grit your teeth and bear it, Chaumbre, because they are an eyesore and a danger.'

'I disagree,' objected Chaumbre. 'However, a consignment of alum arrived this morning, and I must see to it at once, as it is worth a lot of money. I shall deal with the pits as soon as I have a spare moment.'

He bowed and took his leave. Tulyet watched him go.

'I know he is your kin, Matt, but there is something odd about that man. For a start, I do not understand why he smiles all the time. It is hardly normal. And I do not believe that Shardelowe was admiring his holes in the ground.'

Unhappily, Bartholomew was inclined to agree.

It was unfortunate that Bartholomew did not corner Morys immediately after the spat on the High Street, because he reached the Mayor's fine mansion only to learn that the man had already left town on business. Rohese told him that her husband planned to spend the night away, but would return in the morning.

'Perhaps you should take the opportunity to leave yourself,' said Bartholomew. 'Your child will begin to show soon.'

Rohese rested a hand on her belly and smiled. 'I will go in a day or two. I have decided to settle in Oxford, because I have always enjoyed the company of scholars.'

Bartholomew had no more luck with finding Ulf, as the boy's entire gang had gone to Girton's summer fair. He considered following them there, but the event would be crowded, and it would be almost impossible to identify the right brats. Stumped, he decided to visit the Great Bridge, in the hope that one of the workmen might have remembered something useful since he had last spoken to them.

He arrived to see that corners galore had been cut in an effort to speed the work along: scaffolding was not secured properly, stones were stacked in unstable piles, and there were dangerous practices involving heavy equipment. Then there was the *ponticulus*, which the workmen had pressed into service as a makeshift platform – it was in the wrong position for such a function, resulting in a lot of precarious reaching and leaning. It was only a matter of time before someone fell off it.

'We have no time for that,' barked Shardelowe, when Bartholomew suggested he implement some basic safety measures; he was with his two lieutenants, and they had been discussing cement. 'Not if we are to win our bonus.'

'It is better to lose money than a life,' argued Bartholomew. 'Your men—'

'They are paid extra for the danger, and they know the risks,' interrupted Shardelowe shortly. 'Now, leave us alone. We are busy.'

'But thank you for your concern,' put in Bernarde, the polite face of the operation.

Lyonnes spat. 'He can stick his concern up his—'

'Did you see what happened when Elsham was killed?' interrupted Bartholomew. 'You have a good view of the ferry from up here and—'

'We have already told you: none of us pushed the stone,' snarled Lyonnes, evidently a man to see accusations and insults everywhere. 'Why would we? We never met Elsham.'

'It is possible that it was not intended for him,' said Bartholomew. 'It might just have been aimed at the boat.'

'We have no reason to damage the ferries,' said Bernarde, more consiliatory than his colleagues. 'They are useful to us – if they did not carry folk across the river, we would have to keep the *ponticulus* open, which would slow us down.'

Bartholomew was becoming exasperated. 'A man was murdered in a place that teemed with people – you three, your entire workforce, ferry passengers *and* onlookers – but not one of you saw who shoved the rock on Elsham. It beggars belief!'

'Does it?' demanded Lyonnes. 'Then why did *you* notice nothing? You were there – I saw you myself. *You* did not see who tampered with the stone, so why do you expect us to?'

It was a reasonable point.

'It was the brats' fault,' said Shardelowe bitterly. 'They were lobbing missiles and larking about on the *ponticulus*. All our attention was on them, and the first thing I knew about the falling stone was when I heard it land.'

'But the children did not push it,' put in Bernarde. 'None of them are strong enough. Besides, while some were on the *ponticulus*, I saw none on the bridge itself.'

'Yet the stone *did* come from the bridge,' Bartholomew pointed out. 'And as no one other than your people should have been there, the guilty party must have stood out like a sore thumb.'

Shardelowe glared at him. '*You* go up there and see if *you* can spot an intruder through that forest of planks and ropes. It would have been easy for a killer to hide. But do not blame us for it – we cannot be expected to know that our scaffolding would attract murderers.'

'Morys,' spat Lyonnes. '*He* hired those brats to make a nuisance of themselves. He wanted to slow us down, so the town will not have to pay our bonus.'

Bartholomew would not put it past him. 'Do you think he arranged for the stone to fall as well? I imagine Elsham's death has cost you time.'

'We made sure it did not,' said Shardelowe. 'But it is certainly possible that your Mayor thinks that a life is a small price to pay for cheating us of our due.'

'Those children,' said Bernarde thoughtfully. 'Their play did not seem natural to me. They appeared uneasy, frightened even. Not Ulf, perhaps, but the others. If you speak to them, go gently. They may not have been acting of their own free will.'

'What nonsense!' exclaimed Lyonnes contemptuously.

'But have you finished interrogating us now, physician? We have work to do.'

Bartholomew spoke to as many labourers as would answer his questions, but learned nothing new. None could shed light on Elsham's murder, they had not noticed Huntyngdon washed up on the riverbank until Bartholomew himself had raised the alarm, and no one had anything to say about Aynton. The process took far longer than it should have done, because most took the opportunity to present him with their aches, pains, cuts and bruises while he was there. Thus daylight was fading into night when he eventually finished.

As he turned to leave, he bumped into Shardelowe again, and as he had forgotten to do it earlier, asked what he had discussed with Chaumbre shortly after his row with Morys.

'I did not speak to Chaumbre,' replied Shardelowe shiftily. 'You are mistaken.'

Bartholomew blinked. 'But I saw you!'

The builder sighed irritably. 'Perhaps we exchanged greetings – I do not recall. My mind was on more important matters – like getting paid.'

'You did not admire the craftsmanship in his dye-pits?'

It was Shardelowe's turn to look startled. 'You mean the holes in the cemetery? Why would I do that?'

He stalked away, leaving Bartholomew confused and uneasy. Both the builder and Chaumbre had lied about the encounter, but why? He found himself fearful for Edith, and wondered if she would agree to move in with Matilde for a few days. He could always use being on hand for wedding arrangements as a pretext to convince her.

In the hope that Ulf and his cronies had returned from the fair, Bartholomew took Isnard's ferry across the river and walked to the hovels that stood around derelict All

Saints' Church. When he heard the sound of smashing, he went to look over the graveyard wall. Sure enough, the children were there, hurling stones at the few remaining panes of glass in the nave windows.

There were perhaps a dozen of them, all barefoot and dressed in rags. They regarded him with wary suspicion, although Ulf swaggered forward, brimming with audacity and confidence. He sported the new hat that Bartholomew had noticed the day before, which was so large that he had stuffed leaves in it to prevent it from falling over his eyes.

'It was a gift,' said Ulf defiantly, seeing Bartholomew look at it.

'From the Carmelite Friary, like the shoes you offered to give me the other day?' asked Bartholomew archly, and when Ulf looked blank, added, 'As payment for helping your grandmother. Did no one ever teach you that liars need a good memory?'

Ulf glared at him. 'No, the hat came from someone else. I do not have to tell you who. My father says the University has no power over us, and that if all the scholars were to leave, the rest of us would live like kings in your Colleges and hostels.'

'Is that so?' said Bartholomew flatly, and turned to his enquiries. 'You were by the bridge when Elsham was killed. Did you see who pushed the stone on him?'

'No, because we were playing,' replied Ulf insolently. 'A game – we run across the *ponticulus*, and the workmen see if they can catch us. They never do, because we are too quick.'

'They do not see it as a game,' warned Bartholomew. 'And it is dangerous. One of you might be hurt. Do not do it again.'

'We will if we want to,' flashed Ulf, although his cronies were silent, and Bartholomew was under the impression that they would happily take the advice if their leader had been anyone other than Ulf. 'You cannot stop us.'

'*You* were not on the *ponticulus* though,' said Bartholomew, declining to argue. 'You were on the riverbank, throwing mud. It was—'

'I got Isnard,' crowed Ulf. 'Right on the arse! It was a perfect shot.'

He did a little dance, drumming his feet on the ground and waving his arms in the air, while the other children watched with closed, expressionless faces.

'Did someone pay you to do it?' asked Bartholomew. 'And perhaps give you a signal, so you would know when to start?'

'Pay?' asked one of the others sharply. Bartholomew recognised him as Isaac de Blaston, one of Yolande's brood. She would not be pleased to learn he was keeping company with the likes of Ulf Godenave. 'You mean someone gave you money?'

'Or a hat,' replied Bartholomew pointedly.

'Well, no one gave *us* anything,' said Isaac, and shot Ulf a reproachful glare.

'Were you forced to play at the bridge?' asked Bartholomew, carefully excluding Ulf from the question. 'Bullied or frightened into doing it?'

'I am not frightened of nothing,' declared Ulf before the others could reply. 'And no one tells me what to do neither. I do what I please, when I please, how I please. Ask anyone. Now, sod off. And if you come here again, I will stab you with a knife. I know where I can get one.'

Bartholomew was reluctant to press the matter when it was clear that none of the children were going to talk as long as Ulf was there. He went home.

250

CHAPTER 13

The next day was the Feast of St Swithun, and dawn revealed a sky that was an unnatural ochre hue. Then it began to rain, a modest downpour that still managed to turn the dust of the streets to a sticky brown paste. Bartholomew could not summon the energy to celebrate the end of the drought, because he had been called out several times in the night to individuals who felt the flux might kill them without his immediate intervention. He was tired and disconsolate, painfully aware that he was no closer to understanding – or preventing – the sickness than when it had first manifested itself.

As he trudged home from tending a patient near the King's Ditch, he saw Ulf and his cronies merrily flinging mud at passers-by. Most folk were too glad to see rain to object, much to Ulf's disappointment. Prior Pechem received a clod of mire in the chest, but when all he did was sketch a genial blessing, Ulf's temper broke. He hurled his new hat at the departing friar and bawled obscenities that had jaws dropping all down the High Street.

Bartholomew arrived at Michaelhouse to find Walter in a foul temper, because someone – almost certainly Stasy, Hawick, or someone in their thrall – had tried to feed his poultry mouldy grain in the hope that it would make them sicken and die. Fortunately, the birds had become fussy eaters under Walter's doting care, and had declined to touch it.

'Are you fully recovered now?' Bartholomew asked him. 'The flux has gone?'

'Enough to let me protect my birds,' said Walter grimly. 'And if anyone tries to poison them again, they will have

251

me to answer to. Of course, I doubt they will attempt it in the next forty days, because it will be far too wet for mischief.'

'Time is running out, Matt,' said Michael anxiously at breakfast not long after. 'It is Tuesday today, and we *must* have answers by Saturday. What if the culprit is a scholar? He may leave, never to return. Aynton deserves justice, and so does Elsham, even if he was a killer himself.'

'I do not understand what is causing the flux, and it is not relinquishing its hold,' said Bartholomew, wrapped up in his own worries. 'There were ten new cases last night – or ten people who called me for help; the actual figure is likely to be much higher – but all I can do is recommend boiled barley water and rest.'

Michael was sympathetic. 'You look as though you could do with some rest yourself.'

'So do you. I saw you return home long after midnight.'

'The business with the vicars-general is more complex than I anticipated.' Michael rubbed bloodshot eyes. 'I had hoped to finish in a day or two, so I could join you in solving the murders, but I fear I shall be tied up for days yet.'

Bartholomew frowned his exasperation. 'I do not understand why whatever you are doing with them is taking so much time. You have never let University business interfere with a murder enquiry before.'

'But I am Chancellor now,' sighed Michael, so heavily that Bartholomew knew he was wondering whether his decision to stand for the post had been the right one. 'I do not have the freedom I enjoyed as Senior Proctor.'

'Such limitations do not seem to bother Donwich. Can you not press the vicars-general to make a quick decision about him? Having an Anti-Chancellor marching around, causing strife and issuing orders that no one wants to follow, is becoming tiresome.'

Michael grinned. 'Which means our colleagues will be even more delighted when the vicars-general send him packing.'

'So when will they? It should not take them long to see his claims are groundless.'

'No,' acknowledged Michael. 'But who should be Chancellor is not the only matter they must decide, as I think you have deduced. I cannot say more, much as I would like to confide in you. Just know that it is important, and that it suits me to have the decision about Donwich delayed for a while.'

'Justice for Aynton and Elsham is important, too.'

'Yes,' agreed Michael, 'which is why I so desperately need your help. You *must* catch this killer before we break for the end of term.'

'I will do my best. However, I only have two more leads to follow, and if they transpire to be dead ends, I shall not know what else to try.'

'What leads?'

'Morys, although I have interrogated him before with no success, so doing it again is likely to be futile. And young Isaac de Blaston – I need to catch him when Ulf is not there.'

'Corner Isaac first,' instructed Michael. 'Now what about Martyn? Have you learned anything new about him?'

Bartholomew was thoughtful. 'Aynton knew that Narboro had gone to Linton, so he almost certainly asked Huntyngdon to take the letter there – not a local delivery, but one involving a lengthy ride. Perhaps he gave another missive to Martyn, and Martyn is still in the process of delivering it to its distant recipient.'

'Possibly,' acknowledged Michael. 'Although the guards on the gates did not see him leave the town. We shall only know the truth if he reappears – dead or alive.'

'I have a bad feeling it will be dead, and that Gille is

the killer,' said Bartholomew soberly. 'Elsham lied about Gille being in the Brazen George when Huntyngdon was stabbed. Perhaps Gille was dealing with Martyn while Elsham dispatched Huntyngdon.'

'I hope you are wrong.'

'So do I, but Gille's flight suggests otherwise. It was not the thefts that drove him away, because he had been stealing exemplars for a while – he ran when Elsham was murdered. Perhaps he was afraid he would be next.'

'He fled to Stasy and Hawick after packing a bag at Clare Hall,' mused Michael. 'So, could one of them be the "friend" who urged Elsham to kill? I had assumed neither was man enough to order a lout like Elsham around, but . . .'

'Them or Donwich, Morys, Brampton or Shardelowe. Those are our only remaining suspects. However, I think the key to understanding everything is Aynton's letter – or letters.'

'Or the bridge,' countered Michael. 'Aynton was killed *on* it; Huntyngdon's body was found *near* it and his murderer was killed *under* it; and Shardelowe is *rebuilding* it, having won the commission by conniving with Morys.'

'Baldok was killed on it, too,' said Bartholomew. 'And Dick still has not given up hope of justice for him.'

'Of course, if I am right,' Michael went on, 'we shall have to cross Donwich, Stasy and Hawick off our list. They have no connection to the bridge whatsoever.'

'On the contrary, it was Donwich's loud mouth at the guildhall that forced scholars to pay more towards its repairs, while my old students will need a good working bridge if their practice is to thrive – a lot of rich townsfolk live north of the river.'

'Then you had better visit them again today, and see what you can shake loose. Do it after you have spoken to Yolande's boy.'

*

254

Bartholomew left the College in an anxious frame of mind, worried about the flux, a murder investigation that he felt was well beyond his ability to solve, his sister's marriage to a man he did not know or understand, and the fact that in four days, he would leave the University and never teach again.

Then he thought about Matilde's school for women and smiled. But of course he would teach, and it would be just as rewarding as educating men. More so, perhaps, as her pupils would enrol because they had a genuine thirst for knowledge, not because they wanted to make fortunes from calculating horoscopes and compiling astrological tables for wealthy hypochondriacs.

It was drizzling as he walked to the de Blaston house, although the rain had done nothing to cool things down. He arrived to be told that Isaac was out with his newest playmates, although Yolande was horrified when she discovered that one was Ulf.

'If you find him before me, bring him home,' she ordered, eyes flashing with anger. 'I do not want him mixing with the Godenaves. They have low morals and are vulgar.'

Which was damning indeed coming from a woman who was a prostitute in her spare time, and whose large brood bore uncanny likenesses to a number of wealthy merchants and scholars.

Bartholomew decided to go to All Saints, to see if the brats had gone there to stay out of the wet. If Isaac were among them, he would drag him back to Yolande and she would certainly make him tell what he knew about Ulf's antics on the bridge.

He passed Stasy and Hawick on the way. They wore new cloaks and fine waterproof boots, suggesting they had already started to make good money from medicine. He wondered how long it would continue if they persisted in crossing Margery Starre, who was not a woman to sit back meekly while liberties were taken.

'The flux is getting worse and we are the only ones who can cure it,' crowed Stasy. 'Your barley water is useless, so people flock to buy *our* remedy.'

Nettled by their arrogance, Bartholomew went on the offensive. 'Why did you order Elsham to stab Huntyngdon, and Gille to kill Martyn? What did Aynton's letters contain that you are so frantic to keep secret?'

Both students gaped at him, and he was gratified to see even the brash Stasy at a loss for words for once. It did not last for long, though.

'We did nothing of the kind,' Stasy hissed. 'And you cannot prove it. You would do better looking to your own business and staying out of ours.'

'You are guilty,' Bartholomew went on relentlessly. 'We know for a fact that Gille ran to you when he felt the net tightening around him.'

'Yes, he came,' acknowledged Hawick. 'You know he did, because you found the book he left behind – the one that belonged to Elsham. But we have "ordered" no murders. Why would we? We barely knew Huntyngdon and Martyn.'

'But Gille will not get far,' said Stasy, his customary composure completely restored. 'There are charms to prevent felons from escaping. And when he returns, he will prove that we are innocent of whatever dark business he and Elsham embroiled themselves in.'

'You cast a spell on him?' asked Bartholomew in distaste. 'Because his antics landed you in hot water and you want revenge?'

'Not revenge,' replied Stasy. 'Justice. We have done nothing wrong, and I am sick of arrogant scholars like you, Michael and Prior Pechem making nasty accusations.'

He strutted away, Hawick in tow, leaving Bartholomew angry with himself. He should have asked his questions more subtly, not raced at his quarry like a rampaging bull. Again, he wished Michael was with him, sure the monk would have handled the pair with more skill.

'They will get their comeuppance,' murmured Cynric, reappearing from nowhere and making Bartholomew jump by speaking in his ear. He looked exhausted from dogging their footsteps day after day. 'Margery will see to that.'

'So you have said, but please do not involve yourself in whatever she plans,' begged Bartholomew. 'You could end up in serious trouble.'

'She does not need my help, boy,' said Cynric, startled by the notion. 'She has far more powerful resources at her disposal.'

'Not the Devil?' breathed Bartholomew, alarmed.

Cynric regarded him coolly. 'Wealthy burgesses, high-ranking churchmen and influential scholars – friends in high places. Besides, she tends not to ask Satan for assistance any more, because his services are unreliable.'

Bartholomew hastened to change the subject before it grew any more disconcerting. 'Have you learned anything useful from following Stasy and Hawick?'

'Not really,' sighed Cynric. 'And it is tedious work. For example, all they have done today is buy green dye from Chaumbre.'

Bartholomew frowned. 'Dye for what? His wares cannot be used in medicine. They are intended for cloth, not human consumption.'

'He told them that, but they said it is to add a nice verdant sheen to their consulting room walls. It is a stupid notion! They will look mildewed.'

Bartholomew met Isnard outside the Hospital of St John. The bargeman was watching a solitary labourer slowly fill the third of the dye-pits. Bartholomew was not surprised the operation was taking so long when he saw who had been hired to do it – Ned Verious, a notoriously lazy ditcher with a penchant for other people's property. He scraped by on the barest minimum of work, and people rarely rehired him, because they soon learned he was not very good value for money.

'The work should have been finished by now,' Isnard told Bartholomew, 'but Verious is making no effort to hurry.'

'Really,' said Bartholomew flatly, wondering why no one had warned Chaumbre to employ someone else.

'Chaumbre should have let me have the job,' sniffed Isnard. 'I would have had those holes filled in a trice, but Verious was cheaper.'

'You sound better,' remarked Bartholomew. 'Your cold has gone.'

'Thanks to your linctus. Of course, Stasy and Hawick claim it was their doing.'

Bartholomew did not want to talk about them. 'Since we last spoke, have you thought any more about the stone that killed Elsham? I know you did not see it pushed, but can you remember anything that might help us to identify the culprit?'

'Actually, I *did* see it pushed,' averred Isnard. 'I saw a pair of arms heaving at it, and when it landed, I saw a fist raised in victory before the culprit scuttled away.'

'You *saw* the killer?' gasped Bartholomew. 'Why did you not tell me at once?'

'Because I did not see his face, and I have no idea who he was.'

'But you must have noticed something to identify him? His size or shape? His clothes? His gait? Was it a man or a woman?'

'Well, he was nimble, but so would I have been, if I had just committed murder in front of half the town. But the rest is a blur. His clothes were like everyone else's – tunic and breeches – and I doubt it was a woman, because they tend to wear skirts.'

'Anything else?' pressed Bartholomew urgently.

Isnard considered. 'He must have been strong, because

258

the stone was heavy. Of course, Elsham had it coming to him. He was a rogue, and I do not know what Rohese Morys saw in him. He was not worth the risk. His friend Gille is no better – he is a thief.'

'How do you know all this?' asked Bartholomew wonderingly.

'I visit taverns,' shrugged Isnard. 'And I listen to what people say in them.'

'Elsham claimed he killed Huntyngdon as a favour to a friend,' said Bartholomew, desperate enough to tap any source of information. 'Do you have any suggestions as to who that person might be?'

Isnard shook his head. 'But I saw Chancellor Aynton shortly before he died. He was stamping towards the bridge in a tremendous temper. Later, John Godenave – Ulf's father – told me that Aynton tried to climb up the outside of Brampton's house, aiming to look through the windows, but he kept falling down.'

Bartholomew stared at him. 'I think I need to hear this story from Godenave himself.'

There were repercussions arising from the incident that had killed Elsham, and one was that Isnard had been forced to withdraw the damaged ferry from service. The other was working, but one boat was not enough to accommodate all the people wanting to use it. To avoid a riot, the builders had been forced to open the *ponticulus* to pedestrians.

'It was good while it lasted,' said Isnard, who had accompanied Bartholomew to the bridge in order to cast a proprietary eye over his reduced operation. 'Even with the cost of mending my boat, I made enough money for a decent St Swithun's Day celebration at the Griffin tonight. I shall need something to cheer me up, if it is going to rain for the next forty days.'

'Then watch your step on the way home,' advised

Bartholomew. 'I doubt Verious will have filled both dye-pits by then, so at least one will still be open.'

Isnard chuckled, then ducked as mud sailed past his ear, missing him by a whisker. 'It is that damned Ulf again!' he cried angrily. 'Why will he not leave me alone? I did not ask for my leg to be sawn off, and he has no right to mock the way I get around.'

Bartholomew glanced to where Ulf was mimicking Isnard's characteristic swinging gait. He sported his fine new hat, although the rest of him was black with wet mud. He had a small dog with him, and Bartholomew was shocked to see the boy had tied its legs together, so he could drag it along. Clippesby was hot on his heels, trying to rescue it. When Ulf drew a knife, Bartholomew hurried to intervene, Isnard swinging along at his heels.

'That animal is *mine*!' snarled Ulf, feinting at Clippesby with the dagger; it looked far too large and sharp to be in the hands of a child. 'You cannot have it.'

Isnard knocked the weapon out of his hand with a crutch, and Clippesby used it to saw through the rope. The moment the dog was free, it leapt into the Dominican's arms. Clippesby lobbed the blade into the river, and strode away without a word, although judging by the way he cocked his head, the dog had a great deal to say to him.

'He stole my hound *and* my knife,' howled Ulf, gazing after him in stunned disbelief. 'He had better pay for them, or I will tell the Sheriff that he is a thief.'

'Shall we go together, then?' asked Bartholomew, indicating the castle with a wave of his hand. 'And while we are there, you can tell him why you created a diversion at the bridge that allowed the murder of—'

Ulf raced away. Bartholomew started to follow, but when the brat turned and did a taunting dance, he thought better of it. Ulf was fast, and not only was it obvious that Bartholomew would fail to catch him, but that he would make a spectacle of himself in the process. However, some good might come out of the encounter: Ulf had run away from the place where his playmates were likely to be, which gave Bartholomew a chance to talk to them without his menacing presence.

As so many people wanted to use the *ponticulus*, Bernarde had been given the task of restricting the number of folk who were on it at any one time, lest excessive weight brought the whole thing down. He smiled and bowed as he counted them on and off, and his good humour did much to soothe the irritation of those who had been forced to wait. On the main bridge, Shardelowe worked with fierce concentration, shaping the keystone with powerful strokes of his mallet.

'I think he will do what he promised,' said Isnard, watching. 'He has made excellent progress, and he still has four days left. I believe he and his crew will win their bonuses.'

'Where is Lyonnes?' asked Bartholomew, aware that every so often Bernarde would stop counting pedestrians to call some cheerfully encouraging remark to the labourers, which did a lot more to inspire them than Shardelowe's terse commands.

'He did not appear for work this morning,' replied Isnard. 'Shardelowe probably dismissed him for being a mean-spirited rogue. Unlike Bernarde, who is a *nice* man.'

Bartholomew hurried to All Saints next-the-castle, but the churchyard was deserted, and an elderly woman called out that the children had gone to watch the jugglers in the Market Square. Thwarted in one line of enquiry, he moved to another, and went to the Griffin. He arrived to find Godenave already drunk and slumped at a table. He prodded him awake.

'If you are here about Ulf, there is nothing I can do about him,' Godenave declared the moment he had gathered his wits. 'He takes after his mother with his wild ways. I cannot say I like him very much.'

'Yet you helped him dodge a charge of attempted murder,' said Bartholomew coolly. 'He stabbed a beadle, and you arranged for a lawyer to defend him – paid for by Morys.'

Godenave peered blearily at him. 'I merely reminded Morys that he would be sorry to lose Ulf's services if the lad was hanged. Ulf has quick fingers, see, and there is no one like him for opening stubborn windows.'

Bartholomew was not sure he had heard aright. 'Are you saying that not only is Ulf an accomplished burglar, but the Mayor hires him for the purpose?'

Godenave shrugged. 'I need to put ale on the table, and if Morys gives me a job . . .'

'You should watch yourself, John,' advised the landlord, overhearing. 'Morys will see you hanged if he finds out you betray his secrets.'

'He would not dare,' said Godenave, taking a deep draught from his jug. 'Ulf would not stand for it. The lad may be young, but no one pushes *him* around.'

With astonishment, Bartholomew saw he was afraid of the boy. He changed the subject to Aynton, although Godenave refused to speak until his jug had been refilled.

'It keeps me healthy,' he explained. 'People who drink stuff made with water get flux.'

'Ale is made with water,' Bartholomew pointed out.

'It is not! It comes from grain and yeast.'

'And water,' said Bartholomew, although he could see he was wasting his breath. 'But never mind this. Tell me about Aynton.'

'I saw him the night he died,' said Godenave, and nodded through the window, which afforded an excellent view of Brampton's house diagonally opposite. 'He was trying to climb up to the bedrooms, but they are too high, and he kept falling down.'

262

'Why would the Chancellor want to do that?' asked the landlord in astonishment.

Godenave grinned. 'That is what I wondered, so I went outside to get a better view. He was muttering about the Master of his College frolicking with a whore, and how he intended to put an end to it.'

'He used those exact words?' asked Bartholomew.

'No, he swore a lot more. He was livid, see, because every time he got close to the bedchamber, he would lose his footing and slip. Eventually, the scholar came out.'

'You mean Brampton? The man who lives there?'

'No – the tall, nasty one from Clare Hall, who Aynton was trying to watch. They argued, and the Clare Hall rogue stormed off.'

Bartholomew was thoughtful. So Donwich had caught Aynton spying on him, and they had quarrelled about it. How curious – and suspicious – that Donwich had neglected to mention it.

Bartholomew escaped from the Griffin with relief. As he was close, he decided to report to Tulyet, feeling that while Ulf was still only a child, the Sheriff needed to know that he was well on the way to becoming an accomplished criminal. Moreover, he was now sure that Donwich was the killer, and he needed to discuss it with someone he trusted. Michael was unavailable, but Tulyet was the next best thing.

He had expected the bailey to be empty, with the soldiers and their lieutenants opting to stay in the dry. Thus he was surprised to find them all in full battle gear, with swords, pikes and cudgels flailing. Sergeant Robin, who came to greet him, said it was Dickon's idea. Apparently, the boy had made the point that all warriors would have to fight in the rain one day, so they should be ready for it, as their generals were unlikely to postpone military engagements because it was wet.

'That will not make him popular,' remarked Bartholomew. 'They will have to spend an age cleaning their equipment afterwards, or it will rust.'

'He is not popular anyway,' said Robin. 'There is not a man among us who cannot wait until he goes to France. Here he comes now, and the Sheriff with him.'

He made himself scarce, and Bartholomew noted that Dickon had not followed his own suggestion of practising in the downpour, and was bone dry. While the boy watched the soldiers with a critical eye, Bartholomew told Tulyet all he had learned since they had last met. Dickon sneered contemptuously when he heard the physician's concerns about Ulf.

'You cannot be afraid of him! He does not even have a knife.'

'Actually, he did,' countered Bartholomew. 'And I am not afraid of him. I just want him taken in hand before the beadle he stabbed is not his only victim.'

Pointedly ignoring Dickon, he explained to Tulyet why he thought Donwich was the killer. It was good to speak his suspicions aloud, as it clarified them in his mind.

'You must be glad to be leaving that deadly University,' said Tulyet when he had finished. 'You will be a lot safer in the town. However, I sincerely hope these vicars-general find in Michael's favour, because I shall resign if Donwich wins.'

'It will not matter what they decide if Donwich is arrested for murder,' Bartholomew pointed out. 'He cannot be Chancellor if he is a felon.'

Tulyet laughed. 'That has never stopped the University before. Of course, I have been spoiled by Michael. He and I work so well together that on the rare occasions when he is away, I find life here much more difficult. I have been offered other posts – easier ones – and if Michael ever becomes an abbot or a bishop, I shall accept one of them the same day.'

'I will be in France,' put in Dickon grandly. 'But I might come back and be Sheriff when I am older.'

'Much older,' said Tulyet, regarding him fondly. 'You should enjoy life before becoming bogged down with administration and law.'

'I shall hire others to do that boring stuff,' declared Dickon. 'All I shall do is ride around keeping order with my sword.'

Bartholomew hoped that would not happen for many years yet. He took his leave, and Tulyet walked with him, saying he had an errand to run in Bridge Street.

'You will miss Dickon when he goes,' said Bartholomew, tactfully not mentioning that no one else would.

'Yes,' agreed Tulyet. 'He will make a fine warrior once he learns restraint. But who did not long to spill an enemy's guts when he was young, strong and felt himself to be invincible?'

'I cannot say I ever did,' said Bartholomew primly.

'Well, I suppose your calling is to keep guts *inside* a body,' conceded Tulyet. 'But for the rest of us . . . well, I am glad Dickon is no shy daisy. Not like your new Senior Proctor. I made a sudden move the other day, and he reared back like a nervous cow.'

'He is not the boldest of men,' acknowledged Bartholomew.

'No, although he is a formidable force in legal and administrational circles. Take the bridge money, for example. He will not have all of it collected from your Colleges and hostels by tomorrow, as Michael promised, but he will certainly have it by Thursday.'

'You sound impressed, but missing a target by a whole day is hardly laudable.'

Tulyet laughed again. 'The last time we were in this position, the money was not handed over for a decade, so an extra day is little short of miraculous. Of course, this same doggedness is ruining his sister's life. No one

265

will marry Lucy now. And do not say Donwich will have her, because he will never abandon his University.'

'I doubt she would accept him anyway. She says they are just friends.'

As they passed All Saints, Bartholomew saw a flicker of movement, and saw children in the graveyard, playing by a puddle – they had returned to their favourite haunt while he had been in the castle. Tulyet spotted them, too, and strode through the dripping, overgrown cemetery towards them. They stiffened in alarm at the sight of the Sheriff bearing down on them, and Bartholomew was glad they did not bolt, because he was in no mood for a chase.

'Do you want Ulf?' asked Isaac uneasily. 'Because he is not here.'

'You were larking about on the *ponticulus* when the stone fell and killed the scholar,' began Tulyet. 'What did you—'

'No, we were not,' interrupted one of the others nervously. 'It was someone else.'

'I saw you,' said Bartholomew wearily. 'So please do not lie. Who told you to do it? Or rather, who told Ulf?'

The children exchanged furtive glances but none of them replied.

'No one will get into trouble for telling the truth,' said Tulyet. 'But if someone ordered you to fool around, to distract everyone while a man was murdered, we need to know.'

'No one did,' replied Isaac, his eyes furtive. 'We played because we wanted to.'

'Do not protect Ulf,' said Bartholomew. 'He cheated you – he was given a nice new hat for his troubles, but you got nothing. Is that fair?'

'No,' conceded Isaac. 'But we do not mind. Honest, sir.'

Bartholomew and Tulyet did everything in their power

to convince them to talk, but the children remained tight-lipped. Clearly, they were a lot more frightened of Ulf than they were of the Sheriff and a physician.

'If I see Ulf, I shall arrest him,' said Tulyet, as they walked away. 'Perhaps they will confide in us once he is behind bars.'

'Only if there is no prospect of him getting out again,' said Bartholomew. 'And given that he stabbed a beadle and wriggled out of the charge . . .'

'True,' sighed Tulyet. 'Shall we go to Clare Hall together? If Donwich really is the killer, he should not be allowed to roam free until Michael has a spare moment to deal with him. He might claim another victim in the interim.'

Bartholomew agreed, but when they arrived at Clare Hall it was to be told that Donwich was out and no one knew where he had gone, although the general consensus was that Lucy was involved.

'His lover!' spat Pulham angrily. 'No matter what he claims about chaste friendships, that association will lead him straight to Hell.'

'I rather think he knows how to get there on his own,' muttered Tulyet. 'We will confront him tomorrow, Matt. Meet me in the Brazen George after breakfast.'

Although Bartholomew had intended to speak to Morys again, the flux intervened. There was a sudden outbreak in the Carmelite Priory, and by the time he had finished, it was too late to visit suspects and expect them to be cooperative. He returned to Michaelhouse, but was called out again almost at once by a potter near the Mill Pond, who had suffered a compound fracture of the leg. Stasy and Hawick had been there before him, but had walked out again when they learned the man was unable to pay for their services.

As Bartholomew left the potter's house, he stood for a

moment to close his eyes and let rain patter coolly on his upturned face. Repairing the damaged limb had been difficult, and he was far from certain the patient would survive – the wound had been filthy, and he knew how quickly such injuries turned bad, especially in hot weather. But he had done his best, with the result that every fibre in his body ached from weariness.

He looked at the Mill Pond, which was fuller than when he had last seen it. The rain was replenishing the river at last, and he hoped it would wash away whatever was causing the flux, so there would be one less problem to worry about.

'The Mayor refuses to open the sluices until the pond is filled to the brim,' said the potter's wife, who had followed Bartholomew outside. 'But I think he should do it now. The water in it is stale and it stinks worse with every passing day. Your Father William has tried to persuade him to do it several times, but Morys will not listen to him.'

'It does stink,' agreed Bartholomew, then frowned as he looked across the Mill Pond's glittering black surface. 'I never realised Hoo Hall was so close to its edge. Will it flood if we really do have rain for the next forty days?'

'Not if the sluices are opened. Of course, no one lives in Hoo Hall, so it does not matter anyway. Well, no one other than that vain man who admires himself so.'

'Narboro,' said Bartholomew absently.

'He refused to marry Lucy Brampton. Poor lady! First him and now that tall, pompous scholar who ogles her like a moonstruck cow. What awful men she attracts!'

As Bartholomew began to walk away, he saw shadows moving by the edge of the Mill Pond. Curious, he started towards them, but by the time he reached the spot, there was nothing to see. Wearily, he trudged home to snatch a few hours' sleep before the daily grind started all over again.

CHAPTER 14

'Perhaps you and Dick are right,' said Michael unhappily at breakfast the following day, 'and Donwich *is* the culprit.'

'Did you speak to him yesterday?' asked Bartholomew. 'You said you would.'

'I tried twice, but he was out, and I did not have time to hunt him down. However, even if he is the killer, neither of us can accuse him without proof. He will say we are only doing it to damage his claim on the chancellorship.'

'So what?' asked Bartholomew, thick-headed from lack of sleep. 'If he is guilty, it does not matter what he brays from the proctors' cells. Besides, I am tired of this case. I want it resolved so I can concentrate on the flux.'

'Not teaching?'

Bartholomew eyed him balefully. 'I think we both know that is now a lost cause. My students have tasted freedom, and I will never get them back now. But how do you want us to deal with Donwich today? Perhaps he will confess when he sees Dick at my side.'

'Very possibly, but our colleagues would riot if we used the Sheriff to intimidate members of the University. The vicars-general will not be very impressed either.'

'I doubt many scholars will take umbrage on Donwich's behalf – he is not very popular. And the vicars-general do not need to know.'

'They would find out,' predicted Michael, and sighed. 'My business with them is nowhere near finished, so they will be here for days yet.'

Bartholomew glanced at him. He looked exhausted, but at the same time, there was a gleam in his eye that suggested he was enjoying whatever challenge the Archbishop's emissaries were posing for him.

'I will concentrate on Brampton instead then,' Bartholomew said. 'He is supposed to finish collecting the bridge money today. Ergo, he is no longer off limits to me.'

'He told me last night that he has "only" gathered ninety-five per cent of it. He will take it to Morys this morning, with a promise that the rest will be delivered tomorrow. I am impressed, as scholars do not readily part with money. I doubt there is another man in the University who could have done what he has, and that includes me.'

'So he is good for something then. He cannot quell brawls, run elections, or keep the peace, but he can squeeze money out of his colleagues.'

'It is a useful talent,' averred Michael. 'And he has others, too, despite what you think of him. But to return to the murders, I think the best way to proceed is to ask more questions in Clare Hall about Aynton, Elsham and Gille.'

'What good would that do?' Bartholomew was sick of the place.

'If Donwich is the culprit, it will make him uneasy, and uneasy men make mistakes. Perhaps taking Dick is a good idea after all, as his presence will certainly unsettle anyone with a guilty conscience.'

'Very well. I will try to speak to Morys again, too. He is not far below Donwich on the list of suspects.'

'I appreciate all you are doing, Matt,' said Michael quietly. 'However, we *must* have answers by Saturday.'

'I do not see why,' grumbled Bartholomew. 'Our suspects list comprises Donwich, Morys, Brampton, Gille, Stasy, Hawick and Shardelowe. None of the first six will leave, because they live here, while Shardelowe will go nowhere until he has been paid in full, and I am sure we can persuade the burgesses to withhold the last instalment for a few days.'

'I want everyone – scholars *and* vicars-general – to go

home knowing the killer is caught. The reputation of our University is at stake. We cannot have them spreading the tale that our Chancellor was murdered and we let the culprit get away with it.'

'I will do my best,' said Bartholomew unhappily.

'I know.' Michael smiled to lighten the mood. 'Incidentally, Lucy went to Edith's warehouse yesterday, and chose some cloth for your wedding clothes. I should warn you that she picked two very startling shades of red. You might want to exchange them for something a bit more discreet, or Matilde will think she is marrying a cardinal.'

Bartholomew hurried to Matilde's house at once, feeling that Tulyet would not mind him being a few moments late at the Brazen George when his dignity was at stake. Again, he wished he and Matilde could be married quietly, perhaps with Clippesby presiding, and no one but Edith and Michael to witness the ceremony. Lucy was turning what should be the happiest day of his life into an ordeal.

He arrived to find Matilde had gone to church, but Edith was there with Chaumbre. They were making march-pane fancies for the wedding, laughing at some joke one of them had cracked. It was a cosy scene, and he saw yet again that Edith was growing increasingly fond of her new husband.

'Matthew!' exclaimed Chaumbre warmly. 'What a pleasant surprise. Do come in.'

'Thank you,' said Bartholomew, although he resented the dyer inviting him into the house that would soon be his home. Loath to dawdle after Michael's plea for haste, he came straight to the point. 'I hear some cloth has been put aside for me. Some very *red* cloth.'

'Lucy picked it,' said Edith. 'I argued for a nice mid-blue. However, she says red will hide the blood you spill while dabbling with surgery, which is a good point.'

'I do not intend to get married covered in gore,' said

Bartholomew stiffly. 'So blue will be perfectly acceptable. But speaking of colours, I understand Stasy and Hawick bought some dye from you, Philip.'

'For their walls,' replied Chaumbre amiably. 'Apparently, sick people find green soothing. I informed them that there are much cheaper ways of colouring paint, but they declared themselves flush with money, so who was I to argue?'

'You believed them?' asked Bartholomew warily.

'Why not? They paid in cash, so there was never any question of credit.'

'Not about the money,' said Bartholomew, although it occurred to him that it was odd the pair could afford to be extravagant quite so soon after establishing their practice. 'About what they planned to do with the dye.'

Chaumbre shrugged. 'What else would they use it for?'

'To put in medicine,' suggested Bartholomew. 'Perhaps in an effort to disguise the fact that most of their wares come from Margery Starre.'

'Impossible! Even a tiny dab in a pot would be too much, because my dyes are highly concentrated. Not to mention unfit for human consumption. If they had wanted something to colour their remedies, they would have gone to the apothecary.'

Bartholomew supposed that was true. He was about to leave when he recalled that Donwich considered Chaumbre enough of a friend to have invited him to his premature victory feast. Perhaps the dyer had noticed something that night that would either prove Donwich's guilt or allow him to be eliminated.

'You were at Clare Hall the evening Aynton was killed,' he began. 'Did you—'

'I was checking dye when the poor man was struck down,' interrupted Chaumbre patiently. 'We have been through this already, Matthew. Why bring it up again?'

'It is about Donwich, not you,' explained Bartholomew, aware that Edith was eyeing him rather beadily. 'Aynton

272

was killed after spying on him, and the two of them fell out when Aynton declined to support his bid for the chancellorship. I want to know if you consider Donwich capable of murder.'

'You have asked me this before, too, and my answer is the same now as it was then: Donwich is opinionated and arrogant, but not violent. However, as you remain unconvinced, I shall accompany you to Clare Hall and we shall speak to him together. It is the best way to resolve this matter once and for all.'

'There is no need for that,' said Bartholomew hastily.

'Nonsense,' declared Chaumbre, standing up. 'I have nothing more pressing to do, and I should like to spend a morning with my wife's brother. We do not know each other very well, and that must be rectified.'

'How did you become friends with Donwich?' asked Bartholomew, aiming to keep him talking until he had devised a way to dispense with his company. 'You had left Cambridge long before he joined the University, so you cannot have known him for very long.'

'A few weeks,' replied Chaumbre, irritatingly jovial. 'But I have made many new friends since arriving back, not to mention winning a wife. I cannot recall exactly what threw him and me together now. Perhaps he bought some dye.'

'It was at the guildhall,' supplied Edith. 'Mayor Morys introduced you as the richest man in Cambridge, so naturally, Donwich was keen to ingratiate himself with you.'

'Are you a Clare Hall benefactor then?' asked Bartholomew. Donwich tended to treat merchants with contempt, but he was willing to conceal his distaste if it meant donations.

'Not yet, but I have promised to think about it.' Chaumbre beamed merrily. 'Shall we go? There is no time like the present.'

'It is kind of you to offer, but I have already invited

273

the Sheriff,' said Bartholomew, smiling in an effort to soften the refusal. 'Three will be too many.'

'Oh, I do not think that matters in the least,' countered Chaumbre, and picked up his cloak. 'Besides, Dick Tulyet is another man I should like to know better. Lead on!'

'Dickon may be with him,' said Bartholomew, desperately trying to put him off.

'Good! It is common knowledge that Tulyet is grooming him to take over when he hangs up his spurs, so there is no harm in making his acquaintance, too.' Chaumbre opened the door. 'Goodness! Look at the rain. If we have forty days of this, we shall all float away.'

With weary resignation, Bartholomew fell into step at his side.

Bartholomew and Chaumbre entered the Brazen George, shaking the wet from their hats and cloaks, to find Tulyet eating a modest breakfast of bread and apples. Dickon was working his way through a platter of beef that looked unusually bloody.

'He asked for it,' whispered Landlord Lister to Bartholomew, and gave a malicious chuckle. 'Or rather, he ordered me not to burn it, so I made sure it was rare. He is not enjoying it, but he is too proud to say so.'

The other patrons were watching the boy warily, and Bartholomew knew that by the end of the day, the whole town would know that Dickon's breakfast of choice was raw meat. He and Chaumbre sat, and the dyer ordered ale. Bartholomew smothered a sigh. He could not afford to sit around drinking while he had a killer to catch!

'I have been busy since we last met,' reported Tulyet. 'But to no avail. I spoke to every sentry who was on duty when Aynton was killed, but no one saw or heard anything of use.'

'And *I* spoke to everyone who was near the bridge when Elsham died,' put in Dickon importantly. 'They are all blind and stupid, because none of them noticed a thing.'

274

'Those silly youngsters!' sighed Chaumbre. 'If they had not been larking about, someone would have been able to identify the rogue who almost drowned me.'

'It is a pity *I* was not there,' said Dickon, shoving his empty platter away with a victorious flourish. 'I would not have let children distract *me*. But shall we go to Clare Hall now and terrify Master Donwich into a confession? I am looking forward to that!'

'You must contain yourself until I have finished my ale,' chided Chaumbre, making himself comfortable. 'And while I drink, we can talk about the bridge.'

'What about it?' demanded Bartholomew curtly, chafing anew at the delay.

'We were right to choose stone,' the dyer began. 'But I am not sure we should have picked Shardelowe for the task. For a start, I suspect he has never worked on a bridge before.'

Tulyet blinked. 'But he told me this would be his fifth.'

'A barefaced lie,' said Chaumbre. 'He claimed to have designed two over the Fleet and two over the Tyburn, so I wrote to a friend in London, asking what he thought of Shardelowe's work. The reply arrived an hour ago: Shardelowe played no role in constructing any of them.'

Bartholomew was horrified. 'So he is repairing our bridge with frantic haste, but he is doing it with no prior experience? What if it collapses because of his shortcomings? People might be killed!'

'We shall discover its failings very soon, if it rains for the next forty days and the river floods,' put in Tulyet, equally alarmed. 'We must confront him about this deception at once.'

'If we dismiss him, we shall be without a bridge until a new engineer can be hired,' Chaumbre pointed out. 'That could take months, so I suggest we let him finish, but withhold some of the money until we are sure that the thing is up to scratch.'

'Yes,' conceded Tulyet. 'That seems reasonable.'

'And perhaps I have worried you unnecessarily,' Chaumbre went on. 'I took Zoone to inspect the work last night, and he declared it to be satisfactory. So far, at least. Oh, look who has just walked in – Shardelowe himself. Shardelowe! Come over here.'

'I *am* coming,' snapped Shardelowe testily. 'Because I need to report that Lyonnes is missing. He did not appear for work yesterday, so I assumed he had gone to buy extra chisels. However, it transpires that no one has seen him since Monday night, and I am concerned.'

'Perhaps he is enjoying the respite from the frantic pace you are—' began Chaumbre.

'He would not have tarried,' interrupted Shardelowe. 'Not when he knows how tight our schedule is. Ergo, something bad has happened to him.'

'Perhaps he fled when he realised your deceit was about to be exposed,' said Tulyet coolly. 'Namely that ours is the very first bridge that you have ever put together.'

Shardelowe tried for a careless shrug, although his eyes betrayed his alarm. 'I cannot help what you choose to believe. I never actually said I built the four others I described. You just assumed I had.'

'Because that is what you intended,' snapped Tulyet. 'You deliberately misled me.'

'Where lies the problem?' demanded Shardelowe, going on the offensive. 'Examine my work – you will find it perfectly sound. And in three days, you will have a splendid structure that will last hundreds of years.'

'We had better,' said Tulyet warningly. 'Although I would rather you took a little more time and did it properly.'

'If I did, Morys would refuse to pay our bonus.' Shardelowe dropped his hectoring tone to become conciliatory. 'However, I do have some money that may encourage you to—'

276

'Do not finish that sentence,' interrupted Tulyet sharply. 'Or I shall arrest you for attempting to bribe a royally appointed official.'

Shardelowe looked confused. 'But that is the way things work in Cambridge.'

'Not in my part of it. I suppose Morys knows about your deficiencies, so you paid him to make sure you won the commission anyway.'

Shardelowe looked pained. 'Only because he said that is how business is conducted here. I gave him money, which he used to pay witnesses to speak in my favour. For example, Master Donwich's remit was to manipulate the new Chancellor into paying a bigger contribution. It all went exactly as Morys promised it would.'

Bartholomew knew that was true, because Narboro had overheard the pair of them discussing it.

'You may continue the work,' said Tulyet coldly, 'but Zoone will monitor your progress, and I shall dismiss you if there is even the slightest suggestion of a defect.'

'Very well,' said Shardelowe, and held out a callused hand to seal the agreement.

Tulyet refused to take it. 'Is this why Aynton was murdered? He wanted a wooden bridge, so Morys arranged for him to die, lest his dissenting voice threatened his pact with you? Or did you kill him yourself?'

Shardelowe was obviously shocked. 'No! That had nothing to do with me.'

'Prove it,' ordered Tulyet, while Bartholomew held his breath, wondering if the case was about to be solved before his eyes.

'I was in the Angel Inn when Aynton died,' said Shardelowe, 'with Bernarde and Lyonnes. We were working on the report I presented in the guildhall last week. None of us left all evening, as the landlord and two dozen of his regulars will attest.'

Tulyet went to the door and hailed a passing soldier,

who was ordered to go to the Angel and confirm the tale. When Shardelowe looked relieved, Bartholomew knew he was telling the truth. The builder and his two lieutenants could be eliminated from the enquiry.

'We were in the tavern until someone came with news of the Chancellor's plight,' Shardelowe went on, eager to be helpful now. 'Naturally, we went to see if we could help, and you know the rest – how we rigged a winch to lift him up. But I have answered your questions, so now you can answer mine: what are you going to do about Lyonnes?'

'You say he was last seen on Monday night?' asked Tulyet. 'Where?'

'The Griffin. He left a little the worse for wear, apparently.'

'Do you want me to organise a search?' asked Dickon eagerly, the potential confrontation with Donwich forgotten in the face of something much more interesting.

Tulyet patted his shoulder. 'Good lad. Collect John and half a dozen men to help. Visit the Griffin first, though, to confirm what you have been told.'

Delighted, Dickon swaggered away, although Shardelowe was horrified.

'You send a boy to hunt for my assistant?'

'My son,' said Tulyet proudly. 'He is perfectly capable, especially with John at his side.' He glanced at Bartholomew. 'Donwich must wait, because I want a word with Morys first. I cannot overlook his corruption any longer.'

'He is away today, visiting his kin in the Fens,' said Chaumbre. 'He told me so when I met him on my way to Matilde's house earlier.'

'He has left the town *again*?' asked Bartholomew. 'He is never here.'

'He is not,' said Tulyet grimly. 'Which makes me wonder what other nefarious schemes he has in progress. But I shall find out, and woe betide him then.' He glanced at

278

Bartholomew. 'We had better go to Clare Hall before any more of the day is lost.'

Bartholomew's thoughts were in turmoil as he trailed along the High Street after Tulyet and Chaumbre. Was he wrong to be so certain that Donwich had killed Aynton? What if Morys – through his rough kin – had done it, to fulfil his agreement with Shardelowe? And Aynton had made it easy for them by wandering about after dark on his own.

'Michael told me not to challenge Donwich without evidence,' he said unhappily. 'All we are supposed to do in Clare Hall today is ask questions about Aynton, Elsham and Gille.'

'To unsettle Donwich in the hope that he says or does something incriminating,' surmised Tulyet. 'Unfortunately, it will not work, because he is too clever.'

'True,' acknowledged Bartholomew. 'We have tried it before to no avail.'

However,' Tulyet went on, 'a witness has just informed me that Donwich accepted a bribe to manipulate the town council. The University meddling in town affairs is something I cannot overlook, and it is my duty as Sheriff to confront him about it.'

Bartholomew was not sure what to think, and only hoped the charge of corruption would not interfere with the more serious matter of Aynton's murder. Unhappily, he knocked on Clare Hall's gate, where a porter took one look at their grim faces and conducted them to the conclave without a word.

The only Fellow at home was Pulham, who was unsettled to receive such a deputation, but hastened to conceal his unease by inviting them to share his breakfast ale. Chaumbre accepted with a gracious smile, but Tulyet refused, while Bartholomew was far too tense to think about drinking. Then the door was thrown open, and

Donwich marched in with Lucy on his arm. Pulham gave a strangled gasp of shock.

'You cannot bring her in here, Donwich. She is a woman!'

'She is,' agreed Donwich. 'But why should I not entertain a friend in my home? Because of some silly rule written a hundred and fifty years ago by blinkered men? Pah!'

'Because of our benefactors,' argued Pulham in a hoarse whisper, as if he feared they might suddenly materialise and see what was going on. 'They will leave us in droves if they ever find out that we entertain our mistresses on College premises.'

'She is not my mistress,' objected Donwich angrily, while Lucy looked acutely uncomfortable and glanced at the door, clearly considering making a dash for it. 'She is a decent lady, and a far more respectable guest than an impoverished physician, a tradesman and a royal lackey. You certainly should not have invited *them* in here.'

'Allow me to escort you outside,' said Chaumbre kindly to Lucy, who was struggling to pull her arm away from Donwich, so she could escape. 'I do not think you—'

'Yes, you *can* get out,' snarled Donwich, rounding on him. 'You promised us a donation, but now you say we cannot have anything until next year. I do not believe you ever intended to oblige. You just wanted access to my College, so you could spy for your new brother-in-law – the man who is Michael's henchman.'

While Chaumbre gaped his dismay at the unprovoked attack, Lucy succeeded in freeing herself from Donwich. She took the dyer's hand, and murmured that they should leave the scholars and Sheriff to their business. He went with her in a bewildered daze.

Pulham glared at Donwich. 'Now look what your reckless disregard for tradition has done! You exposed a nice lady to embarrassment and offended a potential donor.'

'Enough!' barked Tulyet when Donwich opened his mouth to respond in kind. 'I am not here to listen to a spat. I want to know why you took a bribe from Morys in exchange for speaking at the guildhall. Do not deny it, Donwich. We have witnesses.'

Donwich swallowed uncomfortably. 'How do they . . . I hardly think . . .'

'What you have done is illegal,' Tulyet forged on, taking the stammering reply for an admission of guilt. 'And you will answer for it in a court of law.'

Pulham was shocked anew. 'Is it true?' he cried, aghast. 'You were *paid* to say what you did? God's blood, Donwich! It was bad enough to think you spoke out of a spiteful desire to hurt Michael, but to learn you did it for money . . . Worse, your meddling has forced our University to pay far more than what was originally agreed.'

'Rubbish!' blustered Donwich. 'Our colleagues will pay nothing.'

'But they *have* paid,' shouted Pulham angrily. 'Brampton delivered most of the funds yesterday, and the rest will follow today or tomorrow.'

'Then they are fools,' flashed Donwich. 'I told them to wait until I am Chancellor before parting with any cash. Clare Hall will never give the town a penny.'

Pulham closed his eyes in despair. 'Then we will be forever known as the niggardly foundation that failed to pay its share. All our colleagues will despise us, especially those in the poorest hostels, where finding the necessary contribution was a challenge.'

'I do not care about them,' spat Donwich contemptuously. 'I agreed to help Morys because it was best for Clare Hall and best for myself.'

'You did not need to become Morys's lickspittle in order to earn money,' breathed Pulham, shaking his head in incomprehension. 'I would have lent you some.'

Donwich regarded him archly. 'Would you, when I

wanted it to buy gifts for Lucy? She is the best friend I have ever had, and I intend to make sure she knows it.'

'No,' acknowledged Pulham. 'I would not have financed your infatuation. I still hope you will come to your senses, and revert to the man you were before we elected you Master.' He turned to Tulyet. 'Clare Hall *will* pay its contribution to the bridge, Sheriff. I shall deliver it to Brampton myself. He will have it within the hour.'

'You cannot—' began Donwich in spluttering indignation, but Bartholomew cut across him, hoping the Master was sufficiently unsettled by the confrontation to come clean about the murders.

'Aynton followed you the night he was killed. A witness saw you catch him outside Lucy's house, after which you quarrelled – a fact that you have kept suspiciously quiet.'

Donwich barely looked at him. 'Of course I kept it quiet. You would have accused me of killing him if I had told you about it.'

'Did you kill him?' asked Tulyet baldly.

'Of course not! I was angry – hence my lack of composure when I returned to the feast – but I would never have shoved him off the bridge.'

At that point, Tulyet launched into an interrogation that had his victim blanching in fright. Even so, Donwich continued to claim that he had left Aynton alive, and doggedly refused to be shaken from his story.

'Where is Gille?' demanded Tulyet eventually. 'Because I do not believe that no one here knows where he is hiding. Perhaps *he* can throw light on these murders.'

'If we knew, we would tell you,' said Pulham, desperate to be conciliatory in the hope that the Sheriff would not think the entire College was full of lechers and criminals. 'Would you like to search his room? Bartholomew has already done it, but—'

'No!' objected Donwich. 'A secular has no right to invade our—'

'Follow me, Sheriff,' interrupted Pulham briskly. 'Clare Hall has nothing to hide – and nothing to gain by shielding those who have done us a world of harm either.'

Bartholomew thought they were wasting their time, but Tulyet was rather more thorough than he had been, and even stood on a table to peer on top of the ceiling joists. It was there that he discovered a blade encrusted with dried blood. Pulham immediately identified it as Gille's knife, while Donwich gaped his horror.

'Perhaps it was Gille who stabbed Huntyngdon,' said Tulyet to Bartholomew, 'which would make Elsham's deathbed confession a lie.'

'No one killed Huntyngdon with that weapon,' said Bartholomew. 'It is too wide.'

'He probably used it to cut his meat,' blustered Donwich. 'And as it is clearly valuable, he put it up there for safekeeping.'

'Of course he did,' said Tulyet flatly.

Bartholomew was glad to leave Clare Hall. He and Tulyet hurried outside, where Chaumbre was waiting for them, although there was no sign of Lucy. The dyer looked pale and forlorn.

'She went to the Mill Pond,' he explained, although neither Bartholomew nor Tulyet had asked. 'She was mortified by what happened in there. So was I.'

'So she has gone to recover her composure,' surmised Tulyet. 'Although I can think of better places to do it. The Mill Pond reeks and is always busy.'

'Actually, she went to see if the rain has filled it yet,' explained Chaumbre. 'If so, she intends to petition Morys to open the sluices, so that clean water can wash away all that is stinking and unclean.'

'Like Clare Hall,' muttered Tulyet venomously. 'Donwich has not heard the last of this. He *will* answer for his corrupt dealings in the guildhall, and so will Morys.'

'Today, Donwich revealed a side of himself that I did not know existed,' said Chaumbre in a small, subdued voice. 'It hurt me to learn that his friendship went only as deep as my purse.'

'Then perhaps you can use the money you *would* have given him for filling in your dye-pits,' said Tulyet tartly.

Chaumbre attempted a smile. 'Verious is working on the third hole as we speak. Then there will only be one left.'

'That is one too many,' began Tulyet, 'and it is not—'

But the dyer spotted Burgess FitzAbsolon at that moment, and hared off to greet him, leaving the Sheriff talking to himself. Meanwhile, Bartholomew was frustrated by the encounter in Clare Hall. He remained sure that Donwich was the killer, but how was he ever going to prove it? Then he saw Lucy, who had finished her inspection of the Mill Pond, and was heading for the guildhall.

'I am sorry for what happened in there,' he told her as she passed. 'Pulham had no right to speak about you so disrespectfully, and I should have defended you.'

Lucy grimaced. 'Everyone thinks I am Donwich's paramour, even though nothing could be further from the truth.'

'Perhaps you should break off your friendship with him then,' suggested Tulyet curtly. 'It is difficult to believe it is chaste, when he is so obviously enamoured of you.'

'He is,' acknowledged Lucy ruefully, 'although not enough to exchange University life for marriage, which is why he will only ever be a friend. Even so, being with him is a lot more fun than sitting around at home, knowing that everyone is gossiping about my inability to attract a replacement for Narboro.'

'Why not leave Cambridge and start afresh somewhere else?' asked Bartholomew kindly. 'Do you have kin in another town?'

'If I had, I would have gone already. But perhaps a suitable gentleman will come here eventually. Until then,

I am content to arrange my friends' weddings.' She smiled at him. 'But before I forget, Matthew, my brother asked me to give you a message about the flux.'

'New cases?' asked Bartholomew worriedly.

She nodded. 'More beadles. He thinks they caught it from a miasma that escaped from the barrel of ale they shared last night.'

Bartholomew felt a surge of hope. If the sickness could be traced to a brewery, he might finally be able to stamp it out. He began to subject her to a barrage of questions, but she pushed him away, laughing.

'I cannot tell you about the drinking habits of beadles! You must ask my brother. And you are in luck, because here he comes now.'

Brampton was hurrying along, head down. He ignored the calls of passing scholars for news about the ruminations of the vicars-general, and when there was a spat between two rival hostels, he made no attempt to break it up. He pretended not to hear Bartholomew's hail either, obliging the physician to run after him and grab his arm.

'Yes, a few beadles are ill from miasma-tainted ale,' he said, freeing himself impatiently. 'But I cannot natter to you about it now. I am on *pressing* University business.'

If Bartholomew had not been so tired and frustrated, he would never have allowed Brampton's remark to aggravate him. However, the inference that collecting money was more important than the beadles' health was too galling to ignore. Forgetting Michael's instruction to leave Brampton alone, he launched into a curt interrogation about the ale, and when Brampton professed to know no more about it, he turned to Aynton's murder instead.

'You are a suspect for killing him,' Bartholomew said baldly. 'So is your friend Donwich. You also overheard an argument between Aynton and Chaumbre that you failed to mention.'

Brampton was outraged by the allegations. 'You should *thank* me for not exposing that quarrel! It might have seen your brother-in-law charged with the Chancellor's death. Indeed, it still might. He—'

'You spied on Aynton.' Bartholomew cut across him. 'But you said nothing about it when we were desperate for information about his last hours – information that might hold clues about his killer.'

'I monitored him on Michael's orders,' Brampton flashed back. 'It is common practice for junior proctors to watch certain scholars, as you would know if you were not so engrossed in medicine. *You* were watched in the past, when complaints were made about you.'

Bartholomew regarded him in mystification. 'What complaints?'

'Extolling the delights of anatomy, claiming that horoscopes are a waste of time, practising surgery when it should be left to barbers, washing your hands with disconcerting frequency. Shall I go on?'

'No,' said Bartholomew wearily.

'Many scholars thought your ideas were dangerous, so you were very closely observed for years. Of course, nothing has been done about you since Michael made himself such a force in the University. No one would dare.'

It was discomfiting news, but Bartholomew was not about to let it sidetrack him even so. 'Where were you when Elsham was killed?' he demanded. 'I know you were near the bridge shortly afterwards, because I saw you.'

'Yes, but I did not kill him,' replied Brampton coldly. 'And I can prove it, because I was with that ass Narboro. A workman had jostled him, causing him to drop his mirror, which then broke. I was persuading him not to make a formal complaint, because it would have turned our University into a laughing stock.'

'That is untrue. I saw you with Donwich, not Narboro.'

Brampton smiled thinly. 'You asked where I was when *Elsham was killed*, and the answer is that I was with Narboro. However, I brought that conversation to an end when I heard the commotion following the stone dropping off the bridge. I hurried to the river, where Donwich came to stand next to me.'

'I will visit Narboro today, and ask him to confirm what you have told me,' said Bartholomew, somewhat threateningly.

'Please do. And when you have done that, speak to Father Aiden, Mistress FitzAbsolon, Widow Deschalers and Prior Pechem. All were close enough to have heard my exchange with Narboro, and will also corroborate my story.'

Such disparate witnesses, all respected members of the community, were unlikely to lie, so Bartholomew reluctantly conceded that the Senior Proctor was telling the truth. He struggled to hide his disappointment. He would not have minded at all if Brampton was the killer. Reluctantly, he crossed him off the list of suspects, because if Brampton had not killed Elsham, then the chances were that he had not pushed Aynton to his death either.

'So did you see who dislodged the stone?' he asked shortly.

'Of course not,' snapped Brampton. 'I was too far away. Besides, I was concentrating on Narboro. I had to choose my words carefully, lest the wrong phrase should impact negatively on the case I am bringing against him for dishonouring my sister.'

'Your lawsuit is doing her a lot more harm than Narboro's breach of promise,' said Bartholomew, nettled enough to speak out of turn.

Brampton sneered. 'She thinks she can still win herself a husband, but she is too old, and no suitor wants another man's leavings. My lawsuit will not affect that one way or the other. Now, may I go? If I do not collect the last of the

287

money, Morys will bray that we have broken our word, and the town louts will use it as an excuse to do battle with us.'

Bartholomew watched him scurry away with a sense of rising frustration. Every lead he had seemed to be turning into a dead end.

Hopeful that the beadles' sickness might provide him with answers about the flux at last, Bartholomew hurried to visit one of them. He found out where the ale had been bought, and strode briskly to the brewery.

'Yes, we sold a barrel to Beadle Brown yesterday,' said the brewer. 'But it came from the same vat as nine others, all of which were returned empty this morning. The beadles are the only ones to report any ill effects, so the problem lies with them, not my ale.'

Perplexed, Bartholomew went to Beadle Brown's house in Shoemaker Row, and learned that the barrel had stood in his yard for several hours before it had been broached. Had it soured because it was left in the sun? Or did the problem lie with the bucket of filthy water that Brown and his cronies had used to wash their hands and faces after finishing work?

'I fetched that water from the Market Square well,' groaned Brown, clutching his stomach. 'But Mistress Starre got one at the same time, and *she* is not ill.'

Bartholomew sagged, feeling answers slip through his fingers yet again. Then he saw a familiar figure slinking past. Narboro. He hailed him, and the Peterhouse man stopped so abruptly that the baker wheeling his barrow behind slammed into the back of him. Narboro staggered, and the baker released a stream of pithy obscenities.

'That hurt!' whimpered Narboro. 'I am going to sue him.'

'You have done a remarkable job of disguising your black eyes,' said Bartholomew, peering admiringly at his handiwork. 'The bruises are almost invisible.'

Narboro flashed a pleased grin. 'Your fiancée said the same, and asked me to show her how I did it. That woman is a gem – you should treasure her.'

'I do,' said Bartholomew, and turned to business. 'I understand you had a mishap with your mirror shortly before Elsham was killed.'

Narboro nodded. 'A workman jostled me, and made me drop it, so I stopped Brampton to make a formal complaint. Look at it! Ruined!'

Bartholomew was startled when Narboro fished in his scrip and produced a handful of large, jagged shards. Anyone else would have thrown them away. He said so.

'A couple of pieces are still big enough to use, and they are better than nothing.' Narboro replaced them carefully. 'Thank God I have ordered a replacement from Linton, or I should be in a pretty pickle!'

'Was this before or after you saw Morys pay Donwich for his help at the guildhall?'

'Before,' replied Narboro. 'And after that, Elsham was toted past me and the sight made me sick. So – Brampton, Morys and Donwich, and Elsham – in that order.'

'I wish you had seen who pushed the stone,' said Bartholomew wearily.

'So do I, because I dislike the notion of a vicious killer walking free, poised to strike again. I shall not breathe easy until the rogue is safely behind bars.'

For the rest of the day and well into the evening, Bartholomew was inundated with people who wanted him to visit flux-afflicted loved ones. He was tempted to make a public announcement about how to care for the victims, but realised this would be a bad idea when one patient transpired to have something else entirely – something that would have become a far more serious problem without timely medical intervention.

The only light on the horizon was that everyone

between Milne Street and the High Street was recovering, and there had been no new cases there for two days. He did not care that Stasy and Hawick claimed their remedy was responsible. He was just glad that the sufferers were getting better.

It was nearly dark by the time he had seen everyone who had summoned him. His feet were sore from traipsing around in wet shoes, his back ached from leaning over beds, and he had eaten nothing since breakfast. He stopped to buy a pastry from a baker, touched when the man waved away payment on the grounds that Bartholomew had once mended his daughter's broken arm for free. He was just finishing it when Tulyet and Dickon hurried past.

'Good,' said Tulyet, skidding to a standstill. 'Now I do not need to send a messenger to Michaelhouse. Come with us to the Chesterton lane – we have a report of a body.'

'Lyonnes?' asked Bartholomew, recalling that Shardelowe had reported him missing.

'No,' replied Dickon, all ghoulish delight for the task they were about to perform. 'His men think *he* has gone to London, because there was a big row between him and everyone else on Monday, and they all called him a bad-tempered bully.'

'That is why he was in the Griffin,' elaborated Tulyet. 'Soothing his ruffled feathers with ale. None of the others would jaunt off for an evening in a tavern, not when it might mean the difference between everyone getting his bonus or losing it.'

'Who found this body?' asked Bartholomew, more interested in that than the antics of the surly builder. He allowed Dickon to grab his arm and pull him along with them.

'They did.' Tulyet nodded to where Isaac de Blaston and his friends trailed along behind. All were drenched, but chattered excitedly among themselves. Then Ulf joined them, resplendent in his new hat, and they immediately fell silent.

Feeling he should tell Michael what was happening, lest the victim transpired to be a scholar, Bartholomew hailed a passing beadle, but the man pretended not to hear and scuttled down a nearby alley.

'He is the one Ulf knifed,' explained Tulyet, casting a glance behind him to where the boy skipped along with his friends. 'And as we failed to see justice delivered, he doubtless prefers to keep his distance from the brat. What did you want him for? To tell Michael about the body? Dickon will do it.'

'I would rather see the corpse,' objected Dickon, his face falling.

'Then you had better hurry,' said Tulyet, unmoved. 'Off you go.'

Neither he nor Bartholomew spoke as they trotted along. Their determined pace and grim expressions attracted attention, and soon it was not just children who fell in behind them. They acquired more followers as they crossed the *ponticulus,* and by the time they reached the barren track that led to the village of Chesterton, they had collected quite an entourage. Morys was among them, and Bartholomew was tempted to interrogate him there and then, but it was hardly the time or the place; absently, he noted that the Mayor appeared to have been in a fight, because there were three long, deep scratches down his left cheek. Isnard was there, too, braying his opinions as a man who knew the river and its ways.

'There is a pool by the elms,' the bargeman announced to anyone who would listen. 'The body will have washed up there. They usually do.'

He was right. Unfortunately, the victim was floating in the middle of it, so Tulyet sent a soldier to the castle to fetch ropes and a hook – and lamps, too, as it was now completely dark. When they arrived, it was Isnard who stepped forward to do what was necessary.

'It is Martyn,' said Bartholomew, once the victim had

291

been retrieved and was lying on the bank. 'Stabbed – some days ago, judging by the state of decomposition.'

'He has been somewhere else since he died, but the river runs faster now we have had some rain, and it dislodged him,' said Isnard with confident authority. 'The Cam always yields its treasures in the end. It gave up Huntyngdon and now here is his friend.'

'*Were* they killed at the same time, Matt?' asked Tulyet.

'I cannot be sure, but there is no reason to suppose otherwise.'

'I suspect this one was buried in a shallow grave on the bank opposite Michaelhouse,' Isnard went on. 'And his killer did not realise he would be flushed out when the river returned to its normal levels.'

Bartholomew looked around for Dickon, who had gabbled his message at Michael, then raced to rejoin his father. Now he was at Tulyet's side, agog with interest.

'You cannot have conducted a very thorough search,' he said, feeling that Tulyet should not have entrusted the task to him in the first place. He was still a child, after all.

Dickon was stung. 'Yes, I did! Besides, Michael's beadle did not find him either, so the killer must have hidden him really well.'

'You should have asked me to do it,' said Isnard grandly. 'I would have known where to look. Beadles and children are no substitute for men who know what they are doing.'

'Both were stabbed in the back,' noted Tulyet, bringing an abrupt end to the discussion, and Bartholomew saw he did not appreciate his son's shortcomings aired in public. 'Does this mean that Elsham claimed two victims, rather than the one he was ready to confess?'

'He wanted to unburden his conscience,' replied Bartholomew, 'so I think that if he had killed Martyn, he would have confessed it. Besides, the wounds are different, so the same weapon was not used to dispatch them both. Martyn's is much wider.'

'Caused by the bloodstained blade we found in Gille's room?' asked Tulyet, and pulled it from his scrip.

Bartholomew measured it against the hole in the victim. 'A perfect match, which means that Gille dealt with him, while Elsham stabbed Huntyngdon. It seems likely that Martyn was carrying a letter from Aynton as well.'

He began to search the body for it, aware that he was being watched by dozens of eyes, as people pressed forward for a better view. It was not a pleasant task, and all to no avail, as there was nothing to find – Martyn's purse had been torn from his belt, and there was nowhere else for a missive to be.

'Sheriff!' came Morys's voice suddenly, unnaturally shrill with alarm. 'Quickly! There is another one – another body. And it has no head!'

Tulyet grabbed a lamp and ran towards him, although it did not require much light to see that Morys was right. There was indeed a headless corpse in the reeds. Isnard retrieved it, then flailed around with a crutch in an effort to locate the missing part.

'Who is it?' demanded Tulyet, watching Bartholomew inspect the body. 'Gille?'

'His tool-belt and callused hands suggest a builder,' said Bartholomew. 'I suspect this is Lyonnes. The rumours about him going to London in a sulk are wrong.'

CHAPTER 15

It took a long time for Bartholomew to examine both bodies, then arrange for them to be taken to their parish churches. While he worked, Tulyet questioned the onlookers, but when the two of them met in the Brazen George some hours later, neither had anything significant to report. Michael arrived, too, his face pale and weary in the flickering lamplight. He stayed just long enough to devour a hasty bowl of meat pottage, then left to break the news to Martyn's landlord in the Cardinal's Cap.

Bartholomew trudged home alone, only to be told that there were patients who needed to see him, so it was nearly dawn before he finally reached his bed. He flopped on it fully clothed, and slept through the bell summoning scholars to morning prayers. He slept through breakfast, too, and his students let him be, afraid that if he woke, he would subject them to a gruelling round of classes and lectures.

He might have slumbered until noon, but Walter's peacocks set up a tremendous racket when Stasy came to demand the return of the fees he had paid for the degree he would never receive. The noise was deafening, and even Bartholomew – the deepest sleeper the College had ever known – was unequal to drowsing through it.

He rose slowly, muddle-headed from tiredness, washed in the water Cynric had left for him, then donned a clean tunic and tabard. They felt clammy and cold, the heatwave already a distant memory. He was just restocking his medical bag when Michael walked in.

The monk looked every inch a Chancellor in his spotless habit and neat tonsure. He was freshly shaven, and possessed a natural authority which Donwich lacked. He could not disguise the lines of strain etched into his face, though, or the dark smudges under his eyes that showed Bartholomew was not the only one who needed a decent night's sleep.

'Dickon has been arrested for the murder of Lyonnes,' he reported without preamble. 'His father came to tell me just now.'

Bartholomew wondered if he had misheard. '*Dickon* arrested? On what grounds?'

'The fact that he publicly threatened to cleave Lyonnes' head from his shoulders, and that seems to have been what happened. Lyonnes left the Griffin in a drunken haze on Monday evening, and the general consensus is that Dickon struck then. Naturally, he protests his innocence, and is terrified by the situation in which he finds himself.'

'*Is* he innocent?' asked Bartholomew, struggling to come to terms with the tale.

Michael shrugged. 'He is nasty, bullying and ghoulish, and no one likes him, but murder? That takes a certain courage – which he does not have.'

Bartholomew agreed. 'He is a vicious little brute, who longs to be in France where he thinks he can run amok. But there is a big difference between terrorising strangers in a foreign land and killing people here. Moreover, whoever beheaded Lyonnes did it badly, but Dickon's sword is extremely sharp . . .'

'In other words, you think he would have made a better job of it,' said Michael drily. 'I hardly think that will be seen as much of a defence.'

'Has anyone examined his sword?'

'Sergeant Robin did, and declared it to be blood-free. But Dickon is proud of his weapons, and is forever polishing them, so that is no defence either. Incidentally, Meadowman is back at work, thank God. He can take over the Senior Proctor's duties until Brampton has collected all the bridge money and has written up an official account of it.'

'So Meadowman will investigate the murders now?' asked Bartholomew hopefully.

'That task would be entirely beyond him. However, he did learn something on his first visit to a tavern since becoming ill – the identity of the "saint" who has been donating money to paupers and beadles. The rector of Holy Trinity got drunk with him and let it slip.'

'Who is it?' asked Bartholomew, intrigued. 'A scholar?'

'Chaumbre,' replied Michael. 'Which explains why he has been so slow to infill his dye-pits – his wealth is being channelled into more pressing causes.'

'*Chaumbre?*' echoed Bartholomew, stunned.

'He also lent some to Shardelowe when Morys refused to pay his bargemen. And it is a good thing he did, because Morys continues to default, despite being ordered to settle the account by the end of Monday. You witnessed Shardelowe and Chaumbre discussing the details of the arrangement after the spat on the High Street.'

Bartholomew frowned. 'And both of them lied about it: Shardelowe denied it ever took place, while Chaumbre invented some nonsense about the builder admiring his dye-pits. Why did they not just tell me the truth?'

'Because Chaumbre begged Shardelowe's discretion. It transpires that your brother-in-law is a humble man, who has no desire for gratitude. Perhaps he *is* a saint. No other burgess asks for his generosity to be kept quiet – they all want to be feted and admired.'

Bartholomew pondered the revelation. 'Does Edith know?'

'No one does, other than the priests, and they are sworn to silence. We would still be in the dark if Meadowman had not plied the only unreliable one with ale. When I went to inform Chaumbre that his secret will soon be out, I asked why he had gone to such lengths to maintain his anonymity. The answer is Edith.'

'Edith?'

'Apparently, he has loved her since they were youngsters, and he left the town with a broken heart after she married Oswald – he was not rich then, and your parents insisted she took a wealthy husband with a promising future.'

'They did,' acknowledged Bartholomew. 'She had no say in the matter, but they chose well. She was happy with Oswald.'

'When Chaumbre heard she was a widow,' Michael continued, 'he decided to move back to Cambridge, and was delighted to step in and save her from her profligate son. He knows she married him out of need, not affection, but he claims to be the happiest man alive.'

'He certainly smiles a lot.'

'He told me that the very sight of her makes his heart sing, and thinks God has finally given him the only thing he has ever really wanted. In return, he vowed to help the poor and needy with his wealth – not for his own glory, but for God's.'

'*Is* he wealthy? At one point, Morys jibed him about having no money, and you told me that Edith had to buy her own wedding kirtle. He even tried to borrow some from me.'

'Apparently, settling your nephew's debts took most of his available cash, then he was hurt by the theft from his Girton house. Despite this, he refused to break his oath, even though finding enough to meet his charitable obligations was a serious challenge.'

Bartholomew thought about the huge number of people who had benefited from Chaumbre's largesse, not to mention the heavy purse that had arrived for his paupers' medicine. 'It must be costing him a fortune.'

'It is, but he is solvent again now, because the monks

at Ely have paid for a massive consignment of cloth, and the money has arrived from the sale of his London mansion.'

'Do you believe this tale?' asked Bartholomew, not sure what to think.

'Well, every parish priest – and Shardelowe – confirms it, so yes,' replied Michael. 'And if either of us ever considered him a rogue, we misjudged him badly. He is irritatingly cheerful, but that is not a crime.'

'No,' acknowledged Bartholomew. 'Perhaps I should have trusted Edith's judgement – she would never have married him if he was unsavoury, not even to save her business. She recognised something in him that I failed to see.'

'Then it is a good thing that he wanted to marry her, not you,' said Michael, and glanced up at the sky to gauge the time. 'I have a few moments before meeting the vicars-general again. Come to my rooms for something to eat before you resume your enquiries. It will be a lot nicer than anything you can beg from Agatha.'

Michael was right: his personal larder was far better stocked than the College kitchens, and Bartholomew was presented with fresh bread, crisp apples and creamy cheese.

'I am no closer to finding the killer than I was when I started, Brother,' the physician said unhappily as he ate. 'You will have to help me if you want a culprit in three days.'

Michael winced. 'I wish I could, but my dealings with the vicars-general have reached a critical stage, and I cannot abandon them now. Who are your remaining suspects?'

'Donwich, Morys, Stasy and Hawick. And we need to find Gille, so he can answer for what he did to Martyn. Brampton is eliminated as a suspect, too.'

'Yes, I heard you ignored my express orders and interrogated him anyway. Luckily for you, it did not interfere with him collecting the bridge money – he took the bulk of that to Morys last night, and the remaining few marks will be delivered by noon today. He has performed nothing short of a miracle, and the University has kept its promise to the town.'

'I am disturbed by the violent nature of Lyonnes' death,' said Bartholomew, unwilling to listen to Michael singing the praises of a man he did not like. 'I wonder if—'

'You do not have time to explore a town murder,' interrupted Michael in alarm. 'Concentrate on Aynton, Martyn, Huntyngdon and Elsham. Your colleagues.'

They both jumped when the door was flung open and Cynric burst in, dragging Clippesby behind him. The Dominican had a chicken on his shoulder, which flapped frantically as she fought to keep her balance. William brought up the rear.

'Francis of Assisi here has something to tell you,' announced William, jerking a grubby thumb at Clippesby. 'Information from a sparrow, but important, even so.'

'Tell him, Master Clippesby,' urged Cynric. 'Go on. Quickly now.'

'The sparrow lives in Shoemaker Row,' began Clippesby obligingly, 'so he often sees Stasy and Hawick, who have opened a dispensary there—'

'They recite prayers to Satan every night,' blurted William, unable to wait for the Dominican to come to the point. 'And the consulting room at the back is not for seeing patients, but is where they store their demonic regalia.'

'In chests,' elaborated Clippesby. 'Concealed from the casual visitor. The sparrow—'

'Pentangles, spell books, black candles and bits of dead animals,' listed William furiously. 'Worse yet, Clippesby

299

now reveals that they worshipped Lucifer while they lived here in the College, although he never thought to mention it to the rest of us.'

Michael was horrified. 'But if anyone had found out, we would have been suppressed! You should not have kept such dangerous knowledge to yourself, Clippesby.'

The Dominican shrugged. 'They asked their dark lord for all manner of favours, but none were ever granted. Ergo, I concluded that they were not really his disciples, but silly boys who would eventually come to their senses.'

'That was not for you to decide,' cried Michael angrily. 'You should have told us. Moreover, they are on our list for murdering Aynton.'

'Perhaps they did,' said Clippesby, unruffled by his colleagues' ire. 'Although the sparrow has no knowledge of that, one way or the other. However, he is not convinced that Dickon killed Lyonnes – he thinks the boy would have chosen a cleaner mode of execution.'

'So does Matt, but opinions will not exonerate him,' said Michael. 'He needs—'

'It is time for me and Margery to deal with Stasy and Hawick,' interrupted Cynric, more concerned with the danger posed to the College by the ex-students than exculpating the Sheriff's unlikeable son. 'Do not worry – we know what to do.'

'No!' cried Bartholomew, alarmed. 'Leave them to . . .'

He trailed off. Leave them to whom? Michael was busy with the vicars-general, Tulyet would be frantically trying to prove that Dickon did not decapitate Lyonnes, Brampton was worse than useless, and he himself had a killer to catch. Cynric nodded knowingly when he stopped, and left without another word.

'I cannot do this alone, Brother,' said Bartholomew, suddenly overwhelmed with the enormity of the task that lay ahead of him. 'I need help.'

'Then take William,' suggested Michael. He shrugged

at Bartholomew's instant horror, although the friar gave a grin of delight. 'Desperate circumstances call for desperate measures, Matt, and besides, he is good in a fight.'

'You anticipate fighting?' gulped Bartholomew, more daunted than ever.

'Your suspects include a corrupt mayor with a violent family, two warlocks and the ambitious Donwich,' replied Michael drily. 'So yes, I would say a spat might be possible.'

'Do not worry, Matthew,' said William grandly, drawing himself up to his full height. 'I will protect you. Shall we tackle Morys first? I have never liked him.'

'Dick will want to be there when we do that,' hedged Bartholomew, trying to think of a way to ditch the Franciscan, sure he would be more hindrance than help.

'You will have no help from Tulyet,' predicted William. 'Not when he is trying to save his nasty son. I wish him luck with that! The boy is a hellion, and the only thing that surprises me is that he has not beheaded someone sooner.'

As William categorically refused to be left behind, claiming he had been appointed to the investigation by the Chancellor himself, Bartholomew saw he had no choice but to accept his services. Together, they left Michaelhouse and headed for the guildhall in the hope that Morys would be there. It was raining hard and rather cool, so both wore cloaks. Bartholomew glanced down one lane at the river, and saw it flowing faster than it had done in weeks. He was glad that the filth accumulated during the drought would finally be washed away, although he prayed that no more corpses would appear.

'Morys still refuses to open the Middle and East dams,' grumbled William, who had mentioned the matter several times already, so Bartholomew saw it had become an obsession with him. 'He wants to make sure that his own water needs are met first, so the only one he deigns to unlock is the West Dam, which feeds the spillway to his mill.'

'If it rains like this for another day, it will not matter,' shrugged Bartholomew. 'The Mill Pond will be full, and there will be enough water for everyone.'

'He is a selfish rogue,' William went on, growing angrier the more he thought about it. 'He has done something to the sluice gates, to prevent them from being unfastened without his permission. Well, I hope the burgesses elect a *decent* Mayor next time, and that he fines Morys for hogging the water that God meant us all to share.'

There was no reply to his sharp rap on the guildhall door, but it was open so he marched inside, evidently feeling that being asked to explore the murders gave him the authority to go wherever he pleased. Bartholomew followed more cautiously, and saw the Mayor deep in discussion with Narboro at the far end of the main hall. Morys's cousin John was a menacing presence at his kinsman's side. As he watched, Narboro handed Morys a purse. Morys opened it, and his indignant expression suggested that it contained less than he thought it should. He and Narboro began to quarrel.

'We must find out what they are saying,' whispered William, eyes agleam.

'Why?' asked Bartholomew, startled. 'It will not concern our investigation and—'

'You cannot say that for certain until you know what has set them at each other's throats,' interrupted William firmly. 'Now, follow my lead.'

To Bartholomew's utter astonishment, the friar dropped to his hands and knees and began to crawl towards the squabbling pair, using benches to conceal his approach. Bartholomew did not like to imagine what would happen if he was caught – the University would never live it down. With an irritable sigh, feeling that William was wasting their precious time with something that was irrelevant, he hurried outside to a conveniently placed window, where he could eavesdrop from a rather more dignified position.

'It is no longer enough,' Morys was declaring. 'The stakes have risen.'

'They have not,' objected Narboro. 'They are exactly the same as when we started.'

'If you do not double this, you will regret it,' warned Morys. 'So I strongly advise you to reconsider. It is the way things work in Cambridge.'

'It is while you are Mayor,' muttered Narboro sourly.

He gulped his alarm when John stepped forward, and hastened to slap a second purse into Morys's waiting palm. Then he turned and fled. Bartholomew held his breath when his route took him very close to where William was hiding. Fortunately, he was so intent on leaving that he looked neither to left nor right, and the friar escaped notice. Bartholomew sagged in relief.

Meanwhile, Morys chuckled with pleasure as he counted the coins he had acquired. 'I shall have everything he owns before I am done with him,' he crowed. 'He is a fool.'

'I disagree,' growled John. 'There is something about him . . . I sense he is not the dullard you imagine, cousin. You should treat him with more care.'

'Nonsense,' sniffed Morys. 'But we should put our winnings somewhere safe. Come.'

They left the same way as Narboro, and Bartholomew watched in alarm a second time as they passed within inches of where William huddled like a great grubby grey slug. Fortunately, John was still trying to convince Morys that Narboro was not all he seemed, while Morys was more interested in the feel of his new money, so they also passed without spotting anything amiss. The moment they had gone, Bartholomew darted back to where the friar was brushing dust from his habit.

'Did you hear all that?' William demanded, pleased

with himself. 'I offer to assist you, and within moments, we uncover evidence of a vile plot.'

'All we learned is that Morys is extorting money from Narboro, but we cannot investigate why, because we do not have time.'

'The Mayor is involved in a shabby scheme with a scholar,' countered William. 'Ergo, we have a moral obligation to look into it. We shall speak to Narboro first, and demand a—'

'No!' interrupted Bartholomew sharply, heartily wishing Michael had never suggested working with him. 'We came to talk to Morys about the murders. Everything else must wait.'

William shrugged. 'So we force Morys to confess to those, *then* demand an explanation of his sly business with Narboro. I have no objection to doing it that way around.'

By the time Bartholomew and William emerged from the guildhall, Morys had disappeared, although John could be seen in the distance, striding towards the castle. William pointed to a narrow lane near the Round Church.

'He must have gone down there – it runs near his house. Come on.'

When they reached Morys's mansion, he hammered imperiously on the door with his fist. There was no reply, so he gave it a hefty shove. It swung open, and he marched inside before Bartholomew could remind him that barging into the homes of influential townsmen was not the same as entering a public building like the guildhall, and would bring all manner of trouble down on their heads. Reluctantly, he followed him in.

The house was silent. It was also empty, and not so much as a stick of furniture or a scrap of rug remained anywhere. Bartholomew was astonished, recalling the sumptuous décor he had admired when he had tended the ailing Rohese four days earlier.

'His term of office expires soon,' said William, looking around, 'so I suppose he has decided to rent somewhere more modest. It is odd though – I know most of the burgesses, and none have mentioned him decanting to different lodgings.'

But it looked to Bartholomew as if Morys was not so much moving house as leaving the town altogether, and the fact that he had spirited his belongings away without informing his friends told him exactly what the man was up to.

'He ordered the University to pay all the bridge money by yesterday,' he mused, 'while the funds raised by the town – probably including the King's contribution – are in his cellar. I saw the chest when I tended Rohese.'

William frowned. 'What of it?'

'I think that as soon as Brampton hands over the last few marks from the University, Morys will disappear, taking it all with him.'

William gaped his disbelief. 'Not even he would dare commit theft on that scale!'

'It *is* a fortune – far more than he could make from bribes. And he clearly *does* intend to sneak away. Why else would he strip his house without telling anyone? Moreover, he has been away a lot recently, "on business" or "visiting kin". I suspect what he has really been doing is spiriting his furniture away, ready for when he vanishes with all our money.'

He did not wait to see if William was convinced, feeling time was too short to say more, and inside the lion's den was no place to do it anyway. Motioning the friar to silence, he crept towards the cellar door. It was open and the stairs were lit by a lantern. He descended stealthily, William at his heels. They arrived in a deep stone-built basement that was even cooler than the ground floor of Hoo Hall. No wonder Morys had been able to store ice for his sherbets, he thought.

305

There were now two chests, and Morys was kneeling next to them. The lids of both were open, and he was weighing purses in his hands, his face bright with greed. Bartholomew saw one pouch sewn with Michaelhouse's crest, proving beyond all doubt that this was indeed the bridge money.

'Going somewhere, Morys?' demanded William, pushing past the physician to stalk into the cellar and stand pugnaciously with his hands on his hips.

Morys leapt up in alarm, although his consternation was quickly masked, and the first thing he did was kick shut the lids on the boxes, concealing their contents from sight.

'Yes, I shall return to the Fens in a few weeks,' he replied, struggling to sound nonchalant. 'My term in office expires soon, so I shall leave this house for my successor. Perhaps it will be my cousin John, although he will have to canvass for votes.'

'Buy them, you mean,' said William in distaste. 'Like you did. But you cannot fool us, Morys. We know you plan to make off with all that money.'

'It is why you refused to pay Shardelowe for supplies,' put in Bartholomew, cutting across Morys's blustering denial. 'Why you *still* have not paid. You aim to keep everything for yourself.'

'It will be a pretty sum when added to what you have amassed through corrupt practices,' said William, eyeing him with revulsion.

'What corrupt practices?' demanded Morys indignantly.

'We have just seen you with Narboro,' retorted William. 'He *paid* you for a favour.'

Morys shrugged. 'It is the way things work in Cambridge. You pay me, I pay others, and together we get results. He wants planning permission for a house.'

'What happened to your face?' asked Bartholomew, noting again the three scratches down the Mayor's left cheek. 'Did one of your victims decline to pay, so you fought him?'

Morys touched the wounds with a tentative finger. 'Rohese has a new kitten, and it does not know the strength of its own claws.'

'You pressed for a stone bridge not because it is best for the town,' said William, more interested in his accusations than Morys's injury, 'but because it will require more money than repairing the wooden one. Money you intended to steal from the start.'

'Prove it,' challenged Morys.

William faltered, but confirmation came from an unexpected source.

'I brought the cart, cousin,' came John's voice from the top of the stairs. 'You carry the chests outside, while I keep watch. Then all we need to do is wait for Brampton to bring the last few purses, and we can be away, free and clear.'

Morys shot the two scholars a weary glance. 'Very well, you have caught us fair and square. How much will it take to buy your silence? Ten per cent? It cannot be more – starting a new life will be expensive, and we did not go through all this to live like paupers.'

His words alerted John to the fact that all was not well. There was a sharp hiss as weapons were drawn, and the knight came down the steps with a sword in one hand and a dagger in the other. Bartholomew fumbled in his medical bag for a surgical blade, although he knew it would be of scant use against such a formidable opponent.

Meanwhile, William untied the rope cincture from around his waist and whirled it around his head. It was clearly intended to convey menace, but instead looked ridiculous, and Bartholomew might have laughed had their predicament not been so dire.

'They know our plan, John,' said Morys hoarsely. 'So

307

kill them, and we will leave at once. We shall have to abandon the last of the University's contribution, but better that than be caught. Now, hurry!'

CHAPTER 16

John came towards the two scholars with murder in his eyes, and Bartholomew gripped his little scalpel in an unsteady hand, sure the knight's brutish face was the last thing he would ever see. He experienced a lurch of regret at the pain his death would cause Matilde.

But he had reckoned without William, who continued to whip the cincture around his head. Then he lashed out with it. One of the knots caught John square in the eye, and while the knight yowled in pain, momentarily blinded, William leapt forward and punched him. John crashed to the floor senseless.

'Bind him, before he wakes up,' the friar ordered, tossing the cincture to Bartholomew. 'I will deal with his slippery kinsman.'

Bartholomew caught the cord in a daze, stunned by the speed with which the balance of power had shifted. He quickly bound John's hands and feet, then looked up to see William holding Morys by the scruff of his neck. He was about to suggest sending for Tulyet when he spotted someone lying in the farthest, most shadowy corner of the cellar. Cautiously, he went to investigate.

'Rohese!' he exclaimed in horror. 'She has been strangled.'

'Rohese is dead?' cried Morys, allowing his jaw to drop. 'My beloved wife! Who could have done such a terrible thing?'

'*You* could,' said Bartholomew, regarding him contemptuously. 'Do not deny it. Three of her fingernails are full of blood and skin, and you have three scratches on your face.'

'Those came from her kitten,' objected Morys. 'It is—'

'I am a physician,' interrupted Bartholomew angrily. 'I know the difference between marks made by claws and wounds from human nails. Moreover, Rohese is packed in ice – the ice you imported at great expense for sherbets. You aim to ensure that the smell of her decomposing body does not alert anyone until you are safely away.'

'Lies!' cried Morys, although there was a dull gleam of defeat in his eyes.

'I imagine we will find other evidence, too, once we start looking,' Bartholomew went on, regarding him with revulsion. 'And we know why you did it: she carried another man's child. I warned her to leave before you found out . . .'

'You will hang for murder, Morys,' said William, giving him a shake. 'Your thievery is nothing compared to killing a mother and her unborn child. But you can avoid the noose if you confess to all your crimes.'

Bartholomew was not sure he could, but Morys leapt at the frail strand of hope anyway.

'Yes, all right, we did intend to slip away today with the bridge money,' he gabbled. 'But it was not my idea – it was John's. He has always been greedy, and I am terrified of him. I had no choice but to obey his orders.'

'Very noble,' said Bartholomew, his disgust intensifying. 'Blaming an unconscious kinsman for your crimes. But never mind the money. We want to know why you killed Chancellor Aynton.'

'But I never did!' gulped Morys. 'I know you think I had reason to – he did not want a stone bridge, so his opinions stood between me and this fortune – but I have an alibi for his murder, albeit not one that shows me in a very good light . . .'

'Yes?' prompted William, giving him another shake.

'I was at Chaumbre's house in Girton,' whispered Morys, and nodded towards John. 'With him and a couple

310

of the Godenave children. I knew Chaumbre kept money there, and it was easy to break in when the only guards were two elderly servants.'

'So you stole the money he was using to help the poor and flux-stricken,' said Bartholomew, more repelled than ever by the man's selfishness and greed.

'I did not know he used it for them,' objected Morys. 'Obviously, if I had, I would have stayed my hand.'

'Of course you would,' said Bartholomew flatly. 'But you are still lying, because you were at the Clare Hall feast that evening – and then among the spectators who gathered to gawp at Aynton's body later.'

'Yes, but I left Clare Hall when I saw Chaumbre arrive,' explained Morys. 'If he was there, he could not be in Girton, so it seemed like a good time to strike. Ergo, when Aynton died, we were off a-burgling. I happened across the commotion surrounding his mishap on my way home. Of course I stopped to see what was going on.'

'Was Ulf one of your accomplices?' asked Bartholomew, supposing the claim was possible, but unwilling to give Morys the satisfaction of saying so. 'His father said you have used the boy before – it is why you arranged for him to wriggle out of the charge of stabbing the beadle.'

Morys licked his lips uneasily. 'Ulf does own certain useful skills that I employ from time to time, but I never condoned what he did to that beadle. However, none of us were on the bridge at compline. Ask John and the Godenave boys – they will all tell you the same.'

'You expect us to believe felons?' sneered William. 'Your alibi is worthless!'

Morys thought fast. 'Elsham! Assuming that whoever killed him and Aynton are one and the same, then I have another alibi. I *was* near the bridge when the stone fell, but I was with Prior Pechem of the Franciscans. I was urging him to contribute a little extra to the bridge fund. Talk to him – he will tell you.'

'Pechem would never lie,' William told Bartholomew. 'So if he says this snake was with him, then it will be true.'

Morys's face turned from fearful to calculating. 'Perhaps you and I can reach an accommodation. Not money, as I see you are honest men, but information. I know something important, and I will tell you if you let me go.'

'You will tell us anyway,' growled William, and gave Morys so vigorous a shake that Bartholomew heard his teeth clack together.

'Dickon!' gasped Morys dizzily. 'He did not behead Lyonnes and John can prove it. Take us to the castle, and we will strike a deal: our lives for his.'

'You will not escape that easily,' snarled William, preparing to shake him again.

'Then the Sheriff will lose his only son,' shouted Morys quickly, and smirked when the friar hesitated. 'He will let us go when he hears what we can do for him.'

They all turned in alarm at a sound from the stairs. But it was only Brampton, who stood with a heavy bag in his hand: the last of the University's bridge money.

'You will never be released, Morys,' he said coldly. 'I heard your entire confession. You are a murderer and a thief, and you will answer for all your crimes.'

'Then Dickon will hang, even though he never hurt Lyonnes,' blustered Morys. 'You have no choice but to accede to my demands. If you do not, Tulyet will never forgive you.'

Brampton smiled nastily. 'That assumes he will find out. I shall ensure he never does.'

Morys shook his head in incomprehension. 'You would sacrifice an innocent boy in order to hang me? Why? What has Tulyet done to make you turn against him so cruelly?'

Brampton looked at the body in the shadows. 'It is not Tulyet who has earned my hatred, and not Dickon either. It is you. Rohese did not deserve to die, just because you are not man enough to keep her affections.'

'You were her lover, too?' breathed Morys. 'God's blood! Is there no scholar in the University who did not make a cuckold of me?'

'I did not,' put in William. 'Nor did Clippesby, although I think Zoone and Aungel—'

'Enough, William,' warned Bartholomew sharply, feeling it was not the time for the Senior Proctor to learn that he had been nothing special to the fun-loving Rohese.

'You are going to the proctors' cells, Morys,' said Brampton icily. 'Where there will be no Sheriff to make bargains with you.'

Bartholomew agreed to guard the prisoners while William went to fetch armed beadles. Brampton stayed, too, stony-faced and silent. Bartholomew examined John, who had regained his senses, but stood well back when the knight started to struggle against his bonds, sincerely hoping William's cingulum did not snap, or he and Brampton were going to be in serious trouble. Angry and defeated, Morys began to taunt his captors, knowing it was all the revenge he was likely to get.

'You will never find Aynton's killer, because you are clueless and stupid. But he was a weakling, so who cares about justice for him anyway? Or for Elsham, for that matter? My wife displayed poor judgement by coupling with him.'

The blood drained from Brampton's face. 'She took Elsham as well?'

'You did not know?' jeered Morys, sensing weakness and homing in on it. 'She had dozens of lovers, starting with Burgess Baldok back in the spring.'

But Morys had miscalculated, and Brampton's anguished expression turned to one of savage triumph. 'You should have kept your mouth shut, Morys, because gloating about Elsham has just provided me with the clue I need to solve the case.'

'What clue?' demanded Bartholomew, wondering what he had missed.

'Rohese mentioned something that Elsham had divulged to her – namely that he and his friend Gille knew the identity of the killer. I did not believe her. Why would I? As far as I knew, she and Elsham had never met, let alone exchanged that sort of confidence.'

'But now you know there is a possibility of pillow-talk . . .' prompted Bartholomew.

'It must be true. So go and find Gille, and *he* will tell you the culprit's name.'

'Find him where?' demanded Bartholomew, disliking the way Brampton felt he could order him about. 'He has not been seen since Elsham died, and no one knows where he went.'

Brampton was thoughtful. 'Then ask Narboro. I saw Elsham and Gille corner him in an alley the day after Aynton was killed. It was a curious encounter, and I kept meaning to question them about it, but I never did. Perhaps he will have some ideas.'

'I thought Narboro was in Linton, then,' said Bartholomew, but then realised he was mistaken: the Peterhouse man was away when Huntyngdon and Martyn had gone missing, but was home by the time Aynton was killed.

He was relieved when William returned with a pack of beadles, plus Sergeant Robin and some of his men, who had agreed to take the bridge money to the castle. John had not spoken a word, but his malevolent glare was unnerving, while Brampton had kept glancing at Rohese's body, as if considering whether it warranted a dagger in Morys's black heart. Bartholomew had been on tenter-hooks the entire time.

The beadles baulked when they saw who they were expected to conduct to their cells, and only a sharp word from William reminded them of their duty. The friar decided to go with them, lest Morys talked them into letting him go, or they allowed themselves to be intimidated by John. When beadles, prisoners, soldiers and money had gone, Brampton addressed Bartholomew again.

'Run to Tulyet if you must, but I will not relinquish Morys to save Dickon. The boy will hang sooner or later anyway, and Rohese will not be deprived of justice on his account.'

'Of course I must tell Tulyet. Dickon is his only child.'

'Go, then,' snapped Brampton. 'I will stay here with Rohese.'

Bartholomew had misgivings about abandoning a grieving man with his lover's corpse, but Brampton was insistent on remaining, so the physician sprinted towards Bridge Street, keen to report to Tulyet, then return to his enquiries before any more of the day was lost. He glanced at the bridge while he hammered on the Sheriff's door, and noted that Shardelowe had made astonishing progress since he had last looked. Perhaps it really would be functional by the day after tomorrow.

Tulyet wept tears of relief when he heard Bartholomew's account of what had transpired with the Mayor and John, although his wife's reaction was more difficult to read.

'Morys *will* tell me what he knows of Lyonnes' murder,' Tulyet assured her. 'And when Dickon is free, we shall send him to France at once. He will be safe from unfounded accusations there. Thank you, Matt! I shall go to the proctors' gaol at once.'

Bartholomew walked with him, hoping the Senior Proctor was right to suggest that Narboro could shed light on Gille's whereabouts, because he had no other leads to follow.

'Brampton meant what he said,' he told Tulyet as they went. 'He will not allow Morys to buy his freedom with information to help Dickon, so how will you persuade Morys to talk? He will want something in return and you have nothing to offer.'

315

'Oh, yes, I do,' countered Tulyet. 'A chance to confess to me. If he refuses, I shall threaten to send Dickon to him instead. That will loosen his tongue.'

'Would that be ethical?' asked Bartholomew uneasily.

'More ethical than Morys withholding information that could save an innocent life. Look at Chaumbre over there, admiring those wretched dye-pits. The third is filled at last, but the last one is the biggest and deepest. He should have done that one first.'

Bartholomew supposed the abrupt change of subject was Tulyet's way of telling him that he did not need advice about how to deal with awkward prisoners.

Unfortunately, Bartholomew was called to assess a new outbreak of the flux, so it was William who went to Peterhouse to speak to Narboro. When the friar had finished, he tracked Bartholomew down in a house on Piron Lane, where he was struggling to feed a sick baby.

'Narboro was out,' William reported tersely. 'His colleagues have no idea where, so now what? Who are our remaining suspects?'

'Donwich, Stasy and Hawick,' replied Bartholomew, most of his attention on the child. 'So try cornering our resident warlocks, Father. You may prise more from them than I have done.'

Delighted with an opportunity to interrogate a pair of heretics, William hurried away at once. But when he and Bartholomew next met – at the affluent houses near the Franciscan Priory, where there was yet another outbreak of the sickness – dusk had fallen and the friar's shoulders were slumped in defeat.

'I could not break them,' he confessed, tired and frustrated in equal measure. 'I grilled them for hours, and even threatened excommunication, but they only laughed at me.'

'Well, they would,' said Bartholomew drily. 'They are not Christians.'

'I can report that Shardelowe and his crew did not kill Lyonnes, though,' William went on. 'Lyonnes had great skill with cement, and his death has led to worrying delays at the bridge. Too much money is at stake for them to have done him harm.'

'You are supposed to be looking into *our* murders,' snapped Bartholomew, exasperated. 'Lyonnes is the town's responsibility.'

'I *was* looking into our murders,' William shot back. 'I was at the bridge, asking questions about Aynton and Elsham. The information about the cement just came up.'

Bartholomew rubbed his eyes wearily. 'I am sorry. It has been a long few days.'

William patted his arm, an awkward gesture to show he understood. 'I met Tulyet not long ago,' he said after a moment. 'He told me that Morys is almost frantic to confess his crimes in the hope of escaping the noose. Much to Brampton's fury, he transferred Morys and John to the castle, which he says is more secure.'

Bartholomew sincerely hoped that Tulyet had not done the unthinkable, and promised to let the unsavoury pair go in exchange for proof of his son's innocence.

'And Dickon?' he asked uneasily.

'Free again,' replied William. 'Apparently, John took him out into the Fens on the night of Lyonnes' murder, to teach him how to hunt in the dark. The tale has already been verified by fishermen who have no reason to lie. Moreover, John claims that all Dickon's weapons would decapitate a man cleanly, whereas Lyonnes suffered some serious hacking.'

'He did,' said Bartholomew, who had made that point himself.

'So Dickon is now strutting around like a cockerel, vowing revenge on his accusers.'

'We should visit Hoo Hall,' said Bartholomew, although

317

every bone ached with fatigue and all he wanted to do was go home and sleep. 'Narboro may be home by now.'

It was raining hard as Bartholomew and William hurried towards Peterhouse. Water sluiced from tile roofs and dripped from thatches, and the streets were emptier than they usually were for the time of day, as everyone was keen to be indoors. Some houses had fires lit within, which was rare for July, and the smell of wood-smoke mingled with the scent of cooking and the ever-present reek of human sewage and animal dung.

'I tried to open the dams earlier,' said William as they went. 'The Mill Pond is almost full, and Morys is not in a position to stop me. Unfortunately, I cannot work out what he did to jam them shut.'

'You had better ask him then,' said Bartholomew, aware that it might become a problem if Morys was the only one who knew what to do. Perhaps he would use *that* as leverage to secure his release – the town would flood if the sluice gates could not be controlled.

'I did, when I took him to the proctors' gaol,' replied William. 'He refused to tell me unless he got something in return. I offered absolution from his sins, but he said that was not enough. Let us hope the Sheriff prises it out of him before we get too much more rain.'

They arrived at Peterhouse, where Gayton informed them that Narboro had sauntered in not long before, and had gone straight to his room to dry his hair.

'I am glad his Fellowship terminates on Saturday,' he said fervently, 'because his vanity is embarrassing. Can you make your own way to Hoo Hall? I would rather not go out in this weather. Do not cross Coe Fen, though, because it will be too wet. Use the road instead.'

Blinking rain from their eyes, Bartholomew and William hurried down the lane, grateful for the lamp Gayton had lent them, as their route was muddy and full of potholes. Ahead, Hoo Hall was a black square against the night sky, although light spilled from the dormitory window on the upper floor. Just as they reached the front door, it opened.

'What do you want?' asked Narboro in surprise. He was immaculately clad in an expensive oiled cloak that would keep him dry even in the worst of deluges.

'To accuse you of—' began William so belligerently that Narboro promptly bolted.

Bartholomew groaned, loath to race about on such a foul night. 'Now what?'

'Chase him!' howled William, snatching the lamp and haring after his quarry in a flurry of flailing habit and cincture tails.

Reluctantly, Bartholomew followed. Narboro reached the Trumpington road, turned left and streaked through the gate so fast that the guards there were too startled to stop him. He disappeared into the blackness on the other side.

'Where did he go?' asked Bartholomew, catching up with William, who was frantically shining the lantern down the alleys at the sides of the road.

Before the friar could reply, Narboro exploded from the doorway where he had been hiding, and raced away up the High Street. William set off after him, and Bartholomew saw them both dart into the churchyard of St Mary the Great. He arrived there just in time to witness the spectacular sight of the Franciscan launching himself horizontally at his prey. Narboro shrieked and spat, but he was no match for the burly friar. He was hauled upright, after which William whipped off his trusty cincture and looped it over Narboro's head, pinning his arms to his sides.

'I want one of those,' murmured Bartholomew, impressed. 'They come in very useful.'

'Let me go!' screeched Narboro. 'You cannot assault me! I am a favourite of the King.'

William smacked him around the back of his head. 'Stop squealing and tell us what we want to know. Why did you run?'

'Because of *you*,' cried Narboro, shying away from him. 'Everyone knows you are a fanatic, prone to making wild accusations. I was frightened.'

He did not look frightened, but it was difficult to tell in the gloom, so Bartholomew indicated that William was to take him into the church, where plenty of lamps were lit. It was also out of the rain. Inside, one or two people knelt in private prayer, and Michael's chief clerk was busy with his ledgers, but the building was otherwise empty.

'I suppose you aim to rail at me again for not marrying Lucy Brampton,' said Narboro sullenly. 'Well, I am sorry I called her old and ugly, but—'

'We do not care about that,' interrupted William briskly. 'We want to know where you are hiding Gille the murderer.'

It was not the way Bartholomew would have broached the subject, but it had the desired effect. The blood drained from Narboro's face and he began babbling in alarm.

'But I am *not* hiding him! I heard he was on the ferry when Elsham was killed, and I watched him scurry away afterwards, but I have no idea where he went.'

'We have witnesses who say that you met him in alleys, and that you were on very good terms with each other,' lied William. 'But he is a felon, and so was his friend Elsham.'

'I know,' gulped Narboro. 'I realised that when the pair of them hauled me into a dingy little lane, and insisted that I buy one of their obviously stolen exemplars. I refused, but Gille threatened to cut my face with a knife unless I reconsidered. So I did.'

The tale had a ring of truth about it, and Bartholomew sagged in disappointment. It was yet another dead end, and they had squandered precious time following it.

'Why did you give money to Morys in the guildhall today?' demanded William, less inclined to admit defeat. 'And do not deny it, because Matt and I saw you.'

'It is payment for his help with Brampton,' replied Narboro, and gave a nasty little smile. 'He will tell Brampton to drop his lawsuit against me, or be exposed for leering at Rohese. Senior Proctors are supposed to set a good example, so Brampton will have no choice but to comply.'

'He did a lot more than leer,' muttered William.

'Morys's help was costly, but only a fraction of what Brampton aims to take from me – *he* wants me in debt for the rest of my life. Morys said that if anyone asks about our arrangement, I am to claim that I paid him to arrange planning permission for a house.'

Bartholomew felt hope for a solution to the murders drain away even further, but William was still not ready to give up.

'Morys is under arrest for murder, theft and corruption, and anyone who bribed him will join him in the castle dungeons,' he blustered. 'You will be among them, unless you make it worth our while to let you go.'

'But I do not have anything left,' objected Narboro. 'Morys took it all.'

William fixed him with a baleful eye. 'I do not mean money, and you impugn our honour by suggesting it. We want information.'

Narboro thought fast. 'In that case, I do know something that may interest you, but you must promise to forget my arrangement with Morys.'

'We might,' said William haughtily. 'It depends what you have to offer.'

'It concerns the *real* cause of the flux: I know what is causing it. Do we have a deal?'

'Yes,' said Bartholomew eagerly, speaking over William's equally emphatic 'no'.

'The culprits are Stasy and Hawick,' declared Narboro. 'I have seen them pouring something into the town's water three times now. I imagine it is a substance to make folk ill, so they can then sell their cures. As they work, they call on Satan to help them.'

Bartholomew did not believe him. 'My book-bearer has been following them. He—'

'They do not let *him* see what they do,' interrupted Narboro scathingly. 'They let him think they have retired to bed, then sneak out once he has gone home.'

Bartholomew remained sceptical. 'So why have you not reported it? Or challenged them yourself?'

Narboro regarded him askance. 'Because they are warlocks, of course! I do not want them cursing me. They hexed you, and you have not cured a cold or a case of the flux since.'

'But you are willing to cross them now?' asked William incredulously.

'Well, yes,' replied Narboro, as if the answer were obvious. 'The choice is that or being incarcerated, but dungeons are unwholesome places and people die in them. Even you must see that displeasing Stasy and Hawick is by far the lesser of the two evils.'

'Can you prove these allegations?' asked William archly. 'Or are we just to take your word for them?'

Narboro sniffed huffily. 'It is the truth, but if you doubt me, go and catch them at it. They always act at midnight – the witching hour. Follow them then.'

'No,' said William, shaking his head. 'Not even Stasy and Hawick would stoop that low. You are lying.'

But it was all beginning to make sense to Bartholomew. 'They have already earned a fortune selling remedies. And if they are responsible for creating the symptoms, then they will know exactly what to include in their "cures" to make people feel better.'

'Precisely!' agreed Narboro.

'I should have seen this sooner,' said Bartholomew, angry with himself. 'The beadles caught their flux from a barrel of ale – a barrel that was left unattended in a yard at Shoemaker Row. And who now lives in Shoemaker Row?'

'Stasy and Hawick,' replied William, although the question had been rhetorical.

'They also made Walter ill,' Bartholomew went on, answers coming thick and fast. 'It would have been easy to slip into the porter's lodge and poison his ale while he was fetching treats for his birds. I imagine they aimed to strike at the whole College, but Agatha and the peacocks stopped them.'

'How?' asked William.

'She refused to leave the kitchens during the heatwave, making it impossible for them to gain access to our supplies. Then Stasy made an enemy of Henry, who now creates a racket whenever he comes near.'

William grinned suddenly. 'I feel like a nocturnal adventure, and no warlock will ever best a godly Franciscan. Shall we do what Narboro suggests, and see if we can trap them as they go about their evil business?'

It was not solving murder, but Bartholomew was a physician, and if Stasy and Hawick were responsible for the sickness that had hurt so many people, then they needed to be stopped. He nodded assent.

Cynric was furious to learn that he had been tricked, and readily agreed to be part of William's scheme to catch the ex-students. Unfortunately, so did Margery Starre, who claimed she had intended to strike at them that night anyway, but declared herself happy to fall in with whatever the scholars had planned instead.

'I told you she had the matter in hand, boy,' said Cynric. 'And she has already recited all manner of spells, so I know for a fact that we shall emerge triumphant tonight.'

323

Fortunately, he had spoken softly, as Bartholomew knew that William would baulk if he thought the venture was under the auspices of whoever – or whatever – Margery liked to call upon in times of need.

Meanwhile, the physician was relieved that a solution to the flux might be within his grasp at last, although he appreciated that he had failed dismally in the matter of murder. He only hoped Michael would understand that eliminating an illness that had debilitated so many people, including most of the beadles, was just as important.

'We will watch their shop,' he determined. 'And when they come out—'

'They will know you are there,' interrupted William impatiently. 'Just like they did Cynric. I do not know how – sorcery, most likely.'

'Nonsense,' declared Margery firmly. 'I imagine they pay the neighbours to keep a lookout for them. I do it myself on occasion.'

'When Narboro saw them,' said William, ignoring her, 'they visited two water butts and a well, then went on to the Mill Pond. I recommend we forget the wells and butts, as there are too many to monitor. But they will almost certainly visit the Mill Pond tonight, because the rain will have diluted their poison, and they will need to top it up.'

'Very well,' said Margery, and began to issue instructions regarding who was to do what. William objected to her assuming command, and they quarrelled all the way along the towpath, both turning periodically to Bartholomew for support. He was too tired to devise diplomatic replies, so it was fortunate that neither was very interested in his opinion anyway.

However, even William conceded that her suggestion of using Meadowman's cottage as a hideout was a good one. Not only did it afford excellent views of the whole pond, but it was also out of the rain. Meadowman let them in, but immediately left for St Mary the Great, where Brampton was waiting for him to organise the beadles' nightly patrols.

Trusting Cynric to keep watch through the window, Bartholomew sat at the table, rested his head on his arms and went straight to sleep.

What felt like moments later, William shook his shoulder – vigorously, as Bartholomew was notoriously difficult to wake once he was napping. He struggled up from a bizarre dream in which the headless Lyonnes wallowed in the Mill Pond, while Morys informed him that there was a tax for anyone who wanted to swim there.

'They are here,' hissed William, his voice unsteady with excitement. 'Come and look.'

Sure enough, Stasy and Hawick were at the edge of the water. They carried a large leather bucket between them and it looked heavy. The Mill Pond was deserted, but they prudently waited in the shadows for a long time before deciding it was safe to emerge.

They aimed for the East Dam, which, conveniently for those watching, was almost directly outside Meadowman's door. Thus Bartholomew could not only see what was happening, but could hear, too.

'Dark Lord, hear us,' the pair chanted. 'May your will be done tonight, and may your black powers work inside all who drink this offering.'

There followed a hymn of praise to Satan so sinister that Bartholomew felt a chill run all the way down his spine. Equally unsettled, William and Cynric crossed themselves, although Margery sniffed her contempt for the ritual. Then the singing finished, and the warlocks lifted the pail, ready to deposit its contents into the water. Bartholomew could not allow that to happen.

'Stop!' he bellowed, so loudly that everyone jumped in fright – his helpmeets as well as the culprits. The bucket wobbled perilously. He flung open the door and raced forward to grab it before it tipped. 'Enough!'

Aware that the contents of the pail would see them in serious trouble, Stasy fought to upend it before Bartholomew could examine them. He almost succeeded, but was forced to stop when Cynric slipped up behind him and put a blade at his throat. William surged forward to lay hold of Hawick, while Margery brought a lamp and peered into the bucket.

'This is sewage!' she cried, recoiling in disgust.

'Mixed with crushed berries,' said Bartholomew, wrinkling his nose as he recognised the distinctive aroma of several hedgerow fruits that were known to cause diarrhoea and vomiting. 'And God only knows what else. The mixture is green, so I think we know why they bought dye from Chaumbre – dye that is unfit for human consumption.'

'Nonsense,' blustered Stasy, trying to push Cynric away. 'Chaumbre told us that it contains verdigris and alum, both of which are beneficial to health. And do not think for a moment that our combination of carefully selected ingredients will harm anyone – it is intended to *purify* this filthy water.'

'We were worried by the ever-increasing number of flux cases, you see,' added Hawick with an unconvincing smile. 'Not even Margery or Bartholomew could cure them, so—'

'Because *you* cursed them both,' growled Cynric.

'That was no curse,' sneered Margery. 'This pair are no more warlocks than Father William here, so do not give them an importance they do not deserve. They are frauds.'

Hawick opened his mouth to argue, but then closed it again, evidently realising that contradicting Margery would do him no favours with William. Stasy remained full of bristling defiance.

'You cannot prove that we caused the flux,' he declared. 'This is the first time we have tried to cure the disease by—'

'You were seen on three separate occasions,' said Bartholomew, wondering how two lads who had studied with him for years could have devised such a dangerous scheme. 'There is nothing you can say to exonerate yourselves.'

'*And* you poisoned Walter and the beadles,' put in William. 'You would have done the same to Michaelhouse, but Agatha and the peacock thwarted you. Now you are caught, and you will answer for what you have done.'

'You cannot detain us,' averred Stasy, still trying to move his neck away from Cynric's blade. 'We are no longer members of your University.'

'But you are still subject to the authority of the Church,' said William, 'and *I* am a Franciscan. We have all the jurisdiction we need.'

'Donwich will let us go when he is Chancellor,' said Hawick, doing his best to emulate his friend's smug defiance, although his frightened eyes betrayed him. 'He knows who remained loyal to him in the face of Michael's cheating. So think of *that* as you sip your wine in St Mary the Great when the vicars-general declare him the winner.'

Stasy shot him a furious glance, which told Bartholomew exactly why they had been in the church during the election. Fortunately, no one had touched the celebratory wine, because Donwich's challenge to Michael had brought a premature end to the proceedings. However, it meant that whatever his ex-students had added to it was still there, and Bartholomew made a mental note to make sure it was poured away.

'I suppose your intention was to step forward with a miracle cure, once all the Regents fell mysteriously ill,' he surmised. 'Thus earning you a fortune, and establishing a name for yourselves at the same time.'

327

The truth was in Hawick's sheepish expression, although Stasy continued to bluster.

'You cannot prove *we* did anything to the wine – not now it has been sitting around unattended for days on end. Anyone might have tampered with it. Besides, our potions have done no real harm, so why make a fuss? It will make you look petty and sour.'

'They *did* do real harm,' countered Bartholomew between gritted teeth. 'Beadle Meadowman nearly died.'

'That was because he refused to drink anything,' said Stasy with a shrug. 'You cannot blame us for his stubborn stupidity, and he is better now anyway.'

Bartholomew shook his head in incomprehension. 'You swore an oath to do no harm, yet you pour this . . . this *filth* into people's drinking water.'

Stasy laughed mockingly. 'An oath? You mean those stupid sanctimonious words you ordered us to recite when we first came to study with you? We do not consider *those* binding! There was not even any letting of blood or animal sacrifices.'

'You ridiculous boys!' spat Margery disdainfully. 'Blood-letting and animal sacrifices indeed! You know nothing about—'

'Aynton,' interrupted Bartholomew before she could say anything too incriminating in front of William. 'Why did you kill him? Because he found out what you were doing and threatened to expose you?'

'We did not kill him,' cried Hawick, alarmed. 'And we have alibis to prove it.'

'For each other,' recalled Bartholomew. 'Unfortunately for you, that does not count.'

'No, we were in White Hostel,' said Hawick desperately. 'Nine Cistercians will tell you that we stayed with them the whole evening, and only left after we had celebrated compline together. We were selling them—'

He stopped abruptly when he recalled why he had been

328

unable to use the alibi when asked for it the first time. Stasy shot him another furious look.

'Selling them stolen exemplars,' finished Bartholomew. 'You did not want us to look too closely into why you – two self-confessed Satanists – kept company with monks.'

'If those texts do transpire to be stolen, blame Gille,' said Stasy promptly. 'We had no idea that he obtained them dishonestly, and no one can prove otherwise. We—'

'Enough!' barked William. 'If you try to convince us of your innocence one more time, I swear I will let Cynric slit your throat.'

'So what happens now?' asked Hawick, in the silence that followed. He licked dry lips. 'We are former members of Michaelhouse, so you will not want this matter made public, lest it reflects badly on your College. The most convenient solution is for us to pack up quietly and slip away under cover of darkness.'

'As you pointed out yourselves, you are no longer under the University's jurisdiction,' said William, 'so the Sheriff can have the pleasure of dealing with you. His cells are a lot less comfortable than the ones in the proctors' prison, of course . . .'

'But before you go,' said Margery, pointing a gnarled finger at each young man in turn, 'may all the curses you have uttered rebound on your own heads. I ask this by all I hold holy, and in the hearing of the ancient gods.'

'*No!*' screamed Hawick in terror, a reaction that revealed he had wished some very nasty things indeed on other people.

CHAPTER 17

It was nearly three o'clock in the morning by the time
Bartholomew and William arrived at the castle with their
prisoners. Hawick was cowed with fright, but Stasy
continued to hiss curses and threats. The fortress was
mostly silent, although there were sentries on the gate
and Dickon strutted back and forth barking unnecessary
orders. Anyone else who had been incarcerated for
murder might have been subdued by the experience, but
Dickon was aware that the town owed him an apology for
assuming the worst of him, and was louder and more
confident than ever.

'Perhaps he is up early because Tulyet is sending him
to France today,' remarked William, once the would-be
warlocks were safely locked up. 'I hope so – he may not
have beheaded Lyonnes, but we all believed him capable
of it, and the sooner he is gone, the better.'

Bartholomew heard his name called, and turned to see
Michael hurrying towards them, having heard the news
about Stasy and Hawick from Cynric. The monk looked
pale and tired, and Bartholomew saw he remained
anxious about whatever he was discussing with the
vicars-general.

'The townsfolk will be outraged to learn that two former
scholars gave them all the flux,' he said worriedly. 'Let
us hope that any reprisals come after the vicars-general
have gone, because we cannot afford to let *them* see us
in flames.'

As far as Bartholomew was concerned, creating a bad
impression on visitors, no matter how important, was the
least of their problems. 'The good news is that there will

be no more sickness. I was right: there was no miasma, just buckets full of nasty ingredients.'

'Good,' said Michael. 'Because term ends in about thirty hours, and we *must* have the killer before our colleagues disperse for the summer. Forget about medicine and concentrate on that – which is what you should have been doing anyway. Who is left on your list now?'

'Just Donwich. I am sure he is the author of all this trouble – the "friend" who ordered his henchmen to kill Huntyngdon and Martyn. When we find Gille, he will confirm it.'

'Of course, it could be someone you have not yet considered,' warned William.

Bartholomew glared at him, agitation and tiredness turning him testy. 'Such as whom?'

The friar shrugged. 'Someone who dislikes scholars. Some drunkard from the taverns perhaps, or a townsman who resents the power we hold and wants us gone.'

Michael looked as daunted by that possibility as Bartholomew felt. 'I shall order the beadles to listen for rumours in the ale-houses,' he said tiredly. 'At least, the ones who have recovered from the flux. Damn Stasy and Hawick! They have done us more harm than they can possibly know by depriving us of our eyes and ears in the town.'

'We will catch the culprit for you,' said William reassuringly, although even his natural ebullience was dampened, and Bartholomew saw he did not really believe what he was saying.

At that moment, there was a commotion near the gaol, and they turned to see Tulyet angrily berating some of his guards. One started to make a defiant response, but Dickon surged forward menacingly, hand on the hilt of his sword, and the man backed down. Tulyet saw the scholars and hurried towards them. With one final glare at the soldiers, Dickon turned to scamper after him.

'How long have you three been standing here?' Tulyet demanded tightly.

'A few minutes,' replied William cautiously. 'Why?'

'Because Morys and John have escaped. My fool of a gaoler is not sure when it happened, but it was after midnight – which I know because I visited them then myself.'

'Escaped?' echoed Bartholomew in dismay. 'How?'

'Bribery, no doubt, although the gaoler denies it and so do the sentries on the gate. But Morys is a wealthy man, and I should have predicted something like this would happen. It—'

He faltered at another rumpus. This time, Cynric was the cause. The book-bearer had been too restless to sleep after the events at the Mill Pond, so had gone to do what he loved best – prowling the dark streets to see who was out and what they were doing. He bulled his way through the gate, shoving away guards as he went.

'I have just found Mayor Morys,' he reported tersely when he reached Bartholomew. 'Dead – by the dye-pits.'

'*What?*' cried Tulyet, while Bartholomew, Michael and William gaped in disbelief. 'Are you sure?'

'Oh, yes,' replied Cynric. 'His head is hacked clean from his body.'

'It was not me,' blurted Dickon at once. 'I have been here the whole time.'

Tulyet ignored him. 'And John?'

'I only saw Morys,' replied Cynric. 'But who knows what a search will reveal?'

It was raining hard as Cynric led Tulyet and the scholars down the hill to the High Street, where Beadle Meadowman was guarding the scene of the crime. Lest anyone thought to point accusing fingers at his son again, Tulyet had ordered Dickon to stay in the castle, where he was to help

Sergeant Robin find out exactly how the Mayor had contrived to escape.

They crossed the *ponticulus*, noting that the bridge above was lit with dozens of lamps as work proceeded apace. Builders scampered over the wet, slick scaffolding like monkeys, soaked to the skin and shivering, but unwilling to stop even for an instant. Shardelowe was bawling at an apprentice for making the mortar too wet, ignoring the lad's stammering response that rain had leaked into it.

'Sheriff!' called Bernarde as they hurried past. 'What are you doing about Lyonnes' killer now your boy is proved innocent?'

Gradually, the frantic hammering and knocking faded to silence as men stopped working to listen to the reply. Soon, all that could be heard was the hiss and patter of rain.

'Everything possible,' replied Tulyet shortly. 'But first, I have other duties to attend.'

'Morys has been killed by the same lunatic who beheaded your friend,' put in William, who did not know when it was better to keep his opinions to himself, especially as an official cause of death had not yet been declared.

Shardelowe's jaw dropped in such abject shock that Bartholomew immediately knew that he had had nothing to do with Morys's demise. His workmen were similarly stunned.

'Morys is dead?' breathed Bernarde, the first to recover his voice.

'But what about our money?' gulped someone else. 'Will the town still pay us?'

'It must,' said Shardelowe, although his voice was anxious. 'I will speak to the burgesses first thing in the morning. But who killed Morys, Sheriff? Someone who objected to the way he tried to cheat us?'

'That is an interesting point,' pounced Michael. 'So where have you been all night?'

'Here,' replied Shardelowe. 'I cannot afford to let anyone wander off, if we are to finish the day after tomorrow. None of us left, not even for a moment. We have food brought to us, we sleep in shifts under a tarpaulin, and we use the river as a latrine.'

His people clamoured to say that he was telling the truth, and it was obvious that anyone slinking away would quickly be missed by his fellows. Ergo, none of them had been responsible for whatever had happened to the Mayor.

'You all must have seen him though,' said Tulyet. 'He left the castle after midnight, and he is now at the dye-pits. He almost certainly used this *ponticulus* to get there.'

'There were two friars, cloaked and hooded against the rain,' recalled Bernarde. 'We called out for their blessing, but they ignored us. Do not tell me one of those was him?'

Tulyet grimaced. 'Him and John, I imagine.'

'Now we have even more reason to finish this bridge quickly,' Shardelowe told his men. 'No one is safe in this dangerous little town. As soon as the last cobble is laid and we get our money, we are off. And I hope none of us ever have cause to set foot here again.'

There was a rumble of agreement from his people, after which they returned to work with even greater urgency, taking what Bartholomew considered to be stupidly reckless risks in the process. He glanced over the side of the *ponticulus*, and saw the river flowing smooth, fast and black below, swollen by rain. If one of them fell in, he would drown, because he would be swept away long before he could be rescued.

'I hope the river runs in full spate soon,' muttered Tulyet, as he and the others hurried on their way. 'I want

334

the bridge to suffer a good battering before we let Shardelowe go.'

'That will not happen unless all the sluices are opened,' said William. 'But now Morys is dead, he cannot tell us how to unlock them, and the water will back up until it submerges everything to the south – Peterhouse, the Gilbertine Priory, St Mary the Less, the Hall of Valence Marie . . .'

'He cannot have done anything too complex,' said Bartholomew, tired of hearing about it. 'And I doubt he did it himself, anyway, so someone else will know how to—'

'But what he did *is* complex,' snapped William, exasperated. 'I have tried to open them several times, but they are stuck fast.'

'We will sort it out,' promised Tulyet to mollify him, 'just as soon as we have ascertained what has happened to Morys.'

'Assuming it will not be too late by then,' muttered William darkly.

The Mayor was at the bottom of the fourth and largest dye-pit, looking oddly elongated with a gap between his head and the rest of him. Bartholomew climbed down to examine the body, sincerely hoping he would be able to clamber out again, and a donkey would not have to be hired to haul him up, as had happened with Narboro. Above, he heard Tulyet begin directing the hunt for John, first searching among the graves, and then detailing patrols to look further afield. As several beadles had been attracted by the commotion, Michael told them to help.

Morys had been killed the same way as Lyonnes – decapitated with a shocking degree of clumsiness. Bartholomew imagined it would have taken the culprit an age to do. Fortunately, a cracked skull proved the victim had not been conscious when it had happened.

'Do we now have two killers at large?' asked Tulyet worriedly, when both parts of the Mayor had been lifted from the dye-pit and were lying on a bier. 'Morys and Lyonnes suffered frenzied attacks by a lunatic with a blunt blade, while Aynton and Baldok were shoved off the bridge. We need not include Huntyngdon and Martyn, given that we know Elsham and Gille were responsible for them.'

'Do you think John is dead, too?' asked Bartholomew, glancing around uneasily. 'Or did he kill Morys – a falling-out among thieves?'

'Soldiers know how to make a clean kill, and John was among the best,' replied Tulyet. 'So he is not the culprit. But who is? Someone enraged by Morys's attempt to steal funds that many folk struggled to raise?'

'If so, you will have a whole town to interrogate,' muttered Michael. 'However, I doubt anyone was surprised when he was exposed as a felon. His corruption was an open secret.'

'There is a big difference between bribery and grand larceny,' argued Tulyet. 'And if Morys's plan had succeeded, everyone would have had to pay the bridge tax a second time.'

'A *third* time,' corrected William. 'Baldok stole the first lot, did he not?'

'Some of it,' acknowledged Tulyet. 'But a mere fraction compared to what Morys aimed to make off with.'

Michael's face was pale in the light of Tulyet's lantern. 'We cannot help you with Morys and Lyonnes, Dick. It will be dawn soon, which means Matt, William and I only have one more full day to find whoever dispatched Aynton and Elsham, and ordered the murders of Huntyngdon and Martyn.'

'It must be Donwich,' said Bartholomew wearily, aware that he had let Michael down. 'So we will tackle him again today. Of course, we still have no solid evidence . . .'

'I think we should redouble our efforts to locate Gille,' countered William. 'If he is not in the town, we shall conclude that *he* is the culprit, and Michael can announce the news tomorrow. Everyone will go home happy in the knowledge that the case is solved.'

Bartholomew blinked. 'But it would be untrue! Gille was on the ferry when the stone was pushed, and if he did not kill Elsham . . .'

'But he did stab Martyn, so it is not as if we accuse an innocent man,' argued William. 'And we cannot let our colleagues disperse carrying the news that our Chancellor was murdered and we failed to win him justice.'

'I will not do it,' said Michael firmly. 'I want the truth, not a scapegoat.'

'You may not have a choice,' said William soberly. He turned to Bartholomew. 'I suggest we visit Clare Hall first, and question the servants. Perhaps they are more familiar with Gille's habits than his colleagues seem to be.'

The four men parted company, each with the sense that there was simply not enough time left to find the answers they so desperately needed.

It was still dark when Bartholomew and William reached Clare Hall, although there was a faint glimmer of light in the eastern sky. Bartholomew's head throbbed with tension and fatigue, and his stomach felt like acid. Even the usually ebullient William was subdued, and Bartholomew sensed he also knew they were unlikely to catch the killer in the allotted time.

The rain was coming down so hard that it drummed on Bartholomew's hat and leapt up in lively splashes as it hit the ground. It sluiced down roofs and walls, and splattered noisily into puddles, before flowing into the ditches that ran down the sides of the road. The drains were full and running fast, carrying away weeks of accumulated filth. Whatever else happened that day, thought

Bartholomew, at least they would be left with a cleaner town.

The Clare Hall porter pulled a sour face when they asked to speak to the staff, and they soon learned why. In a brazen flouting of University rules, Donwich had ordered his Fellows to leave early for the summer recess. None had wanted to go, but he had threatened to dock their stipends if they stayed. The only ones left were Pulham and March, who had nowhere else to go. With only three scholars in residence, a large staff was redundant, so Donwich had dismissed them, too, retaining only the porter as a general factotum.

'He ousted them in case the vicars-general order another election,' the man explained bitterly. 'He knows they would all vote for Brother Michael, see.'

Bartholomew's headache intensified. He had not really expected answers from the staff, because the beadles had already questioned them thoroughly, but he felt as though he was trying to swim against a flood that was carrying him and William further from the truth with every passing moment. Everything seemed to be conspiring against them.

Equally fraught, William interrogated the porter until the man was close to tears, but learned nothing new about Gille's private life. Then Donwich appeared, Pulham and March in tow. Bartholomew braced himself for another unpleasant confrontation, but the Master's mind was on other matters.

'My spies in St Mary the Great have just sent me a message,' he declared smugly. 'The vicars-general will announce their decision within the hour. When they declare in my favour, I shall set about rewarding all those who supported me, and punishing those who did not.'

Bartholomew was desperate enough to launch one last, frantic assault on him. 'No murderer will ever be Chancellor,' he declared hotly. 'We know you killed

Aynton, and that you ordered your henchmen to dispatch Huntyngdon and Martyn.'

'Donwich did not kill Aynton,' said March wearily, before his Master could react to the bald accusation. 'I told you that when you first spoke to us.'

'Saying something does not make it true,' retorted Bartholomew.

'*Donwich did not kill Aynton,*' repeated March, so vehemently that everyone looked at him in astonishment. 'I had hoped to avoid this conversation, as it is hardly commensurate with my standing as Clare Hall's Senior Fellow . . .'

'What have you done?' asked Pulham in alarm, while Donwich's eyes narrowed.

March winced and looked at his feet. 'Aynton was not the only one to follow our Master to Lucy Brampton's house that night. So did I.'

Donwich gaped at him, while Bartholomew recalled that March had already admitted that he had not been with the other Fellows – he had claimed to be in the chapel, praying for Donwich to revert to the man he had been before he was Master.

'How dare you!' cried Donwich, when he found his voice. 'You have no—'

'I did it for Clare Hall,' interrupted March, angry in his turn. 'My only home. You have been behaving like an ass, and Aynton was no better – climbing up walls to peer through windows at his age! Anyway, we all heard your quarrel with Lucy, when she spurned your advances that evening.'

'So you eavesdropped, too?' Donwich was outraged and shocked in equal measure.

'"We all"?' pounced Bartholomew at the same time. 'Who else was there?'

'We did not need to eavesdrop – you were yelling like a fishmonger,' March informed Donwich coldly, then

339

turned to Bartholomew. 'I lied about being in the chapel, but not about the company I was in. Our two chaplains went with me to Brampton's house. Speak to them – they will confirm what I say.'

'We *will* speak to them,' put in William warningly. 'And if you are lying again . . .'

'When Lucy repelled him, Donwich stormed out and virtually collided with Aynton.' March ignored William and continued to address Bartholomew. 'Then *they* quarrelled, after which Donwich stalked home. The chaplains and I followed him at a discreet distance.' He winced. 'If one of us had stayed with Aynton, he might still be alive.'

'So why did you leave Aynton?' demanded Bartholomew, struggling to mask his exasperation. True, the tale showed March in a less than edifying light, but this was a murder enquiry, and the man should not have put his dignity above catching a killer.

'Because he would have been mortified to know that he had been spotted scrambling up the outside of the Senior Proctor's house,' explained March wretchedly. 'We aimed to spare his blushes by allowing him to make his way home alone.'

'And what about *my* blushes?' demanded Donwich indignantly.

'Yours we did not care about,' flashed March. 'Aynton was acting for the good of the College. You were satisfying your carnal desires.'

William exploded. 'We have been trying to catch a murderer, and your half-truths and omissions may have allowed him to escape. You should have mentioned this days ago!'

'But I *told* Bartholomew that Donwich was not the culprit,' argued March. 'I assumed he had taken my word for it. How was I to know that he considered me a liar?'

'But you *are* a liar,' snarled William.

'You must have realised that I still had reservations,'

said Bartholomew angrily. 'Why else would I have kept coming back to ask Donwich questions?'

'I assumed it was to learn more about Elsham and Gille,' replied March, although he had the grace to look sheepish. 'And as I said, the chaplains and I are not proud of what we did that night. I cannot tell you how much we wish we had not tried to play the spy.'

'So did you see or hear anything that might lead us to Aynton's killer?' demanded Bartholomew, fighting down an almost irresistible urge to punch him.

March shook his head. 'If we had, I swear we would have informed you at once, even if it had meant exposing ourselves to ridicule.'

'So there you are, Bartholomew,' said Donwich nastily. 'I am exonerated, and you are exposed as an incompetent fool who failed to see that March was leading you astray. I am glad you will leave the University tomorrow, because it will save me the trouble of expelling you.'

'I hardly think—' began March.

'And do not think you will escape unscathed either,' snarled Donwich, fixing him with an icy glare. 'I shall expect your resignation as a Fellow of Clare Hall the moment the vicars-general find in my favour.'

March went so white that Pulham hurried forward to take his arm, although Bartholomew was hard-pressed to feel sorry for the man. He turned to leave, unable to look at the gloating expression on Donwich's face any longer. The gate opened before he and William reached it, and Beadle Meadowman hurried through.

'The vicars-general will announce their verdict in less than an hour,' he said in a low voice, and waved a sealed letter. 'I am sent to deliver this to Donwich, so he will have warning before they make their public statement in St Mary the Great. You two might want to be there, because I have a bad feeling that Brother Michael may need you.'

'You do?' asked William in alarm. 'Why?'

341

'Because I have never seen a man look more utterly devastated,' replied Meadowman grimly. 'He fought with all he had, but his bloodshot eyes and trembling hands tell me that it may not have been enough.'

CHAPTER 18

Michael was not in St Mary the Great, and his chief clerk said he had gone back to Michaelhouse. The vicars-general had returned to their accommodations in King's Hall, where they were relaxing for a few hours before starting the long trek home to Canterbury in the morning.

'What did they decide?' asked Bartholomew anxiously.

The clerk looked away unhappily. 'No one knows, other than them and Michael. All we can do is wait for Teofle to make his speech.'

Bartholomew and William hurried home through the teeming rain, fearing the worst. Michaelhouse's yard was a square of liquid mud, and it was a treacherous journey across it. Bartholomew flung open the Master's door without knocking, then stared in surprise.

Michael was entertaining Brampton and – somewhat surprisingly – Lucy. His eyes were indeed bloodshot, and he looked as though he had not slept in a week. However, his face was split by an enormous grin that told Bartholomew all he needed to know. He sagged in relief.

'You won?' asked William tentatively. 'The vicars-general confirmed your election?'

Michael raised his eyebrows in surprise. 'Of course! That was never in question.'

'Oh, yes it was,' countered William. 'Every scholar in the University has been on tenterhooks for days, and you have been scuttling around looking fraught and anxious.'

'Because of other matters,' explained Michael. 'I was never worried about the election.'

'What "other matters"?' demanded William, and

343

pointed a grubby finger at Lucy before Michael could answer. 'And why is Donwich's mistress here?'

'I am not his mistress,' objected Lucy crossly. 'I never have been and I never will be.' She stood. 'And if I am to be insulted here, like I was in Clare Hall—'

'He meant no offence,' said Bartholomew quickly. 'He is just surprised to see you here.' He glanced at Michael. 'So am I, to be honest. What is going on?'

Lucy sat again. 'My befriending of Donwich was part of their plan,' she said. 'Michael's and my brother's, I mean.'

'Do not tell me that you recruited her to compromise Donwich's morals, and thus strengthen your own claim, Brother!' exclaimed William. 'That was underhand. Well done!'

Michael was indignant. 'I would never stoop to such low tactics! I secured Lucy's help over something far more important than who will be the next Chancellor.'

William was bemused. '*Is* there something more important than that?'

The monk's plump face broke into another happy grin. 'I have been negotiating an arrangement with the vicars-general – namely, that all the priests in the Canterbury Province should only be permitted to study *here*. Any cleric wanting to go to Oxford during the next decade must apply for a special licence *and* pay us compensation.'

He laughed with the sheer giddy joy of it, while Bartholomew supposed he should have guessed that Michael had been working on something huge when all three vicars-general and their retinues had arrived. Clearly, such an enormous party would not have been needed to pass judgement on the legitimacy of an election.

Brampton hastened to elaborate, also smiling. 'It means we shall have a steady and reliable flow of students for the next ten years, not to mention the fact that our pact comes with a substantial donation from the archbishop's coffers.'

William blinked stupidly at Michael. 'So you have not been defending yourself to the vicars-general these last few days? And the chancellorship—'

Michael interrupted with an impatient gesture. 'Do you really think important men like Teofle would waste time examining an election organised by me? A man they know and trust? Of course our meetings were not about that!'

'Donwich played right into our hands by challenging Michael,' crowed Brampton. 'I could have kissed him! It gave us the perfect excuse to fetch them here early. Now we can recruit new students over the summer, instead of waiting for the next academic year – which we would have had to do if the vicars had come in August, as they originally intended.'

William continued to look bewildered, although Bartholomew began to appreciate why Michael had considered his work with the Archbishop's agents more pressing than catching a killer. He was not surprised that it had caused him sleepless nights, as it was clearly one of the most significant coups the University had ever won.

'So you knew Donwich was innocent of murder,' surmised William, 'but you let Matt persecute him anyway, to distract him from what you were really doing.'

The smile faded from Michael's face. 'No, I would never have done that – to Matt or to Donwich. Matt genuinely believed that Donwich was the most likely suspect for Aynton's murder, and I had no reason to doubt his assessment.'

'Unfortunately, we have just learned that Donwich has an alibi,' said Bartholomew, and explained how the Master of Clare Hall had been shadowed home by March and the chaplains.

'Pity,' sighed Michael, 'although I am not surprised. He is unpleasant, but I cannot see him as a killer, even so.'

345

'You should have told us what you were doing, Brother,' said William accusingly. 'We are your friends. We might have been able to help.'

'I wanted to, believe me,' said Michael quietly. 'But everyone involved in the negotiations swore oaths of secrecy – at my insistence. You see, if they had failed, I wanted to be able to deny they ever happened, so as to avoid everyone thinking that Canterbury considers our little community of scholars a poor second to Oxford.'

'Well, it is done now,' said Bartholomew. 'And everyone will be delighted when they hear what you have won for us.'

'Not everyone,' said Michael ruefully. 'That was part of the problem. Donwich and some of his supporters feel that we are too large already. If they had learned what I was doing, they would have sabotaged my efforts.'

'How?' asked William, bristling at the idea.

'By reminding the vicars-general that Oxford has a lot more to offer. And if the other place had been chosen, it would have been the end of us. We are smaller and more vulnerable, and losing all the priests in the Province of Canterbury would have seen us wither and die.'

'But now Oxford will wither and die?' asked William keenly.

Brampton laughed. 'They are powerful enough to survive without Canterbury for a few years. We are not.'

'It was the most terrifying task I have ever undertaken,' admitted Michael. 'The stakes could not have been higher – the very existence of the University itself.'

'He is the only man in the whole country who could have convinced Teofle, Ely and Tinmouth that we are worthier than a foundation that is older, richer, bigger and more stable,' said Brampton, giving the monk a shy smile. 'You should be proud of him.'

'Do not scowl, Father!' chided Michael. 'Later today, you will have the happy duty of informing your fellow

Franciscans to expect a massive surge in numbers next term.'

'They will be pleased,' acknowledged William. 'But you trusted Brampton and his sister before your Michaelhouse friends. That is hurtful.'

'I am his Senior Proctor,' said Brampton haughtily. 'Of course he confided in me. However, *he* did not recruit Lucy, *I* did. Her remit was to prevent Donwich from bursting in on the negotiations and spoiling everything. I never told her why.'

'It is true, Father,' said Lucy. 'And in return, my brother has agreed to drop his lawsuit against Narboro. Hopefully, it will not be too late for me to find another suitor.'

'But Lucy – and you, Brampton – befriended Donwich long before he challenged Michael's election,' Bartholomew pointed out. 'How did you know he might be a problem?'

'Because, as Junior Proctor, I monitored all the University's most troublesome scholars,' replied Brampton. 'Thus I was able to predict exactly who would need distracting when Michael began his work. It would have looked suspicious for Lucy to bewitch Donwich at the last minute, so I arranged for it to happen in advance.'

'It is true,' said Lucy. 'I admit I was uncomfortable not knowing why I had to inveigle my way into his affections, but needs must. However, I am glad it is over. I did not enjoy deceiving him – he was always kind to me.'

'She is not my only agent,' bragged Brampton. 'I had several other schemes in play, all designed to ensure that powerful or vocal scholars did not make a nuisance of themselves. And none did, even though some of them are very difficult characters.'

'It is what makes you such a good proctor,' put in Michael appreciatively.

'I suppose Ufford and Rawby from King's Hall knew what you were doing, too,' said Bartholomew. 'They were suspiciously eager to fetch the vicars-general from Ely, and then host them extravagantly in King's Hall.'

'My College *will* benefit the most from the arrangement Michael has made,' said Brampton smugly. 'All the wealthiest and most influential of these new students will choose us, so yes, Ufford and Rawby were recruited to help, although, like Lucy, they did not know why. They were just told that it would be to King's Hall's advantage.'

Michael stood abruptly. 'But pleasant though it is to bask in our glory, we have a killer to catch.'

'It is too late,' said William sullenly. 'There are only a few hours left of term, so you will have to be content with winning hundreds more scholars for the University and being confirmed as our Chancellor.'

'I am afraid that is not enough,' said Michael. 'And much can be achieved in a few hours. We have done it before, after all.'

'You will not do it this time,' said William. 'You have no clues left to follow. Ergo, you will announce Gille as the culprit regardless of whether it is true. You mark my words.'

Bartholomew escorted Brampton and Lucy out of the College, while a resentful William gave Michael a more detailed account of what had transpired in Clare Hall. As they went, Brampton confided that when the vicars-general had first arrived in Cambridge, they had already decided to favour Oxford, and had only agreed to listen to Michael's arguments as a favour to an old friend. None of them had expected Michael to change their minds.

'So now you *must* solve these murders,' he ordered peremptorily. 'Because if you fail, it will take the shine off his victory.'

'You do it then,' retorted Bartholomew, resenting the man's presumption. 'You are Senior Proctor.'

Brampton looked startled by the notion. 'But I would not know where to start! My skills lie in other areas.'

'I have something that might help you, Matthew,' said Lucy, and withdrew a piece of parchment from the purse at her waist. 'I found it when I washed Martyn's corpse.'

'When you did *what?*' blurted Bartholomew.

'He had no family or College,' explained Brampton, 'so it fell to me, as Senior Proctor, to organise his burial rites. However, the crone who came to prepare him was drunk, so I dismissed her and told my sister to do it instead.' He glanced slyly at her. 'Another favour in exchange for dropping my suit against Narboro.'

'But I searched Martyn's body,' said Bartholomew, wondering if Brampton could be trusted to keep his end of the bargain when it so obviously suited him to have her at his beck and call. 'I do not believe I missed anything.'

'You probably did not pull the brim off his hat, though,' explained Lucy sheepishly. 'I did not mean to, but I grabbed it too roughly, and it came away in my hand. This note was tucked into the lining, suggesting he intended to keep it very safe. It was soaking wet, so the ink has run, but I have dried it as well as I can.'

She started to pass it to Bartholomew, but Brampton snatched it from her first. He turned it this way and that, then screwed it into a ball and tossed it away. 'It is illegible. What a pity. From the way you spoke, I thought it would be a vital clue. But we cannot stay gossiping here all day. Come along, Lucy. We have much to do.'

Lucy's jaw dropped in dismay at his cavalier treatment of something with which she had evidently taken considerable pains, but he grabbed her arm and steered her through the gate before she could voice her objections. She managed to shoot Bartholomew an apologetic glance over her shoulder, then she and her brother were gone.

Bartholomew bent to retrieve the crumpled parchment.

349

It was wet all over again, which darkened the faint marks that had once been letters, so that one or two words could still be made out. He ducked into the porter's lodge to examine it out of the rain.

He felt his pulse quicken when he recognised the spidery scrawl – all scholars were familiar with their chancellors' writing. So Aynton *had* given Martyn a letter to deliver, perhaps a twin of the one he had entrusted to Huntyngdon. But excitement was quickly followed by disappointment, because Brampton was right: most of it was illegible. One word stood out though – *Baldok*. He frowned. Did it refer to the village that lay to the south-west of Cambridge, or the burgess who had been murdered on the bridge a few weeks earlier?

He peered at it again, and made out *Hunty*, which he assumed would have read 'Huntyngdon'. Then *yet so* in the middle of a sentence, which was meaningless without the rest. And at the top, *y f—d Teof.*

'My friend Teofle?' he wondered aloud. 'Aynton was writing to the Archbishop of Canterbury's vicar-general?'

But if so, why was the message in the vernacular, when Latin was the language of choice for communicating with high-ranking churchmen? Or had Aynton and Teofle known each other well enough to dispense with such formality? After all, Bartholomew did not always use Latin when jotting notes to Michael, and Teofle had mentioned a long-standing friendship with Aynton when he and his retinue had first arrived in the town.

He continued to stare and to think, and the more he did, the more he became convinced that Aynton had written to Teofle with information about Burgess Baldok. Had he learned the identity of Baldok's killer? It was a crime that had never been solved, despite Tulyet's best and continued efforts, and surely, it could not be coincidence that the sender of both letters and their bearers had been murdered themselves?

350

Hopeful for the first time in days, he hurried to discuss his idea with Michael.

The monk was sitting alone with his eyes closed and an expression of intense concentration on his face. William had gone to inspect the sluices again, dragging a reluctant Zoone with him – the engineer had no desire to be out in the pouring rain – still concerned about flooding.

'I am reviewing all you told me about the murders,' said Michael, opening his eyes. 'Hoping to spot something that you have missed.'

'And have you?'

'No.' Michael winced before blurting, 'I cannot tell you what agony it was, watching you struggle, but being unable to help. I am more sorry than I can say.'

'Are the negotiations the reason why Aynton resigned so suddenly?'

Michael nodded. 'He thought they should be led by a strong Chancellor, not a weak one with a Senior Proctor whispering in his ear. I disagree – it would have been easier with two of us. But what is done is done, and I shall honour his memory by helping you catch his killer.'

Bartholomew showed him the letter. 'You can make out part of the names *Huntyngdon* and *Baldok*, part of *my friend Teofle*, and the words *yet so.*'

Michael squinted at it through the glass that Bartholomew had given him some years ago, when he had started to complain about everyone else's illegible handwriting.

'But why would Aynton write to Teofle and Narboro – of all people – about a murdered burgess?' he asked, bemused.

'Because he knew the identity of the culprit,' replied Bartholomew.

'Then why not tell the Sheriff – the man who was investigating the crime? Or me, if the culprit is a scholar?'

Bartholomew had no answer. 'Time is passing, and we cannot sit in here all day. Where do you want to start?'

'At Peterhouse,' said Michael, standing abruptly. 'Martyn taught there on occasion, and he was friends with Gayton and Stantone. Perhaps he talked to them about his mission.'

'Why would he?' asked Bartholomew, feeling it was a waste of time they did not have. 'Huntyngdon never did, and they were both discreet, trustworthy men.'

'Can you think of a better idea?' demanded Michael. 'No? Then let us go.'

The moment they left Michael's quarters, they became aware that something bad had happened. Urgent footsteps hammered in the lane outside, and there was a lot of agitated shouting. The other Fellows were with William, who was speaking in a frantic gabble. Students and servants were running towards them, eager to find out what was going on.

'The crisis will come *tonight*,' William was yelling. 'And it cannot be averted, because the sluice gates are jammed and not even Zoone knows how to unlock them.'

'Poor Peterhouse and Valence Marie,' said Aungel. 'They will suffer the worst—'

'Never mind them!' William raved on. 'If the gates give way under the pressure, a great wall of water will race down the river, destroying everything in its path, including *our pier*! Most of our revenue comes from that, and if we lose it, we shall be destitute again.'

'William is right,' said Zoone soberly. 'Our pier *will* be smashed beyond repair when the gates burst – and I say *when*, not *if*, because they will certainly tear apart unless either they are opened or the river stops rising. And as we are set for forty days of rain . . .'

Michael was pale. 'There must be something we can do to save it.'

Zoone considered. 'I suppose we could build a breakwater next to it, to absorb the brunt of the impact. It will not be easy, but—'

'Do it,' ordered Michael. 'We cannot lose our best source of income.'

Zoone nodded briskly. 'Then I shall need sacks filled with sand, a boat, a large net, and as many willing hands as we can muster.'

There was an immediate clamour as all those listening volunteered their services. The students were ordered to dig sand, Walter was told to find a net, the Fellows and Agatha were ordered to collect sacks, Cynric offered to locate a boat, and Clippesby was given the task of taking all the College's animals and birds to the stables, where they would be safe.

Bartholomew was in an agony of indecision. He could not help Zoone if he was to catch Aynton's killer in the next few hours, but nor could he disappear and leave his colleagues to do all the work. Michael was similarly torn.

'My College or a murderer,' he muttered, taut with indecision. 'You hunt for him, Matt. I will remain here with Zoone.'

But Bartholomew shook his head. 'The case needs fresh eyes. You go; I will stay.'

The monk was not happy, but he hurried away into the town.

The rest of the day was simultaneously wretched and anxious for the Michaelhouse men. The rain belted down harder than ever, making their task more difficult and dangerous with every passing hour. Water poured off the fields upstream and gushed into the Cam, threatening to wash them away as they struggled to follow Zoone's anxious instructions.

Heavy rain was not normally a problem for the town – the dams controlled the flow of the river, and excess water could be diverted into a series of channels and bogs to the west. But now that the East and Middle sluices were locked, and the West Dam was only open just enough to drive Morys's mill, the land to the south was beginning to flood.

At noon, Cynric arrived with the alarming news that still no one had been able to work out what Morys had done to the gates, and that all three dams, along with the road bridges that ran across the top of them, were now in serious danger of being washed away as more and more water backed up behind them.

Zoone and his helpers laboured on with their break-water, and Bartholomew was sure he had never been so physically exhausted. Every bone and muscle ached, but he dared not stop, because it was now obvious even to a non-engineer that the pier would be swept away unless the breakwater was finished.

Disturbing news arrived throughout the afternoon: the Gilbertine Priory, built on a rise, had become an island, accessible only by boat; Coe Fen was submerged completely; the Hall of Valence Marie had been evacuated; and Peter-house was moments away from inundation. On a more positive note, every book from both Colleges had been safely stored in the tower of St Mary the Less.

'And the Spital is lost,' gasped Meadowman, who had come to find Michael. 'The only building you can see is the chapel, and everyone who lives there is sitting on its roof.'

'I told you so,' shouted William to anyone who would listen. 'I *said* the blocked sluices would cause problems, but did anyone believe me and do something about it? No! You all thought I was deranged.'

'He *is* deranged,' muttered Zoone. 'Unfortunately, he is also right. I do not know what Morys thought he was doing, but it will spell disaster for the town – one from which it may never recover. What a pity after all Michael has done for us this week.'

'We have had heavy rains and floods before,' gasped Bartholomew, struggling with a long piece of wood. 'We will survive.'

'That was when the sluices were working,' said Zoone grimly. 'But now they are not.'

It was dusk by the time the engineer finally declared that the breakwater should be strong enough to protect the pier from the imminent surge, at which point Bartholomew was not the only one who reeled with fatigue. Every Fellow, student and servant had given his all, and there was a concerted sigh of relief at Zoone's announcement.

'Now what?' asked Bartholomew hoarsely.

'We wait,' replied Zoone tersely. 'Ah, here is the Master.'

He hurried forward to make his report to Michael, while Bartholomew tended to an assortment of cuts, scratches and bruises on those who had worked with more haste than care. The moment he had finished, he ran to hear how Michael had fared with their investigation.

'Nothing,' spat Michael, all his earlier jubilation leached away. 'I spent an age in Peterhouse, asking all manner of desperate questions about Martyn, and I searched every inch of his room in the Cardinal's Cap, but I learned nothing.'

Bartholomew was not surprised. 'Did you speak to Narboro?'

'No, because he was out, and no one knows where he had gone. He did tell Gayton that he would be home by nightfall, though.'

'It is almost dark now,' said Bartholomew. All he wanted to do was pull off his dirty, wet clothes and lie down, but he knew he would not rest easy if he did. 'We could go and see if he is back.'

'We could, but what can he tell us that you have not already asked?'

'Probably nothing,' acknowledged Bartholomew. 'But I imagine Aynton, Huntyngdon and Martyn would want us to try anyway.'

Bartholomew forced himself into a brisk walk, Michael puffing at his side. People were everywhere, running and shouting. Tulyet had ordered the evacuation of all the houses along the river and the King's Ditch. Some residents refused to go, afraid of looters. Others darted back and forth with their precious belongings – pots, pans, furniture, animals, bedding, clothes. The rain pounded down harder than ever.

Dickon was everywhere, and Bartholomew wondered if his spell in gaol had imbued him with greater authority, because there was no question of anyone disobeying his orders. He set soldiers to stand guard over the refugees' possessions, commandeered St Bene't's Church as an emergency shelter, and meticulously cleared the alleys that led to the river, which were predicted to flood at any moment.

The Trumpington Gate was above water, but the roads that ran to its east and west were submerged and impassable. The Mill Pond lapped at the tops of the Small Bridges, while the banks of the King's Ditch had collapsed near the Barnwell Gate, allowing it to spew its vile contents into the grounds of the Franciscan Priory and the Round Church's cemetery.

Once past the harried sentries, Bartholomew and Michael hastened to Peterhouse. Its scholars were in a clamouring cluster around the gate, some carrying travelling packs.

'They want permission to leave, Brother,' explained Gayton. 'It is not only Cambridge that will flood if it rains like this for the next forty days, and they are anxious to get home before the weather traps them here all summer.'

'They aim to go now?' asked Bartholomew doubtfully. 'In the dark?'

'Some live many miles away,' explained Stantone. 'So every hour counts.'

Michael made his decision. 'All those who have more than a day's ride may leave now. The rest will remain until tomorrow, although I shall bring the graduation ceremony forward to dawn and announce the end of term immediately afterwards.'

'You heard him,' shouted Gayton. 'Those who are eligible, off you go and God's speed. The rest, back inside. I want everything carried upstairs – furniture, rugs, *everything*.'

'Has Narboro returned yet?' asked Michael, as the scholars ran to do as they were told.

'An hour ago,' replied Gayton in disgust. 'We asked him to help us carry our library to safety, but he refused. He is in Hoo Hall, packing up his own belongings.'

Bartholomew was not surprised. Peterhouse had opted not to renew Narboro's Fellowship, so why should he put himself out for colleagues who did not want him? Then Stantone approached. He glanced around to make sure no one else could hear, and began to speak in a confidential whisper.

'The Sheriff has hidden Morys's body in our charnel house. We were not very happy about it, but he overrode our objections. He told us not to tell anyone, but I feel you have a right to know, Brother.'

Michael was bemused. 'Did he say why he feels the need to secrete corpses on University property while the town teeters on the brink of disaster?'

'Because there have been attempts to seize it and string it up in revenge,' replied Stantone. 'Word is out that Morys tried to steal the bridge money, while everyone knows our current crisis is his fault for meddling with the dams. Tulyet wants us to keep it safe.'

'Have you remembered anything new since we last talked?' asked Michael, far more concerned with his investigation than the security of Morys's mortal remains.

'Just one thing,' said Stantone. 'Narboro gossiped to us several times about Baldok, apparently fascinated by the fact that he was murdered on the bridge. But Aynton was murdered on the bridge, too, and as you say he tried to send Narboro a letter . . .'

'We must corner Narboro again at once,' said Bartholomew urgently to Michael. 'I have said from the start that Aynton's letters hold the key. We know the one he gave Martyn was about Baldok, and if Huntyngdon's – intended for Narboro – contained the same information, we may have our connection.'

'Yes,' acknowledged Michael cautiously. 'Although it is only a *significant* connection if Narboro knows something about Baldok that the rest of us do not. If he just likes nattering about another man's violent end . . .'

'Which is probably all it is,' put in Stantone warningly. 'I seriously doubt that empty-headed fool knows anything important.'

'I will take my chances,' said Bartholomew, breaking into a run.

The only way to reach Hoo Hall now that Coe Fen was under water was via the lane. However, they had not taken many steps along the Trumpington road towards it when they were hailed by Tulyet, soaking wet and muddy from his fruitless battle with the sluices.

'Do not go too far, Matt,' he warned. 'We will need you soon. When the river breaches the dams, it will flood everything between it and Milne Street. Some folk refuse to leave their homes, so there will be injuries and drownings for certain.'

'Why not just smash the sluice gates?' asked Michael.

'Then all the excess water can be safely channelled away.'

'Zoone says that breaking them now will allow the water to rush through so fast that it will destroy everything in its path anyway – houses, jetties and our expensive new bridge. The only way to avert disaster is to crank them open slowly, but Morys's selfish tampering has stolen that option away from us.'

'Perhaps Zoone will think of something else,' said Bartholomew hopefully.

'There *is* nothing else,' snapped Tulyet. 'But now your breakwater is finished, he has agreed to stay at the Mill Pond and monitor the situation. I begged Shardelowe to do likewise, but he refuses to leave the bridge.'

'He is still working on it?'

'Creating "starlings" to funnel the worst of the water to either side of the piers. But never mind that. I need you two to retrieve Morys's body from Peterhouse and put it somewhere dry.'

'We cannot,' objected Michael. 'We are too—'

'Please, Brother,' said Tulyet hoarsely. 'I cannot trust my men with this – they know his tampering with the sluices has put their town in danger. Dickon offered to do it, but you will appreciate why I cannot have him associating with headless corpses.'

'Why does Morys need to be dry?' demanded Bartholomew, exasperated. 'It is not as if he will drown.'

'No, but he might float away, and I shall need a body to exhibit when the crisis is over, or folk will say he escaped justice and we shall have a riot. Please do it. Here is a lamp.'

Bartholomew resented the waste of time, but he understood why it had to be done. The moment he and Michael turned back towards Peterhouse, Tulyet took off at a run, yelling for Dickon to check the water levels round the houses in Luthborne Lane.

'You find Narboro, Brother,' said Bartholomew tiredly. 'I will see to Morys.'

'You cannot carry his body on your own,' said Michael. 'And I doubt Narboro will have answers anyway, despite your near-frantic optimism.'

Bartholomew set off towards the charnel house, stomach churning in agitation. It was already surrounded by calf-deep water, and they opened the door to find Morys partly submerged: Tulyet was right to fear him bobbing away.

'His killer was deranged,' said Michael, recoiling anew at the sight. 'No one should feel safe as long as that madman walks free.'

Bartholomew was too exhausted to think about it. There was a bier leaning against one wall, so he laid it on the floor and took hold of Morys's shoulders, indicating that Michael was to grab the feet. As they lifted, something caught his eye – something that glinted near the stump of Morys's neck. He plucked it out and inspected it more closely. It took a moment to identify, but when he did, it answered several questions and raised others.

'A shard of glass,' he breathed, holding it up for Michael to see. 'Reflective on one side and painted on the other.'

'So?' asked Michael blankly.

'It is part of a mirror – a *lover's* mirror! And I know of only one person who has one.'

Michael regarded him uneasily. 'You think that shard came from Narboro's? But how did it get inside Morys?'

'We had better find out,' said Bartholomew, a small flame of hope igniting within him. 'Come on!'

'But what about Morys?' asked Michael.

'We shall put him on the highest shelf and retrieve him when the waters recede. He will not float away if we lock the door, and he cannot get any wetter than he is already.'

*

360

The rain continued to hammer down, and even while they had been inside the charnel house, the situation had changed. The Mill Pond, Coe Fen and the river were now one continuous sheet of water, so it was impossible to see where one began and another ended. Lamps had been lit in order to monitor the rising flood, and their reflections shimmered across its surface.

The lane down to Hoo Hall was becoming impassable, and the flood was knee-deep in places. At one point, Michael accidentally veered off to one side, and yelped in alarm when he found himself in water up to his thighs. Bartholomew hauled him out, and they struggled on.

'We should wait,' Michael gasped, when they passed the last of the houses and were faced with a lake. The lane was invisible beneath it, rendering the rest of the journey to Hoo Hall precarious, to say the least. 'Narboro will not be going anywhere tonight.'

But Bartholomew shook his head. He had not slept properly in days, and had spent most of the last week chasing his own tail over the murders or the flux. Every bone in his body burned with fatigue, but new energy surged through him at the prospect of answers at last. He refused to listen to the voice of reason at the back of his mind that warned him against heaping so much hope on a piece of glass. He ploughed on, feet aching with the cold.

'This is madness,' snapped Michael, grabbing Bartholomew's arm to wrench him to a standstill. 'Even if we do manage to reach Hoo Hall, we will not get out again – the flood is rising by the moment, and the only way to escape will be by boat.'

Bartholomew knew the monk was right, because he could feel the tug of a current around his legs – more water *was* flowing into Coe Fen with every minute that passed. But a sort of madness had seized him at the prospect of a solution, so he shook off the monk's restraining hand and forged ahead. He would *not* give up now!

They waded on. Michael was silent and Bartholomew knew he was worried – the monk could not swim, and had always been afraid of drowning.

'Thank God!' he breathed, when they finally reached the house. He stretched unsteady hands to touch the wall in relief. 'We made it.'

They ploughed towards the door to find water pouring through it – Bartholomew had forgotten that the bottom floor was below ground level. He raised the lamp and saw tables and benches floating around inside, some still piled with the food that had been stored there. Then he almost lost his footing as the force of the water increased all of a sudden, almost certainly as a result of some blockage breaking free upstream. For the first time, he appreciated the danger his reckless single-mindedness had put them in.

'We should abandon this foolery and go back,' said Michael unsteadily, more alarmed than ever. 'Narboro must wait.'

'We cannot,' said Bartholomew, staggering again as the water surged faster still. 'It is too late. You were right – we should not have come.'

Michael's face was white in the lamplight. 'Then I sincerely hope you have a plan to keep us safe, because if I drown, I shall haunt you for eternity.'

Bartholomew nodded towards the stairs on the far side of the hall. 'We have to reach those and go up to the dormitory. We should be safe there, and Narboro can answer questions while we wait for rescue.'

'You mean *swim*?' gulped Michael in horror. 'But you know I cannot!'

'It is not very deep yet,' said Bartholomew. 'We can wade. Come on.'

He climbed down the steps into icy water that covered his knees, then his thighs, then his waist. By the time he was on the floor, it was up to his chest, although the

362

gushing flow from the door suggested it would not stay that way for long.

'Quickly,' he ordered Michael. 'Just follow me.'

He held the lantern high with one hand, and shoved aside the furniture that bobbed in their way with the other. The water was agonisingly cold, and yet again, he realised that his frantic desire for answers had been stupid. Then something flashed ahead of him – another lantern. Narboro was coming down the dormitory stairs. He carried a saddlebag and wore a travelling cloak.

'You are not going anywhere,' called Bartholomew. 'You are a murderer!'

For a moment, the only sounds in Hoo Hall were the hiss of the flood rushing through the door and Michael's agitated breathing. The water now reached their shoulders, and if it rose by more than the length of a man's hand, the monk would drown, because he would no longer be able to touch the floor with his feet. Bartholomew continued to plough towards the stairs, pulling Michael with him.

'We know you killed Morys,' he told Narboro as he went. 'We found part of your mirror in his body. You used a piece of it to saw off his head. Lyonnes', too.'

'I never did,' shouted Narboro, although he drew a dagger, which did nothing to convince them of his innocence. 'But come any closer and I will stab *you*.'

'Hoo Hall is surrounded by water,' said Bartholomew, aware that behind him, Michael was beginning to panic. 'You cannot escape, so you may as well confess.'

'Stop!' snarled Narboro, drawing a second blade. 'One more step and I will lob these – one for each of you. Now back away, against the far wall, *at once*!'

With alarm, Bartholomew saw he meant it. Reluctantly, he began to do as he was told, although the water was now up to his chin, and it was easier to swim than to walk. His arm ached from holding the lamp, but he dared not drop it, because if Narboro retreated back to the dormitory, he and Michael would be trapped in a flooded room in the dark, an outcome that did not bear thinking about.

'Keep moving!' shouted Narboro. 'Right across to the hearth.'

Bartholomew was loath to comply, because that would leave him too far away to launch any kind of attack, but Narboro took aim with his blade, so he quickly did as he was told. He helped Michael to a place where the monk could cling to the top of the fireplace, then turned his attention back to Narboro.

'You lied about your reason for paying Morys,' he called, as his teeth started to chatter from the cold. 'It was to buy his silence about you beheading Lyonnes. I suppose he kept demanding more, so you killed him, too.'

Narboro peered towards the main door, gauging the distance. 'What reason could I possibly have had for dispatching Lyonnes?' he asked, although he sounded distant, his mind on escape. 'I barely knew the man.'

Bartholomew had no answer, but was not about to admit it. 'The shards of your mirror were sharp – you showed them to me – but it still must have taken some serious hacking to decapitate him. You got the idea from Dickon, who had threatened to cleave Lyonnes' head from his shoulders after a row. You knew everyone would think he did it, thus deflecting the blame from you.'

'What nonsense!' cried Narboro, most of his attention still on the door.

'Dickon is a child,' said Bartholomew accusingly. 'What sort of man lets a boy suffer for a crime he has committed himself?'

Narboro sneered. 'He may be young, but the Devil sired him, and no one other than his father was sorry when he was arrested.'

Bartholomew was painfully aware that Michael was beginning to run out of handholds as the water lifted them ever higher. His own legs ached from staying afloat, while his arms burned with the effort of holding the lamp aloft.

'You are a liar,' he went on, trying to keep the desperation from his voice. 'You *do* know what Aynton wrote in the letter that saw Huntyngdon murdered. And that led you to dispatch Lyonnes and Morys.'

'He did not kill them,' came a voice from the door. '*I* did.'

Lucy Brampton was in the doorway, paddling a coracle.

CHAPTER 19

Bartholomew was so stunned by Lucy's arrival that the lamp slid from his fingers and almost fell in the water, while Michael lost his grip on the wall and was forced to scrabble wildly until he found another handhold. Both were too astonished to speak, although a distant part of Bartholomew's mind reminded him that Narboro had been sick at the sight of Elsham's relatively unscathed corpse, so sawing off heads would likely be well beyond him. Lucy, on the other hand, had not baulked at preparing Martyn's decomposing body for the grave.

'You took your time,' Narboro told her sourly. 'And how could you be so careless as to leave a piece of my mirror in Morys's corpse?'

'A proper man would have had a knife to hand,' Lucy flashed back at him, 'but all you could provide was a bit of glass. But never mind this. The river is flooding fast, so if you do not want to drown, jump in and swim to my boat.'

'If I do, Bartholomew will catch me,' gulped Narboro. 'Paddle it across to—'

'It is too wide for the door.' Lucy produced a small crossbow. 'But the scholars will not stop you, I promise. Come, quickly now, before the water rises any higher.'

'I do not understand,' gasped Michael, finding his voice at last. 'You helped us . . . you distracted Donwich, so he would not . . .'

'Yes, I did,' said Lucy shortly. 'And now I am leaving.'

'But why embark on a murder spree with Narboro?' asked Bartholomew, acutely aware that he could not reach either culprit before he was shot or stabbed, so all he could do to delay their departure was talk. 'The man who broke his promise to marry you.'

'Neither of us had a choice, thanks to her damned brother,' spat Narboro.

'His lawsuit will ruin Narboro,' explained Lucy, 'and end my chance of winning another suitor. Rather than let him destroy both our lives, we agreed to work together. Narboro would not have been my first choice of collaborator, but needs must.'

'But your brother has agreed to drop the case,' said Bartholomew, coughing as water slapped into his mouth. 'You did what he asked, so now he will—'

'He will renege,' interrupted Lucy shortly. 'He thinks Narboro's breach of promise reflects badly on him, and he wants to prove that he is strong and proud. He never had any intention of honouring the agreement he made with me, and I was a fool to think he might.'

'So we devised a scheme to steal all his money and disappear to France,' finished Narboro, 'where we shall go our separate ways. I shall find work as a clerk, and she will settle in a town where no one will look at her with scorn and pity.'

'Although I shall go alone if you do not come over here soon,' warned Lucy, struggling to keep her boat at the door and maintain her hold on the weapon at the same time. The water had risen so fast that she had to stoop slightly to see under the lintel.

'But Lyonnes overheard us planning,' said Narboro, too frightened to swim, and so talking to delay it. 'We were in Brampton's house with the window open, and he was working on the bridge outside. He demanded a share of the money in return for his silence.'

'Then he and Dickon quarrelled,' said Lucy, indicating with an exasperated flick of the crossbow that Narboro was to jump at once. 'We realised we could be rid of him, and no one would ever think to blame us.'

367

'But it did not work,' said Bartholomew noting with alarm that his lamp was beginning to run out of fuel. 'Because Morys learned the truth.'

Lucy grimaced. 'We lured Lyonnes to the Chesterton road, but Morys saw Narboro and me hurrying there together, and drew his own conclusions after the body was found. Then *he* demanded money for his silence.'

'I paid some of it,' put in Narboro. 'You and William saw me in the guildhall with him, so I had to devise a quick lie. But when he was arrested, Lucy and I knew it was only a matter of time before he betrayed us in exchange for clemency.'

'So you arranged for him to escape,' surmised Bartholomew.

'Dickon did,' said Lucy. 'We told him that John was going to hang, and as John is the only friend the boy has ever had . . .' She struggled to keep her balance as yet another surge rocked the coracle. 'Come on, Narboro, for God's sake, or I really will leave you.'

Bartholomew swallowed hard when he recalled how much time Lucy had spent with Matilde. She seemed to read his thoughts, and her expression turned vengeful.

'I told her some things about you. None are true, but she will never marry you now, even if you do survive the flood. It is my revenge for you arresting Morys and forcing me to cut off his head.'

'I am coming!' called Narboro, sheathing his knives and preparing to brave the water at last. He descended three steps and stopped. 'Lord! It is like ice!'

'Jump!' Lucy snapped at him. 'Or so help me, I am going.'

Narboro gave a mirthless bark of laughter. 'And forfeit the money I stole from your brother? How will you get to France without it?'

Lucy did not reply, and Bartholomew saw she now had to crouch to look through the door. Soon, the whole room would be underwater and he and Michael would drown.

'And Aynton and Elsham?' he asked, desperately. 'Why kill them?'

Lucy's face was full of scorn. 'Have you not worked out who did that yet? How much clearer does it need to be? The clue is in the letter I retrieved from Martyn's body. It reveals that Aynton wrote to his friend Teofle about Baldok. Aynton's letter to Narboro likely contained the same information.'

'Which I never did receive,' put in Narboro. 'However, I *do* know he wrote to me because of my Court connections.'

'But your tales of being the King's favourite are vainglorious lies,' rasped Michael. 'I asked Teofle, and he said you were so lowly as to be all but invisible.'

'Not so!' cried Narboro. 'The King loves me, and even remembered my name once.'

'The point is not what *you* know about Narboro's standing at Court,' said Lucy, 'but what Aynton believed – which was that Narboro has powerful royal connections. Aynton aimed to use him to get a message to the King, and to use Teofle to get a message to the Archbishop. A message about Baldok.'

'Yes,' croaked Michael. 'But *what* about Baldok? That he was a thief?'

'Work it out for yourselves,' challenged Lucy. 'Just like I did. Not that it matters, because you will die in here and so will never be in a position to—'

There was a great splash as Narboro jumped at last. Bartholomew shoved the lamp at Michael and paddled to intercept him, but he was too cold and his muscles were too tired. A crossbow bolt hissed into the water next to him, causing him to duck, and when he surfaced again, it was to see Narboro reach the coracle and haul himself in.

*

369

There was a moment when Bartholomew considered following Lucy and Narboro through the door, but he knew that would be suicide without a boat, so he resigned himself to taking refuge on Hoo Hall's upper floor. He retrieved the lamp and towed Michael to safety, then scrambled up the steps, limbs numb with cold.

'Find dry clothes,' he gasped, as they stumbled into the dormitory. 'I will call for help.'

'No one will hear,' predicted the monk. 'Dick has evacuated all the nearby houses, and the water is making too much noise to attract attention from further away.'

'I can see people working on the sluices – Zoone, William and others. I will wave the lamp. One of them will come to investigate.'

But the roaring water swallowed his cries, while no one took any notice of a winking light. It was not long before he conceded defeat. Shivering, he pulled off his wet shirt and tunic, and replaced them with some that Narboro had left behind. Michael had already donned a baggy robe, and held a blanket around his shoulders.

'I have a bad feeling we will die here, Matt,' the monk said softly. 'Hoo Hall is a squat building on low-lying land. Unless the sluices are opened, the water in Coe Fen and the Mill Pond will continue to rise, and then even the roof will not be tall enough to save us.'

'Zoone will find a way to do it,' said Bartholomew, doggedly optimistic. He hoped it would be soon, or Michael was going to be right. He turned his thoughts to what Lucy and Narboro had admitted. 'They beheaded Lyonnes and Morys, but deny responsibility for Aynton and Elsham.'

'Do you believe them?' Michael sounded as if he no longer cared, but was trying to make the effort for Bartholomew, who did.

The physician nodded. 'They had nothing to gain from confessing to two murders, but disavowing all knowledge of two others.'

'So *has* Lucy identified the culprit, or was she just trying to make us feel stupid?'

'I think she was telling the truth.' Bartholomew felt warmth begin to flow back into his icy limbs. 'And if she can work it out, so can we.'

'If you say so.' Michael's voice was unsteady as he watched the water lap ever higher outside the window.

'It seems that Aynton discovered who pushed Baldok off the bridge, and decided to tell the Archbishop and the King. He chose to contact one via Teofle, and the other through Narboro, whom he mistakenly believed was a favoured courtier. The secret to the mystery lies in why he elected to disclose his discovery to them, and not to you or Dick.'

'Because the killer is more powerful or influential than us?' suggested Michael. 'Or more dangerous?'

'Who?' mused Bartholomew. 'Morys? One of his burgesses? Another high-ranking scholar? A wealthy—'

He was interrupted by Michael's cry of alarm. Water was bubbling through the floorboards.

'You must leave me,' the monk gulped. 'Swim to safety while you can.'

'I would drown,' replied Bartholomew. 'The water is moving far too fast now. Our only hope is to climb on the roof, and hope that someone notices us.'

'Lord!' breathed Michael, peering upwards. 'Is that possible? I am not a monkey.'

His face was pale as he watched Bartholomew's preparations – blankets knotted together to form a rope, and an oiled cloak to huddle under once they were outside.

With water now swirling around his knees Bartholomew handed one end of the 'rope' to Michael, fastened the other around his waist, and clambered on to the window-sill, aware of the flood running very fast just below. He stood, grabbed the edge of the roof, and hauled himself over it. He slipped once, but was saved by Michael's powerful hand beneath his foot.

Then he was on the roof, wishing it was thatched rather than tiled, as it would have been much less slick. He crawled up it, reached the apex, and secured the rope to the chimney, just as Michael yelled that water was flowing in through the window.

'Tie your end around you, and do not worry about falling,' he called. 'I will pull you back up if you lose your footing.'

He was far from sure he could, given that the monk was heavy and he was exhausted, but Michael did not hesitate. He was more nimble than Bartholomew would have anticipated, and he supposed it was pure terror that prompted the monk to hump up the roof like a portly caterpillar. They huddled behind the chimney, which afforded at least some protection from the driving rain.

'Now what?' asked Michael hoarsely.

'We wave the lantern,' replied Bartholomew. 'Someone will see it eventually.'

'Lantern?' asked Michael weakly. 'Oh. Do you want me to go back and fetch it?'

Bartholomew was too tired to feel exasperated. 'It was almost out of fuel anyway. So now, all we can do is wait – and hope that the flood goes down before we are swept away.'

Bartholomew had no idea how long he and Michael crouched on the roof, trying to stay out of the rain. He tried to listen for church bells, which would give him some idea of the time, but all he could hear was the hiss of rain and the roar of the river. He was aware that, while they waited uselessly, Narboro and Lucy would be paddling to freedom in their coracle, and the chances of apprehending them grew less with every passing minute.

'I cannot stop thinking about tomorrow,' said Michael

softly. 'Or rather today, as it must be Saturday by now. I would have enjoyed announcing the good news about the University's future, and then presiding over my first graduation ceremony as Chancellor.'

Bartholomew felt wretched. 'This is my fault. You said to wait before coming here, and you were right.'

'But had we delayed, we would never have heard Lucy and Narboro's confession,' said Michael generously. 'It was not all in vain.'

'We should have taken Morys somewhere dry, like Dick asked,' said Bartholomew, full of self-recrimination. 'Then the lane would have been too flooded for us to reach this place, and we would not be in this predicament.'

'Look!' cried Michael, pointing suddenly. 'Two men in a boat. We are saved!'

'It is Dickon,' said Bartholomew, straining his eyes in the gloom. 'What is—'

'Over here!' yelled Michael, standing to wave his arms over his head. 'Hurry!'

'He cannot have seen us sitting here in the dark,' said Bartholomew, frowning his puzzlement. 'So how did he know where to come?'

'Who cares?' shouted Michael. 'Dickon! Is that his father with him? No, the fellow is too big. It must be one of his soldier friends.'

It was then that answers crashed into Bartholomew's mind like an avalanche. 'Stop, Brother!' he gulped, hauling the monk back behind the chimney. 'Do not let him see you!'

'It is too late,' said Michael. 'He is waving back. But why—'

'He is not coming to rescue us,' whispered Bartholomew, numb with shock. 'He is coming because he met Lucy and Narboro, and she told him that we have all we need to work out who killed Aynton. And I have: it was Dickon!'

Michael regarded him askance. 'The strain of our

predicament has addled your brain, Matt. Dickon is not the culprit. How can he be?'

'Easily! It was written in the letter that Lucy found in Martyn's hat. Very few words were legible, but *yet so* were two of them. Not an adverb and a conjunction, as I stupidly assumed, but part of two nouns – *Tulyet* and *son.*'

'Lord, Matt! That is—'

'It makes sense! Aynton discovered that the "Tulyet son" killed Baldok, but he could hardly tell the Sheriff, while the Senior Proctor is the Sheriff's friend. He had to appeal to an authority outside the University and the shire – to the King and the Archbishop. But he could not write to them by normal channels, lest the Sheriff and the Senior Proctor found out . . .'

The boat came closer, and Bartholomew could see Dickon's brutish face grinning in triumph. It said more than words to confirm his suspicions. Michael continued to shake his head in disbelief, but Bartholomew knew he was right.

'Dickon killed Baldok,' he went on, 'and when Aynton found out, he killed him as well, along with the messengers who carried his letters. Martyn's was hidden in his hat, too well concealed for his killer – Gille – to find, but Huntyngdon's was in his purse.'

'It was not,' countered Michael. 'The purse was empty – thieves had been there first.'

'Thieves who then left the good clothes and boots?' asked Bartholomew archly. 'However, tell me who swooped forward to cut the thing from Huntyngdon's belt, declared nothing was in it, then disappeared around the end of the bridge to take it to you?'

'Yes, it was Dickon, but —'

'He lied about it being empty. I should have retrieved it myself, then we would have had answers days ago.'

'But all this means that Dickon is the "friend" who

ordered Elsham and Gille to kill,' argued Michael. 'Why would they commit capital crimes on the say-so of a boy?'

'Dickon is not just a boy,' snapped Bartholomew, knowing he had to convince Michael fast, or they would both die. 'He is the Sheriff's son, and his best friend is John Morys. The Mayor knew that Gille and Elsham were thieves – he doubtless told his cousin John, who passed it on to Dickon. The boy *blackmailed* them into doing what he wanted.'

'I cannot accept that—'

'Moreover, Elsham was Rohese's lover. Perhaps Dickon threatened to reveal that, too, unless they did what he asked, and no one wants to be on the wrong side of Morys and his savage Fenland kin. And finally there is the comment Elsham made about his afterlife.'

'That the "friend" might disturb it if he spoke out,' recalled Michael. 'You thought that particular remark referred to Stasy and Hawick, the warlocks.'

'And what does everyone say of Dickon?' demanded Bartholomew. 'That he is the Devil's spawn! It used to be figurative, but these days, folk believe it literally.'

Michael was still not convinced. 'Then who killed Elsham? Not Dickon, if the man was under his control.'

'Of course it was Dickon! Such men can never be trusted, and he is not a fool.'

'But Isnard saw the killer's arms – he said nothing about them belonging to a child.'

'Dickon is already bigger than some adults – Clippesby, Aungel and Cynric to name but three. He gave Ulf a hat in exchange for creating a diversion on the bridge, and he shoved the stone down on the boat – unlike the other children, he *is* strong enough to do it. When I questioned them, I thought it was Ulf who had terrified them into silence, but it was Dickon.'

Michael regarded him doubtfully. 'How can you be sure?'

'Because I later cornered them when Ulf was not there, but they still refused to talk. And who was with me at the time? Dickon's father! Of course they could not reveal who had ordered them to run amok on the bridge! God only knows if Gille is still alive.'

'But Dickon is a child!'

'A very *dangerous* child. And if you need more proof, look at who is with him in the boat – John, released by Dickon from his castle cell.'

Bartholomew recalled the boy's interaction with the wardens who had let the prisoners escape – he had not been menacing them for giving defiant answers to Tulyet's questions, but to make sure they did not reveal his role in the affair. He swallowed hard, aware that John probably held *him* responsible for thwarting the plan to steal the bridge money with Morys, and live the rest of his life in luxury. He would want revenge.

'I suppose this explains why Dickon failed to find Martyn's body when he was sent to explore the riverbank,' whispered Michael. He looked sheepish. 'Perhaps we should have been suspicious when the beadle I sent to repeat the search complained that Dickon unsettled him by dogging his every step, making it impossible to do his job.'

Bartholomew was disgusted with himself. 'Yes, we should.'

The boat bobbed closer, John rowing and Dickon kneeling in the bow. They reached Hoo Hall, and Dickon stood. He could just touch the edge of the roof by stretching upwards.

'Brother Michael,' he called sweetly. 'Doctor Bartholomew. Come down. I will not hurt you, I promise. I just want to talk.'

His voice sent a cold shiver down Bartholomew's spine, and he thought he had never heard anything so wicked.

'How do we stop them from coming up here after us?' asked Michael unsteadily. 'Dickon has a sword, while John is a knight. We cannot defeat them in combat.'

Bartholomew considered quickly. 'It will not be easy to climb from their boat to the roof – the distance is too great. So, we must prevent them from getting a handhold.'

'But how? Moreover, the distance between the boat and the roof will not be "too great" if the water keeps rising.'

'We will face that problem when it comes,' said Bartholomew, although he knew in his heart that his plan would only postpone the inevitable. He pulled a tiny surgical blade from his scrip. 'Meanwhile, let us hope they value their fingers.'

Michael prised a tile off the roof. 'Very well. You cut their hands and I will bruise them. Ready? Because here they come.'

At first, it was fairly easy to fend off Dickon and John. The boy howled when Michael crushed his thumb, while John retreated after Bartholomew stabbed his hand. Then John rowed the boat to the other side of the building, looking for a better place from which to launch an attack. Bartholomew scrambled over the apex, and down the other side, driving the villainous pair away by kicking free two loose tiles that rocketed downwards and nearly decapitated them. They hastily retreated to a safe distance to review their strategy.

'At least they cannot separate,' muttered Michael, as he and Bartholomew waited tautly for the next assault.

The boat eased forward again, Dickon in the prow. The boy's face was dark and angry, while John's was calculating as he assessed the roof for weaknesses.

'Come down,' ordered Dickon sullenly, sucking his bruised hand. 'Or when I catch you, I will chop off your ears and noses before I run you through.'

'You should not be here, John,' called Bartholomew, slithering down towards them, ready to stab again. 'You had a chance to run – you could still take it.'

'He is not going anywhere until we kill Brampton,' shouted Dickon. 'Lucy told us everything – how it was her brother who hit John over the head, and while he lay witless, beheaded Morys.'

'He would have done the same to me,' put in John, 'but I came to my senses before he could start, and he ran away. He let Dickon take the blame for Lyonnes – a man *he* dispatched himself.'

'So when we have dealt with you, we will pay Brampton a visit,' said Dickon. 'Then we will take all his money and go to France.'

'Dickon, enough,' shouted Bartholomew, stamping on the hairy hand that was trying to grab his ankle; John gave a grunt of pain. 'Brampton is not the culprit – Narboro and Lucy lied to you. Now they are escaping.'

'No one lies to me,' declared Dickon. 'I am a brave and mighty warrior.'

'Enough of this foolery,' snapped Michael. 'Think of your parents. They will—'

'I do not care about them,' interrupted Dickon, and smiled at his companion. 'John understands me much better.'

'You killed Baldok,' said Bartholomew, hoping to distract him with chatter while he thought of a way to defeat them. 'That is where all this started. You pushed him over the bridge. Why? For the money in his purse?'

He glanced up at the sky, wondering how long it would be until daylight, when someone might spot what was happening, and race to their rescue. But it was still pitch black, and he knew dawn would come too late.

'He called me an ill-mannered brat,' said Dickon indignantly. '*Me*, a powerful soldier! So I punched him and over he went. If he had stepped to one side to let me pass, like I ordered, none of it would have happened. It is all *his* fault for being stubborn.'

'You killed him because he refused to give way to you?' breathed Michael in disbelief.

'He should not have challenged me,' said Dickon, unrepentant. 'But he was a thief anyway – when I went to look at his body, he had the bridge taxes up his sleeve. John is looking after them for me, and I shall spend them on armour when we reach France.'

Bartholomew glanced at John's brutish face and wondered if Dickon would live that long. If the knight had any sense, he would dispatch this malevolent and unpredictable imp, and keep everything for himself.

'What happened then?' he asked. 'Did Aynton witness the incident?'

'No one did,' said Dickon sullenly. 'But later on, your Chancellor was nagging me about learning to read, and I accidentally threatened to do to him what I had done to Baldok. I tried to tell him it was a joke, but the stupid man took it as a confession.'

He drew his sword, and suddenly, it was not chubby fingers that were scrabbling at the edge of the roof, but a very sharp blade that swept back and forth. Bartholomew looked around for something to defend himself with, but there was nothing.

'And as Aynton could not tell your father and your father's friend what you had admitted,' he went on, 'he wrote to Teofle and Narboro—'

'He was a dimwit!' smirked Dickon. 'He *told* me what he was going to do, because he thought it would make me sorry. So I told Gille and Elsham to kill the messengers – said I would tell everyone about their thievery otherwise. I took Huntyngdon's letter from his purse without you seeing, along with a few coins, but Gille could not find Martyn's.'

'*We* have it,' said Michael, jumping away from the sword

379

and then lashing out with his foot at John. It connected, and the knight swore. 'And it is all we need to hang you.'

'We have more than that,' said Bartholomew, lest Lucy had mentioned to Dickon that the ink had run and was virtually illegible. 'We have Aynton's dying testimony.'

'He never said anything about me,' stated Dickon. 'I was there, remember?'

'You were,' acknowledged Bartholomew, 'which is why he chose his words with such care. He said *he* was responsible for Huntyngdon's death – he would probably have told me about Martyn, too, but you interrupted – which allowed us to make the connection between him and the missing men.'

'Well, he *was* responsible,' shrugged Dickon. 'If he had not pestered me about learning to read, I would not have blurted the stuff about Baldok, and he would not have told Huntyngdon and Martyn to deliver his stupid letters.'

'Then he lowered his voice, hoping you would not hear,' Bartholomew went on. 'I thought he whispered *litteratus* the first time, and *non litteratus* the second. But he actually said neither. The word he spoke was *inlitteratus.*'

'Yes, that might have been it,' conceded Dickon. 'So what?'

'It means ignorant or illiterate.'

'If he called me names, then I am *glad* I killed him!' spat Dickon, jabbing hard with his sword, and missing Bartholomew's leg by a whisker.

'But why did Aynton not just tell you what Dickon had done?' whispered Michael to Bartholomew doubtfully. 'He had nothing to lose at that point.'

'No, but I did,' Bartholomew whispered back. 'Dickon was listening, and Aynton knew that accusing him would put me in danger, too. He did his best to pass a message without Dickon realising, but I did not understand it. Until now.'

He grabbed Michael's tile and used it to swipe at the

sword, knocking it from Dickon's hand. The boy howled in dismay as it cartwheeled into the black water and disappeared with a splash.

'You will pay for that!' he cried, reaching for another. 'It was my favourite!'

'You were fortunate with Elsham,' said Michael, eyeing him with contempt. 'Ulf and his rabble played their part perfectly, and your stone landed right on top of your victim.'

'It was a brilliant shot,' bragged Dickon. 'No one else could have done it.'

'It was a poor plan,' countered John. 'It left him alive long enough to say things that should have been kept quiet, while Gille escaped altogether.'

Dickon was stung by the criticism, so sought to redeem himself with some warlike posturing. He addressed Bartholomew and Michael.

'You cannot escape, so surrender and I will kill you quickly. I have a potion that is almost painless. I already gave some to Narboro and Lucy, and they did not suffer much.'

'You poisoned them?' gasped Bartholomew, shocked anew.

'John reminded me that they would be a threat to us as long as they lived. Just like you.' Dickon turned to the knight. 'I am tired of all this chattering, and the water is high enough for us to reach the roof now. Are you ready to finish them? Yes? Then *charge!*'

CHAPTER 20

Dickon's howled order marked the start of a furious and sustained assault by John. He exploded upwards, ignoring a blow to the shoulder and a stabbed forearm, and forced the two scholars to scramble away fast. Dickon held back until he was sure there was no risk to himself, then followed, another sword in his hand and his eyes glittering with malice.

'*Stop!*' roared a commanding voice.

Bartholomew whipped around in alarm, thinking Dickon had recruited other soldiers to help him, then sagged in relief when he saw two boats ploughing towards them. Tulyet was in the first with four soldiers, while Brampton and five beadles were crammed into the second.

'Bartholomew and Michael murdered Aynton,' shrilled Dickon before anyone else could speak. 'So me and John are trying to arrest them.' He pointed accusingly at Brampton. 'And *he* beheaded the Mayor and Lyonnes. His sister told us, so it must be true.'

While John was distracted, Michael lashed out with his fist. He caught the side of the knight's head, causing him to lose his balance. With a howl of shock, John rolled off the roof and landed in the water. He surfaced, gasping, and Tulyet's men were there to fish him out.

'None of this was my idea,' he spluttered, as he was bound hand and foot. 'It was your hellion son's. You should not have inflicted him on me, Sheriff. He is a monster!'

Dickon gaped his dismay at the betrayal, but John did not so much as glance at him, and only continued to protest his own innocence.

'Dickon,' breathed Tulyet, his voice hoarse with anguish. 'What have you done?'

'Nothing!' snarled Dickon, gripping his sword in both hands. 'But I have to kill these two scholars, because if I do not, they will tell lies about me – just like John is doing.'

'Dickon, no!' cried Tulyet, ashen-faced. 'Put up your sword. At once!'

But Dickon ignored him, and went after Bartholomew with murder in his eyes. Bartholomew scrambled away fast.

'We *know* him, Matt,' called Michael urgently. 'We have his measure. Remember?'

At first, Bartholomew had no idea what the monk was talking about, but then understanding dawned. He stopped trying to escape and turned to face the child, ignoring the exclamations of alarm from those in the boats. Michael was right: they had known Dickon for years, and they *did* have his measure – he was a bully, eager to hurt the weak, but afraid of anyone who fought back. He feinted with the little blade, smiling when Dickon faltered, sudden fear in his eyes.

'Well?' Bartholomew taunted. 'All I have is a tiny knife, while you have a broadsword. Come on – attack.'

Dickon did not move. 'It is a trick. You plan to kill me.'

'How could I?' asked Bartholomew. 'You are a mighty warrior, are you not?'

He lunged again, causing Dickon to squeal his alarm and scuttle away.

'I do not feel like fighting any more,' Dickon declared petulantly. 'Everyone put up their blades, and I will do the same.'

Bartholomew lowered the knife, and, exactly as he had predicted, Dickon charged, weapon raised for a killing blow. He heard Brampton's howl of warning and Tulyet's horrified cry, although Dickon's vengeful scream was louder than both. He skipped neatly to one side, and

Dickon's sword hissed through empty air until it struck the roof, so hard that the boy was forced to drop it.

'That hurt!' Dickon cried, rubbing his hand. 'And you cheated! You—'

He broke off as his father grabbed him by the scruff of the neck.

'I have seen and heard enough,' Tulyet said hoarsely. 'It is over.'

'It is not,' countered Dickon, and twisted around to sink his teeth into Tulyet's hand.

Tulyet cuffed him around the ear, which, judging by the boy's screech of shock, was the first time it had ever happened. There was a resounding cheer from everyone else.

It was not over for the town, however, and the situation with the sluices was now critical. Bartholomew and Michael arrived on dry land to find the streets full of people toting belongings on their backs or on carts. The air rang with urgent shouts, church bells tolled the alarm, and terrified animals milled, as their owners frantically tried to drive them to safety.

'Unless Zoone can open the sluices in the next few minutes, the town will flood,' reported Tulyet. He looked spent – sodden and bedraggled from a night of battling rising water and a terrified population, and devastated by what he had learned about his son.

'Will he do it?' asked Bartholomew.

'I do not believe so. He and William have been struggling for hours with no success. The destruction will be massive, and all I hope is that no lives will be lost.'

'What are you going to do about him?' asked Michael, nodding to where Dickon was being held by a pair of burly soldiers. 'He murdered two people – more if he really has poisoned Narboro and Lucy – and blackmailed Gille and Elsham into killing two more.'

Tulyet could not bring himself to look at the boy. 'I have not decided yet,' he said, pain clear in his voice.

'He cannot be allowed to escape justice,' warned Michael. 'Some of his victims were scholars, so even if I was inclined to be merciful, my University would not permit it.'

'I know,' said Tulyet, allowing Bartholomew to inspect his bitten hand. The physician was shocked to see that bones were broken – Dickon had crunched down with all his might.

'We are all to blame,' he said, not liking to imagine the anguish Tulyet must be feeling. 'We should have taken a firmer hand with him from the start.'

'The fault is mine and mine alone,' countered Tulyet shortly. 'I always knew Dickon was . . . different from other children, but I thought I could channel his flaws into something good, something decent. My arrogance has cost lives.'

Bartholomew was not sure what to say, given that there was a strong element of truth in Tulyet's words, and there was barely a soul in Cambridge who did not think he was recklessly blind when it came to his only child.

'How did you know we were in need of rescue?' asked Michael. 'Did you see us?'

'Matilde did. Lucy said a lot of nasty things to her about Matt – things she knew to be lies. Suspicious and bemused, she followed Lucy, and saw her row to Hoo Hall in a coracle. She kept returning to look at the place, to see if anything was happening, until she eventually spotted you two on the roof. She raced to fetch me, and . . . well, you know the rest.'

He turned as Brampton arrived, also wet and dirty, but more authoritative than he had ever been before.

'I put John in the proctors' gaol,' he reported. 'It is safer than the castle, given that he escaped the last time he was there. He tried to bribe me to let him go – offered

385

me the money Baldok stole. I agreed, but reneged once he told me where it is hidden. He is a dishonourable man, and I have no compunction in tricking his sort.'

Tulyet regarded him askance. 'You should be in politics.'

'Next, he offered to confess all in exchange for clemency,' Brampton went on. 'I agreed to consider it, but only if he told me what Morys had done to the sluices. He says there is a lever on the swing manifold – whatever that means.'

'Tell Zoone,' ordered Bartholomew urgently. 'He will understand.'

He feared it would be too late, but hope filled Tulyet's eyes, and he led the way to the sluices at a pace that forced everyone – including the soldiers who held Dickon – into a run.

It was the darkest part of the night, and lamps had been set to illuminate the three dams, although they only seemed to add to the aura of general chaos as they bobbed and flickered unsteadily. And rain continued to fall.

Tulyet and his followers skidded to a halt near the Middle Dam, where Zoone and William were working, both drenched and black with mud. Defeat was in their slumped shoulders and exhausted faces. Before anyone could speak, Dickon released a peal of jeering laughter, delighted by the destruction that was about to befall a town he had suddenly come to hate. Tulyet ignored him and told Zoone what Brampton had prised from John.

Zoone's eyes lit in understanding. 'That explains . . . Yes! I should have guessed . . .'

He lay flat on his stomach, thrust his arm into the water, and began to fumble with something beneath the surface. There was a tense wait, during which cries of alarm sounded from the East Dam, where water was starting to spill over the top. Zoone did not allow it to distract him, and focused entirely on the task in hand.

'There!' he cried, springing upright as a deep boom resonated from under the water. 'That has done it! The lever is now unlocked.'

'Then open the sluice,' ordered Michael. 'What are you waiting for?'

'If I do, the gates will fly open, and water will rush out in an uncontrolled surge that will do exactly what we want to avoid,' explained Zoone. 'It must be released gradually, using a handle attached to this winch.'

'Unfortunately, the water is now so high,' put in William, 'that someone will have to dive down and manually slot the handle into the drive wheel.'

'I will do it,' said Bartholomew; he was a good swimmer. 'How deep do I need to go?'

'Not very,' replied Zoone. 'But it entails squeezing through a narrow gap, and you are too big. It must be someone smaller.'

'Me,' said Tulyet, beginning to unfasten the belt that held his weapons.

Zoone indicated the Sheriff's bandaged fingers. 'You will need two working hands or you will fail.' He looked Dickon up and down appraisingly. 'Can he swim? If so, he will do. He is a little large, but there is no time to fetch someone more suitable.'

Tulyet addressed Dickon briskly. 'We will tie a rope around you, and drag you out if you get into difficulties. Take off your shoes and cloak.'

'No,' gulped Dickon, his voice unsteady. 'It is dangerous.'

'Yes, it is,' agreed Tulyet, 'which is why you will do it. If you succeed, I will plead clemency for you. You will be exiled, but not hanged.'

Dickon shook his head vehemently, but Tulyet brushed his terror aside. He forced him to remove his cloak and shoes, tied the rope around the boy's waist, then made him repeat the instructions Zoone had given. Dickon obeyed with ill grace.

'Good, now go,' ordered Tulyet. 'Do something brave and generous. Then perhaps your mother will remember you with pride.'

'I do not care about her,' snarled Dickon defiantly. 'And I am not doing it. I hope the river washes the lot of you away and that this whole town is destroyed.'

'Then you will hang for murder, right here, right now,' said Tulyet, so coldly that those listening exchanged uneasy glances. 'Do not test me, boy.'

Dickon's face crumpled. 'But I do not want to,' he sobbed. 'I am frightened.'

Tulyet regarded him in distaste. 'You always tell me you are a bold warrior, so now you are going to prove it. But be warned: jumping in and doing nothing will not save you from the noose, and nor will "accidentally" losing the lever. You will only keep your life if you succeed.'

Dickon looked fearful and rebellious in equal measure, but began to sidle towards the water. William arranged lamps to shine downwards, so the boy would be able to see what he was doing, while Zoone readied the handle. It comprised a long L-shaped spindle that could be fitted into the gate at one end, and attached to the winch at the other.

Dickon sat on the edge of the dam, and opened his mouth to object again, but a glance at his father's hard, angry face stopped the words before they could be formed. With shaking hands, he accepted the handle from Zoone, took a deep breath and slid beneath the surface. He surfaced, puffing and blowing, almost at once.

'I cannot—'

'Again,' ordered Tulyet.

Dickon vanished a second time, and everyone peered down to watch him squeeze himself through the opening that held the turning mechanism. To their surprise, he surfaced a few moments later with a delighted grin.

'It was easy!' he crowed, before it occurred to him that it was a mistake to downplay his achievement. 'Although it required great skill and courage, of course.'

While Bartholomew hauled Dickon out of the water, Zoone grabbed the spindle end, and worked quickly to secure it to the winch with a complex system of ropes and tackle. When he was satisfied, he called to William:

'Try turning it. Gently now.'

William obliged, and there was an immediate explosion of bubbles from the other side of the dam, as the gate opened a crack. The onlookers broke into a spontaneous cheer, although Zoone continued to watch intently, calling warnings to William when he felt the friar was working too fast. Soon, even Bartholomew could see that the water in the Mill Pond had stopped rising.

'I did it!' yelled Dickon victoriously. 'I am a hero! I saved the town.'

'We need to do the same to the East Dam,' said Zoone. 'Bring the winch and another handle. Quickly now!'

Pleased with himself, Dickon trotted towards it almost eagerly. He slid into the water without being told, but surfaced a few moments later shaking his head. Tulyet started to order him to try again, but Dickon had dived before he could finish.

The second time, he was gone for much longer, and when he reappeared – some distance away – he was smirking. Everyone understood why when he waved the rope he had untied from around his waist. Furious, Tulyet stepped forward to leap in after him, but Bartholomew grabbed his arm.

'Let him go,' he said. 'You can catch him later.'

'You never will,' taunted Dickon. 'I shall escape, and you can all go to the Devil!'

And with that, he kicked out with his strong legs, swimming into the darkness and laughing in delight at the dismayed expressions on the faces of those he left behind.

389

'Now what?' whispered Tulyet, shocked that his son had bested him with such consummate ease. 'Who else can we send to—'

'No one,' interrupted Zoone, peering down at the water. 'Luckily, what we have done already is enough to let us control the flow. It will just take longer than it would with three operational sluices.'

'So we are safe?' asked William, and when the engineer nodded, he embraced him in a victorious hug. 'And the rain has stopped, too! We have averted disaster.'

'Then I had better go to St Mary the Great to announce the end of term and the name of Aynton's killer,' said Michael, then grinned. 'Not to mention the good news concerning the Province of Canterbury. Our scholars will go home with a song in their hearts.'

But Tulyet and Bartholomew were staring at the tiny splashes of white that showed where Dickon was still making his escape. They watched them until he vanished from sight.

EPILOGUE

Bartholomew and Matilde were married in St Michael's Church the day after the end of term. Father William and Clippesby performed the ceremony, while Michael gave a sermon that was both touching and amusing. Afterwards, so many people wanted to join the happy couple that Matilde's house proved to be far too small, so the celebratory feast was held in Michaelhouse instead. All Bartholomew's students had stayed on to wish him well, while the Marian Singers had been secretly practising for weeks. The rumpus could be heard from as far away as the castle, but no one complained.

Bartholomew was glad the Tulyets were among the guests: they were pale and strained, but also lighter-hearted, as if a great burden had been lifted from them. He feared Tulyet's bitten hand might fester, but it was still clean and pink, so he was hoping for the best. Tulyet would carry the scar for the rest of his days, although it was nothing compared to the one that Dickon had inflicted on his heart.

Tulyet had sent patrols to hunt for the boy as soon as it was light, but none of his soldiers much liked the idea of being the one to catch the brat, so their searches were not as assiduous as they had led him to believe. When the last one returned empty-handed, he resigned as Sheriff.

'That will be a blow to you, Brother,' yelled Bartholomew, shouting to make himself heard over the choir's deafening rendition of 'Summer is a-coming in'. 'You always say that no other royally appointed official will be as easy to work with as him.'

'And I am right,' Michael hollered back. 'But I have

written letters to several powerful acquaintances, and I am confident that Brampton will be appointed in his place.'

Bartholomew gaped at him. '*Brampton?* He could barely function as Senior Proctor. I cannot imagine him running an entire shire.'

'Quite,' said Michael smugly. 'He will require advice, and has promised to come to me for it. Besides, while he may be feeble at keeping law and order, he is excellent at administration. The King's taxes will always be delivered on time, which is enough to keep us away from unwanted royal scrutiny.'

Bartholomew shook his head in grudging admiration. 'You do not need an abbacy or a bishopric now, Brother. You are Chancellor of a University that will reap students from all over the Province of Canterbury, and you will have a Sheriff under your control. Your authority extends over half the country!'

Michael smiled comfortably. 'Hardly half, Matt, but enough. I shall not have to worry about the Great Bridge either, as Zoone informs me that Shardelowe's creation will last for years. And the money Baldok stole – which Dickon gave to John to look after – was used to pay the builders the bonus they were promised, so everyone is happy.'

'Stasy and Hawick are not,' said Bartholomew. 'They were found dead in their cell yesterday morning. They had died by poison.'

Michael blinked. 'They killed themselves to avoid answering for their crimes?'

'Dickon did it. After they were arrested on Friday, he visited their cell and made them an offer: he would help them escape in exchange for a bottle of poison. You see, even then, he guessed he would need to kill more people to protect himself . . .'

'And God forbid that he should do it in a fair fight,' muttered Michael in distaste.

'Quite,' said Bartholomew. 'Poison: the coward's weapon. Anyway, they agreed, and told him where to find some in their dispensary.'

'Which he then used on Narboro and Lucy,' surmised Michael. 'At least, that is what he claimed, although there is no sign of their bodies.'

'Then he visited Stasy and Hawick a second time, and took them some wine. Not long after finishing it, they realised they had been treated to a dose of their own medicine.'

'But why?' asked Michael, frowning. 'They had done nothing to hurt him.'

'I imagine he wanted to make sure they never told anyone about the poison. Or perhaps to spare him the bother of organising an escape. Regardless, they managed to gasp a confession to the gaoler before they died.'

'And I only find out about this now?' asked Michael, unimpressed.

'The gaoler tried to tell someone, but you were too busy with all the end-of-term formalities, while Dick has been working to put all to rights after the flood. He told me that Stasy and Hawick recanted their witchery in the end, and asked for a priest.'

'Folk will claim they died because of Margery Starre's curse.' Michael was obliged to yell again as the choir reached an unexpected crescendo. 'I should be sorry, but their antics nearly killed Meadowman and made dozens of people ill – all to make themselves rich. They would have done it again, in another town, if Dickon had let them out.'

'I spent years training them,' said Bartholomew bitterly. 'And all for nothing.'

'Then you had better start thinking about what to teach the ladies in Matilde's *studium generale*,' bellowed Michael.

Bartholomew smiled. 'Did you know that the school will occupy Morys's old house? Chaumbre has bought it and donated it to her, so she will never have to worry about paying rent. It is very generous of him, but I cannot imagine where he found the money. I know everything Morys stole from Girton was returned, but even so . . .'

Michael laughed. 'He is richer than ever now, because of a sly trick Morys played on him. You see, before the bridge could be rebuilt, two things had to happen: the town had to raise the capital *and* the project had to be underwritten by an independent body. Morys approached Chaumbre, and asked him to stand as guarantor for the scheme.'

Bartholomew was stunned. 'So when Morys stole the money, he knew Chaumbre would be left with a bill for the entire amount? It would have destroyed him – taken everything he and Edith have!'

'Not quite, because Chaumbre only agreed to under-write *half* the total – he asked Morys to take the rest. However, if one of them died, the other would be liable for the whole amount, so he suggested they made each other the sole heirs to their estates. In that way, neither would be left with crippling debts in the event of a tragedy.'

'And Morys agreed? That does not sound like him.'

'He agreed because he did not expect to die. No doubt he intended to change his will back again the moment he absconded with all the money, but Lucy killed him before he had the chance. So Chaumbre remains his sole legal beneficiary.'

'Lord!' muttered Bartholomew. 'Morys was a very wealthy man.'

'He was, and as most of his money was dishonestly obtained, Chaumbre has vowed to spend it all on charitable causes – Matilde's school, a new library for Michaelhouse, a fund to help sick beadles, and a free medical service for the town's poor.'

'What kind of medical service?' asked Bartholomew, puzzled.

'One where you will be paid a salary to tend them, with money available for the remedies you think they need. Did he not tell you? It is his wedding gift to you and Matilde.'

There was a lump in Bartholomew's throat. Of course Chaumbre had not told him – he would be uncomfortable with the resulting gratitude, and would rather let someone else break the news.

'Edith really did marry a good man,' he managed to say eventually.

'A very good man,' agreed Michael, and glanced to where Chaumbre and Edith sat together; she was laughing at something he had said. 'Their partnership of convenience has turned into one of genuine love and friendship. I predict they will be very happy together.'

'I am glad. They deserve it.'

'I have a wedding gift for you, too. I have decided to make the post of Corpse Examiner a secular one, which means you can keep it. It comes with a modest stipend, the right to give occasional lectures, and invitations to College feasts. You will no longer be a Regent Master, but you will not sever all your ties with us.'

Bartholomew stared at him. 'You can do that?'

'I am Master of Michaelhouse and Chancellor of the University at Cambridge,' replied Michael haughtily. 'I can do what I like. Are you pleased?'

Bartholomew nodded, the lump back in his throat. 'I have done something for you, too, Brother. You asked Zoone to be Senior Proctor, and Aungel to be his junior, but both refused. Well, I have persuaded them to change their minds.'

Michael clapped his hands in delight. 'Excellent! They are exactly what I need. Indeed, I suspect they will transpire to be better than us in time.'

'I remember Aungel when he was no more than a child,' sighed Bartholomew. 'Now he is teaching medicine in my place.'

'He still is a child as far as I am concerned. We must be getting old, Matt. But not too old to thwart killers and deadly diseases, eh? Shall we drink to our continued success?'

Bartholomew raised his cup. Then Matilde came to collect him, and he left Michaelhouse for the last time as a Fellow. He paused at the gate, his wife on his arm, and glanced back. The College looked pretty in the dark, with lights burning in the hall windows. The yard was full of well-wishers – colleagues, patients, students, townsfolk and family, each one of whom he considered a friend.

He would miss his old life, but he had not lost what really mattered. That would be with him wherever he went.

Dickon swam for what felt like an age after escaping at the Mill Pond. He was terrified the whole time – afraid that he would drown, afraid that someone would see him and raise the alarm, and afraid that he would catch his death of cold.

He crawled out of the water eventually, and made his way to an abandoned shepherds' hut in the Fens that John had once shown him. Once there, he began to plot his revenge on the men who had destroyed his fine plans. After all, if it were not for Bartholomew and Michael, he would have been in France by now, killing peasants with John at his side and a fortune in his purse.

Slipping into Michaelhouse or Matilde's house to poison their wine quickly proved to be impossible, because they expected him to try, and took precautions. After a fifth frustrating night, when he was still no closer to his objective, he went to sit in the cemetery opposite the Hospital of St John, to consider his options.

Despite inheriting so much money, Chaumbre still had not paid for the last dye-pit to be filled, although no one nagged him about it, as his generosity had earned him so many friends. Dickon liked the last hole, because it was where he had hidden Narboro and Lucy after he had poisoned them. A thin layer of soil concealed their bodies, although one of Narboro's fingers was visible, and Dickon was amazed that no one had noticed it.

He was not alone for long, and he jumped when Ulf emerged from the shadows, distinctive in his new hat. Dickon did not like Ulf, and he certainly did not trust him.

'You are an outlaw,' declared Ulf, plumping himself down next to him. 'I will get money if I tell them at the castle where you are.'

Dickon shrugged, affecting nonchalance, although his stomach lurched in alarm. 'I did what was necessary,' he said, trying to put a swagger in his voice. 'Now I am back for revenge.'

'On who?' asked Ulf curiously. 'Your father, because he threatened to hang you? You are too late – he went to London today, to work for the King. I think him and his wife were too embarrassed to stay here after what you did.'

'I care nothing for them,' spat Dickon contemptuously. 'But Bartholomew and Michael interfered in my business, so I am going to poison them – along with anyone else who gets in my way.'

'Not me then,' said Ulf confidently. 'I did what you asked on the bridge that day. I helped you get rid of Elsham.'

Dickon inclined his head. 'You did, so have a drop of wine as another reward.'

He smirked his satisfaction when Ulf drained the little flask and wiped his lips on the back of his hand.

'Bitter,' said Ulf, grimacing. 'Did you kill Gille as well? Everyone thinks he ran away.'

Dickon grinned. 'Whoever rents my father's house will have a shock when they explore the stink in the cellar.'

397

Ulf was impressed. 'How did you do it?'

'He accused me of killing Elsham, so I told him it was someone at Clare Hall. Then I gave him some wine to drink while we discussed which one of them it might be.'

'Wine?' asked Ulf, suddenly uneasy.

Dickon laughed softly. 'Elsham, Gille, Stasy, Hawick, Narboro, Lucy, Aynton, Baldok – they all learned what happens when I am crossed.'

Ulf reeled suddenly. 'I feel funny . . . Have you . . .'

'I know you will betray me the moment we part company,' said Dickon coldly. 'So I have taught *you* what happens to traitors, too.'

With a howl of rage, Ulf leapt at him. Ulf was smaller, but he had a knife and he knew how to use it. The blade slipped easily between Dickon's ribs. Dickon gasped in disbelief before toppling into the pit. Ulf fell, too, landing beside him. It did not take long for either boy to breathe his last.

The two men who had witnessed the encounter gaped their shock at the speed with which it had turned fatal. Isnard and Chaumbre had been in the shadows to one side, discussing the last dye-pit. It was an odd hour for such a conversation, but Chaumbre was so busy with his charitable works that it was the only time he could manage.

When Dickon had first appeared, Isnard wanted to race forward and lay hold of him, but Chaumbre held him back. Ever since Dickon had escaped, Chaumbre had been painfully aware that the boy posed a serious danger to his brother-in-law – and if anything happened to Matthew, it would break Edith's heart. Thus he was not about to risk losing the brat by chasing him with a one-legged bargeman. However, he had certainly not expected to hear Dickon's confession, and the boy's ruthless malevolence had chilled him to the bone.

'We should have grabbed him when he first appeared,'

whispered Isnard accusingly, once he had recovered his voice. 'Like I told you.'

'I was afraid he would escape,' breathed Chaumbre, still stunned. 'He is younger and faster than us. I would never have delayed if I had thought . . . Lord! And Ulf, too! I should have known they were in it together when he began sporting that new hat . . .'

Isnard frowned. 'His hat? Why? It is just a black one, like any other.'

'Not to a dyer,' explained Chaumbre. 'There is a hint of red that makes it distinctive to the trained eye. I thought it was familiar when I saw him wearing it on the day that Elsham died. I remember why now – it was Dickon's. Ulf must have demanded it as payment for causing a diversion on the bridge.'

Isnard inched towards the dye-pit, and Chaumbre followed, both afraid of what they would see. Ulf was sprawled just below them, while Dickon lay at right angles to him. The eyes of both boys stared upwards sightlessly.

Chaumbre crossed himself. 'They were children, Isnard,' he whispered. 'And they discussed murder as if it were something they did every day. *Children!*'

'Not very nice children,' said Isnard with a sniff.

'Dickon wanted to poison Matthew,' Chaumbre went on, shaking his head at the horror of it all.

'And Brother Michael,' said Isnard. 'The man who leads the Marian Singers and supplies free bread and ale to half the town. Dickon really was the Devil's spawn, to set his sights on them. Did you hear that Sheriff Tulyet found the Chancellor's letter among the brat's belongings, by the way?'

'The one Aynton gave Huntyngdon to deliver?'

Isnard nodded. 'Which proves beyond all doubt that Dickon was indeed the one who ordered Gille and Elsham to kill the messengers.'

Chaumbre shuddered, but then frowned as he

continued to peer into the pit. 'Is that a finger I see poking through the dirt next to Ulf? Is someone else down there? Yet another victim of Tulyet's hellion son?'

'Probably just an old glove,' said Isnard, disinclined to look more closely.

'Poor Tulyet,' said Chaumbre. 'Now he and his wife will have to bear the news that, on top of all his other crimes, Dickon poisoned another child.'

Isnard was silent for a while. 'Perhaps we should spare them that knowledge,' he whispered eventually. 'Dickon has caused them enough pain, so why let him inflict more? What do you say?'

Their eyes met and plans were made. Within an hour, they were back with a cart of hard-core rubble and two spades. Wordlessly, they began to fill in the pit.

'I shall plant a garden on top of them,' said Chaumbre when they had finished. 'One with fragrant herbs and a bench for people to sit on. It will be a place of peace and tranquillity.'

'And if these bodies are ever discovered,' said Isnard, 'you and I will be long dead. No one will ever know the sorry tale of how they came to be there.'

'A mystery,' whispered Chaumbre. 'For future folk to ponder.'

HISTORICAL NOTE

During excavations by Craig Cessford of the Cambridge Archaeological Unit in 2010, a pit containing four skeletons was discovered. The pit was one of four wood-lined structures, located on the edge of the area used as a cemetery by the medieval Hospital of St John. The precise purpose of these pits has been obscured by time.

The skeletons were those of an adult male, an older woman, a youth of eleven to thirteen years, and a child of six to eight. Carbon-14 dating suggests a burial date of between 1300 and 1415. The woman's teeth were in poor condition – decayed, some missing, worn and with abscesses. She was buried face-down, as if she had been thrown in. All four individuals show signs of a hasty burial, although it is impossible to be sure why. Details of this incredible and fascinating excavation can be found in Craig's freely downloadable report on the Archaeology Data Service website: https://tinyurl.com/4muutjjn.

Most of the people in *The Chancellor's Secret* were real. John Stasy and John Hawick – although they were scholars of Oxford, not Cambridge – were accused of dealing in the dark arts. Hawick lived in the 1380s, and seems to have been acquitted, but Stasy, who lived a century later, was not so fortunate and was executed in 1477, despite his protestations of innocence. Two other Oxford scholars were Richard Gille, who murdered John Martyn in 1389, and John Elsham, who killed William Huntyngdon in 1369, apparently in self-defence. In Cambridge at the same time, there was a Huntyngdon who was an illegitimate son of Guichard d'Angle, the Earl of Huntingdon.

Michaelhouse deeds record that funds were left to the College by one Edith Chaumbre, a widow. College Fellows in the 1360s included Michael (de Causton), William (Gotham) and John Clippesby. Later members were William Zoone, John Aungel, John Islaye and Thomas Mallett. The collegiate church was St Michael's, which still stands on Trinity Street (once called the High Street) and was united with the parish of Great St Mary's in 1908. It was refurbished a century later, and is now the Michaelhouse Centre. It serves as a community hub and art gallery and has a lovely cafe – well worth a visit.

A Peterhouse scholar named Richard Narboro was betrothed to Lucy Brampton in the 1400s, but he spent ten years abroad before returning to Cambridge and deciding he did not want her. The fact that the hapless Lucy had been out of the marriage market for a decade, and was likely now too old to win another suitor, was not the main cause of concern to her kin. What mattered more was that Narboro had left them with the bill for housing her all the time he was away. The case went to court and Narboro was compelled to cough up. There is no record of what became of Lucy. There was a King's Hall Fellow named Thomas Brampton in 1388, but he was probably no relation.

Gerard de Hoo was an early, if not the first, Master of Peterhouse. Other Peterhouse Fellows in the 1360s were William Stantone and John Gayton. King's Hall had a scholar named Geoffrey Dodenho, and its Warden in 1361 was John de Shropham.

Clare Hall, originally known as University Hall, was the fourth College to be founded in Cambridge. It is now known as Clare College, and a new Clare Hall was founded in 1966. Three of University Hall's early Fellows were John Donwich, Peter March and John Pulham.

The Moryses were a powerful Cambridge family in the fourteenth century, and Stephen Morys was Mayor of the

402

town in 1360. There is some suggestion that he was corrupt, although that was probably true of most officials at this time. The Tulyets were another well-known local clan, several of whom were named Richard. Edmund Lister, Hugh FitzAbsolon and John Baldok were fourteenth-century burgesses. John Godenave was a convicted felon who lived in the 1340s. Robert de Blaston was a Cambridge carpenter in the mid-1300s.

Unlike Oxford, Cambridge has very few written records from the fourteenth century and earlier, as they were destroyed during the Peasants' Revolt of 1381. One story is that they were tossed on a great bonfire in the Market Square by a woman named Margery Starre.

By 1360, Thomas de Lisle, the Bishop of Ely, had fled his diocese and was living with the Pope in Avignon. Five years earlier, he had been involved in a very public dispute with one of Edward III's kinswomen, which culminated in charges of murder, assault, kidnapping and theft. He was almost certainly complicit in the crimes, most of which were committed by his steward, but he never answered for them in a court of law, and died, still in self-imposed exile, in 1361.

The Great Bridge (now called Magdalene Bridge) was always a bone of contention in the town. It was used by everyone, but the burgesses were expected to pay for its upkeep. In 1362, the King appointed three commissioners to oversee repairs. These were Thomas de Shardelowe, Gilbert Bernarde and John de Lyonnes. There is no suggestion that their improvements lasted, because the cost of maintaining the bridge continued to cause friction for years to come.

As contemporary and later documents contradict each other, there is some confusion as to who was Chancellor of the University in 1360. Some sources say Michael Aynton (or Haynton) held the post until 1362. Others record that it was Michael de Causton. Michael's election was contested by John Donwich of Clare Hall, who then set himself up as the Anti-Chancellor.

Indignant, two senior and well-connected Regent Masters – John Ufford and William Rawby – appealed to the Archbishop of Canterbury, who sent three vicars-general to sort the matter out. Their names were William Teofle, John Tinmouth and Thomas Ely. They found in favour of Michael, leaving Donwich to lick his wounds until the 1370s, when he put himself forward for the post again, and was lawfully elected.

Bartholomew and Matilde are entirely fictional, but, as a scholar, he would have had to resign from the University if he had wanted to marry her.